"Now," Aranthur said aloud.

Instantly, a massive dome of shimmering gold rose from the precinct line, an impermeable barrier that went up in a single hummingbird heartbeat. Six of Kallotronis' Arnauts were cut off outside, as were several Nomadi and some Yellowjackets on the hillside.

Viewed from outside, the entire Academy was suddenly covered in a bright golden dome that was visible from every part of the City.

A second, rose-coloured bubble emerged from the far end of Tirase Square and covered the terrace like the dome on a child's terrarium.

There was a moment of shocked silence.

The Master of Arts' voice came across the square, hugely augmented.

"Throw down your weapons and do not attempt an act of magic, and you will be dealt with leniently."

Praise for
the Masters & Mages trilogy

"Cameron brings an intimate knowledge of history and warfare to a remarkably complex, real-feeling work of epic fantasy."

—*B&N Sci-Fi & Fantasy Blog*

"Utterly, utterly brilliant. A masterclass in how to write modern fantasy—world building, characters, plot, and pacing, all perfectly blended. Miles Cameron is at the top of his game."

—John Gwynne, author of the Faithful and the Fallen series

"*Cold Iron* is fantastic. It shimmers like a well-honed sword blade."

—Anna Smith Spark, author of *The Court of Broken Knives*

"A terrifically good novel that epitomises how good Fantasy novels can be when done right. This is an author with a tale to tell and the skills to do so admirably."

—*SFFWorld*

"[If] you're a fan of military style fantasy...then you're gonna love this one."

—*Fantasy Inn*

"Cameron is a brilliant writer!" —*Grimdark Magazine*

BRIGHT STEEL

By Miles Cameron

The Traitor Son Cycle

The Red Knight
The Fell Sword
The Dread Wyrm
The Plague of Swords
The Fall of Dragons

Masters & Mages

Cold Iron
Dark Forge
Bright Steel

BRIGHT STEEL

Masters & Mages
Book Three

MILES CAMERON

www.orbitbooks.net

This book is a work of fiction. Names, characters, places, and incidents are the product of the author's imagination or are used fictitiously. Any resemblance to actual events, locales, or persons, living or dead, is coincidental.

Orbit
Hachette Book Group
1290 Avenue of the Americas
New York, NY 10104
orbitbooks.net

First U.S. Edition: December 2019
Originally published in Great Britain by Gollancz in August 2019

Orbit is an imprint of Hachette Book Group.
The Orbit name and logo are trademarks of Little, Brown Book Group Limited.

The publisher is not responsible for websites (or their content) that are not owned by the publisher.

The Hachette Speakers Bureau provides a wide range of authors for speaking events. To find out more, go to www.hachettespeakersbureau.com or call (866) 376-6591.

Library of Congress Control Number: 2019940684

ISBNs: 978-0-316-39939-5 (trade paperback), 978-0-316-39937-1 (ebook)

Printed in the United States of America

LSC-C

10 9 8 7 6 5 4 3 2 1

In all our fighting techniques, we should cover the side that our opponent wishes to strike with a clever parado, *and attack where he is least prepared. If he shows an opening, we should fall on and attack there. However, the first blow should be short, a* rebattimento, *to provoke our opponent to an error, while the second blow should be done fully with a dedicated* assalto. *Beware the afterblow!*

Maestro Sparthos,
unpublished notes to the book *Opera Nuova*

THE GREAT CITY OF MEGARA

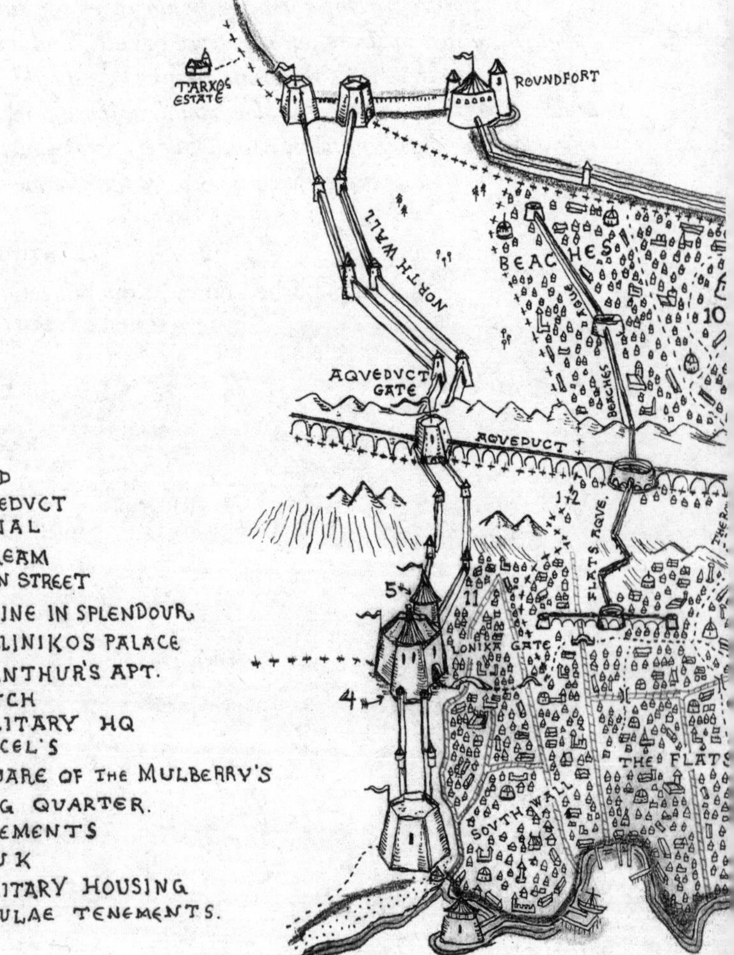

++++ ROAD
AQUEDUCT
CANAL
STREAM
------- MAIN STREET

1. SUVINE IN SPLENDOUR
2. KALLINIKOS PALACE
3. ARANTHUR'S APT.
4. WATCH
5. MILITARY HQ
6. TERCEL'S
7. SQUARE OF THE MULBERRY'S
8. JUDG QUARTER.
9. TENEMENTS
10. SOUK
11. MILITARY HOUSING
12. INSULAE TENEMENTS.

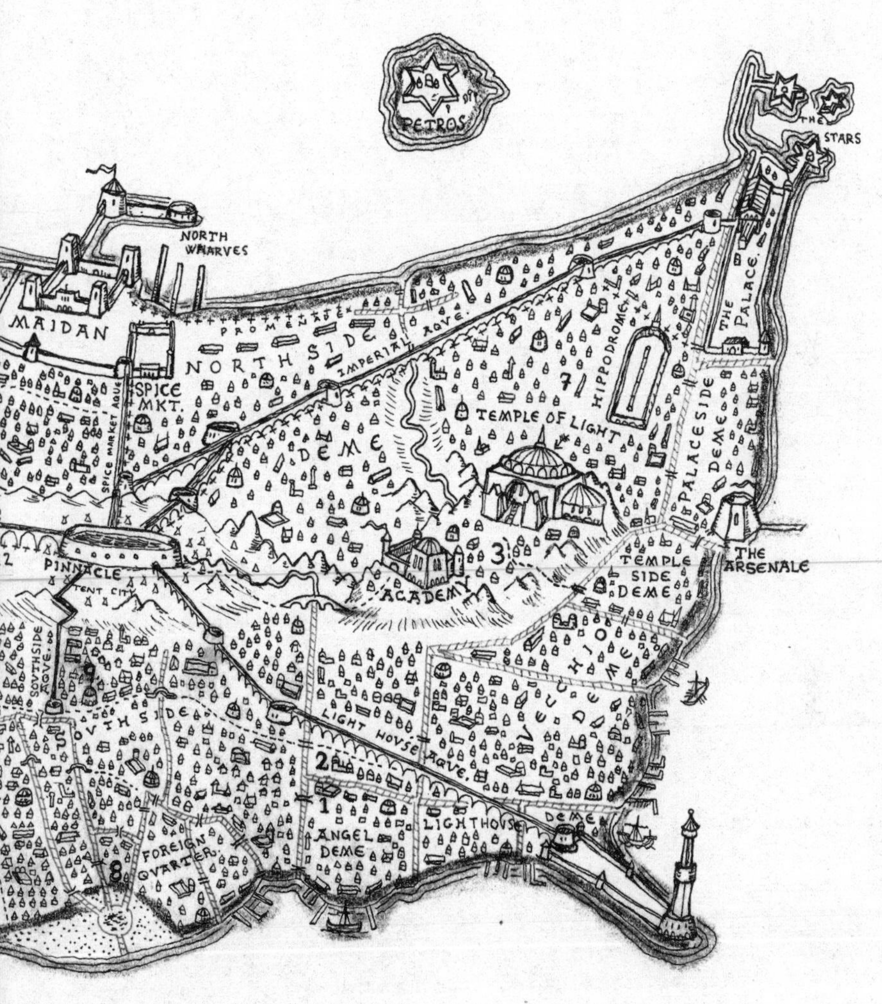
PETROS
THE STARS
NORTH WHARVES
MAIDAN
PROMENADE
NORTH SIDE
IMPERIAL AQVE.
HIPPODROME
THE PALACE
SPICE MKT.
SPICE MARKET AQVE.
7
TEMPLE OF LIGHT
DEME
PALACESIDE DEME
3
THE ARSENALE
12
PINNACLE
TENT CITY
ACADEMY
TEMPLE SIDE DEME
SOUTHSIDE AQVE.
9
SOVTH SIDE
VECCHIO DEME
LIGHT HOUSE AQVE.
2
1
ANGEL DEME
LIGHTHOUSE DEME
8
FOREIGN QVARTER

BRIGHT STEEL

Prologue

Djinar had never, in his twenty-two years, been across the strait to Ulama, but he had become General Roaris' most trusted courier, and he had no objection to the mission; he understood the stakes, how fragile their possession of Megara was, and the importance of communicating with their cells in Atti. When word came that the attack on the Sultan Bey had failed, he volunteered to go.

He also understood, better than most of his peers, how vital it was that they hang on. He knew how badly their Master had been defeated, first in Armea and then at Antioke; how the timetable had nearly been ruined. He knew, because he was an initiate of the first order, how vital it was that the Emperor be killed; and how essential it was that the Sultan Bey be toppled. Out on the high seas, the Imperial fleet was turning the tables on the pirates; at Antioke, another army sent into action by the Master was being ground to bloody pulp by that witch, Tribane.

Djinar knew these things like articles of faith. He also knew that Verit Roaris was no longer himself; that his mortal frame had been seized by the Master because the man would not obey. Djinar knew it, and it filled him with fear, because he, too, had his own devices and desires, and he feared their discovery.

Disagreeing with the creature inhabiting Roaris' body had been the stupidest thing he'd ever done.

Except that he was *right*. The new Disciple was not a native of the Empire; he could no more imagine the politics of the City than peasants tilling the fields could. He was making mistakes…

These are foolish, dangerous thoughts.

Fear kept him strong and alert, or so he told himself. And the mission to the Disciple of Ulama gave him a chance to show his worth, so that his moment of insubordination might be forgotten.

He hired a fishing boat to make the trip across the strait, and the fisherman complained of the change in tides since the emergence of the Dark Forge, the huge rift in the heavens and in the shell of reality that signified the changes to come. Djinar, as an initiate of the Pure, knew a great deal about the Dark Forge, but he hadn't known that it was affecting the currents.

He listened until he grew bored of the fisherman's ignorance of anything not relating to fish.

"Enough," Djinar snapped at the end of his patience. "I hired you to sail, not to talk."

The fisherman fell into a surly silence, but his efforts drove the little boat through the water, and although it took more than four hours, eventually he furled the sail, took to his oars, and brought them close in to the far shore where the reverse current ran, so that they seemed to float against the tide running in from the great sea visible under the rising sun, a sun which also gilded the prayer towers of the Sultan Bey's palace and the majestic Temple of Light that dominated the heights of Megara to their right. Beneath the Temple of Light, the morning sun flashed on the Crystal Palace.

"A remarkable piece of vulgarity," Djinar said aloud, on seeing its great windows.

The fisherman landed them on the beach at the edge of the immense wharf that dominated the Ulama waterfront. Built to accommodate the largest Attian and Megaran ships, it towered almost forty feet above the water, with slum streets concealed beneath the wooden wharves where Ulama's poorest denizens lived and died.

The beach ran straight up to the rows of shacks, built in safety as the Sea of Sud tide never rose more than a foot except in extreme circumstances. Djinar cursed, but after he paid the fisherman he stepped over the side into the shallow water and waded up the beach past a man dying of bone plague.

"Disgusting," he said, glancing at the dying man.

He made his way through the flotsam of the city, trying not to touch them, as if their poverty was a contagion that could infect him. He pulled on gloves and a Byzas aristocrat's mask, and finally found a set of steps leading up out of the slums. He took them the way a drowning man might grab at a floating oar.

But at the top of the shallow wooden steps, he found himself almost across from the so-called Pantheon; the oldest temple in Ulama. He walked north as he'd been ordered, looking for the red chalk mark that would tell him all was well, and he found it, to his own satisfaction, brushed lightly across the belly of Potnia just outside the temple.

He reached up with false piety to touch the mark, her marble belly worn smooth by the thousands of pilgrims who had passed this way. The Master taught that all the gods were false; that there was no god but one's self. But he encouraged outward signs of piety, because *mimicry makes good camouflage*.

He turned east and began to climb the high ridge that ran through the town.

He was crossing a tiny square, the dawn now a fully realised day, the sun rising in showy splendour over the snow-capped mountains of central Atti, when the footpads struck. There were three of them, wielding iron bars stolen from a construction site—crude but fearsome weapons.

Djinar was not much of a magos. Family connections had ensured he received the very best education at the Studion, but he lacked the connection to the sources of power which would allow him to cast complex *occulta.* All the same, he froze one attacker with a weak but well-formed command to the other man's nervous system and he fell like a toppled statue as Djinar got his long rapier clear of its scabbard.

He offered the slim weapon to one of the two remaining footpads, waving the blade at the man until he batted at it with his iron bar, hoping to break the tongue of steel.

Djinar slipped his blade under the heavy blow and stabbed the man in the throat, the needle point punching through his neck even as the point grated on his spine. As the man's knees buckled in death, Djinar raised his wrist and stepped back as if bowing to a dance partner, which, in a way, he was. The corpse fell off his lowered point.

"Your turn," Djinar said.

The remaining man trembled with indecision; the sort of low person

—as the Master taught—who turned to crime from inner weakness. Djinar thought he might be doing the man a favour in killing him; even with the length of a blue-white blade shimmering through the sticky blood of his friend in front of his face, the criminal couldn't decide whether to attack or run.

Djinar tapped the bar with his blade, a sharp *snap* that forced the bandit to move. He raised the bar, his eyes wide with fear.

Quick as a cat, Djinar thrust through one wrist and turned his own, so that the slim blade severed the tendons of the other man's hand.

He screamed and dropped the iron bar.

Like a snake, Djinar struck again, withdrawing the blade and stabbing through his body, and then, as he folded forward, through one eye. The blade came out of the back of the man's skull with a pop.

"Goodbye," Djinar said. "I suspect no one will mourn you."

He stepped back and saluted his two fallen adversaries with an ironic flick of his blade that sent drops of blood flying through the morning air. He started to wipe his blade on a dead man's burnoose, and then shook his head.

"Oh dear," he said.

He walked over to the man whose limbs he'd frozen and smiled, meeting the man's open eyes.

"I wonder if you can break my lock on you," he mused.

He put the point of his rapier against the man's neck under his chin and pushed very slowly, and so discovered his *puissance* was strong enough that the man's life ended before he could break it. Djinar pushed the blade in very slowly, and then withdrew it.

"I wonder what it is like," he asked the morning air. "Death."

He cleaned his blade, and sheathed it in time to pass two veiled women going to the well. He bade them good morning, and smiled when one started to scream.

At the top of the apparently endless steps, he bought a cup of water from a water seller and savoured it, then walked away from the Sultan Bey's magnificent walls and headed south, as he'd been ordered. He found the signs he expected, marks low to the ground in orange chalk, and he followed them through a maze of alleys between the high garden walls and the homes of the very rich. Eventually, when the sun was bright in the sky, he found the gate he sought: yellow with red trim, and a crouching lion in gold. He knocked, and a well-dressed gardener admitted him and took his name.

It can't be this easy, he thought.

But it was. In moments he was summoned, and he climbed to the exedra, the long balcony of a summer palace. He could see through the windows to the apartments within; a dozen rooms for women, and then a long hall which he was led into. It was richly hung with silk carpets and a man sat on a dais, cross-legged on pillows with a naked sword across his lap. There were servants along the walls and a courtier or two, or perhaps they were more valued servants, leaning against the marble pillars that supported the roof over the nave of the hall.

Djinar bowed.

The man on the dais inclined his head.

"My lord, I bring you…"

Djinar looked up and saw the deadliest of his enemies standing in the shadows behind the dais. His hand went to his sword.

"Hold," the lord of the hall said in accented Byzas. "He is no threat."

"No threat?" Djinar asked. "He is our greatest foe."

The lord smiled. "Look!. The serpent has no fangs."

He waved at the figure behind the dais, and the man didn't even blink.

"Gods," Djinar breathed, fascinated. "We heard he was dead!"

The lord had a good-natured laugh, a fatherly one, and he laughed it. "He very much wishes he was dead. Instead, he will serve me forever."

Djinar noted that the Attian lord said "me" and not "the Master."

"I heard that your attack on the Sultan Bey…"

Djinar met the man's eyes and hesitated. His laugh was so at odds with his eyes that the words died in Djinar's throat.

"It was unsuccessful," the lord admitted. "This busybody made too much trouble." He laughed again. "He will have to serve me for many years to balance the chaos he created in one hour." The lord shrugged. "Never mind. You have a message for me, syr?"

"From the Disciple of Megara," Djinar said, taking a sealed parchment cylinder from his bag.

"Even here, in my own house, you should not say such a thing," the lord counselled. He broke the seal with his thumb, and began to read.

The sword across his lap *moved*. It almost seemed to crawl, or writhe like a snake, and Djinar flinched.

Tell me, a thin voice said.

It was like the ringing of tiny bells, or the vibration of a lute string, and the hair began to rise on the nape of Djinar's neck, as if a haunting had crossed his path, or one of the fey.

"Interesting," the lord said. His smile was now quite unfeigned. "Your master speaks highly of you."

Djinar knew a moment of relief. "I'm sure I'm unworthy..." he began.

"Brilliant, ruthless, a true believer. Have you truly memorised *Precepts of a Life of Power*?"

"I have," Djinar said proudly.

"But you have almost no talent for the Art," the lord said.

Djinar sighed. "None."

The lord smiled. "We live in wonderful times. The Old Ones are about to be released back into the world, and life will return to its natural rhythm. The weak shall be slaves, and the strong shall be like gods." He raised his terrible eyes to Djinar. "Do you wish to have the powers of a great magos?" he asked, his voice mild.

"Of course!" Djinar said. "More than anything!"

"How splendid," the lord said. "And how very convenient."

He raised a hand, and the sword seemed to vibrate.

Later, it occurred to Djinar that the sword was laughing.

Four soldiers grabbed his enemy, still frozen in his grey robes—as if paralysed—behind the dais. They dragged him out into the light, and Djinar could see he'd been both defeated and subsequently tortured; the man's nails were ripped from his fingers, and his mouth bled where his teeth had been ripped out.

"We broke him," the lord said. "Not even Kurvenos, the great magos, the Lightbringer, could withstand us." He laughed his happy laugh. "Now I have most of his secrets and, best of all, access to his power."

Kurvenos stood unmoving. Only his eyes betrayed his terror, his horror, his despair.

"When I took him I knew he would make the most powerful Exalted ever created," the lord said. "But I needed a pilot for this mighty warship, someone of impeccable belief...and lo, your Disciple sent you to me."

"Me?" Djinar choked. "Exalted..."

"What is life but the lust for power?" the lord said, quoting from the Master's book of maxims. "Prepare to have more power than you ever dreamt."

Djinar screamed as he met Kurvenos' eyes, and the soldier's hands seized him.

Because, even as the lord and his acolytes began their chant, all Kurvenos' wounded eyes held was pity.

Book One

Parado

It is best in all cases to maintain the initiative, even against a stronger opponent, but when you are over-matched, you must be sure of your parries, covering your body and your hands, maintaining a reserve of tempo for the moment in which you can finally strike from your cover.

Maestro Sparthos,
unpublished notes to the book *Opera Nuova*

1

Megara

Night over Megara; a night with both moons high in the sky, the Red Moon almost full, its tiny disc slightly imperfect, while the Greater Moon, the Huntress, was a mere sickle that looked as if its open arms were ready to catch the smaller ball.

It was the first night of a Mazdayaznian festival, the Dreamcatcher Festival, and the tavernas were open all along the waterfront, despite the presence of the Watch and the unofficial, but heavily armed, black and yellow liveried Yellowjackets of General Roaris' household troops and political adherents. The General, who had taken to calling himself Lord Protector, had declared a curfew throughout the city while his household troops searched the city for "traitors." Despite that, not just Easterners, but every young person in the City seemed to be sitting in a tavern, drinking. The Watch stood by, frowning; and the Yellowjackets patrolled the Northside beachfront and the Southside *fondemento* in small mobs.

On Southside, between the Great Canal and the Low Bridge, under the shadow of the Red Lion, a tall *campanile* of brick, stood the largest inn in the city; the Sunne in Splendour. It towered over the palaces to either side and was surrounded by a sprawl of stables and outbuildings, kitchens, guest houses, and a boat dock on the seaward side and another on the Great Canal. It was a warren of comfort and good cooking, ruled by Laskarina Boulbousa, who, according to the City tittle-tattle, had started life as a prostitute among the notorious Pirates of the Sud. Whatever the truth of the rumour, her Inn was a haven on the waterfront, she paid well, and had the best cooks and the best ostlers in the city. She knew the Emperor, General Roaris and General Tribane personally.

Rumour also said that there had once been a husband, who had owned the original inn in its perfect canal-front location. Whether he had, as rumour claimed, been poisoned and then drowned, or whether he'd died of natural causes, or whether there'd never been a Syr Boulbousos at all, the inn's good reputation and its mistress' slightly colourful reputation tended to keep trouble away. The inn had hundreds of rooms, a dozen commons and fifty snugs, allowing the Lions, Blacks, and Whites to all hold rival meetings in its environs and never come to blows—which was as well, because the proprietress paid her bouncers well, too. When trouble didn't stay away, it was routinely punched in the head and thrown in the Great Canal, after which trouble, in most of its young forms, rarely returned.

The curfew was due to begin in a few minutes. A handsome man in a slashed doublet, black with gold lace revealing a black silk lining and a snowy white shirt that betrayed a slow leak of blood, leant out on a balcony above one of the inn's courtyards. On careful examination one might see that beneath the fashionable cosmetics, the man's face was bruised; and despite silver lines of Imoter *occultae*, his left hand was grotesquely swollen and had no fingernails.

"If he tries to enforce the curfew," Tiy Drako said with something of his usual insouciance, although he slurred his words, "we might retake this city tonight, with no army but offended drunks."

"You should be lying down," Aranthur Timos said.

Autumn had come to the city, and Aranthur was wearing a fine wool doublet—not as elaborate as Drako's, but finer than most, although it couldn't conceal his emaciation. In his high boots and half-cloak he looked like a Byzas gentleman, if a very tall, thin one.

Behind him, Dahlia Tarkas sat on a divan rapidly copying anything Drako said into the flyleaf of a book of translated Safiri poetry.

"He should, but he's a fool," Dahlia said. "Drako, sit down. None of this will work if you faint."

"I want to be *out there*," Drako spat. He was missing two teeth, which gave his voice a sibilance it didn't need. "Roaris is *winning*. Kurvenos is *gone*. Tribane is trapped at Antioke, and the Dark Forge widens every day."

Aranthur came up beside his friend, slipped an arm around his waist, and took him to the divan and into Dahlia's hands.

"I *hate* being cosseted," Drako said.

"You'd hate being dead a lot more," Dahlia said. "You have a touch of the Darkness, and honestly, only my *puissance* and Aranthur's is keeping you on your feet. If I release the pain-blocker…"

"She's not coming," Drako said pettishly.

"She'll come." Aranthur glanced out into the night and pulled the curtains across the balcony windows. "And Tribane isn't trapped. She'll win." He made himself smile. "Drako. We need to know everything about how you were taken. Everything you know about Kurvenos. Please… co-operate. You cannot *go out there.*"

Drako continued as if Aranthur had never spoken. "She needs food, powder, ball, replacements. Food. They all need food, from what you've said, and Roaris' move was brilliant. Even if we topple him, the damage he's done…"

Neither of the others disagreed.

I need food myself, Aranthur thought. He was hungry all the time.

"We should be planning a revolution," Drako insisted.

Aranthur tugged at his growing beard; very fashionable among the Byzas and the Souliotes too.

"Tiy, you know they say that Imoters make the worst patients? Well, spies give the worst debriefings. *We need to know what happened.* I have a plan," he said carefully. "And it doesn't involve starting a revolution. In fact the last thing we need is a wave of violence in the City to rip the bandages off every old quarrel—faction fights, house fights…" He poured himself some wine from a bottle on the side table. "And the first to die would be the Easterners." Aranthur put a hand on Drako's shoulder, and put a little power into his pain-blocker; it already needed reinforcement. "Stop trying to plan. You need serious healing, and to tell us what happened."

"Sophia," Drako said. He glanced at Dhalia. "When did he become so—?"

"Skinny?" Dahlia asked.

"Arrogant," Drako said.

"This from you?" Aranthur asked with a smile. "I made a plan, and I confess that I am now used to being the one to do it."

The two men looked at each other for too long.

Dahlia brushed some breadcrumbs from her doublet.

"Are you going to fight? Because if you do, I'm leaving."

"I'm struggling with the idea of Aranthur as the planner," Drako said.

Dahlia raised an aristocratic eyebrow. "I don't wish to take sides," she said. "But he planned your rescue. And you needed to be rescued. So stop being so fucking high and mighty and tell us what in ten thousand icy hells happened."

Drako winced and sat back suddenly, having encountered some half-Imotered ribs, and Aranthur put a hand to his neck to pass some more raw *puissance* into the healing.

Then he knelt in front of Drako. "Please?"

Drako blinked. "I hate telling the truth. And I hate failing, and this will be a truthful vomiting forth of fucking failure, fully fleshed in folly." He smiled his old smile, and then shook his head. "I have a pile of reports on the money…the money Roaris must be spending on bribes to stop his castle of ice from melting. He's living a gigantic lie—anything can topple him. And I *know* he's paying bribes."

He turned pale, and grunted, a hand across his abdomen, and Dahlia was there.

"Gods," he muttered. "Where is she? I'm dying here…" He looked at the door.

Dahlia looked worried, put more power into her treatment, and frowned at Aranthur.

He shrugged. "I was making this up from the moment the boat landed us here," he said. "I have to hope that our message got through."

Drako scowled up at him. "Do you want to hear this or not? They grabbed Kurvenos in Atti. There was an attempt on the Sultan Bey—well-planned, but someone betrayed it to the Capitan-Bey and it turned into a bloodbath. An open street fight with heavy magic, hundreds of bystanders killed. Kurvenos went to see if he could help. A friend of his was badly wounded…probably another Lightbringer, and no, Kurvenos was no more open-mouthed with me then than with— Sweet Sophia's wisdom! Aphres' flowery gate! Drax's dick!"

He doubled over, the pain of internal haemorrhage leaking through their various attempts at healing. He continued to swear, his white shirt showing the blood very clearly.

They both did what they could, which was far too little.

"If I die," Drako said suddenly. "Aphres. If I die, thanks for the rescue.

I love you two. That's no bullshit. I was going to die a nasty death and fuck, this is hard but it's still better." His head came up as the wave of pain passed. "They hit Kurvenos the moment he landed on the Ulama side, or that's what I heard from my source, who was there. They got the Kaptan Bey; not last night but the night before last…No, it's all too fucking confused now. Anyway, I met someone with access across the strait in Atti. I was going to mount a rescue. And the bastards had already started burning my people—two agents were already dead." Drako looked up. "What are you going to do, Aranthur?"

"I really do have a plan," he said. "Which is to do this with the minimum number of corpses. The stakes are very high, but this isn't a one-time crisis. We need the Empire, and the City, to be stable, even comfortable. We need them to be solid—so I swear to you, if we turn taking Roaris down into a fight we'll be playing straight into the Master's hands."

Drako shrugged. His eyes were too bright. "I know you're right. Because he'll play the factions—"

"Because we'll be weaker. Because there will be more distrust. We can only win by being united. Divided, we'll be crushed."

Aranthur was so close to Drako's left hand that he couldn't help but look at it. It looked as if it had been beaten with an iron rod. The Imoter they'd found on the waterfront had done his best, but had described the hand as nothing but a bag of bones.

Drako leant back. "Pain-blocker is wearing off," he said.

Aranthur shook his head like a reprimanded schoolboy.

"That shouldn't be possible," he said, and reinforced it.

It was like a problem in applied magical mathematics, with diminishing returns. The pain-blocker was going to fail, and his own hunger was growing like a mad thing eating at his vitals.

"Tell me what you plan," Drako muttered.

There was a sound outside; footsteps on the stairs.

"For starters, I plan to land the Black Stone and move it to the Academy, where it will be safe. Where we can use it." Aranthur was lying; he and Dahlia both knew it.

Dahlia's head turned slowly, and her eyes met Aranthur's with flat accusation, but there was, just then, a rhythmic knock at the door.

Aranthur leapt to his feet. In a moment, he had a small puffer in his hand. So did Dahlia. He moved to the door; she rose silently and went to the curtains, her left hand already burning with power, her shields ready to deploy.

Drako lolled on the divan.

Aranthur opened the door. Outside was a tall, cloaked figure in a plain mask and a long cloak—the brown cloak of a priest or priestess of Aploun.

"Cold Iron," the woman said.

Aranthur bowed.

She swept into the room, took off her mask, and stood over Drako. She was neither young nor old, neither beautiful nor ugly; a plain, nondescript woman with brown hair.

"Who are you?" Aranthur asked. He was not quite pointing the puffer at her.

"Drako, you look like all the hells," she said.

She leant over and put a hand on his forehead. He flinched, and a ring sparkled on her hand.

"Myr Benvenutu!" Aranthur said.

The woman turned, and gave Aranthur a slight smile.

"Very perceptive, Syr Timos."

Even as she spoke, her *guise* dropped and she was revealed as the Master of Arts. She wore a silk gown under the brown cloak, beautifully cut. Aranthur had never really seen her as a woman before, or if he had, her form had been buried beneath her authority.

She smiled more widely. "I *do* go to parties," she said.

Dahlia laughed and released her *puissance* and stepped out from behind the curtain, to be embraced by her mentor. Aranthur had never embraced the Master of Arts, so he stood in social confusion as she took his shoulders and kissed him on both cheeks.

"The man of the hour," she said in her deep voice. "Your work on Drako is very good, but he has a high fever, he's on the verge of going into shock and I think that's a touch of the Darkness. I've prepared… friends. For this eventuality. Listen, we have to move quickly. I have reason to believe that Roaris is going to strike against the festival, and has plans to enforce the curfew. And I don't have long—my daughter is pretending to be me a festival ball."

Aranthur had known the Master of Arts for more than a year and had no idea she had a daughter.

To Drako, she said, "Can you walk?"

Drako nodded. "Of course."

"Nonetheless," she said, and there was a controlled burst of power. Aranthur noted that her ease of access to the *Aulos* was as good, or better, than Qna Liras' or Kurvenos'.

"Sweet... Sophia's..." Drako thought better of whatever he was going to say. But he rose carefully. "I'm healed!"

"Not even a little," Benvenutu said. "I'm burning some of your youth to keep you on your feet. You have about ten minutes."

"Oh, gods," Drako said, as if the full extent of his injuries had just hit him.

"There's a chair waiting at the base of the steps," Benvenutu said. "The chairmen are friends. Get in, and trust them."

Drako nodded slowly. "Where are you going?" he asked.

"The Academy," Myr Benvenutu said. "I have to run it. Trust me. You will be well-hidden and taken care of."

She ran a hand over Drako's uninjured side, and suddenly he was *guised* exactly as she had been—as a tall woman with brown hair. She handed Drako her cloak and mask, and he bowed, winced, and steadied himself on the door frame.

"How will I find...?" he said.

The Master of Arts shook her head. "Tiy, you are badly hurt, inside and out. I've virtually cut your pain centres from your mind. It will take expert Imoters at least three weeks to heal you now. Just for once, do as you are told. Get in the chair and go."

"Damn it," Drako said, and then he was leaning against the door frame and Aranthur moved to catch him.

"Damn it," he repeated.

Aranthur put an arm under his and helped him down the steep steps. There were people at the bottom; strangers, a dozen students. One had Yellowjacket livery over his arm. Another, a small woman, had seized his arm.

"You're a fucking idiot if you think Roaris is a legitimate government," she said.

The off-duty Yellowjacket tried to shake her off.

"That's not an appropriate attitude," he said, in a superior tone not calculated to win any argument. "I shouldn't even be with you people—"

"I'll tell you what's not appropriate," spat a young man. "Arresting everyone you disagree with. And I hear a whisper that Tribane *didn't* lose in the East."

"Treason," the Yellowjacket said.

Another young man put a restraining hand on the Yellowjacket's sword arm.

"Jace," he said. "Not everything is treason. We're out for a night of drinking, and you, my friend, are being an arse. When you *fucking promised* to keep your pious aristocratic mouth shut."

Aranthur and Draco had reached the landing and Aranthur didn't think this was the moment to hesitate; he could see the chair and the two men who carried it just past the students at the base of the steps.

"Fuck," Drako said.

"Act drunk," Aranthur said.

"Not a problem," Drako hissed.

Aranthur began easing the brown-cloaked Drako down the last steps.

All of the students turned and looked at them. They were embarrassed to have been so loud, and curious, too, so they fell silent.

"Excuse me," Aranthur said, in a deliberately pettish voice. "I need to get this priest to her chair. And gentles all, there *is* a curfew. Shouldn't we all be going to our homes?"

The chair was sitting on its stretchers: a plain black box. Four very big chairmen stood by it, and all four wore cutlasses.

Most of the students moved from his path, but the biggest of them chuckled.

"No curfew in the Sunne in Splendour," he said.

He was a young man used to getting his way; not particularly belligerent. Merely big.

Aranthur looked past him to the man who'd been called Jace.

"And you a member of the Special Watch," he said, as if shocked. He got Drako into the chair.

The moment Aranthur's head was inside the closed cabin of the chair, Drako's *guised* eyes met his.

"Listen, Timos," he said. "You need some help to pull this off. Go to my office at the lighthouse." His voice was very quiet, and the students were noisy. "Complete works of Tirase—top shelf, volume three. My agent lists. You'll need the whole network to get anywhere."

"Why didn't you give it to Dahlia?" Aranthur asked.

Drako shook his head. "Just remember that someone on those lists fucked me over," he said bitterly. "Someone talked."

"You don't trust Dahlia?"

"I trust you, Timos. Right now, you are a Souliote farm boy, and that means you cannot possibly be playing for the Imperial throne. That's what all this is ultimately about, and I've been too fucking thick to see it," Drako muttered.

Aranthur could see the fever in the man's eyes.

"You need to go," he said.

"I'm not raving," Drako spat. "Damn it, Timos. The world is sinking. Be careful. Be fucking careful."

Aranthur was pulling his head out.

"Dahlia is fucking *related* to Roaris," Drako muttered. "There's a key with my steward at my palazzo. Say *gold rose* and he'll hand it over. Understand?"

"I don't believe it. I don't believe she'd ever betray you." He blinked. "But I understand."

"Someone did," Drako spat. "One of us is bad. Someone betrayed Kurvenos and then me. And she could have motive. Or maybe I'm cutting at shadows. Go with the gods, Aranthur. Do what you can."

Aranthur was reeling at his words, but he got his head out of the chair's box and looked at the chairmen.

The front right-hand man nodded. "We know our business," he said quietly. "We won't let the Cold stop us, and we have Iron in our bones."

Aranthur nodded and turned to the students.

"Well?" he asked, looking at the students, some of whom were actually several years older. "Do you have rooms, or do you just loiter in the courtyards?"

He worried he was overplaying it, but the Yellowjacket was red in the face, and they all shuffled away.

"What an arsehat," someone muttered, but they were going.

The chair had already gone, out of the High Street gate. Aranthur went back up the steps with a forced slowness, but the moment he got to the top, he whirled into action.

"We have to go," he said.

Dahlia nodded and collected her mask and cloak and her wide-brimmed black hat with its beautiful black plume. She'd bought it earlier with the last of Ansu's money.

Benvenutu had made herself another young cavalier, a dark-haired version of Dahlia, complete with a plain, workaday sword.

"We'll walk to the precinct," Benvenutu said. "No use of power to give us away."

Aranthur nodded. He put on his own cloak and hat and his old sword while Dahlia glared at him.

He accepted her glare and went back down the steps, glancing cautiously at the courtyard, but the students were gone, and the three of them hurried through the gate and into the night.

There were sounds of merriment from the other courtyards of the inn, but to the south they could hear chanting, and what might have been breaking glass in the Angel, the open square a whole canal block to the east.

"Straight up the steps," Benvenutu said.

She led the way, taking long strides, and Aranthur matched her, so that Dahlia had to hurry along behind.

"You don't trust *Tiy Drako*?" she hissed.

"I trust you," Aranthur said. "And the Master of Arts. I trust her." He kept going.

"You're insane!" Dahlia said. "You lied to him about the Black Stone..."

Aranthur turned. "Later. Please."

"But—"

"Listen!" he insisted.

Behind them, the chanting had become louder and more shrill, and now sounded like a series of waves breaking on rock.

Benvenutu turned. "Damn his eyes," she said. "Roaris *is* enforcing the curfew."

Indeed, from the first square above the inn, they could see a swirl of crowd activity down on the Square of the Angel, and what appeared to be a fire.

And the telltale sparkle of musket or puffer shots.

"Sophia!" Dahlia said. "He's firing on the crowd." She turned to Aranthur. "It'll be a revolution, whether you think that's a good idea or not."

Aranthur shook his head. "My views stand," he said. "Myr Benvenutu, have you seen the Emperor since he became sick?"

She was still watching the fringe of what appeared to be a riot in the piazza, two hundred feet below them.

"I have not."

"He appears to be afflicted with the Darkness, like Drako," Aranthur said. "Can it be cured?"

Benvenutu nodded, her mask gleaming white in the moonlight.

"Perhaps. Though we're not getting much research done these days."

"Iralia thinks he's been poisoned. In a strange way, I hope she is right."

Aranthur was listening. There were people above them on the steps.

"Blast of Darkness," Dahlia spat. "Poisoned is better?"

"I'd like to go directly to the palace," Aranthur said. "With you. To see the Emperor."

Benvenutu glanced at him.

"If Roaris is moving against the crowd, he's also going to isolate the Academy, if only to arrest students violating the curfew," Aranthur said. "We'll be taken if we go there."

Dahlia nodded, as if in unwilling agreement.

The Master of Arts thought for a long moment.

"Very well," she said. "My daughter is in for a long, dull evening..."

Suddenly the steps above them were full of men and women. Some wore yellow and black livery; a few had armbands, or headbands.

"Halt, in the name of the Protector!" called one.

"This way," Benvenutu said, and rolled over the railing on the steps.

Aranthur turned, and the man on the steps above him called again.

"Halt! Take them!"

Dahlia leapt over the railing and fell to the slope below.

Aranthur followed. He let himself drop, carefully, and landed at the base of the retaining wall that held the steep steps. Dahlia was already sliding away down the slope, and Aranthur had no choice but to follow, as the hill was too steep to stand. He grabbed at trees and slowed his descent enough to not land atop Dahlia, and then his sword tangled between his legs, and he rolled over and got a face full of dirt and old leaves. He rolled again, and his head struck the stems of a decorative bush; not a heavy blow, but enough to stun him. He hung there a moment, and then something gave and he fell free.

He landed badly, knocking the air out of Myr Benvenutu. And he was immediately aware that he'd lost his sword in the long slide down the hill.

There were calls above them, and the sound of more people sliding.

Dahlia glanced at the damage to her hat. "We have to run."

"I'm not leaving my sword," Aranthur said.

He sprang back up the steep hill, grabbing at the brush for support. The hill above him seemed alive; a dozen Yellowjackets and their supporters were combing the bushes.

He raised his magesight and saw the sword; not far above him.

"Ware magery!" called a voice.

Three shields went up on the hillside and a heavy offensive *occulta* flashed through the undergrowth on the steep hill, burning plants.

Aranthur's shields unrolled around him like a fountain springing to life, almost without his volition, and then his reaching hand closed on his sword hilt.

That was stupid, it said.

Aranthur let himself fall back down the hill, clutching the ancient sword. The belt had caught on something and the whole scabbard had been torn away.

This time he landed on the trail with a little more control, and on his feet.

"This way!" Dahlia called.

Aranthur ran to follow her along the bottom of the Cleft, where footpads sometimes lurked and adventurous students went to have privacy.

He turned a sharp corner; one he knew well, just before the trail crossed a wooden bridge over the brook that ran from the leak in the Pinnacle. He saw Dahlia ahead; heard Benvenutu's boots on the wooden planks of the little bridge…and also heard the pursuit at his heels.

So when he reached the bridge, he turned.

His pursuer released a barrage of golden light. It wasn't a very powerful working; the Academy was careful about teaching offensive powers, but most of the older families had their own ancient attack *occultae* despite the legal bans.

Aranthur's layered green and red and gold shields absorbed the attack effortlessly.

The woman behind the first caster also threw something prepared. Hers was a harsher red, and much stronger, and her balefire had heft in the *Aulos*, but Aranthur's shields had withstood—however briefly—attack from an entire military choir at Antioke.

The woman charged forward under the cover of her sorcery, blade in hand.

Aranthur let her come, and covered her ferocious cut with his scabbarded sword.

She passed back into a low guard and cut again, another heavy blow, and this time he covered it with a cross, with a hand at each end of his sword, as if the weapon was a quarterstaff. Then he punched her in the face with his hilt and she fell, spitting teeth. The man threw another golden barrage and Aranthur stepped forward, through it, and kneed him in the groin, then clipped him in the head, dropping him. There were half a dozen more coming, and Aranthur sprang back onto the bridge. He cast at the speed of sword-strokes, creating a plane of force like a standing shield just beyond the little bridge, then he sprang back, off the bridge on the other side, and coated the surface of the bridge and the stones for twenty paces on either side with three fingers of pure ice, and dropped a curtain of darkness over the whole.

He left the standing illusion of his own rainbow of shields pulsing beyond the enhanced darkness.

All in three fencing tempos.

Because he had learned a great deal in three months of war.

He ran. He ran along the little stream for thirty paces before he folded his shields in, and then dropped them, greatly daring. Nothing savaged him. The trail wound on, and he was hit in the face by branches more than once, but he didn't fall.

The trail grew steeper, and he used the wet ground to leave another ice trap under a curtain of darkness, simple *volteie* known to any student prankster, but thrown with a strength and confidence Aranthur had not had a year before. Freezing water was merely the reverse of warming it; darkness was merely the opposite of light.

As the trail became a gravel path, Aranthur caught up with Dahlia and the Master of Arts.

Benvenutu smiled at him.

"Where did those shields come from?" she asked.

"His wife," Dahlia replied.

The Master of Arts shook her head. "I see that you both have many tales to tell for such a short absence," she said. "But if we don't keep running..."

A shout, a scream, and the sound of a body falling. Another scream.

"Ice," Aranthur said. "In the dark. Darkness, enhanced."

Benvenutu smiled again. "What fun," she said, and casually laid an ice wall across the whole path.

Dahlia nodded. "Let's run anyway," she said.

"I'm taking a detour. I'll throw them off your scent," Aranthur said.

Before Dahlia could respond, he was off. He sputtered some excess *saar* as he moved, and left more at the bridge into the Templeside deme when he crossed the palace canal. Then he headed west, climbing back onto the slopes of the city's central ridge; not quite doubling back, but close. The Temple of Light towered above him, its vast bulk and ancient architecture symbolic of the city's durability. The steepest parts of the hillside were heavily wooded; professional foresters tended the hill, the same foresters who maintained parts of the Imperial gardens. The trees were lovingly cared for, but as Aranthur made his way along a path cut into the steep hillside, he found a hollow tree—an ancient holm oak, as tall as the temple and still green, but so hollow that someone could camp inside. He spent a moment investigating; found that inside the hollow trunk, one of the branches was also hollow; there were signs of occasional human habitation. He smiled, took a quick measurement, and then moved on, marking the tree's location by triangulation against the palace, the temple, and the Arsenale at his feet. Then he turned south, into the oldest parts of the city, where the alleys were only four feet wide and the canals wound like blood vessels; the Vecchio.

He took boats twice; the first to cross into the Vecchio, and the second when he got lost, and throughout he worried that he'd wasted too much time. But there were no Yellowjackets in the Vecchio; the neighbourhoods of the city's oldest deme were insular and very protective. Nor were they all poor; many affluent people had their roots in the Vecchio and they tended to protect it.

Aranthur's gondolier dropped him back on the waterfront west of the Angel, almost where he'd begun; if he looked, he could see some of the windows of the distant Sunne in Splendour where they had rented rooms. There were teams of City Imoters, well lit with their characteristic blue magelights, in the great Square of the Angel, which told Aranthur that the Watch had withdrawn and that people had been hurt.

He went the other way, west along the waterfront, past the palaces that lined the Great Canal and then south as the piers curved. It was very late, or very early; he passed several drunks, and a street food seller who was operating out of a tiny alley entrance, obviously aware that he was out after curfew. Aranthur, who was hungry all the time, stopped to buy three excellent fish pies.

"You've made my evening," the pie-seller said.

"I'll just have one more," Aranthur said, watching the waterfront.

The fourth was as good as the other three, and the man smiled.

"Where do you put it, mate?" he said. "You're skinny as a fishing net." He extended a flask. "On the house. You bought four pies."

Aranthur took a swig of a very respectable apple brandy and gave the pie-seller his best Imperial bow.

"You are the very prince of pie-sellers," he said.

"You're the fuckin' prince o' pie eaters," the man grinned.

Aranthur walked away, wondering at the ease with which he'd just spent what would once have been a week's budget. It seemed ridiculous to have so much money. And that he lived in the palace…

He saw two people coming towards him and he reached for his sword. They flinched; he stepped into a doorway to let them pass, and saw a man with a bloody face leaning on a woman…

"Help me?" she asked. "The Yellowjackets attacked us. Oh, Sophia…"

Aranthur looked around, and then led them across the waterside street to where they could get some shelter on the portico of a dockside warehouse.

In the time it would take a priestess of Aphres to invoke her goddess, Aranthur had staunched the man's bleeding. His nose was broken.

"Should I set it?" Aranthur asked. It was something any Souliote child could do.

The man was Byzas. He shrugged.

"Do it!" he snorted through the blood.

"It'll hurt like ten thousand hells," Aranthur said, and then, without warning, put the nose back into place.

"*Arrggh!*" the man gurgled. "Oh, that *is* better."

Aranthur was getting good at pain-blockers, and he'd learned a lot of basic magical medicine in Armea. He did what he could.

"Get him some willow bark tea as soon as you can," he told the woman.

"Who are you?" she asked. "I can't thank you enough."

Aranthur smiled. "Someone who has to keep moving," he said.

"Were you in the...?" She looked away. "It wasn't a riot. It was supposed to be a *festival*." She was not quite sobbing.

"I was close," Aranthur said. "And now I have to go."

"Tell me your name..."

"No."

Aranthur bowed, and walked away.

Ten minutes later, having doubled back and watched his back trail as Drako had taught him, he walked on to the *fondemento* below the Drako family palazzo and demanded to see the steward.

2

Megara

Two hours later, Aranthur sat with Iralia, nervously playing *taraux*, neither of them with their minds on the game. Dahlia was carefully brushing the dirt out of her hat. A pair of palace servants hovered nearby. Aranthur had wood shavings on his hose, from whittling, and Iralia brushed them away like an attentive wife or mother.

"Tell me again why you don't trust Tiy Drako," Dahlia said.

"I do trust Tiy Drako," Aranthur said.

His cards were terrible. He had almost no swords, and swords were trump. It was his lead, and his hand full of low coins betokened disaster. On the other hand, there was a plate of calamari—delicious squid, deep fried in olive oil—and Aranthur's body craved food all the time. He had to keep wiping his fingers to keep the oil off the cards.

"You lied to him about the Black Stone."

Dahlia's voice was flat, calm, without accusation; she merely spoke a truth.

Aranthur nodded. *I will not tell her that Tiy doesn't trust her. Aphres, Armea was easier than this. I knew who to fight.*

Drako's golden rose, the symbol of his Imperial authority, was pressed against his heart, on a heavy gold chain, and with it the key to Drako's office in the Lighthouse by the harbour master's. Aranthur had spent part of the night looking at the lists of Drako's informers and agents, and felt no wiser than before.

He threw his highest card into the suit of coins—the prince.

"We need to look into Kurvenos' death," Aranthur said.

Dahlia made a face. "That's fairly low on my list," she said.

"He was our mentor," Aranthur said. "Also our most powerful magus."

"He manipulated us however he saw fit for his own agenda," Iralia said.

Dahlia nodded at Iralia; one of their rare moments of agreement.

Iralia grunted and tossed the three of coins on the prince, and Aranthur took the trick. He looked over his remaining cards at Iralia.

"My point is that Drako was taken," he said, and tossed in the eight of staffs.

Iralia pounced, took the trick with the queen of staffs and then came back with the queen.

"I want to understand this Black Stone. And Alis' victory... the siege. I want to hear it all."

Aranthur dropped the two of swords to take the trick, and Iralia moaned. He played his queen of coins, and ate more calamari.

Iralia made a face at him and threw the five of coins atop it.

"And?" Dahlia asked. "Let's deal with Drako first, mm?"

"Someone betrayed him," Aranthur said. "And he doesn't know who. So for the moment..." He shrugged. "Listen, Dahlia. He's badly hurt and he's going to get some healing. You saw him. You heard the Master of Arts. And he's not going to be available to us... so..."

Dahlia made a face. "I get it," she said. "I don't like it, but I assumed you were headed somewhere."

She held her beautiful Maguan beaver felt hat up to a carefully produced magelight.

Aranthur played his ten of coins, Iralia trumped it with a low sword, and Aranthur's game was over.

"Surely you plan to bring this Black Stone to the Academy, or to the palace," Iralia said. "What is it, really?"

Aranthur leant forward. "It was the capstone of the Black Pyramid," he said very quietly.

"I could brush that for you, my lady," said one of the two waiting servants. He was tall and blond, with chiselled features; a Northerner, perhaps a Keltai.

"You could," Dahlia said with a smile. "But then I'd have to play cards."

He smiled back.

Dahlia glanced at Aranthur, but his eyes were on his cards.

"It has a number of unique qualities," he said. "We have to keep it safe. Whatever we do, we cannot let Roaris have it."

Iralia looked up with a meaningful glance at the servants. Dahlia was glaring at Aranthur, who had the good grace to look sheepish, and went back to his cards.

Iralia was distracted, knowing that the Master of Arts was examining her lover, the Emperor. She played a staff after a run of wins when Aranthur had one sword left. He took the trick. His coins were useless but he had a few cups; he threw down the nine of cups, his highest card, with a feigned negligence.

Iralia had only one cup, and it was the eight.

With nothing left worth playing, Iralia took all the rest for one point.

"You play too hard," she said snappishly.

"Too hard?" he asked.

She shrugged, rose, fanned herself, looked at the door to the Emperor's chamber, and then poured herself three fingers of brandy and drank it while complaining it would be terrible for her complexion. Dahlia rolled her eyes.

"What can be taking so long?" Iralia asked.

Aranthur was so used to Iralia as a controlled, commanding presence that he was taken aback by her fidgeting and her nerves.

"Worried about your future?" Dahlia drawled. "I'm sure you still have all the necessary talents to find a replacement."

Iralia turned, her face suddenly transformed by anger.

Dahlia smiled mockingly. "I'm sorry. Were you going to say something?"

Iralia stepped up close. "I was going to say that it must be easy for you, as a child of aristocrats who is contemptuous of her own beauty, to despise those who have to use ours. Have you ever known an hour of poverty?"

"My parents are poor." Dahlia was clearly surprised to be challenged.

"So poor you didn't eat? Didn't have shoes?" Iralia asked, and her eyes were like fire. "So poor you had to sleep with strangers to keep your mother alive? That kind of poor, Myr? Or the kind where your fifty-room mansion has a few holes in the roof, and you must bear the shame of struggling to afford matched horses for the carriage?" Iralia leant forward until her nose almost touched Dahlia's. "Shall I tell you what I did when I was twelve, little princess?"

She stood back. Her face was no longer flawless; blotched with anger, and with the almost invisible marks left by the Imoters when they rebuilt her face after the fight in the Square of the Mulberry Trees. Aranthur was struck by her strength, her poise.

"I love him," Iralia said quietly. "I am a courtesan. I fully admit I have a contract. But I have never met a man I like better, and if he dies, I will never be the same."

Dahlia had the grace to look abashed. And then she took Iralia's hand.

"Well, I'm a fool. Isn't that what Aranthur says twice a day? I apologise, Iralia. I have done you wrong."

Iralia gave her usual smile—if not quite so brilliant. She was breathing like a bellows.

"You can't apologise for what you assume," she said. "And you have always assumed I was a whore in my heart. But I accept your apology, Dahlia."

Her face suggested that she was still angry, and Aranthur writhed. Both women were merely expressing the fears that beset them all; about the Emperor, about... *everything.* Aranthur understood that, but he wished that Dahlia hid her thoughts better.

The two women were still glaring when the door opened and Benvenutu emerged, followed by the Emperor's valet, Dakos.

"May we have some privacy?" Benvenutu asked, and Iralia motioned the servants out. Dakos bowed.

"I'd like all three of you to wait right here," Benvenutu said firmly. She pointed to Iralia's antechamber. "In fact, I insist on it."

Dakos looked stricken, but the young Keltai man shrugged.

"As you wish," he said. The woman sat.

Benvenutu closed the door and cast a simple *protection* that made the room relatively difficult to penetrate by sound or sight.

"The Emperor is not suffering from the Darkness." She looked at Iralia. "Or not quite. He has been poisoned. At least once, perhaps multiple times."

"I knew it," Iralia said. "When he fell, I started tasting his food myself, and I've been sick twice." She sat. "I told Aranthur—it's subtle. It's not mortal, it attacks the will."

"It is *aurax*," Benvenutu said. "Subtle and damning. Illegal even to own. The very sort of thing that Lightbringers police, in normal times."

Iralia reached out, and Aranthur took her hand. Her grip was like iron, but her voice was steady.

"And the Emperor?"

Benvenutu poured herself a brandy.

"He will take weeks to heal, and there may be serious damage. As you deduced, the drug is meant to rob the victim of their will. It's usually used in sex crimes and interrogations." Benvenutu's eyes narrowed. "I think he *does* have more than a shade of the Darkness as well, Iralia. The aurax and the Darkness interacted. Or that's how I see it."

"Surely we need an Imoter?" Dahlia asked.

Benvenutu shook her head. "How many people know, for certain, that the Emperor is not...fully competent?"

"The people in this room. And Dakos. The other servants suspect, but they don't know." Iralia shook her head. "I've been as careful as I could be."

Dahlia laughed a bitter laugh. "Roaris must be in a permanent panic. If the Emperor awakens, everything falls apart. His whole takeover explodes. And he can't be sure."

Aranthur was looking into the fire. "If the Emperor dies, who succeeds him?"

"There's no direct heir," Dahlia said.

Benvenutu cast a very significant glace at Iralia, who looked away.

"So there would be an election among the candidates?" Aranthur had barely paid attention in his Constitutional Law course as a first year, but it seemed some of it had, indeed, sunk in. "Is Roaris a candidate?"

"Blessed Sophia," Dahlia said. "Of course he's a fucking candidate."

Aranthur nodded. "So, if the Emperor dies, Roaris has a path to the throne. But if the Emperor is alive, he's locked into his present course, trying to hang on to as much of the machinery of government as he can until either the Emperor dies, or he wakes up and takes the whole thing back."

Dahlia nodded. "And in the meantime, we have to assume that the poisoner is in the palace—along with spies..."

"And we have to wonder about the loyalty of the troops..."

Benvenutu shook her head. "You are getting carried away. The guards are utterly reliable. So are the Nomadi and the Axes."

"Ten weeks ago there was a conspiracy within the Noble Guard," Aranthur said.

Benvenutu blinked.

"That gives me an idea," Dahlia said.

"I have one too," Aranthur said.

"So do I," Iralia said. "First things first. Myr Benvenutu, can you heal my lover?"

Benvenutu nodded. "I think so. And I can bring in some expert help. We've been working on the Darkness since the Dark Forge rose in the sky. But anyone we bring in must stay here, in the palace, until we're done. No one can know." She frowned. "Except my partner. I want her here, along with someone from the Academy."

Aranthur had a moment to savour the implications. He hadn't known that the Master of Arts had a partner.

"If you stay here, no one will know where you are..."

"Yes. That will have all sorts of resounding implications," Benvenutu said. "Blessed Sophia, as Dahlia is wont to say."

"We're going about this all wrong." Dahlia stood up, clearly excited.

"Wait," Benvenutu said. "Those three outside. The servants. Dakos has the best opportunity..."

"Who feeds the Emperor?" Aranthur asked.

"I do," Iralia said. "And I taste everything. I've only been sick... twice..." She looked *harrowed.* "I know aurax—I've been fed it twice." She winced. "This is something different."

Benvenutu drank off her brandy. "Interesting. Iralia, I may want to test you, too."

"Of course."

Benvenutu nodded, thinking. "And we will need to find out who came to the palace kitchens on the days you were sick."

"Cold Iron business," Aranthur said. "The exact sort of thing we do."

"Except that we have no time to do it, and everything takes time," Dahlia said with a touch of petulance. "May I explain my idea?"

Benvenutu gave her a somewhat patronising smile. "Very well, my dear."

Dahlia did not roll her eyes. But it was close. "Secrecy only suits Roaris."

"You're now convinced that he's bad?" Aranthur asked.

"Let me get finish," Dahlia said, "but yes." She looked around. "Listen.

We have... what... twenty Souliote mercenaries who served in Masr. And at Antioke. And half a dozen Nomadi. Right? Where are they now?"

Aranthur knew where they were. He forced himself not to smile. He did not, in truth, like keeping secrets from friends, but that was now his life.

"They are at sea."

"But here... soon?"

Aranthur nodded. "Perhaps as soon as tomorrow."

Dahlia nodded. "But they have been at sea to keep... everything... safe." Aranthur almost writhed. His wife, the demon, had other orders. But Dahlia didn't need to know that. "So when they return... we land our troops and put them in the barracks. They tell their stories to the guards."

"And everyone learns the truth." Aranthur examined the idea. "Roaris' people will damn them as liars..."

"They will. But the problem with *his* story is that it's a lie," Dahlia said. "The destruction of Tribane's army *must* have been a huge shock to the people of this city, and to the empire. How many men and women are waiting, every gods-damned day, to find out if a son, daughter, sister, lover, is lying dead in Armea? All we have to do is spread the news that it was a victory, not a defeat. Say that the casualty lists will be published. And listen—we can even get Tribane to give us the casualty lists. Am I right?"

"Messenger birds. Even a ship. She's five days away." Aranthur shook his head. "You are brilliant."

"Yes, I fucking am," Dahlia said. "In five days, we can pop Roaris like a bubble. Frankly, when the people hear the extent of his lies about their loved ones..."

"I'm totally in favour of this," Aranthur said. "But lies beget lies. Isn't that why Cold Iron exists? Roaris can claim that he was lied to—he must be prepared to have the tables turned like this."

"You have a different plan?" Dahlia said.

"Not all that different," Aranthur said. "I want to use the process of government—to reach the council of seventeen and get them to revoke Roaris' authority."

"He's already arrested six of them," Iralia said.

Dahlia looked shocked. "You know their names?"

The names of the Inner Council were usually kept secret.

"I'm the consort of the Emperor," she said without smugness.

"Eleven of seventeen is still a quorum," Dahlia said.

"But they're all the ones Roaris trusts," Iralia said.

"We can still work with that," Dahlia said. "I agree with Aranthur. And it *is* like my plan. We fight his secrecy with openness and truth. We release Tribane's military dispatches to the remains of the Council of Seventeen. It is, after all, their business."

"And then we take Roaris in an act of treason," Aranthur said.

"We do?" Iralia asked.

The Master of Arts looked at Aranthur and shook her head. "You were such a pleasant, direct boy." She shrugged. "How do we take him?"

Aranthur looked around.

"I like Dahlia's plan. We find the poisoner here. The three of us attend directly the Emperor personally for at least the next few days, and when Inoques comes back, we put our troops in with the palace garrison and send her, if she's willing, back to Antioke with a load of whatever we think General Tribane needs most."

"Food and wine," Dahlia said.

"Agreed. Meanwhile, Dahlia makes contact with the Seventeen and hands over our dispatches. If that fails, we approach the Three Hundred with the same information." Iralia made a face.

"The Three Hundred are the National Assembly," Aranthur began, and Iralia gave him a frustrated glance.

"I know *exactly* what the Three Hundred are," she said. "But it's far from easy getting them to meet and agree on anything."

"This could take weeks," Dahlia said.

Aranthur nodded. "And the rift is widening, and Tribane is still under siege at Antioke. Worse, if Antioke falls then Roaris' lie becomes true. You understand that? If Tribane and her army are lost, we'll have Roaris forever."

"Blessed Sophia, it's like a game of chess."

"It's like three games of chess on three different boards with shifting paths between them," Benvenutu said. "Come to think of it, that could be fun. Regardless, I need equipment from the Academy, and I need Edvin and Janos Sittar, if he'll come. Though Sittar would also have to go back, as someone has to run the Studion. On balance, I'd rather bring Litha here."

Aranthur suspected, strongly, that Sittar was a Lightbringer. "Litha?" he asked.

"My...partner," the Master of Arts said primly.

He nodded. "Where is the *Ulmaghest*?"

"Here," Benvenutu said. "Somewhere in the Imperial Library. I had it sent here with the reader when I thought I'd be arrested."

"Perfect," Aranthur said.

"How do you get a message to the Academy?" Dahlia asked.

"Message stick," the Master of Arts said, and drew one from her hair.

"No," Aranthur said. "In Armea, the enemy had access to all of our sticks."

"What?" Benvenutu spat.

Dahlia nodded. "They had all of our codes. It almost cost us the battle."

"That's why we're not using them to talk to Tribane," Aranthur said.

"We'll have to chance it," Benvenutu said.

"No. Please. The sticks are compromised and we have to think of a new way."

"I'll go," Dahlia said.

"No," Aranthur said. "Almost everyone in the City knows you. Let me go. Myr Benvenutu, may I ask that you only use the stick to contact Master Sittar. Tell him you are going to your country house, and that you are terrified that you have the Darkness?" He was making it up as he went, but he liked it.

She narrowed her eyes. "I've never been terrified..."

"I know, Magistera, but rather like casting a *guise*, this sort of deception will work better if you show our adversaries the kind of person they'd like you to be—terrified and weak—not the person you are."

"Blessed Magdala," Dahlia murmured. "Timos has been possessed by Tiy Drako. Aranthur, you are scaring me." But she smiled. "Myr, I agree."

Aranthur assumed this was Dahlia's idea of praise and shrugged.

The Master of Arts was looking at him oddly, and she grabbed his arm.

"Come here, Aranthur," she commanded.

He obeyed.

She drew him close; almost into an embrace in which she held his shoulders and gazed intently into his eyes for too long. Iralia looked startled, and Dahlia was doing something, and he was...confused.

She let him go. "I'm sorry. That was intrusive and possibly immoral, but I had to know. Do you know why we advise students not to kill, Aranthur Timos?"

Aranthur thought that she had asked him this question almost every time they spent time together. And given him different reasons each time, too.

So he shrugged. "I know all the reasons I've been told," he said.

"None of them are lies, Aranthur. But for you and me, the real reason is that it is too damned easy to kill. Have you ever noticed how few of the *occultae* we teach have genuinely offensive effects?"

Aranthur nodded. "I had noticed. A battlefield is a strange place to discover how little you know about killing." And took a deep breath. "And about *sihr.*"

The Master of Arts nodded, and took his hand, so that her long, bony hand lay across his, and he could feel the cold that seemed to emanate from the ring she wore: the Secret Fire.

"Swords are quick, but magic is faster than thought," she said. "I can kill with *sihr* before I have time to consider, reflect or regret."

"Like a puffer," Dahlia said.

"Yes," the Master of Arts agreed. "With the powder weapons, we have made it possible for every woman and every man to take a life as fast as we can. And that's a warning. This is not a problem faced by the *magi*, but by all of us—that we can kill faster than we can think about it. But for us, we need no device, no powder, no sword, no dagger to do it. The thought is the deed. And every death..." She shrugged.

"Magistera, did Tirase intend to limit our access to power?" Aranthur asked.

Benvenutu squeezed his hand. "He never said anything of the kind," she said. "But he was a very subtle person, and a very arrogant one. For many years now I have thought that the aggregate of his teachings and institutions might have deliberately limited the abilities of the most talented casters."

"It seems a very dangerous course, if none are made aware of it," Aranthur said, staring out of the window. "If we now face another War of Wrath, for example, we will not have the...I don't know the magical term. If we spoke of artillery, I'd call it the weight of metal."

"Yes," Benvenutu said. "It means we don't have the sheer offensive power our enemies can muster."

Dahlia, who had been silent, spoke up. "During the battle, with genuine battle mages—" she looked at Benvenutu—"I was far more powerful than most of them, and—"

"And your house zealously protects its powers, and trains you in otherwise forbidden military magics," Benvenutu said. "Don't deny it. You are not the first Tarka I've trained."

Dahlia blushed.

Aranthur made a slight sound of sudden understanding.

"Oh, yes," Benvenutu said to him. "The old houses preserve some very serious battle lore that we do not teach at the Studion. Why should we? Why would anyone give an aggressive and hormonal adolescent student the keys to a powder magazine?"

She was glaring at Aranthur. "I wanted to teach you some skills. But you kept killing people with swords, and I didn't think you were suitable to learn…" She shrugged. "I had no idea what you two were about to face, and I'm very glad you survived. While we are all here, I will attempt to make it up to you. Dahlia…" She reached out.

Aranthur realised that he was watching what Benvenutu had done to him, and he was not surprised by her ruthlessness, or her skill. She immobilised Dahlia, *subjugated* her will, and glided through her shields while looking into her eyes from so close that a kiss wouldn't have required more than a twitch of her head.

Just for a moment, Aranthur wondered how dangerous Benvenutu really was.

"By the gods," Benvenutu sighed. "I pray that I may claim some credit that you two children have survived this so far with so little darkness. Dahlia has not, but Aranthur—you used *sihr.*"

He thought about lying; she did not have a *compulsion* on him.

"Yes," he admitted.

"Why?" she asked.

Dahlia was looking at him with horror, while Iralia shrugged as if it was of no consequence.

He bit his lip. "I was angry and tired," he said. "And my friends were dying."

Benvenutu nodded. "I have used *sihr*," she said. "It is the first step on a short, steep road which makes *thuryx* addiction appear banal by comparison. But until you have tasted it, you cannot know."

"I…" Aranthur wanted to say, *I will never do it again* and he also wanted to say *I regret nothing.* But he feared he might do it again, and he had bitter regrets. "I hated it."

"And yourself?" Benvenutu said tenderly.

"Yes," he said quietly. His eyes flicked to Dahlia and she looked away.

Benvenutu shook her head. "I am a mother," she said. "And this is how it feels when your child has chosen their path and you cannot change their mind."

She embraced Aranthur, and his eyes filled with tears; some for himself, and some for the Dhadhi and the men he'd killed.

Benvenutu kissed him on the cheek. "We will talk. Even Iralia might benefit from some lessons."

Iralia started. "I thought that *autodidacts* like me were outside your system and could not be taught?"

The Master of Arts raised both eyebrows. "That's interesting. Perhaps a few. But you have a broad range of powers, my dear, and you have had lessons—I can tell."

"Dearly bought," Iralia said bitterly.

"I would not charge," Benvenutu said. "I'm going back to the Emperor."

Iralia took Aranthur's hand. "Tell me she is everything she appears to be."

"I think so," Aranthur said.

Benvenutu reappeared in the elaborate door that led to the Emperor's private apartment.

"What are we doing to find Kurvenos?" she asked.

Aranthur felt as if his head was spinning. "Nothing this instant," he admitted.

Benvenutu shook her head. "If you are our Tiy Drako, find out what people know."

Iralia rose to her feet. "I think I need to speak to the palace staff. We're going to need an unprecedented level of secrecy, are we not?"

"Oh, yes," Benvenutu said.

Dahlia kissed her mentor on the cheek and left through the main door and Aranthur followed her. Iralia was explaining the new system to the three servants, who listened attentively. Aranthur was watching the handsome Keltai man carefully, but if he was guilty of anything, he gave no indication of it.

He followed Dahlia out of the Imperial Apartments and down from the Apex towards their own rooms.

She whirled. "What are you up to?" she asked.

Aranthur had a head full of plots, and he shrugged.

"Where is the ship? You're not a very good liar, and I know your body language pretty well." There was a pause, and both of them blushed.

"Inoques will keep the Black Stone safe," he said.

"And how do you plan to take down Roaris?" she asked. "I noticed you evaded that. When did you use *sihr*?" She was glaring at him.

Aranthur had never felt such a kinship for the ever-deceptive Tiy Drako as in that moment.

"In the Black Bastion," he said with brutal frankness.

"I should have known. You killed…seventy?"

"Too fucking many," he admitted.

She surprised him by taking his hand and squeezing it.

"I don't doubt you, Aranthur. Forget it. But the whole thing with the Stone, and this plan to take Roaris. You are keeping secrets—too many secrets."

"I have a plan," he said. "I promise that I'll lay it out if, and only if, it looks as if we can pull it off."

Dahlia searched his face for a moment and then shrugged.

"Good. What's your plan to getting to the academy?"

Aranthur breathed in relief. "Simple," he said.

Dressed as he always used to, in a short linen tunic belted with a dagger thrust through a ragged purse, and with his Masran-made buckler on his hip, old hose out at one knee, and shoes that seemed at the verge of falling apart, Aranthur looked like any other Souliote worker in the streets of the Temple district, and he crossed the deme bridge and passed the Watch checkpoint without even a word. First he climbed Temple Hill, and after a little wander over the steep and heavily forested hillside, he found his hollow tree again. He took the plug he'd carved in the barracks courtyard and fitted it into the hollow branch. He tried it three times, until it was almost seamless—a hiding place in the middle of the city. The wooden plug made the hollow branch look solid.

Then, having memorised the first three of Drako's lists, he moved across the city looking at signposts. They were not obvious; the Cold Iron drop boxes didn't have numbers. Some of the signposts were just the walls of tenements or old trees that shaded the squares; the signs nothing more than a tack placed in the tree, or a chalk mark on the flying buttress of a local temple, or a red ochre smudge on a white marble statue.

The boxes were just as well-hidden: an envelope slipped between two boards in an abandoned dog kennel; a rusting cauldron, half-buried in mud on the slopes below the temple of light; a brick that moved in a garden wall. Inside a tavern: a small wooden box placed on a plate rail so that it couldn't be seen from the room below. In an outhouse behind the Sunne in Splendour: a tin box hidden in the cobwebbed rafters.

Aranthur noted the signs and emptied the boxes in turn, moving quickly, painfully aware that any of these might be the trap that had taken Drako. And also staggering under the weight of the responsibility. Drako had *been* Cold Iron, and Aranthur felt unequal to the role. He waited for a shout, a rush of feet, the gleam of blades, the sound of a shot.

But none of that happened, and his doublet was stuffed with the gleaning of six drop boxes. He climbed a street by the Academy, wondering how to be less conspicuous, and walked right past two Yellowjackets...

And Djinar. There the man was, briefing his men; Aranthur forced himself to shuffle past, a weary workman facing another day of work, painfully aware that he had a shirt stuffed with incriminating evidence.

Djinar didn't see him. Journeymen all over the city were headed to work, and the Watch posts couldn't stop everyone. But the man looked terrible; haunted, and his face was pinched and almost grey.

A quarter of an hour's walk later and he was in the Square of the Mulberry Trees, his hands still shaking. The violence had happened less than two months before, but the Emperor himself had ordered repairs, and the storefronts and houses, still so new they smelled of lime and new wood, were complete. Beautifully glazed windows with the best of Murana glass gazed out on twenty replanted mulberry trees.

Ghazala's leather workshop had new windows, a new door, and a beautifully painted sign. The new front window showed the family's best work: indigo-blue dyed purses, a magnificent velvet belt covered in fine silver plaques, scabbards, garters, shoulder bags for travel, saddlebags.

Manacher was cutting belts at a new and very solid front table. He looked up, did a double take, and Aranthur was enveloped in a particularly warm embrace.

"*Madhar!*" Manacher called.

"It's a secret," Aranthur insisted, his heart still racing from the encounter with Djinar, and he was still insisting fifteen minutes later, after he'd regaled his former employer with most of the Empire's secrets. He trusted Ghazala and her son absolutely; it seemed to him that if they were to betray the City, there might be no point protecting it. Somewhere in his heart, he thought of Ghazala and her son as *being* the City.

"I need you to get this note to the Academy, to Master Edvin the notary in the Main Hall," he said.

"This had better be good," Ghazala said. "We don't have much work and we can't afford to slack off."

"Everything is bad," Manacher agreed.

While they spoke, half a dozen Easterner children came to the back, in the alley, and Ghazala's housekeeper gave them food.

"We give them food," Ghazala said. "Every day. All we can spare. Almost everyone does. It's so bad, Aranthur. The bone plague is raging up on the Pinnacle. And the Darkness..."

She looked down when she said that, and Aranthur saw that she had a touch herself.

"She never goes outside now," Manacher said, when his mother went to the back room. "She never looks up at the sky or the stars."

"I wouldn't ask if it weren't very important."

Aranthur was tempted to recruit Manacher for Cold Iron, except that, at some remove, he realised that doing so was no favour. Rather the opposite. He wrote a note for Edvin and didn't sign it.

"If you are stopped by the Watch or by the Yellowjackets, tell them everything," he said. "Seriously—I'm a former employee. They'll work out as much anyway."

Manacher looked terrified. But he took a deep breath and walked out of the door.

Aranthur passed the time cutting belts, which he did well enough. Ghazala came to the front when a customer came in, and seemed unsurprised to see him. He had a *guise* on, and she looked right through it, which was one of the most remarkable proofs of how the *guise* really worked he'd ever seen.

"Like old times," she said, examining his work. "You nicked this one. Rub it out, please."

He was almost sick with worry about Manacher: he was trying to save the world, and an old woman was telling him his leather work was below par.

He took a burnisher and began rubbing out his minute mistake. Two minutes later, the error was eliminated by beeswax and a little effort, and Manacher walked in.

"Never doing that again," he said. "By Kerkos, Aranthur. Do you do this sort of thing often?"

"Too often, *dadhashi*," Aranthur said, using the family word for *brother.*

Manacher shook his head. "You speak more Safiri than I do, you woodlouse." He laughed. "And your accent is better than *madhar*'s." He handed Aranthur a folded piece of parchment.

Aranthur popped it open.

Understood

Aranthur dropped the parchment into the coal grate at the back of the shop and watched it curl and burn. It smelled like burning leather, which it was; the stink brought Ghazala out of the back.

"We do not burn parchment in this shop…" she began.

"*Madhar*, not now," Manacher pleaded.

"I'll never do it again," Aranthur said.

"It was very good of you to come to help out," Ghazala said. "I'm sorry to tell you this, Aranthur, because we like you, but we don't have work for you right now…"

Aranthur was afraid she was going to cry. He embraced her.

"Never worry, *madhar.*" The Safiri word just came out, and she looked away. "Look—I am an officer now. I have pay, and I'd like a new sword belt and a set of scabbard fittings."

"New sword?" Manacher asked, suddenly delighted at the business.

"Same old sword," Aranthur said.

"Oh," Manacher said, somewhat deflated. "You can't be doing that well if you still have that ugly sword. But I still have the scabbard pattern—it's right here." He looked up. "What colour?"

"Red," Aranthur said, thinking of the woman who lived in the blade.

He went out into the day, found a quiet shop that sold *quaveh* and sat at the back, one of dozens of customers. He asked for the outhouse and was told he had to go to the baths, so he crossed the street, where a recent emperor had constructed a triple-domed bathhouse with hot water and water-driven privies.

Aranthur sat in unassailable privacy and read the drop box reports before he tore them to pieces and dropped the refuse through into the public sewers. He couldn't write anything down, but happily a whole programme of the Studion was aimed at perfecting memorisation, and Aranthur built mnemonics to remember all six items.

It took two more hours to view all the signposts and clear the remaining boxes. He was virtually high on *quaveh* by the time he was done, and he had learned a great deal about the Watch posts. Too much.

Give me a straightforward fight anytime, he thought.

3

Megara

By nightfall he was back in the palace, by gondola, and Dahlia was sitting by him. Together, they were leafing through the pages of glyphs that Aranthur had largely ignored earlier. He found it much easier to read the *Ulmaghest* now; weeks of speaking Safiri had changed everything.

He and Dahlia were comparing the glyphs in the text and in the margins with the glyphs Dahlia had copied from the enchanted well at the edge of the Kud desert. Edvin Larik was safely ensconced in the palace; Magister Sittar had been and gone.

Dahlia copied out another glyph, and the two of them compared their work.

"Sittar asked where Drako was," she said. "He insisted that he needed to know."

"But we don't know!" Aranthur said.

"Exactly. Myr Benvenutu claims she doesn't know either. But Sittar says he needs to speak to Drako urgently."

Aranthur shrugged. "I don't know either."

Dahlia nodded. "I assumed as much, but I wanted to hear it from you. I find Sittar hard to deal with. A year ago he was my tutor and now suddenly we're peers…"

Aranthur raised his hands. "How do you think I feel?" he asked. "Farmhand to master spy? Everything I do is probably wrong. And Myr Benvenutu and Syr Sittar terrify me."

Dahlia nodded. They were silent for a little while, each working on their own glyph.

"Can we do this?" she asked.

"You mean, work out how the so-called Master manipulated glyphs?" Aranthur asked.

"I was thinking more—can we actually save the world?" Dahlia said. "I think we're close to solving the glyph system and I'd like the Magistera to give us some of her time."

"I'd like to understand this *displacement*," Aranthur said, pointing to an elaborate spell. He'd begun working on it long before, but only now, with his vastly improved Safiri skills, could he read the nuances.

Dahlia shook her head. "Never done a *displacement*," she said.

Aranthur was used to relying on Dahlia to teach him *occultae.* She was more than a year ahead of him, and she was a brilliant practitioner. It always surprised him when she didn't know something.

"I think we should move the reader, the book itself, and our study materials to the Emperor's antechamber," Aranthur said. "We're going to be living this way for days."

"No time like the present."

They moved into the extensive anteroom, seized a magnificently inlaid table and a trio of heavy, comfortable chairs from a palace sitting room, and visited the kitchens for food and wine. Back at the table, they gazed out of the enormous, hundred-paned window at the ocean far below and ate.

Myr Benvenutu came in. She wiped her hands on a magnificent towel and began to eat Aranthur's food—a delicious risotto made with a heavy, dark wine and a sharp cheese.

"Oh, I could get used to that," she said. "Mmmm." She leant over him, tracing the Safiri text. "What does this say?"

Aranthur handed her the *reader*, an ancient artifact that could translate as you passed it over the text...though the translation was not always perfect. Occasionally it was wildly inaccurate, but a clever user could derive meaning from it. Then he passed her his own translation, carefully amended.

She finished his risotto and started on his *polpo*, a rich dish of seafood, mostly octopus.

"Do you know that Danesh Ravos thinks that the larger *Octopodes* are sentient?" she said, chewing away.

"Oh, gods, and we eat them?" Aranthur asked. "You mean to say we're forbidden lamb and beef but not octopus? And who is Danesh Ravos?"

"Syr Ravos to you," the Master of Arts said with a smile. "Master of Natural Philosophy. You would have studied with him this year, if you..." She shrugged and looked away. "If we still had classes. If the world doesn't end."

Aranthur blinked. "We can win this." He was surprised by his own voice. "We should not eat other sentients."

Benvenutu shrugged. "We're hardly kind to our own species, Aranthur. It's only a theory." She paused, looking over his work. "I see it. Can you cast it?"

"Magistera, I don't even know what it's for! This is too..."

Myr Benvenutu usually looked more like a well-to-do cook than a dangerous sorceress, but she shook her head and made a small sign in the air.

"*Displacement* is a very valuable technique," she said. "It's almost always a layer, with something else. Do you know the theory of origins?"

Everything with Myr Benvenutu was a test. He had certainly *heard* of the theory of origins.

"The...spirit world and the *Aulos*..." he muttered.

Dahlia nodded encouragingly behind Myr Benvenutu's head.

"Exactly. Only things with...I'll say *spirit* for the lack of a better word...seem to exist in the *Aulos.*" She smiled. "So, for example, if you *displaced* me to the *Aulos* and went back a year later, I might be starkly insane, barking mad. But I'd still be where you left me." She frowned. "Actually, not exactly, the *Aulos* has some kind of tide, and I might have moved somewhat relative to you. But as long as I was alive and had a *spirit* I could be located in the *Aulos.* As this *reader* is an artifact of the early First Empire, it is deeply imbued with *spirit.* Indeed, one might, if one was in the mood for a nasty enquiry, look deep into this thing and find that it had the stripped soul of some criminal bound to it. The First Empire routinely committed such crimes."

"Ouch," Aranthur said.

Dahlia winced, too.

"I'd like to tell you that people thought differently two thousand years ago." Her glance was distant. "But in fact, if that was true, Tirase would never have happened, would he? Regardless...if you cast a *displacement* on your shoes and placed them in the *Aulos*, you'd never find them again. Because in the *Aulos*, they don't really exist. This is why casting via *displacement* is so difficult."

Aranthur thought about it, his brow furrowed like a newly ploughed field.

Dahlia looked up. "But could you store...a completed *occulta*...?"

Benvenutu smiled. "Exactly the question. It takes a very fine sense of balance, but you can, in effect, develop an entire *occulta*. Even a set of them. Remember your sandbox, Aranthur? It's very much the same idea. In fact, if you have used your sandbox..."

"I have!" In that instant he understood it. "Of course. The storing—the location." He beamed at her with understanding.

She kissed his forehead. "I wish you two were my only students," she said. "And I suppose for a week or so, you will be!"

In the morning, when they awoke, there were Watch posts set on the bridges to the palace. The Lord Protector had declared martial law, and a suspension of the Academy's privileges.

Across the straits, a fire raged on the slopes above Ulama. Something bad was happening in Atti.

"Here we go," Aranthur said.

"And we're just going to sit here and work on the *Ulmaghest*?" Dahlia said.

"Yes," Aranthur replied. "After we make a copy of these dispatches."

"He's suspended the whole Academy!" Dahlia said. "He's trying to undo Tirase!"

"Exactly. That is exactly what he's seeking to do. He's trying to roll back our enlightenment—to take magic from people and return it to a handful of godlike casters. The way things were in the First Empire."

Dahlia groaned. And then went back to work.

But there was more happening in the palace than just study. Edvin's first job was generating copies of General Tribane's dispatches from the Battle of Armea, and then from the Siege of Antioke. After two hours of copying Aranthur practised his *displacement* several times and then, when the first copy was complete, he went to the Guards' barracks. Four storeys of pink marble and white marble trim, statues of Imperial generals and heroes, and the de facto headquarters of the Imperial planning staff. There he found the skeleton staff left by General Tribane, who ordinarily lived in the penthouse on the roof of the barracks; Iralia had given him the key to her rooms. He passed them by, found the planning staff, and gave them a copy of Tribane's dispatches.

They practically interrogated him for several hours in the afternoon, but his centark's commission in the Nomadi, which he had with him, made him almost the highest ranking officer of the guards in the palace. Only the Commander of the Axes outranked him.

The commander was sent for.

Aranthur had never met Dranat McBane, the Keltai warlord who'd risen to command the Axes, before. He was reputed to be the most dangerous man in the City; in person, he was huge, with greying hair and tattooed, muscular arms emerging from the heavy sleeves of his gilded-bronze byrnie. His hair and beard were red with henna, and he reminded Aranthur of the Kaptan Bey of Atti.

"Timos," he said, and extended an enormous hand for a clasp.

"Lord Commander."

One of the staff officers held out a scroll. She was the junior officer, a dekark from the Arsenale seconded to palace duty.

He took the scroll and read it rapidly. His tattooed face didn't even twitch.

"And?" he asked.

"General Roaris' account of the battle is a lie," Aranthur said. "I was there."

McBane's mismatched blue eyes regarded him closely, and Aranthur unexpectedly found himself at a loss. He wanted McBane to say something, to react.

The man stood like a mountain in armour.

"So?" he finally asked.

Aranthur took a deep breath. "I want the staff to consider planning a relief expedition to Antioke. Food, powder, drafts of replacements for the army. I'd like to gather food and wine to fill a…" He almost wilted under those ice-blue Keltai eyes. "A small ship."

McBane never seemed to blink. "I have one role," he said. "I protect the Emperor from outside threats. I have watched Tribane and Roaris squabble for ten years." He glanced at the staff officer. "Let me see your commission."

Aranthur handed it over.

McBane looked at it and nodded. "Promoted once for loyalty to the Crown and once for heroism," he said, looking at the parchment. "You understand that if I let you do this, Roaris has every right to be furious. Get me, son? We're the Guards. He's sitting in the headquarters at the Lonika Gate. He's the army."

"He's—"

"Spare me. Centark Timos is hereby in command of a planning group to raise a relief expedition."

He nodded to the military secretary, a civilian, who began writing the order.

"Thank you, syr," Aranthur said.

McBane nodded. "Keep me informed," he said, and started for the door. In the doorway, where he had to duck his head, he paused. "And, Timos?" he called.

"Syr?" Aranthur answered.

"Next time, you will come and find me. I'm only summoned by the Emperor."

Aranthur found that he had swallowed heavily.

"Yes, syr."

"Good lad," the commander said, and trudged away across the courtyard.

The secretary glanced up.

"Syr? Syr Timos? I was stopped by the Watch this morning. They… asked about you. By name."

Aranthur smiled. "I'm not surprised."

But inside, he froze.

The antechamber of the Emperor's private apartments had become their headquarters. The *Ulmaghest* sat open on the beautiful inlaid table with the First Empire reader, an artifact of incredible power, sitting by it; by noon, both Dahlia and Aranthur had *displaced* the precious thing and brought it back.

On the other side of the same table, Edvin, the Master of Arts' secretary, sat hunched like a skinny spider, writing furiously. He was the fastest copyist Aranthur had ever seen, and he was copying anything that they gave him. Dahlia worked with Aranthur, albeit with a different focus, but she was still the superior practitioner and often she could solve problems that baffled him. Iralia worked directly with the Master of Arts, caring for the Emperor in his private apartment, and Litha, Myr Benventutu's partner, joined them. A pair of wolfhounds and a terrier now resided in the outer room; tasters for everything entering the apartment. They were also amusing companions and an overeager alarm system, and had to be walked, individually, three times a day.

Magistera Benvenutu compiled an impressive list of drugs and alchemical substances they needed, and Aranthur decided that they could not be obtained by sending palace servants to fetch them.

"I agree," Dahlia said. "But Aphres, all this caution makes everything twice as hard."

Aranthur solved the problem by breaking the list into relatively innocuous amounts and substances and despatching guards from the Palace Barracks. The Nomadi were serving in Oltramar, but they still had a full troop—a senior dekark's command—in the palace, mostly new recruits. The old dekark was a one-eyed Gilzai from the Southern Steppes, where they bordered on Safi, called Amad Ilq. He was unimpressed by Aranthur, but he was also a professional.

The really difficult ingredients Aranthur decided to find himself, but for him the challenge was time, of which he had too little. Just the time to walk through the corridors of the Crystal Palace, across the magnificent quadrangle and along the gravel paths to the Barracks Square seemed too long and he had cleared less than a fifth of Drako's total list of spies; in fact, having taken on his work Aranthur now thought that Drako's whole life was explained. And none of the information coming in was particularly useful; most of it had to do with financial matters in the City. Aranthur could already see a pattern around the manipulation of currency and his sources suggested that someone in the Imperial Salt Monopoly was siphoning off a great deal of money. It would have been important stuff, ordinarily.

But nothing to do with the crisis Aranthur faced today, as far as he could see.

He sent his soldiers out after some coaching, and the Nomadi recruits went out into the neighbourhoods they were assigned, passing the Watch posts as they always did to go for a carouse. They gathered the substances he requested and returned. It took two full days and fifteen different errands, and Aranthur used that time to start compiling the various visitor lists and lists of palace servants, and comparing them against the days Iralia remembered being sick, the date on which the

Emperor had failed, the day of the Darkness and the appearance of the Dark Forge.

The low black trabaccolo, his wife's ship, didn't reappear off the "Stars," as the line of seaward fortresses were known, but Aranthur, despite his studies, his work for Benvenutu, and his fledgling investigations, found himself looking out to sea through the Emperor's windows so often that he wasn't getting any work done.

What if Roaris had cruisers or privateers out there, snapping up ships? He must have some plan for returning merchants; his big lie depended on no Great Galley or small merchant coming home from Oltramar. What if Roaris already had the Black Stone? And Inoques?

Aranthur blinked. *What if I'm a complete fool? Why am I in charge? I'm a Souliote farm kid from the hills. A total fake.*

He was sitting alone, sipping superb *quaveh* and unable to concentrate on his work. He was out at sea, flying over the waves…

His head snapped back. Iralia, wearing no make-up, no *guise*, no *enhancement* and a plain dark wool robe, came through the Emperor's door carrying a tray. She struggled with the door and he rose and took the tray, which he took to the hallway. Litha, the Magister's partner, was a tall, brown woman with the face of a Dhadh; she had not hesitated to take on a nursing role, and now she took over, taking the tray into the Emperor's private room and closing the door with a smile at Iralia.

"How goes it?" he asked Iralia.

She shrugged. "He has colour today. Altaria wants something complicated from you—she's very…" Iralia turned her head and smiled. "Commanding."

"Altaria?" Aranthur almost choked.

"Myr Benvenutu," Iralia said with a tired smile. "I'm not a student, so she offered me her first name. But she remains imposing."

"So she is," Aranthur agreed.

Until that moment, he'd never really imagined that the Master of Arts even *had* a first name.

Iralia lingered.

"I feel like an idiot," he said.

"Why? You seem to know how to do everything."

"All fake."

Iralia shrugged. "Sure."

Aranthur had seldom seen Iralia, the glorious Iralia, so tired.

"Are you all right?"

"Oh," she said more brightly, "I'm fine. A little run-down. You know, my *patron* is very sick and I might have to look for a new *contract*, but otherwise, I'm just fine."

Aranthur frowned. "I don't think I deserved that."

"It's what Dahlia believes—probably what all of you do. Aphres, Aranthur, maybe it's true. Two things I have too little experience to judge—happiness and emotional bonds."

"Not guilty. I knew you before you were so important, remember?"

Iralia smiled. "And you've never pushed yourself on me, which is virtually unique in your gender."

Aranthur looked out to sea and tried not to remember a certain moment in the Square of the Mulberries.

"I'm sorry, Aranthur. I'm a mess." She put a hand on his shoulder and he took it, and she clenched it hard. "And I'm pregnant."

"By...the Emperor?" he asked.

Iralia bridled. "Aranthur Timos, I would think that you, of all people, would not need to ask that."

Aranthur looked at her, really looked, and it was obvious, even from his two Imoter classes.

"I'm afraid it is a fair question, given what's at stake. How long has it been?"

"I'm going to say sixty-five days," Iralia said.

"Very precise."

Aranthur was trying to reckon how this might play into the knife edge they were living.

"I am a priestess of Aphres," she said. "I know a great deal about contraception, and conception."

Aranthur nodded. "So, conceivably, you have the next emperor in your womb."

"Conceivably." Iralia smiled. "Nice pun."

"Think nothing of it. All right, that's a crisis for six weeks from now, when you show." Aranthur felt a shiver run through him. Inoques was pregnant. Iralia was pregnant. "You...allowed yourself to become pregnant," he said carefully.

"Of course."

"Discussed?" Aranthur asked.

"Oh, yes. He was quite determined..."

Aranthur took a breath. And another. A vista of plots and counter-plots opened before him, and some of his thoughts were shameful or ugly—or both.

"You realise that for some this will make you a suspect in poisoning the Emperor," he said. "After all—"

"Aphres! That's foul!" Iralia spat.

Aranthur shrugged. "Keep your voice down. It's the first thing Roaris would say," he insisted. "Listen—I'm sorry. Tiy Drako has rubbed off on me…and the Armean War. I'm not sure I even like the new me."

She squeezed his hand. "I'm sorry. I have already thought the same. I just hated hearing it from your mouth."

"Then let me change the subject to something inconsequential," Aranthur said. "Does the Emperor keep falcons?"

"Of course," Iralia said. "He taught me falconry. Really, that's when I started to fall in love with him. I'd never met a man who could teach a skill and not patronise me. I really have a low bar. Men just generally fail to climb over it."

Aranthur nodded. "If we can make time tomorrow, I want to try an experiment. It's something I just thought of."

"I'll teach you to handle the birds. But if you hurt them, we're not friends."

Aranthur nodded. "I promise."

A night and a day, and no Inoques. No trabaccolo.

The Academy classes didn't start.

The watch made another arrest among the Council of Seventeen. This time an aristocratic woman, a member of the extensive Comnoi clan: Stasia Comnas, the dowager countess of Daka.

"She's an old busybody!" Dahlia said. "The kind of harridan who sits at balls making nasty remarks about people's clothes."

Iralia shook her head. "She was virtually the head of intelligence. She collected reports and maintained files on most of the foreigners who lived and worked in the City until the Easterner problems started, and even then, her people did most of the work in fighting *al Ghugha*."

"And Roaris had her arrested?" Aranthur said.

"Yes. So now I worry that if Dahlia hands every surviving member of the Seventeen a copy of Tribane's reports, they will fall into Roaris' hands the next time he arrests one of them."

Aranthur looked at Dahlia.

She shook her head. "No. No, you don't know the city the way I do, Iralia. He's made a mistake. The countess is too powerful, too well-connected, to just arrest. She's a member of his own power base—the old, rich nobles."

"I want to take whatever Edvin's finished and share it right now," Aranthur said. "This is the moment to strike, while all the other Lions are wondering if Roaris is trustworthy."

Now Iralia was shaking her head.

Aranthur glanced at her. "While I have you here," he said, "can you tell me anything about what Syr Sittar is organising? Is he a Lightbringer? Is he... Cold Iron?"

Dahlia raised an eyebrow and played with her hat.

"What is Cold Iron but a support system for Lightbringers? Sittar is one—I heard him referred to as such by Kurvenos."

"Let's ask Myr Benvenutu," Aranthur said, trying to dispel responsibility.

The Master of Arts was standing at a work table, mixing ingredients.

"Janos Sittar is most certainly a Lightbringer," she said. "Although, as an Armean, he is probably not a formal member of Cold Iron."

Aranthur looked at her, but she shook her head.

"I am not in the habit of discussing these matters," she said forbiddingly.

She sent him out of the sick room with a new list of expensive alchemical compounds and orders not to disturb her.

As he backed out, she said, "I need a real alchemist. Iralia needs more rest and Litha and Iralia can't do all the nursing by themselves. We need another, and an alchemist."

Aranthur nodded. "I know where to find both."

"Go, then."

Benvenutu waved a hand in dismissal. She was crouched over an alembic, coaxing it to heat with a simple *volteia.*

Aranthur read down her list: all expensive, and all rare. Then he glanced at Dahlia, who met his eyes squarely.

"This is high risk," he said. "But we're not yet under siege. Let's do it."

"I think you're both mad," Iralia said. "Why the questions about Sittar?"

Aranthur considered both of them. "He's been here a great deal since the Darkness," he said. "And Iralia never mentioned him."

"I saw him once," she admitted. "But he never so much as acknowledges me."

Aranthur grunted.

Dahlia furrowed her brows. "You can't suspect Janos Sittar."

Aranthur shrugged. "I can."

Dahlia shook her head. "Waste of time," she said. "Let's get these ingredients."

"I'm going with you, at least until your first stop. I have to go down to the Spice Market, at the very least." Aranthur shook his head. "Where is Inoques?"

"Where indeed?" Iralia said.

"One more thing," Dahlia said. "My mater..."

"Your mother?" Aranthur asked.

"You thought I'd come home and not contact my mother and my sister? And Oroma, Harlequin's lover?" Dahlia looked at Aranthur as if he was a fool.

He shook his head.

"Aranthur, *Roaris knows we're here.* He's looking for us—two people in half a million. No one likes him; no one will co-operate with the Watch on the best of days, and the Yellowjackets are hated..."

Aranthur had to smile. "I thought I was the rash one and you were the cautious one."

"You are being cautious because you are really a Souliote farm boy and you don't know the big city. I'm not being rash—I'm exploiting the weaknesses in our opponent. He can post a watch on every bridge, but he can't watch the gondolas and he can't stop traffic from Atti, can he? No, he cannot. The rumours on the street today are that Tribane won a huge battle with the Kaptan Pasha as an ally. That rumour is coming across the strait from Ulama and Atti. There's another about civil strife there, and about an attack on the Sultan Bey."

"I've heard," Aranthur said.

"Of course you have. But my point is that everyone in Atti knows perfectly well that everything Roaris says is a lie." She glanced at him. "Which reminds me that we need to look into Kurvenos' death. Damn it...what if he isn't dead?"

Aranthur's head snapped around. "What?"

Dahlia shrugged. "What if it's just more disinformation?"

Aranthur breathed heavily through his nose and tried not to give way to the anger that rose at her tone of superiority.

Iralia put a hand gently on Dahlia's. "Dahlia, you are a hero, and I think you are right. But you really need to learn to speak the truth without quite so much tone."

Dahlia shook her head. "But it's true!"

"Souliote farm boy?" Iralia asked. "Was that necessary?"

Aranthur walked over to his inlaid table and sat. Edvin looked up, gave him a knowing smile, and went back to copying.

Aranthur made himself go back to copying the glyph on which he was working. It was the complex far seer *occulta* that he and Dahlia had developed under fire, at sea. But the two of them had refined it and reduced it to a glyph. He was working it into a small scrap of leather.

Dahlia came over and stood awkwardly.

"I meant no offence."

Aranthur took a breath. "None taken," he lied.

She nodded. "Inoques will come. Let's get out there. I'm meeting my sister at Tercel's."

He sat back and looked at her.

"They took Tiy Drako off the streets of this city," he said. "Dahlia, I want you to think, just for a moment, what they'll do to you if they catch you."

Dahlia reddened with anger. "You think I've never considered it?"

Aranthur shrugged. "It seems possible, since we're going to Tercel's to meet your friends. As if nothing had changed."

Dahlia looked at him.

"Can we wear *guise*?"

"We'll reek of power to anyone looking into the *Aulos*."

Aranthur picked up another scrap of leather. He tied it around his wrist and touched it.

"Oh, my," Iralia said.

In place of Aranthur sat a dark-skinned, red-haired Byzas man.

Dahlia prodded him. "Sophia, that's good." She cast, pale blue fire on her fingers. "Almost nothing shows…"

"Because the glyph is powered by *me*. By my life essence."

Iralia shook her head. "This is brilliant."

Dahlia shook her head. "It's brilliant, but it's why he eats like a horse and looks like a famine victim."

Aranthur shrugged, flushing, making the rapid transition from anger to pleasure.

"Dahlia and I did it together, and my wife played her part too. Once we start manipulating the glyphs...and, you recognise, this is how the enemy magisters operate."

Iralia brushed a wisp of hair out of her eyes.

"Make me one, too," she said. "Make me...plain. And unremarkable."

"Just remember that if a Watch officer or a Yellowjacket refines his Sight as carefully as we did looking for *sigils* in Armea, he'll see the artifact."

Aranthur handed Dahlia a leather bracelet.

She put it on. Instantly, she looked like an Arnaut farm girl, complete to her rosy lips and olive skin.

"Oh, I love it!" she said.

"Finally, I've made you something you like," Aranthur said.

Iralia was laughing. "Aranthur, you have a very subtle notion of revenge."

"Don't I?" he said, with a smile.

Dahlia looked back and forth.

Iralia laughed, a loud bark at odds with her musical social laughter.

"Back to the mines," she said, and went out to fetch a tray of food and fresh water, which she gave to the dogs to taste.

"Poor dogs," Dahlia said.

Aranthur nodded. "You ready?"

"I'll get my sword," Dahlia said.

"Wear it, but don't use it, I beg you," Aranthur said.

"Oh, I'll be quiet as a mouse. I'll put up with insults, I'll do whatever it takes to stay hidden."

Aranthur nodded. "I'll wear a sword too. Now please hurry. I'm hungry."

"You are always fucking hungry," Dahlia said.

An hour later, they were sitting in the massive common room of Tercel's Inn, Brothel, and School of Defence, an institution almost as ancient as the palace, the hippodrome, and the Temple of Light. High overhead in the main hall, massive wooden beams black with age and smoke arched from internal buttresses so old that the base stones matched those at the very bottom of the city wall. Student rumour said that the place had once been a palace, and that it was more than a thousand years old. But then, student rumour also claimed that the basements ran to tunnels that went under the canals, and held a stairway to a subterranean world.

Aranthur was having the strange experience of receiving excellent service. He wore the same good wool doublet he'd worn to rescue Drako, and thigh-high boots, and his sword was in its new scabbard dangling from an elegant belt made by Ghazala, but for all that, he looked much as he usually did except for his darker skin and copper-red hair. And yet, every server in Tercel's seemed eager to wait on him; his wine reached his table almost before he was ready to drink it. Dahlia was having the reverse experience; as a scion of one of the oldest Houses, she affected a plain black doublet and dirty shirt collar and seldom did anything to enhance her tawny skin or bright blonde hair. As a pale Souliote woman in plain clothes and dirty linen, she was invisible to servers, or worse.

She'd ordered wine and it hadn't come.

Aranthur waved vaguely, ready to go to the server's station and fetch someone; he was used to this sort of thing. But the moment he moved, a woman was at his side.

"Syr?" she asked with obvious and obsequious attention.

"My companion lacks wine," Aranthur said. "And I'd like some food."

"I ordered five minutes ago..." Dahlia began, and then trailed off as she was ignored.

"Syr desires food?"

The server simpered, as if Aranthur had said something very clever indeed.

"Surprise me with something," Aranthur said, playing the aristocrat with a casual wave.

"I..." Dahlia sputtered, but the server had walked away.

"By Sophia's wisdom," she spat. "She *ignored* me!"

Aranthur fought the urge to smile.

"Here, syr," the serving woman said, placing a second glass—a fine glass at that—by him, with a plate of pickled figs and cheese, with a flourish. "Try that, syr."

"The wine is for my companion," Aranthur said haughtily.

"Of course, syr," the server agreed, and moved the glass to Dahlia's place. "Would syr like a more private place? We have snugs, and private tables, and a variety of..."

Aranthur smiled. "We'll be fine."

Dahlia shook her head. She looked away, and then looked back.

"Rose might be watching the fencing floor, but at this hour, there's not likely to be anyone engaged," Dahlia said.

Aranthur was remembering Drako's lessons on surveillance.

"Let's just sit here and watch the room. Three of the building's four entrances are here—we can see the clientele."

Dahlia raised an eyebrow. "My wine is sour."

Aranthur tasted his. "Hmm. If it makes you feel any better, so is mine. We've been in the palace for three days and already we're used to a ridiculous level of quality."

He ate a pickled fig and found it delicious, and the old cheese was amazing. Both flavours made the wine much more palatable.

He laughed aloud.

"What?" Dahlia didn't quite spit, but she was none too pleased.

"Have a fig," he said.

She ate a fig, drank some wine.

"What were you laughing at?" she asked.

"Myself."

Dahlia sat back. She shook her head. "That's the thing that makes you tolerable, old boy," she drawled. "What aspect of you shall we mock first?"

"My rapid assimilation to the status of *daesia*," he said. "I was enjoying the taste of the fig with the wine, and then I realised that two years ago, I'd never had a fig, and wine was a rarity." He shrugged.

"I find your impersonation of a Byzas aristocrat a little threatening," Dahlia said.

"I learned it all from you," Aranthur said, sprawling over his chair the way she did.

Dahlia tasted Aranthur's wine and shook her head. "I think you're right. I assumed that little witch gave me inferior wine."

"No," Aranthur said with an easy smile. "She wouldn't want to offend me."

Dahlia laughed aloud.

They sat long enough to hear a travelling singer sing a political song that never named Verit Roaris and yet suggested he was a lying tyrant. It was under the guise of an old bandit ballad, *The Road to Lonika*, and it was well done. Aranthur gave the singer a silver five-piece.

"You know who could help us?" Aranthur said. "Dhadhi. That's who. There must be dozens in the city. Maybe more."

Dahlia was watching people come in.

"Here comes trouble," she said.

Six Yellowjackets came in, pushing past the bouncers.

"Touch me again and I'll cut off your hands," said the leader.

The bouncer, a big Keltai woman with jet-black hair and skin so covered with tattoos it appeared to be blue, stepped back, raising her hands. But she rang a bell.

"What's the bell for?" the leader demanded.

"Orders," the woman snapped. "You have yours, I have mine."

"Syr. Call me syr."

The woman shrugged. "I have my orders, *syr.*" Her use of the word *syr* was unsurprisingly absent of respect.

Aranthur didn't know the young man who came at a run. He too had black hair and pale skin; an Easterner, with Armean features, he wore clothes at the very height of fashion, with wide breeches and the new long coat.

"How can I help you, gentlemen?" His voice was cheerful and if he was anxious or afraid, he gave no sign.

The Yellowjacket waved. "Your singer just sang a seditious song. Hand him over or I close this establishment and arrest you."

"I'm sorry," the young manager said. "A seditious song?"

"Yes."

He smiled. "Go and get a warrant. From a real judge. Bring it here. Better yet, have her explain that there's no such thing as a *seditious song* on the law books of the Empire."

The Yellowjacket looked at the manager for a moment, slapping his gloves against the back of his hand.

"I know him," Dahlia said. "He's a fourth year. Very competent. Nasty piece of work."

The Yellowjacket raised his hand and the young manager's head snapped back and he fell and lay still.

"That's my warrant," the Yellowjacket said.

The common room was not crowded; it was really a great hall and had room in its dusty magnificence for half a thousand eager drinkers, and today, as the lunch bells rang from all the temples, it held perhaps a hundred men and women. But the muttering became ugly; most of the clients were Academy students, and their classes had already been cancelled. Many of them had been drinking since the night before.

A woman went to the manager, touched his face, and whirled.

"He's dead!" she spat.

The Yellowjacket slapped his gloves against his boots.

"And you're next, *lady.* Hand over that singer."

"You *killed* the manager of Tercel's in cold blood…"

"For resisting arrest. And he's an Easterner. Really, no one will mourn him. Now, the singer. Or do all of you want to visit the cells?"

The man's poise was remarkable. Dahlia was already moving.

"So much for staying hidden," Aranthur said to the air.

He picked up the last pickled fig and ate it.

The woman standing by the manager's corpse was scared, but she stood her ground.

"I don't even know who you mean," she said. "But I wouldn't tell you anyway. And before you try whatever you did before, I promise you—my family are not Easterners, and your life will be over."

"Posture away, little witch," the Yellowjacket said.

She drew herself up. "I'm a Cerchai. And since I don't know you, I think it safe to say you are not from a Great House. So—"

He slapped her. "Your houses are all traitors anyway. There's a new world coming, and those with real power—"

Dahlia stepped out from one of the columns that supported the vaulting.

"If you try another *occulta*, I'll drop you," she said.

The silence was suddenly thick.

"Who the fuck are you? Some *Souliote* hedge witch?"

The Yellowjacket snapped his fingers and a slim bolt of red fire crossed the hall.

It vanished into Dahlia's shields.

Aranthur stepped up beside her and cast, placing an oblique wall of his own green fire between the Yellowjackets and their leader. The Yellowjacket raised his shield, which was a simple, heavy red *aspis*.

Aranthur walked forward towards the Yellowjackets.

Their leader loosed a salvo of the red balefire and men and women throughout the ancient common room dived under tables or flattened themselves against the columns. Shields came up around the room; most Studion students knew several shield *volteie.*

Aranthur leapt forward, even as his shields flashed out to meet a third attack. Two of the junior Yellowjackets began to contend with his green fire, trying to bleed it off—the wrong approach.

Aranthur's shields struck the leader's and the man drew his sword as Aranthur's shields overwhelmed the red *aspis*, but Aranthur didn't plan to kill him.

Inside the shields, their swords crossed, but the tall man was still shorter than Aranthur and he carried a small sword, like a reinforced needle of steel. It was fast, but he could not cross a cut from Aranthur's heavy blade, and he retreated as Aranthur seized the initiative with a quick cut.

Aranthur cut again. As he did he leapt forward a second time, slipped his blade around the Yellowjacket's head after forcing his light blade offline, and flung him into the wall. The man stumbled and Aranthur caught his flailing arm. He dropped his own sword deliberately, caught the man's elbow and rolled him down, using the arm lock as a lever, until the Yellowjacket was retching in pain, his nose almost touching the floor.

Loudly, Aranthur said, "I am an Imperial officer. I arrest you in the name of the Emperor for murder, and incitement to violence."

He reached into his doublet left-handed and pulled out Drako's Golden Rose.

"You can't fucking arrest *me*!" the man spat. "Do you know who I am? Every Yellowjacket in the town will hunt you down."

"One more twist and I rip your shoulder," Aranthur said. "That will never heal."

"You're fucking dead," the man spat.

Aranthur tweaked the shoulder joint and the man screamed.

Dahlia was collecting the blades of the other five Yellowjackets, backed by twenty students.

Aranthur hauled his prisoner to his feet and found himself looking into Rose Tarkas' beautiful, widely spaced eyes.

"You two are remarkably inconspicuous," she said.

"Fuck this," Dahlia said.

She pulled her bracelet off and appeared instantly as herself. She leapt up on a table.

"Listen up, friends!" she said. "I'm Dahlia Tarkas. Some of you know me—I'm a fourth year at the Academy. My friends and I just fought in Armea, with General Tribane. We fought and we *won.* The rumours are true—the Empire and Atti stood together and beat the shit out of the Pure. Roaris is a liar. The Emperor is alive. Spread the word!"

"We weren't going to start a revolution, remember?" Aranthur muttered.

Dahlia nodded sharply. "Good point. We *don't* want street riots and blood. But do what you can to disobey the Watch and the Yellowjackets! Change is coming!"

"What about the Darkness!" someone called.

"The bone plague!" another called.

"We can beat the Darkness," Dahlia insisted. "The rift, the Dark Forge? We *know* how to close it. Give us time."

Rose was shaking her head. "Great job, little sister. No one here will remember you," she said with noticeable sarcasm. "Especially not after you shouted out your name."

Aranthur shook his head. "I'm taking these bastards back to the palace. Can you collect a shopping list of alchemicals for us?" he asked Rose. "Before Roaris puts us under siege."

He was annoyed—with himself, and with Dahlia.

She smiled a twisted smile. "My maid can," she said.

The Keltai bouncer was snapping orders; two men collected their dead manager.

"Heads will roll for this," she said. "Need help with the Pisspots?"

"Pisspots?" Aranthur asked.

"Yellowjackets. By Dagda, syr. They should be eradicated." The woman was angry.

"Now is *not* the time for violence, myr. We need to restore the rule of law…"

The Keltai woman shrugged. "Where I come from, if someone kills one of yours, you kill one of theirs. I can start with this Pisspot right here."

"No," Aranthur said.

The black-haired woman looked at him with contempt.

"Fine," she spat.

Getting six men through the streets to the palace was at least as difficult as Aranthur expected, but he couldn't release them, and he wanted them to experience justice. A little pack of students had followed them into the street, including a woman he'd seen in *Practical Philosophy* and two young men.

"We can help," she said. "I'm Thendara Trapezetas. This is Giannis, and this is..."

The smaller man nodded. "Lars Two-Fingers," he said.

Giannis grimaced. "As long as you'll take help from two Arnauts and a Northerner."

Aranthur had a moment of confusion and then remembered that he was wearing a Byzas *guise*. But he bowed.

"Most pleased." He realised to his embarrassment that he didn't have a cover name to go with the *guise*. "I'll keep my name to myself for now," he said stiffly.

They all nodded.

Two of the Yellowjackets were demanding his attention; one was trying to negotiate, drawing on his family. While the three of them babbled the fourth, the only woman, bolted.

Lars tripped her as she passed. He held her, and Aranthur reached out into her *aura* and *subjugated* her.

He'd never done it to a human before. But in a moment he had control of her will.

"*What do Lightbringers do?*" he asked himself. "*This is better than killing her, surely?*"

The winds of power were blowing hard from the rift; Aranthur did what he had to do.

But the three young men carrying their unconscious leader were not cowed; they were angry.

"Fucking *sorcery*!" one spat.

"Traitor!" another muttered.

"Just keep them moving," Aranthur said.

The Northerner threw the woman over his shoulder; he was as big as Aranthur and she was small.

There followed a harrowing half hour as he pushed them into gondolas and shepherded his little flotilla under bridges held by the Watch or by Yellowjackets, waiting for the inevitable discovery or challenge, but none came, and they were dropped safely on the quay at the palace.

"You really are an Imperial officer," Thendara said.

"You sound disappointed," Aranthur said.

"I don't have a lot of time for the Emperor," she said. "It's time that the people made the decisions, not an antique figurehead."

Aranthur smiled. She smiled back.

"You speak your mind. So let me do you the same favour," he said. "Get lost, don't brag about this, and don't start the revolution today."

Lars nodded. Giannis looked disappointed, and then adoringly at Thendara. Thendara shrugged.

Aranthur thought of Drako, of his lists, and all the various threats.

He looked back at the three of them.

"You really want to help?" he asked.

Thendara shrugged. "We helped you cross the city with these arse-hats," she said.

"Come inside," he said.

All three of them balked, standing on the Imperial Quay with the great lion and the triangle looming over them, the gold leaf fresh and brilliant, the rose marble itself imposing.

Thendara was clearly their leader and both men looked at her until she nodded.

"All right."

She passed through the gate, where a detachment of Axes had taken charge of the prisoners. Aranthur showed his golden rose and marched them to the Guards' barracks.

"Cells," he said.

The officer of the day was a newly promoted Dekark of the Axes.

"Charge?" the woman asked.

Aranthur wrote *murder* in the day-log.

"Ouch," the woman said.

She was huge, as most of the Axes were—taller and heavier than Aranthur, possibly one of the most heavily muscled women he'd ever met.

"Tabitha," she said. "MaGinta."

"Aranthur Timos," he said.

"Heard of you." She smiled. "They're all Yellowjackets?" she asked, curiously.

He nodded.

She smiled again. "Good. Hate those fuckers. Can we take 'em all?"

"Not yet, Dekark."

He turned back to his trio of unlikely accomplices.

"Come with me," he said.

He led them to the anteroom to General Tribane's apartments, on the top floor. He had access and a key, and it was private.

They sat, their body language betraying their anxiety, and Aranthur sent for wine.

He stood by the mantelpiece, remembering Tribane's enhanced perfume. He had to smile.

"I'd love some help," he said. "I don't really know you, but I'm prepared to trust you a little. And you don't know me, but you do know I have access to the palace and the ability to give orders to the guard."

All three nodded.

"I need people in the City. People who will report to me, run errands, recruit, collect information."

"Spies," Lars said with some disgust.

Aranthur shrugged. "If you like. But no amount of student idealism alone is going to overthrow Roaris or restore the Academy."

Thendara accepted wine from a wooden-faced Nomadi trooper straight from the Steppes. Aranthur nodded and thanked the man in Pastun.

She looked at Aranthur. "You are wearing a *guise*," she said. "It's good—it took me this long to be sure."

Aranthur nodded.

"I'm in," she said. "I'm about to become an agent of the Empire." She shook her head in obvious disgust. "Serving the Byzas."

"The Byzas aren't so bad," Aranthur said, in Souliote.

Giannis sat back.

Thendara's smile became more genuine. "Ahh," she said.

Aranthur nodded briskly. "All right. We communicate by drops and couriers. You three will meet me and no one else. If you recruit others, they should only know you, and you never mention me. Understand?"

He had to explain the concept of cells several times to Lars; and then he laid out a system by which they could leave messages for each other. His hollow tree on the slopes of the temple became the focus; he explained how to find it and how to leave a message.

He found it very odd to do all the things Drako had done; he felt like an imposter, and the disguise added to his sense of unreality. It was all terribly hurried, and any one of them could be an informer for the Watch or for the Yellowjackets. But the three students accepted his communication plan as if they'd always wanted to be informants, and when he was done, they all drank off their wine and rose.

"My first request is a list of all the students you can identify who are Yellowjackets," Aranthur said.

Lars furrowed his broad brow. "How the hell do we get that?"

But Giannis, the quiet one, nodded. "I can get a membership list for the Young Lions."

"And I can at least list all the Yellowjackets that I know," Thendara said. "I can name all six of those bastards you brought in. Tarquin's a right bastard. And you can't let them go, syr. That has to be a promise."

"I swear," Aranthur said. "Tarquin?"

"The one you dropped in the fight," Thendara said. "You might call him the Lead Lion."

"What family?" Aranthur asked.

"Thanatoi," she said. "A petty branch. He was nobody before the Yellowjackets made him a Watch officer. Still willing to hold him?"

Aranthur shrugged. "I work for the Emperor. The Families don't concern me."

She shook her head. "I don't believe you, but I liked hearing someone say that out loud."

4

Megara

News of the encounter at Tercel's went through the City like a summer fire, and an hour after Dahlia returned, flushed with victory, having visited four of the Seventeen named by Iralia, hundreds of Watch officers and Yellowjackets surrounded the palace enclosure, carrying torches. Many had a poster with her name and a crude woodcut of her likeness, offering five thousand soldi for her capture.

Her balletic sister, plain as a temple mouse in a brown wool *justaucorps*, handed Benvenutu a wooden box which proved to hold a treasure-trove of rare alchemicals.

"I didn't even have to shop," Rose said. "I have friends. One had this lying about." She glanced at Aranthur. "Oroma wants news of Harlequin." She smiled at Iralia. "Hello, my dear. We've missed you."

Dahlia looked at her sister. "Missed?"

"Iralia is very good to actors," Rose said. "And she plays cards and dances beautifully. Where have you been?"

"Fighting a war?" Dahlia growled.

"Another of my *friends* wants you to know that most of the Watch… I won't say loathes, but at least distrusts Roaris. My friend would like to meet one of you."

Dahlia looked at Aranthur. "This could be it," she said.

Aranthur tugged his beard. "I know." He glanced at Rose. "You trust this man?"

"Woman." Rose said demurely. "I vouch for her. She's a straight arrow. And a patron of the arts." She smiled.

Aranthur looked at Dahlia. "Can you take this?"

Dahlia nodded. Her eyes flickered over to Aranthur's and he didn't like what he saw there, but then she turned to her sister.

"I need a moment with Aranthur," she said.

Rose smiled. "Of course. I'll find a gondola."

Rose swept out, leaving Dahlia glaring at Aranthur.

"Where do you go?" Dahlia asked. "I know you leave the palace. Where are you going every day?"

"Errands," Aranthur said.

Dahlia looked at him for too long. "You're running Drako's agents. By Kerkos, Aranthur. Is that what you are doing?"

Aranthur had real trouble lying to Dahlia and he hesitated a moment too long.

"Drako gave *you* his agent lists. And you are..." She glared at him. "Fuck!"

"Dahlia..."

She turned to leave the room, her face mottled with anger.

He caught an arm. "Dahlia! Listen!"

She turned very slowly. "Take your hands off me."

Aranthur did not relax his grip. "Promise to listen," he said.

She released a breath. "Talk," she snapped.

He released her.

"Drako said... No, before I go further, let me say that what Drako said and what I believe he intended are not the same. Yes?" Aranthur was pleading.

"He is the world's greatest liar, I agree. Fuck me, Aranthur Timos. Tiy Drako gave you to the keys to Cold Iron instead of me?" She was hurt, and she didn't hide it.

Aranthur nodded. "Yes he did," he said flatly. "He said that the real issue was Imperial succession and that you and your family were too close to Roaris—"

"Oh Drax, we're electors!" Dahlia sat down suddenly in one of the big leather chairs, as if her sinews had been cut. "We're on the board this year." She blinked. "The Imperial succession. So he believes Roaris..."

"Plans to make himself emperor? I have..." Aranthur was not Tiy Drako and he took the plunge. "I have a number of reports to suggest that Roaris is positioning himself as the only possible candidate for emperor."

Dahlia shook her head. "Of course. The whole big lie is just a temporary cover to buy time. But Kerkos, he must be bribing half the city to keep them quiet and sweet. Where's all the money coming from?"

"Roaris is rich," Aranthur said. "Drako was looking into that. I'm following up."

"Sometimes you are just a farm boy. No one is that rich. Imagine what it costs to bribe half of the customs officers, the Watch, or at least, the senior Watch, someone in the army. Maybe someone on the Seventeen. And gate guards, students..." She looked at him. "Fuck, I still can't believe that Drako chose you over me. I'm sorry. It sounds so fucking petty but I'm..."

Aranthur smiled and knelt beside her chair. "That's what he told me. But... really? I'm expendable, to Drako. And you aren't. Someone on the Agent List betrayed him, and he threw me the ball. Think about it."

She looked at him for a long time.

"Fuck it." Dahlia leant forward and kissed him.

And the kiss seemed like the most natural thing in the world. Dahlia's lips were a home he'd never really wanted to leave...

He broke away.

Dahlia shook her head. "I didn't actually mean to do that," she said. "And it was a terrible idea."

Aranthur cautiously kept his distance.

"Was Drako really protecting me?" she asked, as if she had not just licked his lips.

"Yes." He couldn't think. His head whirled.

"And you wear a *guise* when you check the list?" she asked.

"Of course," he said.

She got up. For a moment, she looked at him from under her lashes—a look he remembered very well—and his whole body seemed to do a flip.

And then she was gone.

Oh, Inoques.

Oh, Dahlia.

I'm an idiot. Aranthur had the briefest imagining of Inoques blasting Dahlia with black sorcery. *Oh, gods.*

*

That evening he wore the *guise* of a tall, heavily built longshoreman, headed home from the Northside piers. He'd laid out a route based on the cover he'd made up for himself, and he checked signals and put messages *into* drops as he worked his way across the city, north to south. He cleared the hollow tree on the slope of the Temple, and sat in the Temple court, reading his way through the reports, before dropping the shreds into the Temple Fire. Thendara and her friends had given him most of the student members of the Yellowjackets.

He'd also worked out which drop boxes Drako had visited on the day he was taken. Nine that had been serviced on the last day Drako was free...and while it was possible that Drako had been followed before that, and that all the sites were compromised, Aranthur had a notion that Roaris and his agents were at least as desperate as Aranthur was.

But it was nerve-racking, and Aranthur had already begun to hate it. It was harder to make himself approach the drops than it was to draw a sword and charge a group of Pindari horsemen in Armea—much harder. Aranthur had been tortured once; he knew that if he was caught, he wouldn't be rescued this time.

He worked his way across the city grimly, leaving his requests in every drop. He fought the fear silently, and drank too much *quaveh*, and wished he had Sasan at his side. Or Tiy himself. Or Dahlia.

Dahlia...

He sat in an outhouse in the Flats, gagging on the smell and working his way through two long reports on the salt monopoly. Above him, a brown hermit, the region's largest and least poisonous spider, was carefully weaving a web. Aranthur kept glancing up at her as she spun; first the visibly heavier web-cords that linked to the rough-cut wooden walls of the stinking little shed, and then the delicate strands that filled in between the supports.

He'd watched spiders before, but this one was large, and her eyes seemed to glow with intelligence, and he watched her spin with the kind of enjoyment he usually reserved for cats and the working dogs who herded his father's sheep.

He watched her until it was getting dark; the long summer evenings were giving way to autumn outside. And he made plans.

*

"Tell me about the salt monopoly," Aranthur asked Iralia.

They were in the Imperial mews, and Iralia had a hawk, a very small sparrowhawk, on her thumb.

"It remains the single largest line item in Imperial revenue," she said. "The salt pans at Evesta and mines in the Daka hills are the largest in the world. The Emperor visits them in person. The salt is sold as far away as Masr."

Aranthur nodded. "There's so much to *know*," he said with a sigh.

"The Salt Farm, that is, the office of collecting the salt revenues, is sold off each year at auction. This year it's held by Syr Ilios Thanatos." Iralia made a moue of distaste. "I went with the Emperor and watched the auction."

"Dahlia's right," Aranthur said in disgust. "I am a Souliote farm boy. I don't know *anything*." He shrugged. "All right. Teach me to be friends with this fine little fellow."

"I'm pretty sure this is a fine little lass," Iralia said.

"Added to my endless list of things I don't know," Aranthur said.

And later, after two hours of basic falconry instruction, he went with Iralia to visit the dragon.

"He's lonely. And angry. He's a guest not a prisoner, but..." Iralia shrugged.

The dragon, an emissary of the fabulous land of Zhou far to the east, had a set of apartments built out of portions of the Imperial mews and kennels. Any implied disrespect had been muted or eliminated by beautiful stonework in golden sandstone, elaborately carved, with esoteric coloured marble accents. The whole had been built in the form of a perfectly snug cave, with a manicured front lawn, and a floor of black volcanic sand, on which the dragon reclined.

Aranthur made his full Imperial reverence. "Greetings, 蟠龍Pánlóng!" he said.

The dragon's eyes opened, and he blinked, and shook himself. He smelled marvellous, like fresh cut hay with a slight tinge of cinnamon.

"Who speaks my name correctly?" he asked.

He rolled slightly and rose to his haunches, and his sinuous neck stretched like that of a waking cat.

"Iralia!" he said. "Ah, now this is a treat."

"You cannot pretend that I don't visit you," she said.

蟠龍Pánlóng shook himself. "I hesssitate to presss my sssuperior intelligencsse and wisssdom on you," he said. "But permit me to sssuggest that I am ssso bored that I sssometimes consssider the wholesssale ssslaughter of..." He coughed. "Never mind. I am awfully bored." He turned his head without moving his long neck—a remarkable show of dexterity. "How isss the Emperor, may hisss name be praisssed?"

"My consort is now receiving better care than I could provide," Iralia said.

"I beg your leave, marvelousssss lady, to doubt you. Indeed, if your consssort happensss to passs from the realmsss of life, I might be forcssed to alter my sssshape to consssole you..." The dragon nodded his head.

Iralia laughed. "You are an old flatterer," she said fondly.

"I am quite a young flatterer as my kind count the yearsss," he said. "That'sss why I wasss sssent." The long head turned back to Aranthur. "I know you, sssir. I know your ssscent. And you have been presssent..."

"We've met three times," Aranthur said. "I am a friend of Ansu's."

It was all Aranthur could do not to render his "esses" as sibilant as the dragon's, so powerful was the great creature's personality.

"I know that 蟠龍Pánlóng craves company," Iralia said. "But I must return to nursing. I'm sure he'd love to hear how Ansu does, and what happened in Armea."

Aranthur retold the entire story, from the Battle of Armea to the Black Pyramid. At one point he thoughtlessly referred to his friend as "Zhu Jingfu," his private name, and the dragon stiffened.

"He has permitted you his name?" the dragon asked.

"Yes, syr," Aranthur answered.

The dragon licked between the talons of his right leg a little. And then looked up, a suddenly human meeting of eyes.

"That isss very good. Good for him—a great honour for you." He nodded. "Let me sssummarise your ssstory. You fear the Old Gods, or whatever they name themssselvesss. You fear they can essscape from confinement and you have no dragon to help you. In addition, thissss *Pure* organisation continuesss to make very human, ordinary war. Finally, here, Sssyr Roarisss isss attempting to usssurp the government, and you sssuspect him of poisssoning the Emperor. Is that correct?"

"All correct," Aranthur said.

The dragon stretched. "I would be mossst help with the Old Onesss.

But I would be delighted to help you in any way I can, the moressso as you have been permitted my friend'sss private name. It meansss he trussstsss you, and we, my dear boy, are not trusssting creatures."

Aranthur tugged at his beard. "I will most willingly…engage you, syr."

"Nicely ssspoken. Come again soon. Boredom is a fearsome enemy, and I am out of interessst with logic problems."

"At your service," Aranthur said. "Are you any good at reading glyphs?"

Darkness was falling over the city; there was still no trabaccolo on the horizon, and Aranthur was sitting outside the Emperor's private apartment with Dahlia, working on the *Ulmaghest.*

"I don't understand," Dahlia said. "The salt monopoly?"

"It's how Roaris is funding his bribes," Aranthur said. "And Drako was on to it. The day he was captured, he was supposed to visit this man." He put a card on the table but kept his thumb over the man's name. He'd written it out longhand from Drako's crabbed hand in the agent list. "Mid-level bureaucrat in the Salt Tax. The original whistle-blower on the whole thing, who hasn't reported in since Drako was taken."

"It can't be this easy," Dahlia said.

"The Emperor is awake," Litha announced, and Iralia appeared behind her, carrying a tray.

Dahlia shot to her feet.

The Master of Arts came in, kissed her partner on the cheek, and looked at something on the tray. Then she waved her hand.

"He is by no means fully recovered," she said. "But I think he needs to see people. Please be brief. Make your bows and go."

Aranthur went in behind Dahlia. Iralia was by the bedside, her face wet with tears.

The Emperor was as thin as Aranthur, his beard overgrown, and a slightly foolish smile on his face. He lay on a magnificent bed in a room large enough to house four Easterner families, with a window of a hundred panes of glass looking out over the sea. They were high in the palace—well above the mighty, modern fortifications that guarded the seaward approach to the city. From here, it was easy to see why they were called the Stars; their sharply angled bastions made them look like stars of pale stone against the wine-dark sea.

The walls behind the Emperor were hung with tapestries of the hunt, and a magnificent Safian wall hanging depicting the sun as the Lord of Light.

McBane stood inside the chamber with three other Axes, all facing in different directions, all wearing a dozen amulets and protections over their armour. None of them even glanced at Aranthur.

"Dahlia!" the Emperor said in obvious delight. "Oh, gods, I dreamt you were all dead. Everyone, dead."

Dahlia made a deep reverence, and Aranthur joined her.

"Apple juice, sire?" Iralia asked.

"Apple juice? Oh, yes," the Emperor said, and drank it off.

"More?" Iralia asked.

"More, please."

"I can get you a doublet if you are cold." Iralia hovered.

"Come to think of it, I am cold, my dear," the Emperor said.

Benvenutu was watching from the doorway and she shook her head.

"Majesty, would you like to drink some warm, fresh goat piss?" she asked.

"Oh, yes, very much so, Altaria," the Emperor said.

Benvenutu looked at Iralia, and then at Dahlia.

"Is that young Timos?" the Emperor asked. "By the gods—I have dreamt such dark dreams. Is all well?"

Aranthur looked at the Master of Arts.

She shrugged.

"No," Aranthur said.

"Then make it well, Timos. I beg you."

Aranthur had an odd moment of affection for this man, whose mind had been broken, but who only wanted his realm to be healthy.

"We are doing all we can," he said.

The Emperor sat up. For a moment, he didn't look like an emaciated priest of Aploun, but like the Emperor again.

"*Do what you must*," he said.

And then the smile returned, and he lay down.

"More apple juice," he said. "Or the fresh goat piss."

Benvenutu ushered them out. McBane gave Aranthur a significant look as he passed and Aranthur nodded.

"Goat piss?" Iralia spat.

"I needed you to see and understand what the aurax has done," Benvenutu said. "I need a real alchemist. He'll live, but at the moment, he'd be the most suggestible, biddable emperor in history, and I do not recommend we allow that."

"Allow?" Iralia asked. "What choice do we have?"

Benvenutu said nothing.

"Get me an alchemist," she said.

Aranthur shook his head. "Ma'am, he should have been here days ago."

When she was gone back to her charge, Aranthur sat back down with Dahlia and Iralia.

"I was waiting for Inoques," he admitted. "And maybe even Tiy Drako. But I think we have to move without them. I have a plan—a whole set of plans. But I have no sense that I'm the one who should run this show."

Dahlia nodded slowly, her whole body rocking back and forth.

"Drako chose you, though," she said.

"You met with Rose's friend?" Aranthur asked.

Dahlia glanced at Iralia. The glance told volumes of Dahlia's failure to trust the other woman, but in the end she shrugged.

"Yes," she said. "I name no names."

"Good," Aranthur said.

"She says the Watch is deeply dissatisfied with the current situation and that several senior Watch officers are either frozen with indecision or actively supporting Roaris. But the Watch, as a whole, is made up of military veterans, and the military is rife with rumours that Tribane is alive and victorious. Some of those rumours are coming from our four contacts in the Seventeen, because some of them saw Rose and Oroma today."

Aranthur nodded.

"I know you don't want an armed revolution..." Dahlia said.

"I don't," Aranthur said. "Do you know for sure that there are people out there who'd like to overthrow the whole government? The city? The Emperor?"

Dahlia stared at her hands. "Of course there are. But I told you, Aranthur, Roaris made a huge mistake in arresting the countess. Everything I heard today confirms it. These aren't students talking—these are my relatives and their friends."

"And you trusted them not to turn you in," Aranthur said angrily. "The reward is now ten thousand silver soldi, Myr Tarkas."

Dahlia stopped and whistled. "And my practical philosophy teacher said I'd never amount to anything."

Aranthur had to smile. So did Iralia.

"We need to strike at him, and they'll rally to us. The aristocrats—the very basis of the Lion's political power. He'll fall like a ripe apple. No revolution. No struggle."

Dahlia was leaning forward; her face was very close to Aranthur's, and he blushed at his own thoughts and leant back.

"I agree," Aranthur said.

Dahlia leant back herself. "You do?"

Aranthur thought for a moment. "I see this..." he began. "I see this like the collapse of a house of cards. We need to pull out the right card."

"We need to rescue the countess," Dahlia said. "That will change everything."

Aranthur nodded. "Again, I agree. But I want to do something first."

"Damn it, Timos, the time is now," Dahlia said.

Iralia glanced at Aranthur. "The Emperor is awake." She shrugged. "I'm sorry, Aranthur, but that news will also spread. And it will hurry Roaris. He will have to act, and there will be fighting, blood, all the things you fear. And I fear."

"I fear them too," Dahlia said. She shook her head. "I agree with Aranthur that we do not want an uncontrolled fire. But when summer is past on my family farm, and all the fields are done, and the rains come..."

"Controlled burn," Aranthur agreed. "We Souliotes do the same."

"Exactly," she said. "Since we can't avoid it, let's control it."

"A perfect image," Aranthur said. "I have an idea, which I can modify for this. Let's try it. I know I'm not the director of Cold Iron. But I think I know how to pull the right card."

Iralia looked at both of them. "I'm here, in the palace. I only went out to try to save Drako. But...what of the rift? The Dark Forge? And everything you told me about Masr? And Antioke?"

Aranthur was riffling the cards of Iralia's beautifully painted tarrocio deck. The cards were so fine that sometimes he had to stop and look at one. The Queen of Love was Iralia herself; he smiled at her.

"He had the deck painted for me when he learned I loved to play," Iralia said.

"If we take Roaris down," Aranthur said, "we can put fifty Studion trained magisters in Al-Khaire and bury Tribane in supplies and if we have to, raise a second and a third army to push into Safi and Armea. Tribane proved one vital thing—militarily, the Pure are no match for the Empire and Atti together. Really, no surprise there. If we knock the wraiths back into the Black Pyramid and Masr enters the war, the Pure can count the hours. I worry about Atti."

Dahlia nodded. "As do I. That's where they killed Kurvenos. The Pure have an establishment there."

"And there was an attack on the Kaptan Bey and his family," Aranthur said. "The road back to victory starts right here."

"You are very persuasive," Iralia said.

Dahlia narrowed her eyes. "I feel like I never really knew you at all," she said suddenly. "You are much deeper and much sharper than I guessed. I'm sorry, Aranthur. I thought you were a peasant boy willing to work his arse off to get ahead. Instead, you're a thinker."

Aranthur flushed. "I'm not sure that I am not both."

Iralia put a hand on her abdomen. "Dahlia, you really do have a way of expressing yourself," she said.

Aranthur looked around. "I'm not offended. Listen, I say we try to pull out a card. I've already asked Drako's network, part of it, to find the countess."

Dahlia clapped her hands together.

"Now we're bloody talking!" she said.

Aranthur smiled. "But the first card is this one." He flipped over the card he'd written the details of Drako's agent on. "Giorgios Litkos."

"Who is he?" Iralia asked. "Sixth undersecretary? He's nobody."

Aranthur picked up the card. "I think he's somebody. If he's still alive, I think he was used as the bait to take Drako. In fact, I bet he's dead. But if he's dead, then my guess on the Salt Tax is correct, and then we strike."

"How?" Iralia asked.

He told them.

Dahlia shook her head. "Remind me never to piss you off," she said. "When did you get to be like this?"

"The Black Bastion," he said.

An hour later, Dahlia and Aranthur sat in one of the palace's dozens of sitting rooms, with the servants waiting on them hand and foot.

"That's better wine," Dahlia said, accepting the whole decanter from the Keltai man who'd waited on them the first day. She smiled at him, and he returned her smile with interest. "So the Stone is back tonight?" she said in a hushed whisper.

"Tomorrow," Aranthur said. "Keep your voice down. We'll need the Master of Arts to move it."

"Are you sure the Academy is the right place to put it?"

"The precinct is sacred ground. Not even Roaris would dare…"

Dahlia shook her head. "He might. Why not move it here?"

Aranthur stood. "Damn it, Dahlia, for once, just do as I fucking say. All right?" He shook himself. "The *Emperor* is here, Dahlia, and if anything happens to him, we're sunk."

Dahlia set her face, flushed red, and then stood.

"Listen to me, *farm boy.* I don't obey. I give the orders. Do what you want. You know nothing of how this place works."

She put her *murana* glass down on the inlaid ivory table with a click and walked out, her boots silent in the deep Safian rugs. She turned at the doorway.

"Call for me when you're ready to take my orders, and not before. And move your precious Black Stone on your own."

Two hours later, Aranthur was moving across Southside, past the Flats. He'd just walked past Master Sparthos' house and wished he had time to take a lesson—even in a *guise*.

The streets were dark, and Dahlia padded alongside him, a Souliote woman, someone's nurse or scullery maid walking home from a long day of work.

"Did I overplay it?" Dahlia asked.

"No, I think we were pretty good."

Aranthur smiled in the near darkness, and hoped Dahlia never knew how clear it was when she said something she half-believed.

"You're sure the pretty Keltai boy is the traitor?" she asked.

"Not at all sure, but he fits the bill in several ways. Anyway, whoever it is, our public spat should do the job."

They were hurrying along a narrow street in one of the City's poorer middle-class neighbourhoods. The Flats were so named because of their proximity to the mud flats south of the City's central coastline. They stank in summer, but they were the cheapest land and every month aggressive developers drove more alder pilings into the mud, built more houses and dredged more canals. They were too narrow for heavy traffic and the islands they created lacked the orchards and parks that made the city beautiful; the developers were too keen on profit to waste their gold on beauty. But a prosperous bureaucrat could buy his own house in the Flats; and the only other option was to live in the lower floors of one of the huge tenements that lined the ancient aqueduct lines. The tenements were nice enough if you lived on the lower floors, but not above, where heat, light, and water were all hard to come by, and so the Flats expanded, month by month.

"We should have come by boat," Dahlia said.

"If this goes badly, I don't want any witnesses," Aranthur said.

"Fair," Dahlia agreed. "This one."

It was nightfall. Every house on the street was lit, some by expensive magelight, but many by candles. Every house but the one they were facing—the yellow house, built in the form of a much more expensive palazzo but only two storeys tall and with a facing much narrower than a real palace. It faced on to a narrow *fondemento* and then a canal.

The canal was busy; two narrow gondolas had trouble passing and the gondoliers were sparring, angry shouts echoing from the wall of the canal. Two houses down, a loggia was full of young people outside eating what smelled like fish and rice. Aranthur's stomach grumbled.

"No lights," he said.

Dahlia nodded. "Let's try the back alley."

They went down to the corner, and Dahlia unerringly led them into an alley.

"You've been here before," Aranthur said.

"Never," Dahlia said. "But there has to be a back entrance. The owners want to pretend they're living in palaces."

"Spoken with all the privilege of an aristocrat."

Dahlia shrugged. "If you like. But they could design their own houses to be convenient for what they really are, and not ape us?"

"Poor things," Aranthur said.

"Shut up," Dahlia said. "This one."

They were standing outside a heavily iron-studded door in a tall wall. The alley was just wide enough for a cart, and smelled like cat's piss.

But it was empty.

The gate was locked, of course.

Aranthur stripped off his doublet.

"This is my idea," he said. "So I'll do the dirty work."

"Good," Dahlia said.

But despite her words, she made a stirrup of her hands and Aranthur was over the wall in a moment. His hands weren't cut by the sharp glass in the top because of his swordsman's gloves, though he did get a gash in his knee before he dropped to the cobbled courtyard. The drop was farther than he'd anticipated; he landed hard, but rolled, and by bad luck struck the same knee he'd just cut. He stifled a yelp.

Then he got back to his feet, and took a step in total darkness. He knew what was around him from the smell, but he misjudged a step and his booted foot sank into something squishy and he swore.

The gate was easy, and he had it open in moments.

"Watch your step," he said. "There's a corpse."

"Kerkos!" She shut the gate and lit her mage fire.

"Oh, gods," they both said.

The smell was explained. There were three dead people in the tiny courtyard. All three had been beheaded, and something had been chewing on them. In the harsh blue-white light, they were a terrible sight.

"Hold it."

Aranthur leant down and examined one corpse and then stood up.

"Servants. And a child." He made a face.

"Kerkos," Dahlia said again.

The back door, at the top of a flight of steps, was not only unlatched but open, and the kitchen beyond was chaotic. Pots were on the floor, and there was flour everywhere...

"Behuts," Dahlia said.

"I know," Aranthur said. "I live here too."

Behuts were mid-sized mammals, like little bears. They were ferociously intelligent, and they would break into anything for food. A few lived in the wild; most of them seemed to live in the City now.

There were behut tracks in the flour, and across the corpse of the cook, whose eyes had been eaten out. The cook must have tried to defend himself; his hands had been cut off, and one, lying on the wooden cutting table, still held a heavy cleaver. Aranthur looked at the wrists and then at a long burn mark in the wall.

He shook his head.

"This is far worse than anything I imagined," he said. "We need to dim our lights."

Dahlia nodded, and they both reduced the power of their magelights to just enough light to render the shadows terrifying.

"These corpses are what, four days old?" Dahlia asked.

Aranthur was already moving, his light moving with him. Dahlia pressed in behind him, and they moved through the first floor, looking into the sitting room, which was empty, and a tiny guest bedroom.

"Up," Aranthur breathed. He wasn't sure why he was being quiet, but it seemed important.

They went up the single staircase with silent caution; Aranthur could feel Dahlia's potent *aura*, her powers already summoned and ready to use, as his were.

Those fifteen steps seemed to take forever.

At the top was a small corridor with pictures hung on good wainscoting. Aranthur turned left; Dahlia covered the right.

Bedroom. Empty. All the drawers in an enormous dresser pulled out and dumped on the bed. Then another room: a dressing room with an armoire that almost filled it. The doors were open, and the clothes dumped on the floor.

That was the whole corridor. Aranthur backed to the stairs and followed Dahlia to the right. There was a shiny puddle on the floor.

"Blood."

Aranthur pointed overhead, where the blood had come through the ceiling.

"Gods." Dahlia turned aside and spat. "Gods," she said again. "You take me to all the best places."

There was a third bedroom. A woman was dead on the bed, cleanly beheaded.

Dahlia just shook her head, but Aranthur looked carefully at the cuts. Burn marks.

"Aphres. Kerkos. Fuck," Dahlia said.

"Pretty much my thought," Aranthur said. "A Scarlet. In Megara."

Dahlia breathed through her mouth for a few breaths.

"I need a pomade ball," she said.

"Me too," he agreed. "How do we get to the attic?"

In the end, Dahlia found the ladder in a bedroom, and Aranthur climbed to the trapdoor.

Giorgios Litkos had hidden in the attic while the Scarlet killed his family—his son, his daughter, his wife, his servants. Maybe he wasn't particularly brave; or maybe just rational, or maybe he tried to get them to come with him. Aranthur stood over his corpse, and wanted to weep, because the man had hidden, and waited, and still failed. Aranthur didn't need any specific identification; he was the right age, and the severed head matched the description in the agent list.

The attic looked like the deck of a war galley after a long battle. Everything was pulled over; much had been cut, slashed apart, and opened.

Dahlia's head was now looking up through the trapdoor.

"The Scarlet was looking for something," she said.

"Yes," Aranthur said. "I don't think they found it, either."

"Can we find it?" Dahlia asked.

"We don't need to," Aranthur said. "Litkos is no longer our only whistle blower. We know about the Salt Tax and how much is missing. And really, if we needed proof, it's lying all around us."

Dahlia nodded. "And it's always good to be reminded that we're on the side of right," she said. "Because this is… fucked."

"Aye," Aranthur said.

"We need to be sure…"

Aranthur was looking at the dead agent: a mid-sized Byzas man with a carefully tended beard, who'd been murdered along with his whole family for knowing that the Salt Tax funds were being embezzled.

He thought for a moment about the Emperor. *Do what you must.*

"We're going to make very sure indeed," Aranthur said.

5

Megara

An hour after the Salt Tax office opened in among the government offices in Harbourside, Syr Ilios Thanatos came in with a pair of servants and a bodyguard. Syr Ilios was a pale-skinned Byzas who might have passed for Keltai, with dark hair and eyes and a pointed beard. He smiled at the doorkeeper, who gazed back more woodenly than usual.

Syr Iios nodded. "Bad morning?"

The man said nothing, and Syr Ilios climbed the broad, official staircase to his office with a beautiful view of the harbour. His secretary was sitting very still, and he only nodded as his master passed.

"Anything for me?" Syr Ilios called, and then he saw that there were two people in his office.

"Drant?" he called to the secretary, who kept his hands folded carefully in front of him.

The two people were well enough dressed, and both wore the familiar yellow and black livery of the Yellowjackets.

Thanatos nodded. "I don't know you. May I help you?" he said, with frosty courtesy.

"You are under arrest for the embezzlement of Imperial funds." Aranthur held up Drako's golden rose.

By his side, Dahlia had a puffer pointed at the nobleman's face.

Thanatos shook his head. "Is this some sort of joke?" he asked. "Do you two idiots know who I am?" He looked at the rose and his pale face flushed.

"You are Syr Ilios Thanatos," Dahlia said. "I know you well enough, and my mother knows you better, syr. And there is no joke."

"Conspiracy to commit murder, and high treason." Aranthur motioned to the others in Yellowjackets. "Take them all. Everyone in the building."

Out in the corridor, half a dozen Nomadi dressed as Yellowjackets prodded the building's entire work complement—twenty-two clerks, the doorman, the cleaning man, the cook—out of the door. A dozen gondolas were waiting for them. It was full daylight, a working day, and hundreds of people in the street saw the Yellowjackets and two Watch officers arresting the entire Salt Tax regime. A few people cheered.

One of the clerks turned to Aranthur.

"But it's collection day!" she said. "People won't pay their taxes! There will be no one here…"

"That's right," Aranthur said.

"People depend on this money," Thanatos said. "Important people."

Aranthur smiled at him. "You mean Verit Roaris?"

Thanatos blinked. "Maybe!" he said. "You are making a terrible mistake."

"Didn't it occur to you, when they killed Litkos," Dahlia said, her eyes bright, "that you were expendable too?"

"Sophia!" the man said. He was shoved into a gondola, with Aranthur beside him and Dahlia and her puffer behind. "This is a terrible mistake."

"I doubt it," Dahlia said with absolute assurance.

"Take me to the Lord Protector!" Thanatos said. "He'll put you right."

"That's unlikely," Aranthur said.

And when the gondolas swung out into the open sea past the Lighthouse and made to approach the sea gate of the Stars fortress, the man went very pale indeed.

"You aren't Yellowjackets," he said.

"That's the first intelligent thing you've said," Dahlia noted. "Here's the deal, Syr Thanatos. You are convicted on the strength of your own words —your treason is obvious. Do you know the penalty for high treason?"

Thanatos was sweating visibly.

"For a commoner, hanging." Dahlia brushed her hand against his neck. "But you are a gentleman, are you not? A member of the mighty Thanatos family."

"Stop," the man said.

"An aristocratic traitor is more of a threat to the public order," Dahlia said. "Isn't he?"

He threw up.

"Hanged by the neck," Dahlia said. "Then cut down. Eviscerated and castrated. Then, if you yet live, pulled to pieces by horses." She nodded. "Utterly barbaric. The sort of thing that makes the Empire look like an ancient feudal state and not a modern nation."

Aranthur smiled.

So did Dahlia. "Still on the books, though, Syr Ilios. Please don't make us use you as an example of bad old laws."

"I didn't do anything..." Thanatos said quietly. "I..."

"You will tell us exactly what General Roaris ordered," Dahlia said, "and then I will guarantee that you won't be tortured."

The boat tapped against the fortress pier.

"Otherwise, we go straight to the torture chambers," Aranthur said.

Thanatos looked away. "No," he said. "I will never speak. I demand my advocate and my rights under the law."

"Good." Aranthur marched the prisoner into a small chamber and glanced at him. "Strip," he said.

"No," Thanatos said.

"I can have you stripped. Your choice."

The man took off his clothes.

Aranthur nodded, and took them. "Goodbye," he said.

"What do I wear?" Thanatos asked. "By the gods! I'm a nobleman!"

"You were a nobleman," Aranthur said. "Now you will be tortured until you talk, and then your body will be thrown in the harbour."

He went out and closed the door.

Dahlia was cleaning her nails with a knife.

"Do we even have torture chambers?"

Aranthur shrugged. "I'm not from here, remember? But not that I know of."

Dahlia nodded. "I hate to think what Drako did. But don't worry. I won't touch him. Naked, I suspect he won't last an hour."

"This is a different Dahlia."

Dahlia shook her head. "A fucking Scarlet loose in my city?" she spat. "My patience is at an end."

*

Somewhere in Southside, the brown hermit moved across her web, savouring the vibrations of the two moths and the mosquito caught on her sticky strands. Aranthur looked up at her from time to time. He had eleven messages; one of them made him smile a great deal.

The spider was sucking the life fluids out of one of the moths.

She stopped, her forelegs brushing her mandibles, a little like a cat cleaning its whiskers.

Aranthur smiled at her. "I have a nice juicy one, too," he said.

"Did he talk?" Aranthur said.

Iralia looked worse, with dark circles under her eyes. The Master of Arts was snoring on the settee.

Dahlia had her boots off and her feet up.

"He sang," she said. She tossed a heavy, cream-coloured folder on the table next to the *Ulmaghest*. "His confession."

"Edvin?" Aranthur asked.

"I hate you all," the notary said.

"No one ever died of writing," Myr Benvenutu said.

"Cruel," Edvin said.

"I brought you spiced *quaveh*," Aranthur said.

Edvin smiled. "You, I might continue to like."

Iralia shook her head. "I understand the confession. But I'm so tired." She slumped suddenly, like a marionette with her strings cut. "Tell me anyway."

Dahlia smiled at Iralia, as if somehow the diminishment of Iralia's beauty made her more likeable.

"I can barely follow the plot myself," she said. "Listen, then. We took the whole Salt Tax office, dressed as Yellowjackets. No one can pay their tax, and no matter how wide the rot is spread, no one will be there to pass it on to Roaris or one of his minions…"

"So tonight, no one gets paid. Actually, no one ever gets paid again." Aranthur's smile was feral. "And we did it publicly, so every man and woman on the take knows that the source of their money just vanished…"

"And we did it as Yellowjackets," Dahlia said, "just to spread more chaos. Even better, because he was stupid enough to arrest the countess, there are plenty of aristos who will assume he's also stupid enough to arrest a Thanatos."

Iralia managed a barked laugh. "I love it."

"And the other part?" Dahlia asked.

Aranthur nodded to Edvin. "Four copies of that confession, as fast as you can. In fact, I'll make one while you make three."

He tossed a scrap of paper on the table and Dahlia snatched it, read it, and her eyes caught fire.

"We can do that!" she said.

"I think so." Aranthur picked up a pen and checked the nib.

Edvin laughed. "Well, that's fair," he said.

"They go to the same councillors to whom you passed the dispatches," Aranthur said, and Dahlia nodded.

"I was not born yesterday." She was doodling. "Why is the countess being kept in a private house?"

Aranthur sat and copied; the Master of Arts snored softly, and Iralia fed the Emperor and then played with the dogs. After a heavy silence, Aranthur looked up.

"Because the Pure have ordered her taken and tortured," he said. "For what she knows as Imperial spymistress."

"Fuck," Dahlia said.

"We go for her tonight," Aranthur said. "Iralia, we'll need the Axes."

Iralia smiled. "To save a woman from torture? I want to come. And I will make sure the Emperor orders McBane along in person."

Aranthur nodded.

"So," Iralia said. "Is Roaris beaten?"

Dahlia nodded. "Yes. But as the man behind the lies, he was always going to lose unless the Emperor died. For now he's like a dangerous opponent who's badly cut. He'll take a little while to bleed out and we just learned that he has the kind of... support... that we most fear. But regardless... I think we've just pulled a lot of his teeth."

Drakas, the steward, came in a few minutes later as the Imperial clock rang six and handed Iralia a note.

She read it and nodded. "Roaris has ordered the army to blockade the palace," she said. "The troops at the Arsenale have received orders to blockade us by sea."

Aranthur nodded. "He should have done that four days ago."

Iralia smiled over the parchment. "The Master of the Arsenale refused the order."

Aranthur looked at the two women. "Which is more important?" he asked. "Saving the countess? Or passing the confessions to the Council?"

Dahlia sighed. "The confessions," she admitted. "Much as I want to help her."

Aranthur shuddered. "I hate this," he said, and then, "I'd do almost anything to get Inoques here. To know..."

Iralia patted his hand. "She's a tough woman. She'll hold out."

Dahlia smiled. "You may not have to do anything to summon your demon lover."

Because the Master of Arts was lying full length on the settee, Dahlia was sitting at the table with Edvin and Aranthur. She got up and pointed out of the window, at the sea.

Out over Atti, a major storm was brewing; lightning flashed, and from this high up, it was possible to see how heavy the dark clouds were, lashing the magnificent city of Ulama across the straits with rain.

Almost at their feet, the Stars guarded the breakwater and the entrance to the Imperial Harbour, and even as Aranthur looked out, the nearer fortress fired a gun—a tiny wink of fire and a blossom of smoke clear against the darkening sea.

And the low black ship, scudding along under its foresail, running before the storm, fired in return and ran up the Imperial signal: three red flags and a single black.

The Great Lion flag, as big as a warship's sail, flying on the Greater Star dipped, and the trabaccolo turned for the mouth of the Imperial harbour.

Aranthur felt as if an iron band was slipping from his heart. He wanted to jump for joy, and in fact, he found himself embracing Iralia, who was pounding his back.

Dahlia's smile was feral. "Now," she said, "we have some fun."

Book Two
Rebattimento

. . . when you use your sword to strike your adversary's in such a way as to deceive him, to open a line, or better yet, to move his blade in such a way that he will overreact, this is a *rebattimento*, and it must be delivered with great precision.

Maestro Sparthos,
unpublished notes to the book *Opera Nuova*

1

Megara

Inoques' kiss still burned on Aranthur's lips as he moved through the darkness.

The house was on Northside, near the Spice Market; it gave Aranthur an almost physical pain to realise that he'd walked past the very house, a tall, elegant blue building on a plain cobbled street, more than once in the past few days.

The discovery of the kidnapped countess's location had been almost happenstance—a foolish error by an over-smart Yellowjacket. The house had belonged to one of Drako's agents, who had not reported for more than two weeks, and Aranthur now assumed he was dead, beheaded or worse, the body dumped in the marshes. But someone had decided the dead agent's empty house would make a perfect interrogation location, where the Watch would not overhear the efforts of the interrogators and demand extra bribes.

Regardless, when he asked an agent to check the house it had only taken her one glance, and a single scream, to understand what she had found.

And so Aranthur, for the second time in twenty-four hours, stood at the back gate of a private house. This time, he stood with Iralia, McBane and Vilna, and Kallotronis' two biggest men, known as Shtaze and Injorancz—Brute Force and Ignorance, in Byzas. They were very large men. Dahlia was in front with four more Arnauts and Kallotronis himself. The Arnauts had a witch, a natural talent, called Dead Eye, and he was with Dahlia to make smoke, which was his best trick.

McBane had an enormous axe in his hands, and he stood with it, poised; Vilna had a puffer and a bell-mouthed *fusil* aimed at the gate, and above them, Chimeg settled on to a nearby garden wall, her long-barrelled *jezzail* aimed at an upstairs window. Nata had gone directly to the palace Infirmary. Despite his protests, Aranthur had arranged for the little Steppe man to get a prosthetic hand, a miracle of Byzas engineering and modern magik.

The thought of lifting the dark cloud of bitterness from Nata made Aranthur smile, despite the pressure of the moment. Habit made him check the priming of the puffer in his left hand. He had the ancient broadsword in his right. It was warm to the touch.

He looked up, at the stars; and saw the flicker of movement he needed to see.

Dahlia's blue magelight flashed once, up into the shaded tree in front of the house.

Aranthur nodded. Even in the darkness, McBane saw the nod, and his hands tensed.

Aranthur looked around; Vilna was smiling.

He pulsed his own dark red light back again.

Instantly, there was a heavy buzz above them, like an enormous humming bee, and leaves and garbage began to flutter around the alley.

"Go!" Aranthur said, uselessly, because McBane's axe, which had artifactual qualities of its own, smashed through the gate as if he was cutting flesh, and came out again. The lock fell, severed, and the gate swung open.

Aranthur had the guard, instantly; a single pulsed *occulta* and he was through the man's shield and into his *aura* and his *subjugation* unfolded…

Vilna shot him dead anyway. He dropped his puffer and swung his *fusil* up. There was a shot from inside the gate and Aranthur's hat flew from his head.

Vilna shot the bell-mouth through the gate—a massive charge of old nails and bird shot. There were screams, and Aranthur went through the gate.

A tirade of *occultae* struck his shields, and then suddenly the entire sending was gone, and the caster stood, amazed.

Aranthur broke his nose and knocked him unconscious with a forehand and a backhand, and then stood over him so that none of the Nomadi would kill him. Three paces away, a Yellowjacket was trying to raise the winds of magik but nothing came between her hands. She was still trying to summon something—anything—when Vilna took her down with the butt of his *fusil*. At their backs, Chimeg's *jezzail* spoke with a flat crack; a window seemed to detonate, and a dark figure staggered. His puffer fired into the ceiling above him and he vanished.

McBane charged past Aranthur, up the steps to the house. An arbalest bolt shattered against his armour, and the force of the blow slowed him for a moment, but then the great axe smashed into the half-door and he was through, bellowing a war cry, with three more Imperial Axes behind him, and Aranthur doubted that there was a mortal force that could stand against them.

He didn't follow them. He went instead to the low bulkhead doors where firewood and coal were delivered, on the hunch that the foulest deeds were done in basements.

He pulled a door open and someone in the basement fired a puffer ball that tore the air past his head. He fired back left-handed as he charged down the stone steps; hit his head with a ringing crash against the low lintel and went down.

Vilna was shorter, and right behind him, and fired at the same time as their opponent, but Vilna's aim was true, and the other man fell like a sack, dead before he hit the ground. Aranthur, running on spirit and luck, rolled to his feet, even though his head felt as if it had a spike driven through it.

He was having trouble seeing properly. But there was a low door, and he unleashed a massive pulse in the *Aulos* through his shields, and his *puissance* shredded the old oak door.

He threw his puffer at the shadowy figure on the other side of the door, but the man, or woman, was so lacerated by the splinters that they could only scream and feel for their missing flesh.

Vilna's sword flickered up, more in mercy than aggression, and punctured the screaming thing's throat…

There was a table in the low room beyond. The old countess was strapped to it, and it was terrible; and yet her eye met Aranthur's, an eagle's eye and not any kind of prey, and then he saw the Scarlet on the other side. The thing was bent almost double in the low-ceilinged basement, and the heavy table and its occupant blocked it from moving. It had clearly just came down the steps from above.

It killed the old woman with a casual flick of a blinding white sword.

Aranthur cursed. He'd dropped his sword when he hit his head.

"Back, Vilna!" he yelled.

He grabbed the Pastun by the coat and pulled him back through the door. The Scarlet raised its swords, and nothing happened as it tried and failed to throw a bolt of balefire.

Aranthur backed through the inner door. But the cellar was dark as pitch now, a single lamp guttering on the floor where one of the tables had been overthrown, and the Scarlet burst through the opening, crouched low…

Aranthur cast his *enhancement.* He had it ready, *inside* his own private *Aulos*, so it worked.

Everything seemed to go very slowly.

Except the Scarlet. It turned; again it attempted balefire and failed, and Aranthur used the wasted tempo to move, but he could not find the sword and nothing was coming to his magesight.

The Scarlet's sword burned like torches, and it came after him.

"Out!" he roared at Vilna.

The Pastun had drawn a dagger. Game to the last, he was turning slowly, so slowly, to face the Scarlet.

Aranthur *threw* him up the steps.

The Scarlet struck. Its swords cut through the space that Vilna had occupied, and then, apparently shocked to be balked of its prey, it sprang forward and tripped over the corpse.

Aranthur didn't hesitate. He leapt on top of the thing, hands reaching for its sword hands, knees on its abdomen.

The thing's parchment skin burned…

Its eyes…

Aranthur spoke the binding. It was not the unbinding he'd concocted at Antioke. It was a darker *occulta* altogether, and the Scarlet collapsed under him.

Its eyes…*their* eyes locked with his.

"No!" they said, quite clearly, in Byzas; four, or six, voices in a terrible disharmony.

Aranthur's hands were burnt, and he could barely see, and something was wrong with his breathing.

"Imoter," he moaned, as he rolled off the Scarlet…

…that he had *captured.*

*

"We lost her," Dahlia said. "Fuck them. I will personally peel the skin off Roaris, relative or not."

She threw a blanket over the ruin of the countess's body.

"I have four of their magi," Iralia said. "All alive." She smiled grimly.

"She was still in charge of herself when the Scarlet killed her," Aranthur said. "I…She…" He was having trouble talking.

"All the more reason we should have saved her. I had a shot at the Exalted at the top of the stairs…" Dahlia was shaking.

"She chose to save me instead," Kallotronis said. "For which, lady, I thank you."

"Why'd you take that thing alive?" Dahlia spat.

Because I want to be a Lightbringer.

Because it's like Inoques.

Because…

"I couldn't get to my sword," he said.

"What the ten thousand hells do we do with a captured Scarlet?" Dahlia said.

"Show it to the Council of Seventeen," Aranthur said thickly.

The Imoter was a very small man, and his hands were fast and sure, spreading a thick white paste over Aranthur's hands. His head hurt, and he was having trouble with his vision.

The leaves and garbage fluttered, and then went into a mad dance as a massive cyclone seemed to fall on the yard.

蟠龍Pánlóng landed in the cramped space, his long, narrow wings reaching far behind him and beating frantically.

"That," he said, "was the most fun I have had since coming to this damp land."

Iralia smiled and ran a hand down the dragon's long nose. Dahlia bowed.

"I don't think I have had the pleasure of a formal introduction," she said.

"We have been comradesss in combat twicsse," the dragon said. "Isssssn't that a fine sssubstitute for formality?"

Vilna and Chimeg were flattened against a far wall; Chimeg's eyes were round as saucers. Kallotronis was trying his level best to look unimpressed.

"This is why they had no *sihr*," he said.

蟠龍Pánlóng allowed a hint of fire to pass his teeth. "Ah, even with my youth and inexperiencsse," he preened, "I managed to ssstrip away mossst of their power. Thisss, hmm, thisss Exsssalted conssstruct isss the mossst remarkable." The dragon put a foot on the imprisoned Scarlet and it writhed. "I want to ssstudy it."

"I do, too," Aranthur said.

Dahlia picked up Aranthur's sword. "Damn!" she said. "The hilt is hot!" And then she looked at him. "It's talking to me."

"She's talking more and more," Aranthur agreed. "But never enough to have a conversation. I worry…"

"You worry too much…"

"I worry that she's stronger every time I kill something," he said.

"Aphres, Aranthur. You're married to a demon and you have a sword that powers itself on death?"

"And we're the good guys," Aranthur said.

Kallotronis laughed.

"Now for the complicated bit," Aranthur said.

"We're still going to do it?" Dahlia looked around the crowded courtyard.

"It will still take us days… *days,* if Roaris plays to the end. This way is fast."

"And the end justifies the means?" Dahlia asked. "If we show the world what we took tonight, Roaris will fall…"

"Imagine that there's a Servant, or another Exalted. Or, gods save us, a Disciple. Imagine that it's not Roaris calling the shots, and all they want is to cause chaos and ruination. Imagine bombs in the fortresses and terror in the streets…" Aranthur spread his hands.

"I hate the way you think," Iralia said. "Not Roaris?"

Aranthur took a deep breath. "Imagine," he said, "that the Pure have replaced Roaris."

Dahlia nodded. "Why do you think that?"

"You said it—when he took the countess, he made a terrible mistake. The City is buzzing with it. Only someone who doesn't care would have done this to one of his own supporters, and Roaris cares. Roaris is one of… you. A Byzas aristocrat. He'd never have done something so stupid. The Pure are under threat. They're desperate."

Dahlia nodded. "You know I'm in. But this will be messy."

"With 蟠龍Pánlóng to contain their sorcery, with the Axes and the

Nomadi…" Aranthur shook his head. "We should have overwhelming force."

"We could kill two hundred people. Civilians, Yellowjackets, the Watch." Dahlia stood very close to him. "I'm in. But we're talking about starting a fight in a public place."

"I have one card I haven't played. Or rather, Myr Benvenutu does."

Dahlia looked at Aranthur's hands. "Can you hold a sword?"

Aranthur took the old sword. The moment the warm hilt touched his hands he felt better. "Yes," he said.

What do you want? he asked. *I've meant to ask that for weeks.*

I was tasked with the preservation of the Empire, she said. *I have come to have more elaborate goals.*

You are waking up, aren't you?

Yes.

Why now? Aranthur asked.

Because two years ago the one you call the Master released one of my… brothers. I am not the only living sword. I'm merely the only one who is not insane.

Aranthur looked at Iralia, and then at the dragon, but they were all talking.

I will explain. But you have… urgency?

I do.

Then I will help you now, and you will help me later.

"Your hands are healed." Dahlia shook her head. "The sword is as scary as Inoques."

"Later," Aranthur said.

"What if you ended up being very dangerous?" Dahlia asked softly. "We all underestimate you, farm boy."

Aranthur smiled. "Yes. You do."

Two hours later the long, low black ship slipped into a pier on Northside that had just been cleared of fishing boats by a dozen sailors from the Arsenale. They had cleared a spot for the trabaccolo by cutting the fishing boats free of their moorings and pushing them away with poles.

The trabaccolo threw a gangplank across to the pier immediately, and a pale nimbus sprang up over the entire ship and her captain as she engaged her defences.

A dozen Arnauts formed a perimeter on the pier, their *jezzails* and *carabins* primed, searching the darkness. Then Haras, the Masran priest, came down the plank with some hesitation; he made a magelight and then cast it on several distant objects, and a large container like a sedan chair moved off the ship, carried by four sweating Masran sailors. The moment they were on the pier the Arnaut vanguard began to move, headed south and east, the sedan chair following them. Another dozen Arnauts closed in behind, and the whole procession moved at a brisk pace.

Iralia lay behind a wall. Dahlia was inches away, flicking roaches off her legs with the tip of her arming sword; above them, in what would ordinarily be a flea-bitten student lodging, Chimeg was invisible, perfectly still, but the very tip of her long weapon peeped through the window's embrasure.

A light rain began to fall.

"Tell me again why Roaris will attack here?" Dahlia asked.

"He can't know where we'll land the Black Stone," Iralia said. "He can only know where we're taking it. Or that's what Aranthur said."

"Pretty thin," Dahlia said. "Besides, rain *and* bugs? Take me back to defusing *stigals* in Armea."

The small red roaches continued to move out of an opening in the ancient wall.

Dahlia felt the coin in her hand vibrate.

"Places!" she whispered.

All around her, people moved in the darkness.

"If Roaris knows what the Stone is, and who we are, won't *he* bring an overwhelming force?" Dahlia asked.

"Yes," Iralia agreed. "I wondered the same. Dahlia... if I die here..."

"Perish the thought," Dahlia said.

Iralia shook her head. "I have dark thoughts. Tell the Emperor I loved him. I've never told him—I can't. He paid for me... perhaps he likes it that way. But you know him..."

Dahlia rolled over and put a warm hand on Iralia's cheek.

"Tell him yourself. I mean it." She kissed the other woman lightly. "I think this will work, Iralia."

The consort nodded. She raised her hands, and they were shaking.

"I was never like this, until I faced the Servant," she said. "My nerves are shot. And I'm in love." She shook her head. "This is not the way I used to be."

Dahlia smiled grimly. "Everyone's in love." Her bitterness was unhidden. "Now, quiet!"

The procession of Arnauts and the Masran priest came to the end of the neatly laid out streets of the Northside neighbourhoods and started up Temple Hill, into the Cleft that separated the Temple Hill from the Academy.

"This way," Thendara indicated.

The whole party turned south, into the maze of trails that generations of students had made on the hillside. But the main trail ran along the outflow of the reservoir of the Pinnacle, and Thendara led the Arnaut soldiers along the stream, and through the trees.

Aranthur watched them come. The woods at the base of the Cleft were, to him, the most dangerous chokepoint on the route before the obvious ambush point. His experiences in Armea had taught him a few things about laying an ambush, and he and Vilna and a dozen Nomadi had combed the woods since the Morning Star had risen by the Red Moon, indicating the hour after midnight in the heavens above.

They moved through the woods to either side of the Arnauts, all the way to the Steps. And then, as the Arnauts and the sedan chair started up the Steps, the Nomadi began to haul themselves up the steep slopes on either side.

The Arnauts, heads up and looking right and left, trotted up the endless steps; past the Third Landing where couples went to "court" amid the rose gardens, and past the Second Landing, which was a large as a racecourse, where the students studying Practical Agriculture had their field and greenhouse.

Aranthur began to think that he had guessed correctly.

But off to his left, in among the tall trees and tangled underbrush of the slopes of the Academy Hill, someone lost their nerve, hearing the steady approach of the Nomadi working their way up the steep slopes in the darkness.

A wink of fire—a sharp *bang*.

Far too soon.

"Go!" Aranthur shouted.

The Arnauts bounded forward, even up the seven hundred steps.

They were mountaineers and they powered forward even as Haras layered his shields over them. Off to Aranthur's left, *Spasmeno*, which in an Arnaut dialect meant Cut Face, the smallest and most vicious of the Arnauts, shot into the dark and his lean, scarred, mustachioed face was illuminated by the flash of his priming. Beyond him, Stilcho, the best singer among the Arnauts, roared an order.

Another shot—a blossoming of shields in Aranthur's Sight, like the sudden culmination of a field of wildflowers. A dozen bursts, and more.

蟠龍Pánlóng swept in from high above, his long tapering wings beating the air to a froth as he devoured the enemy shields and robbed them of the *Aulos*. Unlike the fight in Southside, this time the dragon ripped through; he interrupted casting, shattered shields, and flew past, leaving chaos in his wake.

The Arnauts made it to the Terrace—the almost sacred space under the golden statue of Tirase, pointing east. There were shots; despite shields and amulets, an Arnaut woman was hit, and fell, her heels kicking futilely at the matched marble paving stones as she bled out.

Aranthur was running up the steps, the palanquin just behind him, moving as fast as the sailors could run.

A single aimed shot, and one of the bearers was down. An Arnaut leapt forward and took the falling handle and lifted, and they were moving again. The sedan chair passed over the gold line in the marble that marked the precinct of the Academy.

蟠龍Pánlóng returned, slower, and attacked the newly emerging shields in the Terrace.

"Now," Aranthur said aloud.

Instantly, a massive dome of shimmering gold rose from the precinct line, an impermeable barrier that went up in a single hummingbird heartbeat. Six of Kallotronis' Arnauts were cut off outside, as were several Nomadi and some Yellowjackets on the hillside.

Viewed from outside, the entire Academy was suddenly covered in a bright golden dome that was visible from every part of the City.

A second, rose-coloured bubble emerged from the far end of Tirase Square and covered the terrace like the dome on a child's terrarium.

There was a moment of shocked silence.

The Master of Arts' voice came across the square, hugely augmented.

"Throw down your weapons and do not attempt an act of magic, and you will be dealt with leniently."

A massive pulse of *puissance* slammed into the pink and gold bubbles. It burst a hole through the pink and burst against the gold wall, but could not penetrate it.

Instantly, the dragon banked, turning sharply over the head of the statue, pivoted on one wing tip, and breathed.

Ice, fire, steam, smoke, and raw power burst across the square. More than a dozen men and women threw down their weapons, or released their shields; some were butchered by their own comrades, and others simply crossed their arms and waited, or lay flat, protecting themselves. But there were fifty more who unleashed whatever they were capable of—at the pink walls; at the Arnauts; at Haras, who stood his ground, his dark green shields emanating smaller shields like the riotous growth of a jungle; at the dragon, passing so low his wing tips almost brushed the brick pavement. Many of their emanations were weak, or under-trained, but the volley they created was staggering.

Aranthur raised his shields. The moment he did, adversaries identified him and a fusillade of sorcery, most of it red balefire, came his way. Once again, 蟠龍Pánlóng came over; this time he flew *through* the shields, which should not have been possible, and their opponents faltered along his line of travel, cut off from the *Aulos.* A dozen sendings failed; a second-year student casting above his talent fell to his knees, vomiting blood.

Aranthur understood in that moment by how much he had underestimated his opponents. Despite the dragon, there were dozens of magi and while the shock of the counter-ambush had shattered their cohesion, they still had the advantage of numbers. Those unaffected by the dragon's rapid passage continued to cast.

Despite that, Aranthur had a moment to assess. Secure behind his massive shields he could survey the battlefield, and for the first time note the difference in magical auras between new casters and the deadly pair at the centre of the enemy.

Trees were blown to splinters, and the splinters made a lethal hail that killed men and women on both sides. A strike of raw *puissance,* mishandled by an under-trained caster, destroyed him. It also evaporated the decorative pool at Tirase's feet in a flash of superheated steam that went through the permeable shields of two Yellowjacket students, killing them instantly, and burnt an Arnaut so badly he could only lie screaming.

Aranthur pushed aside his doubts and ran towards the towering figure of the first caster, the one who'd tried to punch a hole in the Academy shield. The one whose *aura* appeared somehow *hardened.*

As he took his first steps a dark figure targeted him. Aranthur felt the man's attack; he was very close…

Somewhere above them, Chimeg put her front sight on a dark figure with a red *aspis*. The *aspis* was facing the Arnauts.

She pulled the trigger. The magos' head snapped back, and his shield went out, and he fell.

Aranthur ran on. Off to his left across the square, Dahlia and Iralia continued to advance. Iralia rolled forces off the rings on her right hand like a puppeteer controlling puppets, and her blows stung her adversaries through their shields, or dropped them, unconscious, or in one case, dead, blood flowing from her eyes. She walked forward from the shadows at the Academy side of the square, a radiant, untouchable figure, and the ambushers closest to her ran.

By her side, Dahlia maintained an interlocking web of shields over both of them, flashing open a portcullis of light to allow Iralia's next working out, and then slamming it shut. The Yellowjacket magi could not match them, and many of them ran. A young woman, her hair streaked with fire, stood her ground and cast a black balefire that scarred Dahlia's shields. Iralia concentrated on her for a count of three, and her blue-white fire lashed the woman, burning though her shields, touching her arm. The woman flew twice the length of her own body until she struck a wall and lay still, her left arm burnt beyond recognition.

Iralia walked on, seeking her next target.

Dahlia reached into the *Aulos* and unleashed a multilevel complex *occulta* from *displacement.* A dozen lethal forks of lightning, faster than sight, blazed along invisible paths and left a blue-white impression burnt in every onlooker's retinas. One of her targets fell, clutching his leg where the lightning had grounded, screaming in shock at what his leg had become.

Aralia Benvenutu was the first to reach the original attacker. She reached out, punched a hole in his shield, and entered with a *subjugation.* Janos Sittar, close by her side, caught the counter-strike on his flawless hemisphere of crystal and he bent the balefire straight back down its line of attack to strike their adversary, but he missed.

Aranthur was still twenty paces away when the Disciple revealed itself. It was behind Benvenutu, and its shields went up in the *Aulos,* the smooth, metallic-seeming shield that Aranthur remembered from the Battle of Armea. There was a ripple; Sittar's shields and the Disciple's spun off the fractal effects that Aranthur had seen before. There was a massive *displacement* and Sittar was down, apparently dead, and Benvenutu stood over him, her shields rising to cover them both.

The Disciple, now revealed, was a tower of white light that rose from the marble surface of the square to the very edge of the glowing salmon pink ward over the terrace. And it poured attacks: a rain of power down on Aranthur's shields, on Dahlia's; a torrent of power on the Master of Arts, no longer covered by Sittar; a fine beam of coherent scarlet light at the dragon, driving it off; a massive concussion as it unleashed something titanic into the shield above, blowing through the pink ward, so that it collapsed, leaving the gold untouched.

The defeat of her rose pink ward cost Benvenutu and she stumbled. Her shields flickered, and the initial target of her attacks closed with her—blue fire against red, staff to staff, *enhancement* to *enhancement*, *subjugation* to *subjugation*, force on force.

Aranthur watched in horror as the Disciple brushed past the desperate fight, passing on an opportunity to overwhelm the Master of Arts. The combat had become general. The whole square seemed to pulse with light and heat; dozens of *occultae* flowered in every heartbeat, and the wind of magic was drained by fifty hands where the dragon left some *puissance* for use.

A simple kinetic blow from the Disciple staggered Aranthur, failing to penetrate his woven shields but ripping the bricks from under his feet so that he fell, and the Disciple blew past, overwhelming Haras at point-blank range and wounding him instantly. The red fire penetrated the priest's shields in a dozen places and he fell silently, still mouthing his next casting, his body scorched.

The Disciple wanted the artifact in the sedan chair, and it ignored the almost defenceless Masran priest and eviscerated two sailors to clear its line of approach.

It punched a white-hot hand into the sedan chair. And gave a shrill scream.

A little charred black appeared at the edge of its blinding whiteness.

Dahlia, despite being hard-pressed by a dozen magi, gave a nasty smile.

Aranthur rolled to his feet and drew the sword.

Oh yes, she said. *Now we strike home.*

Aranthur stepped over Haras. Behind him, the Master of Arts was bending her adversary's shields, gradually collapsing them and the internal reality they protected.

Aranthur triggered his own *enhancement.*

The Disciple took a shot from an Arnaut and killed the man with a tendril of power, but a dozen more soldiers were firing into the swirling, blinding shields. Vilna fired twice, once with each hand, carefully, coldly into the very centre of the spinning light. He already seemed slow, but his poise was magnificent.

The Disciple flinched, and Aranthur was on it. Close in, its emanations rippled like the very rays of the sun, so fast that Aranthur could never, under ordinary circumstances, have held them, but the shields Inoques had built him rippled, buckled, folded, and stood.

It attacked the stones under his feet, but Aranthur had seen that before; he defended the very stones. He *was* the stones. And they held.

Another pace forward and the Disciple was moving to the side, back towards the Master of Arts. Again and again it punched gouts of *power* at the golden Academy wards. Now it sprayed chaos with reckless abandon, striking Aranthur's shields, Dahlia's, Benvenutu's; another red beam touched 蟠龍Pánlóng. Again, it threw an incredible bolt of force into the Academy ward, and its projection burned like the sun.

It is trying to escape.

Aranthur was at the edge of the thing's shield.

"You really aren't too bright, are you?" he asked, conversationally. "It's a trick. You fell for it, and now you are *done.*"

The Disciple drifted silently towards Benvenutu, stalking her, ignoring Aranthur.

"The Stone isn't even here."

Aranthur cut with the sword. It burst into bright fire, opening a hole in the Disciple's shield.

Benvenutu's contest came to its inevitable conclusion. For a moment, her adversary was there, manifest, his shields shredded; for a single heartbeat, the thing wore the likeness of General Roaris, and then Benvenutu's *occulta* stripped away the last of its defences. Her staff came up, as the fanged thing's head turned. A child, or what had once been a child—black, black eyes, and long fangs like something from a nightmare.

Faster than the strike of a cat's paw, it bit at her, and her staff erupted. The monstrous thing burst, spraying black blood.

The Disciple stopped retreating.

Benvenutu sat suddenly...and the Disciple began to move, sensing an opening.

Iralia's web of force stopped it dead. Iralia and Dahlia stood between the Disciple and Benvenutu, and it threw gouts of force.

The women endured.

Aranthur sprang forward; a long, gliding double lunge to follow his retreating adversary, and he cut its shield from head height to the marble pavement and went *through*.

Mine.

Aranthur feared the sword, at a remove, but the Disciple was there, the same sort of small, pale creature that he'd seen pinned by Harlequin's staff. It was impossible to judge if it was human or something else; its shields cast no light on it, so it was only lit by the calamitous firelight of the battle outside the shields.

"Wrong again," Aranthur said, and the tip of his sword led his *imbrocatto*; his blade passed through it, and it gave a thin, weak scream. The sword immolated it so that it fell off his blade as charred chunks of roasted meat.

Ahhhhhhh.

In the moment of its real death, the Disciple's shields fell, and it was revealed.

Silence fell across the square. The golden statue of Tirase was toppled, the pointing arm broken away after a thousand years, and under it was crushed the broken body of a Nomadi recruit. Dahlia cursed the wreckage of her fine beaver hat, ruined by fire, and tried to beat it out against the cracked marble decoration of the Terrace's paving. Iralia's eyes were as bright as the fires that burned along the edge of the square, and in that moment she didn't look like the Emperor's consort, but like one of the heroes of the War of Wrath, her hair like flame behind her and fire flowing from her hands as she held the power of her next strike within her. Both women looked up at the Great Ward of the Academy. But the Golden Ward held, supported by forty magi singing in the Hidden Temple above them in the Academy, and not a lick of fire had crossed the Precinct boundary.

Aranthur motioned, and Vilna put a trumpet to his lips, and the Wards retreated, and fell away, and a dozen Imoters pushed through the barrier from outside.

Despite the titanic energies that had destroyed the City's most beautiful square, not a building beyond the square was touched; not a civilian had been hurt.

Aranthur was already moving to the Master of Arts. She was lying, glassy-eyed, at the base of Tirase's fallen statue, most of her gown burnt away. Her hand and arm were black to the elbow, and the black was moving up her biceps to her shoulder even as Aranthur watched.

She met his eyes. "Well done," she said. "We felled the Disciple."

Aranthur knelt by her. She raised her good arm.

"I have perhaps a minute," she said. "I wouldn't go any other way. I defeated the Disciple, whatever it was, and I have no regrets. Tell Litha I loved her."

The black moved inexorably up her shoulder, and touched her neck.

"So fucking cold," the Master of Arts said. "Did it have to be cold?" She raised her good hand. "Take my ring, Aranthur. Do not let anyone else touch it. Is Janos alive?"

Aranthur could scarcely take his eyes off her, but he put a hand on the fallen Lightbringer's neck, and there was a pulse.

"He lives! Imoter!" he roared.

The sound of feet pounding across the square.

Screams; the smell of a battlefield; the burnt soap smell of expended *sihr* and *saar*, the sulphur smell of black powder...

He took her hand and kissed it, and she gave a slight smile.

Help her! Aranthur thought it, mouthed it.

The sword was warm in his hand. *Against the Serpent's Bite there is no cure. This is an ancient weapon, and a terrible one.*

She raised her head. "Sophia!" she murmured, and the spreading black moved up her neck.

The young Imoter knelt by Aranthur, who was holding the unpoisoned hand and already crying. Aranthur didn't just cry; he found that suddenly his weeks of tension had become a fountain of tears, and he wept. He had no control over it. He tried to staunch the flow of tears and nothing happened, and if a second Disciple had eventuated next to him, he would have died crying.

After a while he was aware of Iralia's arms around him.

2

Megara

The hardest thing that Aranthur did in the next hour was to go into the palace, climb all the way to the Emperor's private apartments, and face the tall, quiet woman who had helped them tend the Emperor. There were others who could cleanse the square and heal the wounded, like Haras and Kallotronis, and arrest the guilty: Janos Sittar was already in the Chapel; Dahlia had rounded up the unwounded Yellowjackets.

But Aranthur would trust no one else to do this.

He found McBane on duty at the door.

"Myr Litha?" he asked.

"Inside," McBane said. "You're here—I assume we won."

"Yes," Aranthur said.

"High cost?"

Aranthur met his pale eyes. "Isn't there always?"

As he spoke, he happened to see Edvin, the notary. The man blinked and looked down.

The Captain of the Axes nodded. "Always." He stepped out of the way.

Aranthur went into the Emperor's presence and bowed. Litha had turned her head at the first voices, and so had the Emperor. He smiled.

She understood immediately. She blinked once, and then her face crumpled and collapsed like an infant's, and she began to weep.

In a moment, the Emperor was also weeping.

And again, Aranthur felt an imposter. What did he know of grief?

Of the loss of a partner of a life? He embraced Litha and stood with her, and could think of nothing to say that could possibly penetrate her grief.

Finally he said something true.

"I loved her too," he said.

Litha made no answer.

And after another minute, when Iralia came in, she embraced Iralia and left Aranthur to contemplate his own uselessness. But his brain marched on, independent of grief, independent of feeling, as if it had its own agenda, and as soon as Iralia was able to disengage herself, Aranthur took her hand and led her out into the anteroom where Edvin was still copying.

Edvin looked up. "She's dead, then," he said.

Iralia nodded.

Edvin's lips curled. "Damn you both."

Iralia shook her head. "She faced the Servant and triumphed, Edvin. And she fought, fully knowing what we faced." She glanced at Aranthur. "More than I did."

"We need to strike back right now," he said. "I'm sorry, Edvin. But we're not done. We've barely started, and we still need you."

Iralia moved her own grief aside with a disturbing fluidity and nodded sharply.

"Yes." She looked at Aranthur. "How?"

Aranthur took a deep breath. "If the Emperor will authorise this, we need to seize the Towers at Lonika Gate, so they cannot be used against us. We need to disarm the Yellowjackets immediately—I have a list of them. Djinar of the Ultroi—he wasn't in the square, but I saw him the other day. We need to take him. And...we need to strike a number of private houses before anything can be moved."

Iralia looked down. "Is that her ring?" she asked.

"Yes. She ordered me to take it." Aranthur shrugged.

Edvin cursed. "All right. I'll help."

He sat again, and began copying. His tears hit the parchment and he wiped them away impatiently, as if his weakness disgusted him. Aranthur went over to him.

"Leave me be," Edvin snapped.

Iralia nodded and stepped into the Imperial apartments.

Dahlia came into the anteroom, followed by two Nomadi, all three carrying trays of food. She had a pair of Imoters with her, who immediately went to work on her cuts and abrasions.

"I need clothes," she called to some distant servitor. "How's Litha?" she asked Aranthur.

He just looked at her.

She nodded. "Right, stupid question," she admitted. "Sorry, Edvin. Combat."

Iralia came back out and handed Edvin a document; he spat a dark curse, pushed his work aside and began to copy her document.

"Here. This is the appointment, and this is the title," Iralia demanded.

Edvin looked up, his eyes red-rimmed. His eyes met Aranthur's, as if he doubted what he saw, and then he copied the document, ending with a long flourish. He began copying it a second time.

"Sophia," Edvin whispered. "But she would have wanted it."

Iralia nodded sharply. One of the Imoters was going over Aranthur's body; he had a marble chip in his right forearm he hadn't even felt, a sword cut on his left hand, and a burn. Sitting down had been a mistake. He felt…

Horrible.

"Haras?" Aranthur asked through the numbness.

"In for a great deal of pain. He'll recover soon enough." Dahlia, relatively unhurt, was untroubled by the Masr priest's pain.

Iralia picked up the finished documents and went back into the Imperial apartments. She reappeared before Aranthur had his shirt back on, but the anteroom was strewn with bloody garments and weapons.

Iralia handed Dahlia a sheet of parchment with a heavy purple and gold seal appended.

"Myr Tarkas, you are an aristocrat of noble blood?" she asked.

"You know it," Dahlia said.

"You are hereby appointed to fill the seat on the Council of Seventeen vacated by the death of the Dowager Countess of Daka." Iralia nodded coolly. "Aranthur Timos, you are a commoner?"

"Last time I checked," he said.

"You are hereby appointed to fill the seat of Myr Aralia Benvenutu on the Council of Seventeen. Signed by the Emperor. The assignments are temporary, and must be accepted by the Assembly. This Imperial assignment is valid for one year."

Dahlia looked at the florid wording in High Liote and shook her head.

"My mother will never believe it," she said.

"Think of what *my* mother would say," Aranthur put in. "A Souliote on the Seventeen? The sky will fall."

Iralia looked at him, her face serene.

"The sky *is* falling, and we will yet triumph, regardless of who we were before this started," she said.

Dahlia nodded. "Well said." She peered at her document. "Do we need to convene the council?"

"Eventually," Iralia said.

"But for the moment, we can act," Dahlia said.

"Then we need to think like soldiers," Aranthur said. "We won a battle, and after the battle comes the *pursuit.*"

Dahlia gave a small, hard smile. "Yes. Pursuit. Let's hunt them to extinction." She glanced at Aranthur. "Where is the Stone?"

Aranthur looked around; then, very quietly, he said, "The Inn at Fosse."

Dahlia laughed out loud.

Dahlia looked at Iralia. "Are you appointing yourself to the Seventeen?" she asked.

"Yes," Iralia said. "There were seven seats to fill. Tiy Drako gets another."

Dahlia nodded.

Aranthur looked out of the window at the Imperial harbour far below.

"We need an agenda. A set of priorities."

"Exactly," Iralia said.

Dahlia started to shrug into a doublet. "I'm with Aranthur—we need to seize the Towers at the Lonika Gate."

"We need to send a relief expedition to Antioke," he said. "The planners should have everything gathered—"

"Except that we have no ships, and those come from the Arsenale, and we need to order them to release whatever they have."

Both of them looked at Iralia, and she shook her head.

"No idea," she admitted. "We have the trabaccolo..."

"Inoques will not be making courier runs," Aranthur predicted. "She and Haras will want to retrieve the Stone immediately. By the way,

Haras is the alchemist that Myr Benvenutu…" He stumbled over her name, and suddenly choked a little. "That she wanted." He looked at Iralia. "Do you know what she wanted an alchemist for?"

Litha came up behind Iralia. "I do—I know exactly."

"You getting this?" Dahlia asked Edvin.

"Oh, naturally, I'll just sit here and take notes," he said. "I have nothing else to do."

"So we need what, two ships? Seize merchant ships?" Dahlia asked.

"No news from the fleet," Aranthur said. "Something's wrong out there. We can't assume that two unarmed ships would make it through to Antioke. We need armed ships and a convoy…We need our own supply of warded shields. We need steel cables…"

"What?" Dahlia asked. "What's a steel cable?"

Aranthur smiled. "Do great ladies not keep up on the developments of the mere tekne?"

"Spare me your class warfare," Dahlia said.

"Steel wire can be woven into cables. Like a more extensive version of the wire-wrap on your sword hilt."

"Why do we need it?" Dahlia asked.

Aranthur glanced around. "Remember what burnt when we put a sigil in the deck of a ship?"

Her eyes widened. "Steel cable," she said, and wrote it down.

Iralia looked up and met the eye of one of the Nomadi recruits.

"Taras, fetch me the Admiral of the Arsenale," she said. "In the name of the Emperor."

Young Taras saluted and left.

"Suddenly this room is full of servants," Dahlia said.

Iralia nodded. "I ordered the detention of everyone on Aranthur's suspect list, and then I let the rest back in, led by Dakos," she said. "There's no longer anything to hide. Roaris is dealt with, and the Emperor is alive."

Dahlia and Iralia met, eye to eye.

"And you just appointed me to the Council of Seventeen," Dahlia said. "For life, if approved."

"Yes."

"You…are taking the throne yourself?" Dahlia said.

"No," Iralia said, proudly.

Dahlia shook her head. "He's so full of aurax he'll do what he's told, and you are the one closest to him. In effect, you are the Emperor now."

Iralia nodded. "It is an emergency. We need to act."

Dahlia looked at Aranthur. "Do you trust her?"

Aranthur didn't even shrug. "Yes."

Dahlia looked back at Iralia, and managed a smile.

"Well, well," she said. "Isn't this going to be interesting."

And you don't even know about the baby, Aranthur thought. *I suspect that Iralia always intended to be Empress. And yet...*

"What about Masr?" Dahlia asked, changing the subject.

"You take that one," he said. "The planning staff should be ready to rattle off orders for the relief of Antioke. But only you can plan the Masr thing. The Studion...I'm a junior third year student." He tried not to meet Litha's red eyes. "I thought Myr Benvenutu would lead the expedition. I don't really even know the players."

Iralia shrugged.

Dahlia laughed. "No. You are a terrifying member of the secret Seventeen." She shrugged. "But I accept—I want the Masr business. I'll start picking magi. I know most of them and my sister will know everyone."

Iralia said, "I really can't leave the palace. I can oversee the Emperor's recovery, and he *will* recover. I can also plan for the relief of Antioke."

"I'll secure the Towers," Aranthur said. He picked up his puffer, which lay, loaded, on the divan. "I'll need McBane and all the Guards available. The more people I have, the less chance of resistance."

Iralia nodded. "I can make sure of that."

Dahlia frowned. "And then what? After the towers?"

"After the towers," Aranthur said, "I plan to see my wife. And ask her to drop me in Ulama."

"Ulama?" Iralia said. But Dahlia understood immediately.

"We have an impressive haul of prisoners," Iralia said. "What in a thousand hells do we do with them?"

Dahlia glanced at the others. "Edvin, stop writing," she said.

He put his pen down. "Oh, at your service, Myr Tarkas."

"This is all illegal," she said. "So tomorrow, we need a real meeting of the Seventeen. In their Chambers. Have the Emperor summon them. With luck they will approve everything and we can roll."

"We can do all of this from inside the palace," Iralia said.

Dahlia shook her head. "No, Iralia. I mean, yes we can—there are even precedents. But that way lies a new tyranny. No one will trust us after ten days, and Aranthur's burning to say that there's already revolutionary talk. We started this to hide as little as possible, right? The Seventeen are secretive as it is. Let people know that the machinery of government, real government, is working. Set a date for the Assembly. Let's do it right."

Iralia turned and looked at Aranthur, who was already buckling on a cuirass. Dranat McBane stood in the anteroom's doorway, looking impatient.

"I entirely agree with Dahlia," Aranthur said.

Dahlia smiled warmly. "Why, thank you, syr."

Iralia shook her head. "You trust these politicians," she said. "I doubt we can get a quorum by tomorrow. Maybe three days, if you insist."

Dahlia nodded. "I do. I trust the whole of the government. Not just me or just you."

"And if they balk, and refuse to send aid to Antioke?" Iralia asked. "My way, whatever happens, the ships will sail and the magi will go to Masr."

That stopped Dahlia for a moment.

There was a silence.

"Iralia?" the Emperor asked.

He was on his feet, clad in a green silk khaftan lined in wolf fur, and he wasn't smiling.

"My love?" she said, and she took his hands.

"I couldn't help but overhear," he said. "Always, always trust the government. We are servants of empire, not masters." His face was curiously open when he spoke—the face of a grey-haired adolescent, not an aging emperor. "My mother taught me three things about ruling. The first was that I should never give an order unless I knew it was going to be obeyed. The second was that it was always easier to build consensus than to practise tyranny. But her third rule was to remember that we are not the empire. The Empire is all the people—we only act in their name."

He said all these things with the simple conviction of youth, and the speech sounded odd from the mouth of a rumpled man over fifty.

Iralia bent her head, and so did Dahlia. But Aranthur found himself on one knee before the Emperor. Perhaps for the first time, he felt loyalty to the man.

"Yes, majesty," all three of them said in chorus.

Dahlia smiled.

Iralia was crying. But she wiped her eyes with a clever gesture, tossed her head, and took the Emperor's hand.

"Come, my lord," she said.

She led the Emperor back to his apartment.

Dahlia looked at Aranthur. "Damn. I took her point. We're playing for everything." She shrugged. "But he..."

Aranthur looked around for Drako's half-cloak, which he'd adopted. *I'm becoming Tiy Drako*, he thought.

"I think we should...obey the Emperor."

Dahlia nodded. "I'm bred to it. It's different for you, eh?"

Aranthur nodded. He thrust his puffer into his sash and tested the draw of his sword.

"All the more reason to do it right. And remember...we don't know that this is a short war—a single emergency. This could go on for years. I think the Empire and Atti were built for this emergency."

Dahlia nodded. "I agree. And it always worries me when we agree too much."

"You coming?" he asked.

"With a little luck, my sister's friend will hand us the Watch. She's the Tower duty officer starting at sunup."

Aranthur nodded. "Best news yet."

McBane nodded. "I assume I take my orders from you?" he said. "The consort and the Emperor were not too clear."

"You do," Aranthur said.

McBane nodded. "I like to be sure. If the army resists, do we fight?"

They were moving through the palace corridors, and there were almost a hundred guardsmen following them, mostly Axes.

Aranthur shook his head. "No," he said. "On no account will we use violence. If they choose to hold the gate, we'll retreat and explore other options."

McBane bridled. "What the fuck are we here for then?" he asked. "You can get my people killed for nothing."

"Yes," Aranthur said with brutal frankness. "You are a show of force. And of the Imperial will."

McBane nodded curtly. "Huh. Why are you in charge, Centark?"

Aranthur met the older man's stare. "I have no idea."

*

The Lonika Gate was a fortress set into the City wall. The wall itself was a double wall with carefully tended fields of crops between; food that would help feed the population in the event of a siege, although no siege had happened in six hundred years. The two walls were a long bowshot apart, and had enormous towers spaced to cover the angles. Each tower was a small fortress on its own, and most of them couldn't actually be entered directly from the wall walks, making any kind of sudden assault almost impossible, except that some sections were crumbling and whenever the Empire was poor, the maintenance of the walls suffered.

But the Lonika Gate was a different kind of fortress altogether. The inner gate faced on a canal which functioned as a moat; at the far side of the Gate Bridge, which had three spans that could be raised, stood an independent bastion that could *also* be held. Coming from Lonika, the city to the west, an invader faced the Outer Gate, a sixty-foot high octagonal tower a hundred paces across and with walls fifteen feet thick and reinforced with earth. Once inside the gate tower, the attacker would be between the Two Towers, one of which held the administration of the army, and one the command of the Watch. In between was a magnificent courtyard through which tens of thousands of people passed every day, but an invader would be stopped by the inner gate and the canal beyond it, and trapped in the crossfire of two masked batteries of heavy guns firing grapeshot at waist height. Despite their penchant for beauty, neither the designers of the gates, nor the succeeding Councils of Seventeen, in charge of the empire's security, had chosen to hide the power of the towers or the rows of cannon. Any visitor was welcome to examine the iron teeth of the city.

There was a jam of traffic, dozens of carts, hundreds of animals and at least a thousand people, crowded into Lonika Road, and more on the broader avenue under the Great Aqueduct. They grew silent as the Imperial Axes filed past them. Some hurried away, others hid in doorways; but some cheered. It had been a long night and an anxious morning; dozens of voices asked Aranthur and McBane and Dahlia for news.

"The Emperor is alive and the government has survived a difficult time," Aranthur said, over and over.

The sun was rising by the time they reached the great fortresses.

Aranthur arrived at the Canal Bastion with his heart pounding. The city gates were closed; an almost unheard of event. He'd guessed as much from the jam of traffic.

McBane rested his enormous arms on the long-handled puffers in the belt of his heavy maille.

"Your orders?" he asked.

Aranthur wished that he had Vilna, or Kallotronis, and he wondered if life was nothing but an endless process of proving himself to other people. He was tired, and every time he let his thoughts wander he was scared, and the Master of Arts was still dead. Her death had pierced him like a thrust from a sword.

His head ached as if he'd been to a first year party.

"Wait here," Aranthur said.

"With pleasure," Dahlia said.

Aranthur walked up to the Canal Bastion. The gate was closed, but there were people on the wall above the gate; they had muskets, and he could smell their lit match.

"Centark Aranthur Timos, Imperial Nomadi, to see the officer of the day!" he called. He held up his Golden Rose. "I speak in the Emperor's name!"

A woman's voice, shouting. And a man's voice above his head.

"Sent for my officer!" he called. "Our orders were to close the gates and admit no one."

"I'll wait," Aranthur called.

The minutes dragged by. Aranthur was aware that someone above him had a loaded musket pointed at him. The smoke of the match twirled away, but he could smell it, and see the wink of the gunmetal when he looked up.

Then the little postern in the greater gate opened.

The man inside was a regular army dekark who looked as if he hadn't slept.

"Yes, syr?" he asked. "Dekark Dramos. Border Regiment."

"I'm Centark Timos of the—" Aranthur began.

"I know who you are," the officer said. "I have orders to arrest you." He shrugged, as if he knew the order was invalid.

His shrug told Aranthur a great deal.

Aranthur held up his Golden Rose. "I am here in the name of the Emperor." He pointed back behind him. "That's Vanax McBane, the

Emperor's bodyguard, if you doubt me. If I must, I suppose I might summon the Emperor himself, although he's still recovering from the Darkness. Dekark, I need you to open this gate and surrender the keys of this bastion."

The man looked past Aranthur. He was a professional—a full-time soldier; Aranthur guessed that meant he'd be above petty politics. Maybe.

"General Roaris is no longer in command," he said softly.

"I guessed that," the dekark said. "Syr, what happened?"

Aranthur knew he should say he was not at liberty to share. He looked back.

"General Roaris has been dead for some time, as best we can discover. Please, Dekark—these are secret matters." He looked at the man. "He was being...used. By the enemy."

"Thousand hells," the dekark said. "Sorcery?"

"Yes."

Aranthur beckoned to McBane and Dahlia. They came forward with six Imperial Axes. If McBane resented the order, he now gave no sign; he came to a point less than three feet from the gate, stopped, and leant on his huge axe.

"Dekark?" he said.

"Syr!" The dekark snapped a salute he had not given Aranthur. "Damn. I have orders not to open the gate for anyone."

Aranthur nodded. "In my eyes, orders from the Emperor must override any others."

The man looked harrowed. "I'm not even supposed to talk to anyone. Orders was to shoot anyone who approached the gate."

"Orders about which you had your doubts," Dahlia snapped. "Good for you, syr. Now open the gate."

The man hesitated, and Aranthur knew that Dahlia's tone had not helped.

Gently, Aranthur held up the Golden Rose.

"You know what this means," he said.

"I know," the man said with weary resignation. "All the gods be damned. I hate this." He looked around. "I have some very...aristocratic...militia under my command," he said very quietly. "I beg you, go easy. And no reprisals."

Aranthur looked at Dahlia. "That's acceptable," he said.

The dekark nodded. "Right."

He stepped back, and before he could change his mind, McBane went through the postern behind him. Aranthur went next, and then Dahlia.

"Open the gates," the dekark shouted.

Aranthur could hear shuffling; wooden floors in a stone tower echoed like drumheads.

There was a shot.

"No!" someone screamed.

Aranthur ran for the inner stairs. He wasn't sure why he was running, but he could feel the tension, and smell the tang of powder in the air.

"No reprisals!" shouted the dekark. "Everyone put up! Put up!"

Aranthur had the sense to raise his heavy red *proaspismos* as he went up the steps. Halfway to the top, someone opened the door and shot at him. The musket ball penetrated the *occulta*, and struck his shoulder, but was robbed of much of its force. Nonetheless, it hurt like the kick of a mule, and he grunted, almost lost his footing, and kept going.

The soldier at the top slammed the door shut.

Aranthur blew it open, unmaking the door in a single word, a summoned glyph. His bindings and unbindings came more easily these days, after Benvenutu had made him practise every day...

All the splinters flew inwards, killing the soldier through her maille armour.

"It was her!" shouted another man.

Aranthur had summoned fire, and his hands itched with the *puissance.* There was a dead man on the floor, the back of his head a messy red crater, and the woman he'd just killed, and two more soldiers with their hands in the air.

"She shot you!" shouted one.

"We'll open the fucking gate," said the other. "Kerkos, syr! Don't fry me!"

Aranthur felt...like a man who'd just killed again. He wanted to vomit; his working against the door had flayed most of the flesh from her face and hands.

"Gods," he spat.

Dahlia came through the ruined door frame.

"Just get the gate open," she said, her chest heaving from the run up the steps. "Nice trick with the door, Timos." She bent over. "Do you attack everything that resists you?"

"Yes," he admitted.

"Why do I ever follow you?" she asked. "And to think that this is just the outwork. Ready to do it all again?"

They opened the outer gate, and the Axes took the bastion. The regular army soldiers were rounded up; the militia were paraded and disarmed. The woman who'd tried to hold the gate was from a House militia.

The bridge was open and Aranthur found that a sign for hope, and he led the way, opening the north gate of the bastion and then walking, alone, across the heavy planks of the bridge.

"Open, in the name of the Emperor!" he called.

All was silent for a dozen beats of his heart, and then…

The drawbridge began to move. Aranthur had to struggle back over, ignominiously slipping down one side and then leaping to the stone buttress of the bridge to avoid being dumped into the canal.

McBane nodded. "They didn't shoot," he said. "Tells you something."

Aranthur glanced at Dahlia, who was not laughing.

"Damn," she said. "What do they hope to gain?"

"Time," Aranthur said. "Time in Masr. Time in Antioke. Time everywhere."

"I'm worried about my sister's friend," Dahlia said. "We should have taken this gate."

"Remember how we left?" Aranthur said. "What, five days ago?"

Dahlia shook her head. "It'll never work."

"Let's pay a gondolier and find out."

An hour later, it was not a gondola but a grain barge that floated up to the barracks kitchens. There was no challenge and no shots were fired, and Aranthur leapt ashore with a rope, secured the heavy barge to a bollard, and then stepped into the kitchens through one of the great floor-to-ceiling windows.

A dozen military cooks stood gaping; closest to Aranthur, a big Arnaut man with an apron over the uniform khaftan turned on him with an air of authority.

"No deliveries allowed. Ain't you heard…?"

His words trickled away as McBane came in through the dockside doors, and then another dozen Axes.

"Fuck me," the soldier said.

McBane's mouth twitched under his moustache.

"Corridor secure," said an Axe. He had a *carabin* in his hands and not an axe at all.

Aranthur felt like an imposter, but he nodded to the cooks.

"We are here in the Emperor's name," he said. "Put your tools down and you will not be harmed."

"Posedaos' throbbing spear!" the cook spat.

But he put his cleaver down on his cutting board and sat on the slate floor with his hands behind his head.

Aranthur moved past him. He stepped into the corridor, expecting a shot, but the corridor was silent, and there were already two Axes at the far end, the doors that Aranthur had last passed in the *guise* of General Roaris. He went through, into the lower barracks hall, McBane at his shoulder and six Axes behind him, and the off-duty soldiers snapped to attention. Most of them wore only shirts and braes, regardless of gender; they were cleaning their armour.

"Who the hells…?" someone shouted and then was silent.

Aranthur's thoughts raced. Obviously these soldiers were not expecting an attack. It told him some of what was going on, but it also made no sense—as if someone was trying to hold the Lonika Gate without putting the soldiers on any kind of alert.

What the hells, indeed?

"I'm missing something," he said aloud.

He'd done dozens of drill days in this fortress: he'd first signed on to the Select Militia here; he'd met Centark Equus; put his horse in the stables that took up most of the space between the walls, along with the musketry range where he'd fired…

Fired…

"Kerkos!" He whirled on McBane. "Powder magazine."

"Gods!" McBane flushed and then paled.

Aranthur ran for the stairs. He knew where the magazine was.

McBane pounded along behind him, with the Axes.

They burst into the Inner Gate entry hall. A dozen soldiers stared.

"Stand where you are!" roared McBane. "Stand in the name of the Emperor!"

The soldiers hesitated; the Axes didn't. Their weapons were aimed with intent. The soldiers looked at each other.

"Muskets on the floor. Extinguish your match," McBane was ordering.

Aranthur was out of the gate and into the great courtyard.

There was a company of militia doing drill. Across the courtyard, in front of the Watch barracks, a full company of the Watch stood, round shields on their shoulders, partisans in hand, watching the militia drill.

Aranthur ran for the magnificent entrance to the military tower. He passed the row of heavy guns, the northern battery; four regular soldiers sat under the carriage of a massive gun, playing dice. But they had a linstock with a lit match, and the tools of the artillerist's trade were all around them.

It was a battery of great guns, and Aranthur's limited military knowledge suggested it had to be connected to the powder magazine, however distantly. Big guns ate powder. He knew that.

He leapt over the stone wall at a run, and landed competently inside the battery; his knee twinged where he'd cut it on glass, what seemed like a lifetime before. The four artillerists all looked up.

Aranthur could now see, from inside the battery, that there was indeed a low doorway at the far end of the battery, going into the army tower. He flashed his Golden Rose.

"Emperor's business," he said.

The four artillerists hesitated like the soldiers at the Inner Gate, and Aranthur was on them.

"Centark Timos, Imperial Nomadi!" he spat. "Gambling, on duty? Lit match near a powder bag? All on report."

They stood as if carved from stone.

He continued past them. "Come with me," he said. "You, Dekark. With me. The rest of you, look sharp."

The dekark was looking at the Golden Rose as if hypnotised.

"Syr…" he began, but Aranthur was already heading for the dark portal at the far end of the battery.

"Take me to the powder magazine," Aranthur said.

"Yes, syr," the artillerist said. "What's going on, syr?"

Aranthur did not feel that it was the time to tell the truth, as it had been with the dekark at the gate.

"Special inspection," he said.

His militia unit had been threatened with "special inspections" so he assumed they were real.

"Gods," the artillerist said. "Syr, nothing ever happens here."

"Magazine!" Aranthur snapped in his most peremptory tone.

"This way," the soldier said.

They were under the main tower; lightless spaces with only a handful of people. They passed a woman at a table lit by four candles, writing. She didn't look up. Then along a gradually sloping tunnel. A large sign proclaimed, in Liote and Arnaut and Byzas, that no fire nor lit candle could pass this point.

"Oh, gods," the soldier gagged.

The door at the far end was open, and there were two dead men and a dead woman outside.

Aranthur didn't spare them a glance.

He stepped over the woman's body and slammed his good shoulder into the massive door. It was already ajar, and it swung open.

"Oh, gods," the artillerist repeated behind him.

Aranthur had been to the magazine during drills. The long tunnel protected it from sparks, and outside the magazine itself was an anteroom where paper cartridges were prepared and filled, and where young dekarks waited for the ammunition their troops would fire off in exercises.

In one heartbeat, Aranthur realised that the anteroom had another function. It held a magical barrier, a ward. He'd never looked for it before, but now he understood it all—including why he was still alive.

The anteroom had heavy double doors into the magazine itself. They were open. An artillerist lay between the doors, his face a death mask of surprise. And beyond him, a portcullis gate. In normal times, this kept unauthorised people out of the confines of the magazine. Powder could be handed through the openings or moved on a dumb waiter that moved on sparkless felt ropes.

Today, it was locked. Beyond it was the narrow corridor that led to the main powder store, with its six or eight tons of military grade black powder.

And burning along the corridor, a long fuse of match-cord.

Aranthur grabbed the portcullis. It rattled, but it did not move.

"Locked," he grunted.

He tried to throw a simple *volteia* through the portcullis.

But of course, there was the ward.

"Darkness falling!" he snarled. So damned close.

The fuse burned.

Aranthur ran back to the outer door and closed it. The artillerist was kneeling by the corpse of a woman who had been his comrade, and perhaps more. His face had the same collapsed look that Litha's face had worn.

"I need water," Aranthur said.

The man was crying. "Who would fucking do this?" he moaned.

Aranthur shook him. "I need water. A large quantity. Towels, rags—a bow. Arrows."

He shook his head. There was no time.

He ran back to the portcullis. He could see the rising smoke from the match-cord; in the near darkness, he thought he could see the ember. It was perhaps a hand's breadth from going under the door at the far end.

He had one puffer.

He drew, aimed.

Blinked, and aimed again.

Squeezed the trigger.

The snaphaunce misfired. The pan fired—a dangerous flare of fire—but the weapon didn't kick.

A terrible moment—fumbling with a priming horn in his sash. His hands were trembling. He re-primed, cocked, slid the frizzen's hammer back into place.

Aimed.

Fired.

The puffer slammed back into his hand; the ball ricocheted off the stone floor, the ceiling, the walls.

The tiny ember burned on, almost invisible in the powder smoke.

"Fuck," Aranthur said.

Perhaps two fingers' width to go to the doorway.

Aranthur reached into the *Aulos* and summoned *puissance*. He blinked, imagining the first *volteia* he'd ever learned, standing by a well in his village with his mother patiently instructing him on the use of the family *kuria* crystal. The moment when the local Byzas nobleman had noticed him—the moment his life had changed.

Because almost everyone, with a *kuria* crystal, could make clean water.

But Aranthur had *summoned* water and cleaned it. He'd brought it from the well, without any instruction; enough to drench his mother and the two impatient sheepdogs who'd followed them.

A much older and better trained Aranthur *summoned* water from beneath the fortress—from the canal outside the wall, really only a few dozen paces away. And it came. He summoned it to his side of the ward.

And the tunnel sloped down.

He drenched the floor, pouring water and power together into the tunnel, and the water ran downhill past the ward. The ward might stop an *occulta*, but the emanation of magic was real water, and it flowed—first at the centre of the corridor, and then, at his command, along the same edge where the ember burned.

The water ran downhill; first in a mighty flow, and then in rills.

Aranthur poured more power into the spell, and more water came, and the water ran.

It was a long corridor; the other side of the portcullis was perhaps fifteen paces. The slope down wasn't steep enough to accelerate the water…

The ember vanished under the door.

Aranthur waited to die. But he poured the water from his hands the way he wept for Aralia Benvenutu. He thought of her, and he closed his eyes, and poured the water into the tunnel.

"Who the hell is that?" shouted a woman's voice. "Take him!"

Aranthur tossed a wall of force across the door to the magazine's anteroom.

"Halt! Stop! Whoever you are! Damn my eyes, get me a musket."

Aranthur didn't turn around. "There's a fuse," he said. "Laid to the magazine."

"What the hells?" shouted the woman. "Musket!"

"He didn't kill these people," said the broken artillerist. "We—"

"Who the hell is he?" asked the woman.

Aranthur was staring at the doorway, still waiting to die, still pouring water. By now, he was almost sure that he could see the reflection of light from the far end of the corridor—a puddle. Success, or stalemate; he couldn't tell either way.

It took an effort of will, but he let the *volteia* go. He turned, trying to sound calm, but his voice broke with the effort.

"There's a fuse that may still be alight. I need you to get the portcullis open."

The woman was an officer, he could see that now. She had a *gorget* on; she was probably the officer of the day.

"Centark?" he asked.

"Yes. Who the fuck are you?"

"Centark Timos, Imperial Nomadi…"

"Aphres, how the hells did you get in here?" she spat.

"Myr, I didn't do this, and if we fuck up, we all die. Please listen to me. There's a fuse laid to the powder magazine."

She hesitated.

The artillerist said, bravely, "I was with him when we came in. He didn't kill these people, ma'am. And that means someone else did."

The officer nodded, her dark face barely visible in the gloom.

"Very well."

Aranthur opened the outer door. "Don't make a breeze," he begged.

The centark moved carefully. She was readying her keys; she pulled out a complex metal key.

"I'm supposed to arrest you, Timos," she growled.

"The world has changed since that order was given."

They went down the corridor together, their boots splashing in the shallow water.

"The right-hand door," Aranthur said.

"It ought to be open," she spat. "All our ready powder. Who the hells would close…?"

She put the key to the lock.

"Plugged," she said. "Aphres. Someone broke the key off in the lock."

Aranthur raised one hand, summoned power, and cast. He rewrote it on the fly, an unthinkable level of skill two months before; he removed the fire from his working and inserted ice.

The door cracked open, and the lock popped open.

Quick as thought, Aranthur summoned water and dumped it through the door even as the centark opened it.

The match-cord ran, unburnt, across the room to a pile of powder and wood shavings, already turned to black sludge by Aranthur's water.

"Who the fuck did this?" the centark spat.

Aranthur took a deep breath. "Thank the gods, it was someone with no talent for sorcery whatsoever. Or someone who didn't think it through."

"Why?" she asked.

He shook his head. "Whoever it was lit the match at the outer door. A student would have lit it by power at the ward." He breathed. "And we'd all be dead," he added.

"And so you saved us by dumping water on my gods-damned magazine." She shook her head. "I suppose I shouldn't arrest you, then."

"You are the officer of the day?" he asked.

"I am."

"In that case, I must ask you to surrender the Tower to me. In the name of the Emperor."

"Fucking perfect," she said.

3

Megara and Ulama, capital city of Atti

Back at the palace, Aranthur went to the infirmary to check on his wounded, and was told that the drake had been hit—the first he knew of it. But he didn't go directly to the drake's enclosure; first he visited Nata, who was asleep after the surgery to replace his hand. Aranthur took the time to admire the metal and leather prosthetic on the pillow, and the near perfect join of the arm to the wrist. He looked in on the wounded Arnauts, and then walked along the gardens at the edge of the barracks until he found a team of Imoters gathered at the enclosure that housed the drake.

蟠龍Pánlóng had been hit repeatedly; some wounds in long slashes, or repeated punctures where his shields had burnt through. Right now he looked more like a piece of equipment being repaired than a being; there was a ladder with an Imoter working by magelight, and two more lay under the drake's belly where it was supported by wool sacks, one with physical bandages, one with a pale fire burning from his fingertips.

"He's asleep," a lead Imoter said. "Don't wake him."

Aranthur went back to the palace to find food. It was almost all he thought about these days.

Aranthur sat at the long, narrow table in the cabin of the trabaccolo, Inoques across from him. He was on his third cup of wine, served in broad-bottomed wooden cups that didn't tip in rough seas. He'd eaten his way through a small feast and he was now on to honeyed almonds.

"First food I've had," he muttered with his mouth full.

"And now we have to go all the way back to your backwater inn to retrieve our Stone," she said.

"Yes," he said. "It had to be safe."

She smiled. "It was safe at sea on my ship. But I understand that Haras does not trust me."

"No," Aranthur agreed.

She smiled, and the tattoos on her face seemed to glow. "And so, in the end, they surrendered the gate?"

"Dahlia's sister had a friend in the Watch. She surrendered the south tower…Well, she took over the Watch in the Emperor's name."

"Dahlia," Inoques said, as if tasting the name.

Aranthur knew a moment's unease.

"Dahlia, Dahlia, always Dahlia. Tell me, *husband.* Do you love her still?" Inoques sounded amused.

Aranthur's stomach flipped. He'd thought that he was too tired to react to anything, but…

Inoques leant across the table. "I am no longer a god," she said. "But I am still a jealous spouse, my dear, and you swore an oath. I would not like to tell you what retribution I might exact." She licked her lips.

"I…" Aranthur began.

She raised a hand. "I make no accusation. But I would prefer to see you two…" She shrugged. "Separate. Tell me why we're crossing the strait. It is more difficult than it looks."

It had taken Aranthur less than a week to forget how fast Inoques went through topics and challenges.

"Have you heard us mention Kurvenos?" he asked.

"That bastard," Inoques said. "I know him."

"How?"

Inoques' brown eyes were bright as lanterns in the gloomy cabin.

"I was sent to do a thing for him."

Aranthur leant forward. "What *thing*?"

She rose, went to the chest stowed at the stern of the cabin, and poured more wine for them both. This time she did not sit across from him, but next to him.

"You are so naive," she said. "So passionate. You think this…incident in Masr, this Master, these Pure—you think these are great events, moments of extreme peril? And perhaps they are." She rested her forearm against his on the table. "But there is always something. Both mortals and immortals play for power—the power to dominate, to effect change. The power to dream, or to deny others their dreams. But these power games define…everything."

Aranthur thought of his family, in the Souliote Hills, which seemed very far away.

"I don't think everyone thinks that way," he said.

His demon lover smiled, her eyes only half-open. "I think they do. They cloak their desire to dominate others in the rhetoric of fashion, whether that be religion, faction, nation…" She shrugged. "I know Kurvenos the meddler. Always with a finger in the soup—always, afterwards, wringing his hands over the corpses."

Aranthur nodded. Sometimes, when friends dislike each other, it is best not to comment.

"I have to find him. There is a rumour that he is dead."

Inoques raised an eyebrow. "Ah. I do not wish him dead. I think that he is a hypocrite, but not an enemy. First he calls me an abomination, then he sends me on a mission." She smiled. "Unlike some of our Masran priests, who call me an abomination and then lust after me." She laughed mirthlessly. "If I am ever free," she mused.

"What mission?" Aranthur asked.

She opened her mouth and blinked. Her face became still and then she licked her lips.

"I am, quite literally, bound to secrecy. So this is your new fixation? You will now go to Atti, and run around until you find the Meddler?"

"Fixation?" he asked, trying to keep his voice mild.

"Each task they give you, you run to perform, like a good dog."

"I chose this task," he said.

She smiled. "Of course."

He blinked, anger flooding him. "Inoques, you are old, and wise, and possessed of a deep pool of cynicism—"

"As is usual in slaves," she said calmly.

"But you have no idea what—"

"What is at stake? Spare me."

"What would you have me do?" Aranthur asked.

She spread her hands. "Sometimes you make me feel old—even foolish—with your total assurance." She looked at him fiercely. "I am sick of slavery. I want to be free, and by the gods, your foolish, infantile gods, I *will* be free, and there will be a reckoning."

"This is not me you are angry at."

Inoques shrugged. "No. At Haras. He *added* to my binding," she said, showing him a new whorl of tattooed glyphs on her arms, almost to the top of her left bicep.

Aranthur took a breath, and released it, as Myr Benvenutu had taught him; Sparthos too, come to that.

You threatened to escape, and he took precautions, came to his mind with a coldness that frightened him. *What am I becoming?*

Aranthur looked at his wife, and at the tension in her arms, the straightness of her shoulders, the fire that lurked in her eyes.

"You plan to escape." He immediately wished he had not spoken.

"Yes." She leant over. "Yes. Will you help me?"

Aranthur leant back. Harlequin's words came to him with almost perfect clarity, and now he understood them.

If you elect to spend the rest of your life teetering on the edge of the abyss, then you are a Lightbringer. Some jump. Some retreat. Only a few stay.

"I will," he said. "Under certain conditions."

She smiled. "Aha. Not so naïve then."

She kissed him. Actually, the very tip of her tongue licked his lips.

Instantly, he was afire for her, but something inside his head remained unchanged—assessing. Calculating. It was as if some remote, terrible judge sat above him, watching her poise, her passion, her sudden eroticism as she straddled him on the cabin bench, her mouth over his.

He regretted the distant judge.

A little later, as he pulled his shirt over his head, he said, "You have taught me a great deal."

She sat back on her haunches; naked, and indifferent to her own nudity.

"Too much, I sometimes wonder," she said.

And later still, he leant on one elbow.

"Why is the voyage to Atti difficult? Even little rowing boats cross the strait."

"I think your brain can be too much like something made of cogs and gears," she said lazily. "When I use this body like this, I do not want to think. Let all the busy plotting go."

Whereas I never seem to let go any more, he thought.

She rolled on her side. "When the rift opened, more than magikal winds were released. The currents have changed. I asked about it on the docks yesterday while you were arresting people." She shrugged. "I have to sail all the way to Tolos on this wind to have the... angle... to beat back down against the new current. It might actually have been easier in a smaller boat. Anyway, I'll have you ashore by morning."

"Do you think the currents have changed everywhere?"

His hands seemed to have their own intent; they were wandering her body, and she smiled.

"*Everywhere*," she said, meaninglessly, and they floated away again. And later, she said, "Everywhere is such a beautiful word."

But that part of Aranthur's mind that would not let go wondered about the fleet, and about Ansu, sailing for Zhou.

And much later, he asked into the darkness, "Are the storms worse?" and she rolled over so fast that he thought she might strike him.

"Have you been waiting all this time to ask me that?"

He decided to use one of her weapons against her, and he put a hand on her belly.

"What will our child be like?" he asked.

"She will be very, very strong," Inoques said. "And you make me worry that she will never sleep, and will never stop asking questions." After a silence, she said, "Yes. The weather is growing worse. I have... ways of feeling these things. My kind have always loved your rough weather. Perhaps that is why I love the sea. But this is... worse."

Aranthur nodded in the darkness.

The morning dawned, a magnificent red sunrise over the Atti highlands far to the east, where white, snow-capped mountains rose: shadowy, almost purple in the haze.

Closer in were the red-tile roofs of Ulama.

"It's good to see you sleep," Inoques said.

She was dressed differently from her wont, in billowing trousers of white cotton and fine leather slippers, and a magnificently embroidered vest over a white linen shirt with sleeves that each seemed to have ten yards of cloth; on her head she wore a small red felt cap with a jaunty plume, a fine red gold brooch, and a veil that hid her face. She had a good knife in her belt; an Attian yataghan.

"You have never been to Atti, I think," she said.

"Never," he admitted.

"I will help you, in part because you ask nothing of me but a ride across the strait." She laughed. "Get dressed."

He dressed in Arnaut clothes, not unlike her own: a good brown jacket of fine wool over a *fustinella*, and his sword in its new scabbard with his Masran-made buckler hung over the hilt, and new boots he'd bought in Megara across the way. Beautiful boots that buckled halfway up the leg.

Inoques admired him. "You really are beautiful," she said. "Where did you acquire the ring?"

Aranthur had forgotten Benvenutu's ring.

"A friend," he said.

"What kind of friend?"

He raised an eyebrow. "The kind who is dead."

She was watching the waterfront. There was no room at any of the piers, and she'd had to anchor out at a buoy and was waiting for a paid boat to fetch them.

"I'm sorry," she said. After a pause, "I ask because it is redolent with *power*. Very few people have friends who give away such things, and it will mark you to anyone who can see it." She shrugged. "Which, in truth, is not so many people."

"When did you become so jealous?" he asked.

She smiled. "When I realised that you meant more to me than a marriage of convenience, obviously," she said. "Our pilot said there was another attempt on the Sultan Bey. We have to go to the harbour master to sign some papers and perhaps get some news."

Their water taxi came and they were rowed ashore; dropped at the stone steps that led up to the harbour master's office, which had once been a magnificent, tiled stone building and was now more than a little decrepit, with sagging wooden shutters almost devoid of the handsome blue paint that had once graced them.

They had to wait in a long line of fisherfolk, who were signing a heavy book.

"A new regulation," Inoques said. "They are attempting to track all the boats entering and leaving the harbour. The small folk, who row for their livings, are upset by the waste of time and money."

Aranthur thought of Roaris, or whoever had replaced him, trying to control the flow of gossip across the strait.

"I can understand some of their Armean," he said. "And I understand everything I read."

Inoques nodded. "Well, they write in Safiri and most of them speak Armean, but it's not the Armean I know—too fast, too full of Liote and Byzas."

Indeed, the same might have been said of the people. After an hour in the harbour master's office, Aranthur could see that the aphorism *Between Ulama and Megara there is only wine* was very true. The Attians looked the same as Megarans: the same faces, the same smiles; most of the fisherfolk would have been called Byzas across the strait, and most of them had grey eyes and rich brown skin. But there was the same riot of difference, too; there were olive complexions and there was blond hair and there, jet-black hair over blue-black skin, just like Megara.

Eventually they made their way to the front of the line, where the harbour master's officer, a woman wearing a mailled shirt and with her peaked helmet on the table by the book, asked them some questions while looking at the scroll Inoques handed over.

"Masr?" the woman asked. "How long?"

"Three weeks," Inoques said.

"Hmm," the officer said. "You have a cargo?"

Inoques smiled. "Tawed hides," she said. "Not a full cargo, but enough to make a little. I'm hoping to buy saffron."

"Go with the grace of Posedaos." The woman made the sign of the stallion in the air and put a wax seal on Inoques' papers. "You were in Masr when…the Dark Forge appeared?" she asked, as if it was a question of no import.

Inoques had a rare moment of indecision.

"Yes," Aranthur said.

"Someone from the Sultan may wish to see you," the officer said. "Would you return here after noon?"

People behind them in the line were grumbling; a short woman with oars on her shoulder was already quite loud about her wasted time.

"Yes," Aranthur said.

Inoques gave him a look to suggest she didn't agree, and they went out.

"You can't be serious," she said as she passed under the magnificent tiled arch of the entrance.

He shrugged. “I need to contact someone in their government at some point,” he said. “Why not make it simple?”

“If this were Megara you’d be talking to the Watch, and three days ago it was controlled by Roaris. You have no idea who is in government.” She smiled, and her teeth showed like those of a dangerous animal. “Your governments come and go so quickly.”

“Let’s get a cup of wine,” Aranthur suggested.

“*Quaveh*, my dear. Wine is...not forbidden, but not encouraged.”

Inoques took his arm and they walked down the dock together, and then turned onto the *fondemento* that ran along the waterfront in a graceful curve. The docks under their feet were enormous, built of white oak and cypress, wider than a Megaran street and well off the water. The curve, Aranthur thought as they walked, was probably the line of the beach, and the sand of the beach must be under the old pilings...

“Is there sand down there?” he asked.

“Sand, and people,” Inoques said. “The poorest waterfront dwellers live under the docks.”

Aranthur paused, as if he could look down between the perfectly fitted, massive beams.

“How do they get down there?”

“There are stairs, if you know where to look. Look, there’s a *quaveh* seller with tables.”

“When were you last here?” he asked her.

She smiled, blinked. Looked at him.

“Not so long ago,” she said. “Perhaps some years.”

They settled into cushions at low tables. A boy brought them a pipe, and stock; Aranthur paid him in Byzas soldi, and the boy brought change in Attian silver sequins. An older man brought a brass tray laden with little dishes in a brilliant blue glazed ceramic.

Inoques took her first cup greedily, and Aranthur sipped his.

“Delicious,” she said. “*Quaveh* is just better here.”

Aranthur discovered that he was surprisingly patriotic.

“It’s different,” he said.

“Better, stronger, fresher beans,” she said. “What do we do now?”

“I thought of asking for an audience with the Kaptan Pasha,” Aranthur said. “I was with him in Armea.”

She nodded. “I see the sense in that.”

"First I'd like to visit the souk," Aranthur said, using the Armean word. "The bazaar. The covered bazaar."

Inoques got up, leaving some silver sequins behind.

"Not what I expected you to say. What are we doing there?"

Aranthur put a hand in the small of her back and feigned a broad grin.

"We're finding out if we're being followed," he said. "I think we are. My... source... suggested that Kurvenos was betrayed coming off his boat."

"Ah," Inoques said. "Any other little details you may have neglected to share?"

Twenty minutes later, Aranthur had a fine steel-hilted yataghan in his sash; he'd bought the most magnificent turban cloth he'd ever been able to afford, and he was positive they were being followed.

He grew more concerned as he fingered the finest maille he'd ever seen—rings so small and light that he wasn't sure he believed that they would stop a blow. But his purse was full of money, and he needed armour; so he bought the maille and a pair of damascened gauntlets with flexible wrists and beautifully articulated fingers. He watched the street while two boys and a girl stitched gloves carefully fitted to his hands into the cuffs of his new purchase while the master smith reseated the finger lames to perfectly match his long fingers.

It was at the watchmaker's that he was sure. Inoques loved mechanical gadgets, and the watchmaker had a stall of marvels: mechanical nightingales; tiny jewelled turtles who crawled along with visible patience; a very small, very fat bear who sang. The watchmaker was a wide woman with tiny, mouse-like hands and enormous, round glasses and half a dozen apprentices who all appeared to be her in miniature, and her watches, in tortoiseshell and gold, were like fabulous technological eggs that told time.

Aranthur was distracted by the military potential of knowing the exact time when he saw a beggar-woman he had seen outside the harbour master's office. She was his confirmation; he already had a dozen suspects, but a beggar-woman with an unlikely gold stud in her nose was an absolute identification, and her guilty start as his eyes passed over her was further evidence.

"We're under close surveillance," he said. "As many as twenty people."

Inoques leant against him. "Then why don't I sell my hides and buy some saffron? If I get enough for my hides, I'm buying the bear." She smiled. Softly she said, "You are good value in a husband. Any day with you is an adventure."

Another woman might have been mocking him; Inoques was perfectly serious. She was *enjoying herself.*

Aranthur smiled. Inoques could be patronising and she could be ambiguous, but her passion for the minutiae of human life could be intoxicating, and he enjoyed watching her. And for the first time in Aranthur's life, he had money, in quantities that seemed ridiculous to him. An account at a Byzas bank.

"If you buy the bear, I get a watch," he said.

Inoques clapped her hands together. "Only if I get to open it," she said. "By Sun and Moon, I love them. This *craft* is something you *people* have done that is new. And the watch? A machine that measures time instead of killing people?" She spread her hands in mock amusement. "Perhaps there is hope for you yet."

They walked along the waterfront until they came to a shed that seemed to sell rugs, but Inoques asked a few questions and was shown to a man in a fine khaftan and boots—like a nomad, not a merchant. He was the first Attian Aranthur had seen with a sword.

He called for tea and sat with Inoques. The rest of the men and women under the awning seemed to assume that Aranthur was her muscle; they were polite, but no one talked with him. He looked at the rugs with their marvellous weaving and intricate patterns.

He grew bored, and wandered a little, exploring the awnings on either side, never moving so far that he could not hear the musical drone of Inoques' voice. Eventually, she said "No," very firmly, and rose, clapping her hands, and Aranthur stepped back under the awning.

"Mistress?" he asked.

She nodded coolly. "With me," she said, and walked out with her usual dancer's step.

"Not enough?" Aranthur asked.

She flashed him a smile. "I'm fairly certain he'll be my buyer, but not in one cup of tea."

"You enjoy this?"

"Very much. Being a slave to Masran priests is both dull and dangerous. Being a merchant is my cover, and is much, much more fun." She glanced at a stall full of Zhouian silk. "Are we still being followed?"

"I assume so," Aranthur said. "I can't tell, and I don't want to be too obvious."

He followed her into another awning—this one inside a fine sandstone caravanserai, Aranthur's first.

Inoques pointed up at the apex of the magnificent arched door.

"In the old days, they were built for protection," she said.

Inside the huge door was a succession of arched bays filling all four sides; each bay had its own dome, and held a shop, a little like the arcaded malls of Lonika, but built of stone.

"Caravans used to open here for business, with their animals safe in the centre," she said. "The merchants could guard the one entrance easily. This one is very old."

Aranthur followed her around the courtyard. She visited two of the bays; each one was a shop or stall, and the whole building seemed to be dedicated to leather workers, which interested him.

But he never stopped looking at the lone entrance, and his fears were confirmed; first the beggar woman with the gold stud, and then a longshoreman, surprisingly out of place, and wearing a bright blue turban that was just a little too noticeable. Aranthur had seen him at the *quaveh* seller's.

"You like my purses?" asked a man. He smiled.

Aranthur's Armean wasn't as good as his Safiri but he tried.

"They are very good. Very..." He struggled for the word. "Well-making."

"You are Byzas?" the man asked, and Aranthur smiled.

"Souliote," he said.

"Ah," his new friend said. "The cattle thieves." He grinned. "I am Yusef. You work with leather, yes?" he asked in Byzas. "No one else looks at a purse the way we do."

Aranthur bowed. "I do, sometimes."

"You are a guard, heh?" Yusef asked. "I knew Souliotes when I was a Yaniceri. Good fighters." He leant over. "Good leather workers?"

Aranthur laughed. He had a small purse dangling from his belt and a buckler on his hip he'd made himself, and he showed the purse.

"Not bad. Nice blue dye," Yusef said. "Really good dye."

In moments, he and Aranthur were deep in a discussion about

dyeing leather blue. Aranthur drank a red tea with the man, watched him make a sale, and confirmed two more probable stalkers.

Inoques rose, and Aranthur shook Yusef's hand.

"Another time," he said.

The former Yaniceri squeezed his hand. "Please, my friend. Please."

Aranthur followed Inoques out into the sun. The deep arches and the domes were easily explained.

"Can the autumn sun be stronger on this side of the strait?" he asked.

Inoques shrugged. "It's all cold to me. Take me back to Masr, where the weather is normal. Or a storm at sea. I would like to make love during a storm at sea," she added, and Aranthur's heart all but skipped a beat.

"Any interest?" Aranthur asked.

"The woman with the good hides made me a very reasonable offer. The other one wanted to sleep with me but didn't want my hides." She shrugged. "You are not asking about Kurvenos."

"If he came here, he went straight to the Sultan, I'm guessing." Aranthur shook his head. "I feel foolish."

"You often do. It is endearing."

"Thanks," Aranthur said. "How do I find an Attian Lightbringer?"

"You didn't think to ask that on the other side of the water?"

"There wasn't anyone to ask," he said.

She blinked. He'd seen her do this before on several occasions; just the night before, when he asked…

About the mission Kurvenos sent her to perform.

"When did you last see Kurvenos?" he asked.

She blinked. "I don't think I can say."

"Let me guess," Aranthur said. "Two years ago."

She blinked again. "Please stop this. It is like a physical pain." And then she said, "Perhaps a little worse."

"He sent you to Atti," Aranthur said.

She blinked, and her face froze.

"I'll stop." Aranthur's head reeled with a new set of theories, conspiracies, and alignments. "Did Kurvenos go to Masr?"

She met his eyes without blinking. "At least twice," she said.

"I'm done," he said. "Harbour master?"

She shook her head. "I'm going back to the first merchant to see if he'll match Elsbet's price. If they take you, I'll come and get you." She smiled. "Listen, Aranthur. Do not use *power* here. It is not like Megara in this sense. They are much more…shy…of *baraka.* Understand?"

Aranthur had received a similar warning from Dahlia, so he agreed.

"The ship?" he asked.

"No, no. The first to finish goes to the other. If we miss each other, sundown at the watchmaker's." She raised an eyebrow. "Be careful."

"I think I'll be safe going to the harbour master. They're no doubt his people."

He kissed her, and her lips were warm and soft.

"Oh, my," he said.

"And that's another thing I like about you," she said. "Don't get killed."

He entered through the magnificent tiled arch, which he stopped and admired. This time, however, the officer came and took him out of the line, which was no shorter than it had been before. He was taken to an office with two fine carpets on the floor, and a set of cushions around a brazier; an incense ball was hanging from a chain, lit.

A very fat man sat on a pile of cushions with a very thin man reclining beside him, smoking from a water pipe.

"Incredible," the fat man said. "He came. It was stupid of you to let him walk away, Maryam."

The woman in the maille shirt bowed her head.

"My lord," she said, in what seemed to Aranthur to be mock humility.

The thin man allowed smoke to trickle out of his mouth. He had a piece of creamy paper in his hand.

"You are Aranthur Timos of Megara?" he asked in near-perfect Byzas.

"Yes, syr," Aranthur answered.

The fat man nodded. "Interesting," he said. "Until yesterday you were a wanted man across the strait."

"Yes, my lord," Aranthur said in Armean. "Today I am not."

The fat man took the pipe. "Would you like *quaveh*?"

"I would."

"You are an Imperial officer?" the fat man asked.

"I am," Aranthur agreed. "Indeed, I served in Armea with the Kaptan Bey."

Here the fat man looked at the thin man.

"Now, by Wad and Warah," he said.

"Where is thy woman?" the fat man asked.

"She is a merchant, and is doing her work," Aranthur said.

"You mean she is a spy," the thin man said. "And she is spying even as you are spying."

Aranthur shrugged. Another man might have bridled, but it was really no different from being a Souliote confronted by the Watch in Megara.

"My lord, she has hides to sell, and she is selling them."

The fat man snapped his fingers and the officer came in. He whispered to her and she left again.

A boy came in with *quaveh*. Aranthur put sugar in his as the officer returned.

"How many people know he is here?" the fat man asked.

"Too many," she said. "How was I to know he was some famous fighter?"

The thin man nodded. "We must try and get him to the palace," he said in Safiri.

"That is for thee and not me," the fat man said. "I do not like these strenuous activities." In Byzas, he said, "You like our *quaveh*?"

"Very much," Aranthur said agreeably.

"No one likes to expose a weakness," the fat man said. "But we are having...difficulties. Not dissimilar, I think, from those your government is experiencing." He stroked his magnificent beard. "Several very important people are missing—people who help the Sultan Bey run the government. The Kaptan Pasha, who directs the Sultan's foreign policy. Gone, with his entire family, two days ago. I need to ask you to go with my colleague to the palace."

"For an interrogation?" Aranthur asked.

"Please!" The thin man held up his hands theatrically. "Let us not use so barbaric a word. We need to talk. We are fighting in the dark, and you may bring us some light."

"Are the streets so dangerous?" Aranthur asked. "Is there anything out there I can't finish with cold iron?"

The thin man smiled thinly. "Cold Iron indeed, my friend."

"At your service, then," Aranthur said.

"Al-Malat be praised," the fat man said. "I am Ismail. This is Suleiman. And we are *just a little desperate* right now." He drank off his *quaveh*. "Our organisation is being disassembled. We have a traitor—indeed..." He looked at his partner.

"In honesty, we've had a traitor for some time," Suleiman said bitterly.

"We have one too," Aranthur said carefully. "I am reasonably sure I know who ours is."

Suleiman leant forward. "You do?"

"I think I do." Aranthur raised his *quaveh* to his lips. "How can I help you?"

"You should move. I will cover for you, as I am the size of any two men." Ismail raised an eyebrow.

He held out a small tray covered in curious candies, each like a thick jelly covered in powdered sugar.

"Have one," he said. "I recommend them."

Aranthur bit into one and had a near-religious experience.

"Delicious!" he said, and drank more *quaveh*.

"Indeed." Suleiman ate two. "I think we will walk."

"No, take chairs. Much less conspicuous. By now, they'll have agents around us, and they'll know who he is."

Aranthur was far from trusting the two of them, although the gentle mockery of the mailled officer and the fat man's confidence and humour suggested that they were worthy of trust.

"My partner will miss me," he said.

"We will find her," Ismail said.

Aranthur nodded to the fat man. "Do you know the Lightbringer, Kurvenos?"

The two men looked at each other.

"Yes," Ismail said.

"I'm here to find him," Aranthur said.

"We'd like to find him, too," Ismail said.

"I think he's the traitor," Suleiman said.

"What?" Aranthur snapped. "I don't believe it."

Both of the Attians shrugged.

"He is, though," Suleiman said.

Aranthur said, "And am I being held?"

Suleiman bowed slightly. "You are *not* being held, and we will help you. If you insist, you can go back on your ship. In fact that might be the best course. But the Sultan Bey has need for information, and we serve him, and just now, we know nothing."

"Tell him," Ismail said.

"Later," Suleiman said.

"Now," Ismail said. The humour was gone, and he spoke with enormous authority.

Suleiman met Aranthur's eyes. His own were deep and very dark.

"Your Kurvenos tried to kill one of our Lightbringers, Ahbar Jakal. And the Sultan Bey. And he kidnapped or killed the Kaptan Bey and his family."

"What?" Aranthur spat.

Suleiman nodded. "So you see our problem."

Aranthur narrowed his eyes. "The rumour on our side of the strait is that he is dead."

Suleiman shook his head. "That would be news to us," he said. "Do we tell him...?"

"Not yet," Ismail said.

Aranthur sat back in shock.

Aranthur got into a chair. It was the first time he'd ridden in one in his life. It was private: an enclosed box that smelled slightly of the former occupant's patchouli oil and spikenard. The cushions were leather, and worn to a shiny finish, and the bearers looked too small to carry his weight. But as soon as Suleiman gave directions in rapid Armean, they plucked his box off the ground and went through the harbour master's gate at a rapid walk.

The chair had small windows on both sides of the box, and Aranthur watched the streets go by. They left the docks immediately, climbing rapidly, and his chairmen carried him up a long series of steps cut straight into the rock. He could see the trabaccolo at her moorings in the deep bay, and beyond, Megara shining in the sun, her own red-tiled roofs as familiar as his Souliote home, and the new gilding of the Temple of Light shining like a beacon. To the south, the tall *campanile* of the "Red Lion" stood like a brick needle in the sunlight.

They cut back so that he could see the street beneath him, and then they were over some sort of barrier and moving on a broad avenue with temples and beautiful houses on one side and a cliff-side promenade on the other. The view was magnificent; he was almost level with the Pinnacle on the far side of the strait. He was trying to see the Academy when he realised that the woman with the gold stud was just turning away down an alley.

And just emerging from between two of the fine palaces with

magnificent shuttered balconies above street level was the longshoreman with the blue turban, now utterly out of place amid the rich clothing of the upper Ulamans—the only barefoot man on the whole broad avenue except a very young water seller.

Aranthur tried to tell himself that these were the harbour master's people and he should feel safe, but the gold stud in the woman's nose troubled him.

Expensive jewellery.

Aristocrat, slumming.

Her posture was excellent, as was that of the longshoreman in the blue turban.

"Stop!" Aranthur said in Armean.

He pounded a fist on the top of the chair and the bearers stopped in the middle of the avenue. He opened his door and waved at Suleiman, but the man's chair turned into the next major street and started uphill.

"Damn it!" Aranthur spat.

He was halfway out of the chair, and he looked back. The bearer's eyes were wide, and Aranthur threw himself at the ground and rolled.

He came to his feet drawing the yataghan. The rear bearer was dead, a crossbow bolt in his gut; he sat with his legs splayed like a broken doll, his eyes wide open, the stretchers of the chair keeping him from falling back.

Aranthur couldn't see the crossbowman.

A man shouted; a child screamed.

Aranthur couldn't see anyone to fight. He turned away, back the way they'd come, and another bolt *thudded* into the side of the chair. It went right through.

Aranthur got his feet under him and ran.

Screams pierced the air; a woman was down across the street, her long veils like a shroud over her. Aranthur smelt the burning match and he ducked as a puffer fired, very close. The long-bearded priest he'd been pushing past gave a choked grunt and fell, and Aranthur turned and ran between two buildings.

Are they invisible? he wondered.

The buildings on either side were palaces, at least by Megaran scale: big houses with gates and walls and servants. All along the street front, shutters were slamming closed. The screams and cries remained loud.

Aranthur came to the alley behind the palaces and turned right. He was looking for a place to hide, but it was too soon; he could hear footsteps.

He ran along the back of the sandstone palace, looking for an open door or a gate on either side of the stinking alley. He could smell garbage—old vegetables, uneaten fish, many days old.

A puffer spat. The ball ricocheted off stone and Aranthur turned… and saw no one.

But he could smell. He could smell the burnt powder, and there was a tiny curl of smoke where the weapon had fired.

Aranthur leapt over a quagmire of old garbage—the source of the foul smell. Then he ran as hard as he could, breaking his stride to make a difficult target.

He could think of a dozen *occultae* to throw; but Dahlia and Inoques had both impressed on him the relative rarity of displays of power in Ulama. It wasn't that he feared attention; it was that he understood that if these people were Pure they'd be on him in seconds once he revealed himself in the *Aulos.*

Not many choices.

He found what he was looking for—an old shed in the alley, once the stall for a horse or mule, and now just a shed packed with…

He ignored the refuse, the garbage, the cat piss and the sharp feral smell of rats. He wedged himself into the space behind the rickety door and watched the filthy puddle outside the door through the crack at the misplaced hinges.

And, as he both expected and feared, he saw the puddle disturbed as if by magic. An invisible foot stepped in…

Aranthur fired through the door. His puffer was small and easy to conceal and threw a small ball, but the door was old and rotten and the ball passed through it.

Blood spattered the ground.

Aranthur slammed the rickety door into his enemy and went forward, yataghan in his right hand. He clipped something with the barrel of his little puffer and slashed at that target with the yataghan. His pursuer fell heavily and gurgled, and the filthy puddle turned red.

The man, if it was a man, remained invisible.

Aranthur wiped his yataghan on a scrap of old cotton bedding and slipped the sharp thing into its scabbard. His pursuer was dying at his feet; Aranthur was all too familiar with the sounds.

Still invisible.

Aranthur shook his head in frustration and then stepped over the invisible body and walked on, dusting off his shoulders where he'd rubbed against the garbage, or perhaps chicken scree, in the shed. He knew that pursuit must be close; even his little puffer had made a sharp crack when it fired.

He kept to the alley behind the palaces, stopping to listen occasionally. There were screams—another shot. He moved on for several blocks, and then turned towards the sea.

But something was wrong. He emerged from between two fine houses, neither as big as the palaces, saw that he'd come downhill, and that the street he was emerging on to was lower on the hill than the steps his bearers had climbed.

He was lost.

He kept going. He had to believe that down would take him to the water: like Megara, Ulama was surrounded on three sides by water.

He went into the next alley that went downhill and found himself in a very narrow street enclosed by high walls. The street was crisscrossed with hanging laundry, and he moved down it briskly and then looked back, confident that even an invisible pursuer would have to move the sodden cotton and linen in the alley aside.

He saw no sign of immediate pursuit; the screams and cries were faint, and perhaps not even to do with him.

He grabbed a large, pale-blue cotton burnoose off one of the laundry lines and, after another hundred paces, pulled it on over his Souliote finery, making himself both anonymous and genderless, and continued down the hill. The alleys and streets were very steep, and the tenements and little slab-sided houses were very poor. He passed people, mostly women with wide-eyed children on their hips; a shoemaker made sandals at a tiny *corte* where three alleys came together, and a small boy sold orange juice.

Aranthur was parched, and he stopped to buy some, and was thankful for the Attian change he had from the *quaveh* seller.

"How much?" he asked in rough Armean.

"How much do you want to pay?" asked the young daredevil with the orange juice. "Ah, wise Hakim, please pay what this unworthy one needs, and not what one desires."

Aranthur lacked the energy or the language to have a lengthy debate. He produced a pair of silver sequins and the boy tried to snatch both, and Aranthur held one back.

"Fool!" spat Aranthur, the only epithet he could remember in Armean.

"I'm not the one dressed like a woman with a sword as long as my dick trailing on the ground," laughed the boy.

Aranthur winced, swallowed the juice, and walked on, the boy's laughter trailing behind him. As soon as he was clear, he belted his sword close by his side and pulled up the voluminous hood. A street later he left it on a laundry line and took a black one, sprang over a wall into a tiny *corte* and then leapt another wall into yet another alley under the watchful gaze of a one-eyed tomcat.

Now the side of the cliff was so steep that houses were on stilts and the alley itself was cut into the cliff face. He came to steps; once, they had been maintained, but the treads were worn to a slippery polish and he felt his way down carefully.

The steps turned at a narrow platform to run along the cliff instead of straight down it; and there, restoring Aranthur's faith in his sense of direction, was the sea, sparkling in the late afternoon light. There was Megara in the haze across the strait, close enough to touch, and so far away that he wondered if he would ever live to see it.

There was the sound of footsteps on the stairs coming up to the landing, and the sword hilt was hot in his hand.

Ware! said the sword.

There was nowhere to hide on the landing so Aranthur stepped forward, more boldly than he felt, and guessed, or perhaps felt, the presence of someone coming up the steps. He tried to act like a man going about his business, and went straight down the stairs.

He heard the breath—the dry dust on the steps and the movement of flies was some help—but he saw no one.

Aranthur was very close when the invisible man moved, the sword flashed a warning, and Aranthur's arm shot out. He misjudged it. The man pulled the trigger on a puffer, perhaps by mistake. Aranthur's flailing arm found the hot pistol barrel and then both of them were falling down the steps.

There was no plan, no fight. Aranthur fell atop his assailant—if the man had even planned to attack him—and they fell all the way to the next landing. Aranthur cracked ribs on the hilt of his own sword, but the other man screamed and then went limp.

They're tracking me, the sword said.

Aranthur was straddling a dying man. He was invisible; nonetheless Aranthur knew he had a beard, and Aranthur was holding his expended puffer. He shoved it under his burnoose into his sash with his other *gonne* and drew his sword.

Make him visible.

Yes.

Aranthur tapped the injured man, and there at his feet was a man in a nondescript brown cloak and equally common white trousers and a small cap.

Aranthur shook his head. "Fuck it," he said, and raised his magesight.

Now you are a beacon, the sword said.

The man had some sort of *saar* powered artifact on a thong around his neck; Aranthur took it, and noted that the man also had a fine large *kuria.*

His eyes fluttered open.

The moment their gazes crossed, Aranthur registered the man's fear, and cast with the same ruthlessness he had seen from Benvenutu; this was not the time to be squeamish.

He cast his *subjugation* and then his *compulsion*. He did it the dark way, using the man's terror to command him. It was ugly; it was grotesque to watch the dying, terrified man crawl to him.

It was also efficient.

"Who are you?" Aranthur asked.

"Daud in-Salud," the man said.

"Why are you following me?"

"I was ordered to."

"By whom?" Aranthur asked.

A moment's hesitation. Aranthur leant on the terror in his compulsion and the man shuddered.

"The Servant. She ordered it."

"Do you work for the harbour master?" Aranthur asked.

The man shook his head. "No! We work for the Servant, and…" He froze.

Aranthur would not be blocked, and bore down.

"No," the man pleaded.

Aranthur was pitiless.

The man screamed. "The Disciple!"

He choked, as if the words themselves were killing him.

Aranthur was sure he was out of time.

"Did you kill Kurvenos?"

The man was lost to questions. Too much terror; his mind was literally shredded, or perhaps someone had put a powerful block on him and now it was released. Either way, he chewed his tongue until blood flowed and said nothing but obscenities.

Aranthur got off the dying man. He ignited the man's *kuria*, so that it burned like a small hermetical sun; then he tossed the man over the edge of the landing. He fell almost a hundred feet and lay there, the *kuria* still sending out a magnificent and empty flare.

Very clever.

Thanks, Aranthur said, and went back up the steps.

He had at least two broken ribs, and his legs ached, and it took all his will to climb to the next platform, but he needed to go farther, and he did; up again, until he found another set of steps leading down, and then down again, aware that he was going farther and farther from the harbour master's office and the trabaccolo.

"I should just leave you leaning against someone's door," Aranthur subvocalised.

I beg you not to, the sword answered. *You know what's at stake.*

"Do I?" Aranthur muttered. "I am just your puppet, am I not?"

Never, the sword insisted.

"I bet you tell that to all the sword-bearers. You missed the attack in the street. No warning."

I am not all-knowing, and my... brothers... are here. I was fooled. You were not. Take comfort in that.

"What brothers?" Aranthur asked.

We swords were made by the mad emperor, from the souls of his paladins. And now the other six are as mad as he was, and bent on... revenge.

Aranthur walked on. "That was your longest sentence. Tell me, can you speak to Inoques?" he said softly.

I suppose I might. She is as much an artifact of the Aulos *as I am.*

"Tell her that I will meet her on the ship."

The sword seemed to vibrate in his hand. *It is done.*

He walked on, but when he tried to talk to the sword, it didn't answer.

Down, and down. He bought water for a copper and swallowed it, and got lost in a maze of transverse alleys. It shouldn't have been possible to be lost on a steep hillside, but he was. He could see the ocean, but he couldn't be sure what he was looking at; he could be looking south, towards Armea.

Then down again, with darkness falling. His fine boots were as out of place here as his long sword; these were poor people, and they were patently afraid of him, even the water seller and the orange-robed *Siddhartha* monk he passed. And the lower he got on the hillside, the poorer and the more temporary the hovels, so that the houses he'd passed far above, built out on stilts, seemed like fine homes by comparison. Here, at the edge of darkness, the only light came from cheap oil lamps, or just wicks in little pools of oil on a plate; some of the little mud houses were already dark as he went by. He made too much noise; he was too big, too loud, too foreign. And he was painfully aware that there were no other emanations of power here; his enemies must know where he was.

But he couldn't leave the sword. Perhaps it was controlling him—he was increasingly aware of how much the sword had done. In some ways, he began to suspect that the sword, and not he, was the author of all his plans.

If you're so brilliant, get me out of this, he thought.

Leave me, the sword said. *They can't see you precisely. And the cliff side distorts both distance and magic resonance. And stop complaining. You are doing very well. If only one of us can survive, it should be you.*

Really? Isn't all this your plan? I just unwittingly execute...

Aranthur Timos, I am the fragment of a soul of a person who has been dead two thousand years, trapped in a piece of metal. Do tell me how fucking hard your life is.

Almost unwillingly, Aranthur smiled.

"I take your point. Tell me your name," he muttered.

Once, I was called Lyda Orsin.

"You are not just one of the Six. You are Myr Orsin, the Paladin of Paladins," he whispered, awed. There was guessing, and then there was knowing.

I am the fucking Six. All the others are raving monsters.

Aranthur looked down at the darkening docks below. There, at the edge of one of the many harbours around the outside of Ulama, stood a magnificent temple; a pale blue dome rose between a pair of beautiful towers as fine as anything in Megara. The blue dome was lightly gilded by the sun setting over Megara.

Aranthur took a deep breath. *I have a plan*, he thought.

4

Ulama and Megara

An hour later, Aranthur was just above sea level. He couldn't conceal himself here; he'd reached a broad avenue along the waterfront. Aranthur had to hope speed would be its own deception, and he moved quickly—quickly enough to draw stares. The sun was setting; there were long streaks of red across the strait as the very last peep of scarlet showed *under* the distant aqueduct across the water.

A priest was just closing the iron gates of the magnificent temple as Aranthur ran up to him; his desperation was unfeigned. He threw himself on the ground in supplication and his ribs punished him for it.

"I beg a boon, wise one!" he said in fair Safiri.

The priest nodded. "Well spoken, lad," he said. "Need to pray all of a sudden, do you?"

"Yes, *hakim.*" Aranthur bowed again.

The priest was older, and indulgent.

"Probably something depressingly frivolous," he said. "Don't tell me. Come in, come in! To what god or goddess do you make invocation?"

Aranthur had to guess wildly. "Pallas."

The priest raised an eyebrow. "That sounds serious, my son. Not Aphres? Not a prayer for some...fair friend..."

"No, wise one. Pallas."

Pallas, at least in Megara, was the goddess of the Arts of Magik; sometimes she had become the Lady, and sometimes she was Sophia, but in Ulama, she went by her old name.

"Well," the older man said. "Better come in, then."

He took Aranthur into the main body of the temple, under the dome. The great nave had twelve sides, and each one held a chapel dedicated to a god or goddess. The whole nave was lit with lamps hanging high above, and some of the chapels were also lit, with enduring magelight as well as candles and oil lamps.

Aranthur inhaled the beautiful scent of the incense and brushed his mage sense against the nave. Most of the chapels were redolent with power; his gamble was going to pay off, but only if he was very quick.

"May I make a private prayer?" he asked, and gave the priest an entire Imperial soldi.

Even in the dark, the man knew the size of the coin, and he grunted.

"A prayer can be bought for less than this," he said with a smile.

But the coin vanished, and Aranthur heard his footsteps retreating across the huge marble floor, worn perfectly smooth by a hundred generations of worship.

Aranthur unclipped the sword's hangers from his belt, leant over so that he was hidden from the priest, and placed the sword carefully under the silk altar cloth. He managed to place it... *her*... exactly under a magnificent gilded-bronze dolphin set with *kuria* crystals as eyes that *burned* with *puissance*.

He hoped that the flare of power was utterly camouflaged by the array of powers and artifacts that surrounded him.

Goodbye, he said.

Brilliant. Do come back for me.

I hope to be back in less than a day. He glanced over his shoulder. *Do you know anything about what Kurvenos was doing in Atti?*

No. I only know that at least one of the Six swords is here. Think of them as versions of what we faced in Masr, embodied in swords.

Aranthur shuddered and let her go.

He completed his working, closed his pocket of the *Aulos* and stepped back to the rail of the Lady altar.

Aranthur knelt and prayed to the Lady, and the Eagle. And then he turned and left as quickly as he'd entered.

The priest was at his shoulder.

"A heavy burden?" he asked.

"You don't know the half of it," Aranthur replied.

He went out into the broad dockside, and began to walk. Without the sword he felt odd—lonely, even. And afraid.

But he walked rapidly back to the stairway he'd taken down the cliff side. He'd noted that it went down into the darkness under the dockside, and he followed his hunch. No one attacked him; twice he passed suspicious knots of men, and just as he came to the steps, he brushed past another invisible adversary. They hurried by, cursing under their breath.

"Where is he?" they said aloud.

A cat paused, washing itself, and then bolted.

"Not here," said another disembodied voice.

You must take him tonight! said a new voice.

"Yes, lord. But there is no *baraka.*"

Make no excuses unless you wish to be my next sacrifice.

The only answer was silence.

Aranthur managed a slight smile as he took the steps, into the darkness of Underside.

Underside Ulama was better lit than the cliff side. Voices were loud down here, in half a dozen languages; there were lamps all along the beachfront, and if it smelled a little more like old seawater and dead fish than the topside did, it was also cooler. The dockside echoed hollowly above; the towering docks were only forty feet above them, and most of the hovels lining the beach were built without much in the way of a roof, or even supporting timbers. Some were nothing but rotting old nets suspended from the dock above.

Aranthur had only been in Underside for a few minutes before he saw his first bone plague victim, her swollen flesh bruised and swelling as her bones melted away and she began to drown in her own fluids. Everyone stepped over her, and she made terrible noises, those of a despairing infant or an old cat.

Aranthur knew there was nothing he could do for her, but he felt more pity for her than for the men he'd killed in the upper town, and he knelt by her.

A moment later he realised he was not alone. A small man, or perhaps a woman, knelt by him in a shapeless brown robe.

"I can't do anything to help," Aranthur said with brutal honesty. "Except kill her."

The priest, or monk, shrugged.

"Nor can I, brother," she said. "I can only hold her hand as the bones soften, and hope it is quick." She sounded bitter, not graceful. "What kind of gods would allow this?"

Aranthur thought of all the answers he'd learned in various classes and none of them was suited to the reality of this bloated, ugly remnant of what had once been a human woman.

The dying woman gurgled.

Aranthur thought he heard pleading.

"I could put her out of her misery."

He looked into the eyes. The skull was usually the last thing to go, although the loss of the rib cage killed most victims.

"I won't stop you," the nun said. "This is the Underside. You could kill me without comment, much less this poor bag of flesh."

Aranthur blinked and looked away.

And then he drew the yataghan. The eyes blinked.

Aranthur was fastidious; death was instantaneous.

The nun rose, dusting her hands together.

"I seldom meet a killer with enough empathy to kill them. I can't do it," she admitted with something that sounded like self-loathing. "I can't leave, and I can't stay, and I can't help."

Aranthur nodded. He cleaned his yataghan on the dead woman's robes and sheathed it, offering the nun his hand.

"Sarduk," he said, offering her an ancient name of his people. He was sure that he shouldn't share his real name.

She didn't smile, but nor did she scruple to clasp the hand he'd just used to kill the poor woman.

"Alla," she said. "I am a Brown."

"I know," Aranthur said. "I've met other Browns."

"You are from Megara."

"True," he agreed.

She was aware that his eyes were everywhere—that every time someone came down the steps, he flinched.

"You need to hide?" she asked. "And you are not afraid of the bone plague?"

"Yes," he said. "And I am afraid of it." He glanced at her. "But I know what causes it."

She shrugged. "Come with me, if you like." She started to walk away, then turned and looked back. "I'll save you if I can. I'd like to save something. All people do here is die."

She said the small Temple of the Browns was close, so they walked along the waterfront. People cried greetings to the priestess, and some came and kissed her hand.

She smiled easily, and she clasped their hands, kissed them, smoothed the hair of one, offered a clean handkerchief to another.

"Come to the temple and we'll feed you," she said to a third. He was a big man with only one hand.

He turned his head away.

"The gods did not place you here to die of shame," she said sharply. "Get up and come with me."

The man looked resolutely out to sea.

Aranthur knelt by the man. "Come with us," he said in Armean.

The man's face twitched. But then he looked at his right arm, and the stump, and looked away.

"He was found guilty of stealing and they took his hand," she said. "Now he is unclean, and cannot eat with any of his sect—they are all Mazdayanians in his village."

"How do you know all this?" Aranthur asked.

She shrugged. "I know everything down here. Even when I don't want to."

Aranthur nodded.

"He will starve himself to death. I suppose that's what the judge intended anyway."

Alla got to her feet, her anger obvious.

Aranthur made one of his spur-of-the-moment cavalry charge decisions, partly because the man reminded him of Sasan, somehow.

He was still kneeling by the man.

"You weren't guilty, were you?" he asked.

The man looked at him for a moment. His eyes were not pleading, not angry, not desperate. It was the flat look of absolute despair.

Aranthur knew it from Antioke.

"I am guilty." The man's voice was dignified, careful. "When the Dark Forge came, the Darkness took my children, and my wife was sick." He met Aranthur's eyes in the near dark. "I did what I could, and they took me for it. Now she is dead, and I am here."

Aranthur put a hand on the man's shoulder.

"What if I could get you another hand?" he asked.

"Don't make him an empty promise," Alla spat.

"What if you could avenge your wife and children?" Aranthur asked.

"You are playing with fire," Alla said in Byzas.

"You want to save someone?" Aranthur realised that he, too, wanted to save someone.

"You would not lie to a man so wasted as I?" the handless man asked.

Aranthur shook his head. He put his hands together over the stricken thief's left hand.

"If I live, and you live, then I swear that I will give you a new hand of leather and sinew and bone, in five days, in Megara."

"You are a magos," Alla said.

"Yes," Aranthur said.

"Aploun," the woman said.

The handless man got to his feet and swayed as if, having once lain down to die, he had lost the ability to stand.

"I am Ardvan," he said.

Aranthur supported the man down the waterfront, to a low building constructed entirely of ship's timbers and planking; it had an organic look, but it was very solid. The floors planks were solid and clean; inside were a dozen people sitting on woven mats in a front room under a fine painting of Aploun and his harp.

"Are you an Imoter?" Alla asked him.

"No," Aranthur said. "I can perform several Imoter tasks but I have not studied the healing arts..."

"Will you look at some of my people?" she asked, ignoring his answer and leading him through a screen of hanging beads into a second room. This one had a tiny wood stove made of iron and an open hearth, and there were twenty people lying on pallets that smelled of salt and the sea—bags of dried kelp. "I will fetch food."

Aranthur glanced at Ardvan. "Sit and eat."

The man bowed his head. "As you command, *huzoor.*"

Aranthur made a circuit of the room. There were simple cases: two men with broken arms, and a woman with a newborn on her chest, fast asleep. There was one case of bone plague. As was becoming increasingly common, only part of the man was affected: one arm hung from him like a sack. The rest were diseases: two children, almost blind from some form of *optamalia* and a woman with stomach worms.

And six people who lay still and stared at the ceiling.

"Darkness," Aranthur said aloud.

"Yes," Alla said. "And this is only a tithe of the victims—someone left each of them here, the way people sometimes leave us unwanted babies." She managed half a smile and she stroked one of the lithe tortoiseshell cats. "And cats."

The Brown's temple came with four other priests and priestesses and a colony of cats; several were the thin, very clean tortoiseshells, but Aranthur was drawn to the enormous orange tom who sat by the door. He had very little left in the way of ears; Aranthur scratched him, and was bitten for his trouble.

"One of the Darkness victims is still bleeding," said a Brown priest. "Alla says you are a magos. Can you stop it?"

"Show me," Aranthur said. In truth, he'd flinched away from the Darkness victims.

Now he knelt next to a beautiful young woman with an obvious knife wound in her left thigh and slashes across both arms, deep cuts that had injured muscle.

All of the cuts showed the red inflammation that Aranthur knew indicated various fires in the blood, and the steady flow of blood from her thigh was the most immediately life-threatening. He summoned his trance as Dahlia had taught him and dived in, and examination showed that her artery was *just* touched, so that she was losing blood steadily. Aranthur focused, finding his way into the web of life force that remained and making the *alteration* required.

He'd had plenty of practice lately. Once he was in the correct state, he didn't release himself back to the real but worked his way up her body and went to work on her arms. She was very strong—a swordswoman or a dancer or both—and that was why she was still alive. He touched her with a pain-blocker and used a little more *puissance* to strengthen her in the *Aulos*, as he'd seen Myr Benvenutu do with the Emperor.

Then, as his inner state was solid, he entered his own inner complexity and went to work on his own ribs.

He emerged to find Alla standing beside him with a bowl of lentils.

"You stopped her blood flow," she said.

"Yes," he agreed.

"And closed the wounds."

"They should still be bandaged—these repairs can burst open under stress."

The necessity of his investigations had caused him to pull back her robes to expose her legs and abdomen. Alla began removing the old bandage, and Aplos, the youngest priest, stood by with clean ones.

Aranthur was looking at the gold stud in the woman's navel. He took one of her hands, and turned it over; they were soft, and very neat, the nails well cared for. A faint trace of henna decorated the back of her hand in elaborate whorls.

Alla saw the stud too.

"Yes," she agreed, as if Aranthur had said something.

"Someone *brought* them to you," he said.

"Yes. All six were left on the portico. She was bandaged."

Aranthur went to the heavily bearded man; he was well-muscled and neither his hands nor feet showed the signs of hard physical labour.

"This man is somebody," Aranthur said.

"They are all *somebody*," Alla corrected him.

He nodded and went to the next man, who had the calloused hands of a professional soldier, or just possibly a gentleman farmer. He too was badly cut—not stab wounds, but slashes on his back and arms, as if…

As if he had been defending something or someone.

Aranthur went to work.

"This woman," he said, indicating an older woman who was deep in the Darkness, "is clearly that young woman's mother." Her eyes were sunken, but the features and the near-perfect *quaveh* skin were the same. He finished with the man he'd mentally christened the Soldier. "And all of them wore rings until recently," he added.

Alla shrugged. "Yes. I agree. Aplos noted most of this when we brought them in off the portico." She shrugged again. "Eat your soup before it gets cold."

"This man is a soldier. I believe that's the number of his Yaniceri regiment in Safiri, along with an astrological sign," he added, pointing at the elaborate tattoos on his back.

Aranthur took the bowl and began to eat. The lentils were good; they were followed by chick peas in a delicious, spiced oil.

"You know everything that passes on the waterfront," he said.

Alla shook her head. "Only to the poor."

"Do you know the ships?"

Aplos smiled grimly. "I do," he said. "I treat sailors."

"Do you know the black trabaccolo from Masr that came in last night?"

Aplos shook his head. "No."

"I need to know if she's still at her moorings," Aranthur said. "And I need a boat."

"Who are you to give us orders?" Alla asked.

Aranthur finished the chick peas.

"That was delicious," he said. "Friends, I cannot tell you who I am. I can only tell you I'm trying to end the Darkness, and if you can put me in a boat with these six people, Ardvan and a rower, I think I will be one step closer."

Alla glanced at Aplos.

"I know some fisherfolk," Aplos said. "I suspect they can borrow a boat."

"Why do we help you?" Alla asked.

Aranthur put five solid gold byzants on the table next to the wooden bowl he'd eaten from.

"We're on the same side," he said. "And I can be a good friend." He looked back at both of them.

Alla narrowed her eyes. "I was prepared to see you as a victim," she said. "Now, you seem more like one of those busy bastards who create the broken bodies we attempt to repair."

Aranthur tugged at his beard in frustration.

"Did you know Radir Ulgul?"

She had picked up the five gold coins. Now she froze.

"Of course," she said, as if he was a fool.

"We all knew him," Aplos said.

"I knew him too," Aranthur said. "I tried to save him. From *al Ghugha*."

Alla shook her head. "You're an Imperial officer?" She took a step back. "That's all we need. Half the locals think we are Imperial spies already."

Aplos' brown eyes met Aranthur's. "You know he was a living saint to us," he said.

Alla smiled bitterly. "He never lost his faith, no matter how much shit was poured on him."

"He was remarkable," Aranthur said. "He helped me save a good friend... from *thuryx*."

Aplos glanced back at Aranthur. "Then I know who you are," he said slowly. "Radir spoke of you..." He had gathered up the wooden bowls, and now he stood by the beaded curtain to the kitchen, as if he needed to defend the kitchen. "You are lying about your name. And you are a wanted man."

Aranthur took a deep breath. "Appearances may be against me. But I am Cold Iron, and not hot metal."

Aplos smiled. "I know that story. Tirase, I think?"

"Yes." Aranthur was disappointed that neither of them responded to the code words, but the Browns made every attempt to disassociate themselves from politics.

Alla was looking down at the middle-aged woman lost in the Darkness.

"Can you actually help them?" she asked.

"I think so," Aranthur said. "On the other side of the strait there is a team working on the Darkness and cures for it. They have had some success."

"Who are they?" Alla asked.

Aranthur sighed. "It is too dangerous for you to know. I want you to let me go without any questions, and don't, for the love of the gods, ask my name. And please, I have another favour."

"In for a penny, in for a soldi," Alla said.

"I'm guessing that you have many sources of information."

She smiled.

"Please, share anything you can learn about a man called Daud in-Salud. He's local—he's dead."

"How do you know that?" Aplos asked.

"I killed him," Aranthur said. "I need to know who he worked for, who his friends were, his lady friends, his parents, anything."

Alla looked at Aplos. "Not a common name," she said. "I'll see what I can do. I know people at most of the temples."

Aranthur leant forward. "This is not some matter of Imperial economic policy. We are going to save the world. Right now. From the Pure, and from the Darkness, and from the Forge. You want to save someone?" he asked Alla. "Save everyone. Help me."

She didn't take her eyes off him.

"I knew you were a bastard," she said.

*

Two hours later, he was in a boat with six apparent corpses, a man with one hand, and three terrified fisherfolk—two women rowing and a man at the steering oar. Their oars were muffled to reduce the noise, and they had no lantern lit, so when an official launch powered by an *occulta* swept by, they were almost cut in half. Only a ruddy light from deeper in the harbour saved them, lighting the low black launch as it darted by.

After ten further minutes of rowing, Aranthur's worst fears were realised. The ruddy light was a ship on fire.

And it was the trabaccolo.

Black despair settled on Aranthur.

"Our ship?" asked Ardvan. He asked in a matter-of-fact voice; a man for whom disaster had become commonplace.

"Yes," Aranthur choked out.

Even as he watched, something in the forward holds caught, and the fire roared out of the hatches. They could hear it even at this distance, half a mile away.

Aranthur's whole body screamed with rage and fatigue and loss.

She cannot be dead.

They attacked the ship. Of course they did. They must be looking for the Stone the way I'm looking for them.

Think! Think!

"Oh, well." Ardvan turned his head away.

Aranthur looked west, where the lights of the palace shone across the water. He was out of options...and he thought they could reach it.

He drew both of his puffers—his own, and the one he'd taken off his victim in the fight on the steps.

The two oarswomen looked at him.

He cocked them both, and pointed west.

"Start rowing," he said.

"You fucking bastard," one woman said. "If we're taken, they'll gut us and throw us to the fish."

Aranthur nodded. "West," he added. "Row for the lights of the palace. I'll see you richly rewarded."

In Armean, the steersman said, "We can take him. And a thousand curses on Alla that she brought us to this. Aplos said he could be trusted!"

Aranthur sat back in the bow, and a wave caught him as the boat turned west into the chop.

"I speak Armean," he said. "And I don't want to kill you and row this boat by myself. If you row, I will see you richly rewarded."

"How richly?" asked the woman on the left. She was big and had dark hair and was missing two teeth.

"Twenty gold byzants," Aranthur said.

The two women exchanged glances.

"Really?" the man in the stern asked. "Or just a lot of sweat, and our bodies dumped in the harbour?"

Aranthur checked the priming on the two puffers; left, then right. He put one into his sash, under the black burnoose, mostly safe from ocean spray. He let them see the yataghan in his belt.

"I swear by Sophia, by the Eagle, and by my father's honour and my mother's name," he said. "You will not be harmed. If I can arrange it, you will return here in a way that will excite no comment."

"Fuck!" spat the woman missing teeth.

"We're all fish food anyway," said the other woman.

And the steersman shrugged. "Agreed."

Aranthur wanted to search for Inoques. His whole body demanded it; his gut roiled.

But there was no time. In the boat, he had a key to the the puzzle of the world; in his head, he now knew who was the traitor. And Inoques was not a maiden in a tower who needed rescuing. If she was alive, she was more powerful than most of the forces arrayed against her. If she was dead…

The distant judge took over and gave the orders.

"Row," he commanded.

The light fishing boat had an easier time with the new currents than the trabaccolo had had. They rowed steadily south and east, and the current bore them north and west, and they inched their way closer and closer to the City, which rose before them until its lights finally towered over them—the brilliant white magelight atop the Temple of Light an intentional beacon for mariners.

Aranthur showed his golden rose to the Axes on duty at the Sea Gate of the palace.

"Get me ten Nomadi," he said, and stood on the sea wall, stretching.

Only then did his hands begin to shake; only then did he let himself think about it all.

Vilna came in person, his arm in a sling. Aranthur hugged him anyway. Right behind him was Kallotronis.

He raised a hand, forestalling stories and explanations.

"We're going back at last light," he said. "I want six of your best—Chimeg for certain. Reward these three—twenty gold byzants for each of them, a meal and a place to sleep."

"And...?"

"And don't let them go anywhere," Aranthur said. "We need them to get back in."

"Where's Inoques?" Vilna asked.

"Gone. The ship's burnt, and we were betrayed. Atti is sinking into the hands of the Pure."

Kallotronis frowned. "Inoques? I'll miss that one."

"I pray she's alive," Aranthur said.

Kallotronis grinned. "My ducats are on the woman. Ulama is in the hands of the Pure? And we're going there tonight? Excellent." He looked down into the boat. "Who are the dead people?"

"Not dead. The Darkness," Aranthur said. "I believe this is the Kaptan Pasha and his family and bodyguards, kidnapped by the Pure and left for dead by someone too soft-hearted to kill them."

Kallotronis grinned at Aranthur, beaming approval. "And you just tripped over them?"

"Pretty much," Aranthur said. "Is Haras working the alchemy that Myr Benvenutu..." His voice cracked. "That Myr Benvenutu prepared?"

Vilna nodded.

Aranthur took a deep breath. "Then carry these poor people up to the palace. With a little luck, the wind is about to change."

He slept for six hours, and read through the *Ulmaghest*, and found Litha directing the care of his Darkness victims. Haras had taken over two big rooms in the palace to work on the alchemical suggestions that Myr Benvenutu had left behind; he still found time to grumble to Aranthur about his fears for the Black Stone. The burns he'd taken facing the Disciple were swathed in bandages, and his temper had not improved.

The whole lower hall of the palace, the magnificent nave under the arcing crystal canopy that was the palace's central feature, was full of beds—hundreds of them—and on them lay the victims of the Darkness. Dahlia and Iralia had agreed to concentrate the city's efforts in the palace, and the Imperial servants had become nurses and attendants.

Aranthur found Ardvan sitting up in a bed with clean sheets. Around him were people who, for the most part, lay still, eyes open, looking at the patterns in the glass above them, or looking at nothing at all, or staring into some terrible personal Darkness. Ardvan, in contrast, was sitting up, flexing a mechanical hand.

"It is incredible," he said to Aranthur.

"A good piece of work," Aranthur said.

A cursory review showed him how good: the mechanical hand was powered by *kuria*, and unlike many prosthetics, it was exactly the same size as the man's missing hand, and nicely coloured.

"I cannot afford the crystals to power this," the man said.

Aranthur nodded. "You are in my household, if you wish it. It will be dangerous, so I do not require it of you."

Ardvan touched his new hand to his forehead. "Lord, I will serve you into hell."

Aranthur flinched. "Don't call me lord," he said. "I am no one's lord."

Ardvan shrugged. "Sure. I want to work. If I lie here, all I do is think of my wife." He looked at Aranthur. "I hate them," he said suddenly. "Will you let me have my revenge? May I strike my blow against those who do this?"

Aranthur took a breath. "Yes," he said. "If I can, I will help you strike a blow."

The man threw off his sheets. "Let me serve you, lord."

Aranthur shook his head. "Not lord. Syr, if you like. My name is Aranthur."

"Yes, lord," Ardvan said.

"All right," Aranthur said. "You need clothes. Follow me."

Aranthur wanted to talk to Inoques. Or Dahlia. Or Tiy Drako, or even Iralia. He felt isolated; he wondered if this was an effect of being separated from the sword.

He thought of Benvenutu every ten minutes, because he missed her and he missed her tutoring. He suddenly had a dozen questions an hour about the working of the glyphs.

He ended up standing in the anteroom of the Emperor's private apartments with a cup of *quaveh* and a heaped plate of fried calamari and various extravagant desserts, all provided without question by Drakas, who was lecturing Ardvan in the next room. He was eating, and trying not to get his greasy fingers on the vellum, when Iralia came in.

She looked surprisingly like her old self; her hair was brilliant, her make-up perfect, her eyes glowing with life.

"I heard you were here," she said. "Keep eating. What's happening?" She sniffed. "Aphres, you smell like the bottom of an old boat."

Aranthur knew he had to trust someone, and no layout of the last two years seemed to place Iralia in a position to be an opponent.

"I think one of the Lightbringers is a double agent," he said. "Worst case, several of them. The Attians think it's Kurvenos."

"Impossible," she said flatly.

"Are you sure?"

"Yes. He's duplicitous, and he's manipulative. But he's the best man I know—he *believes.*" She met his eyes. "Honestly, Aranthur, if he's tainted... don't tell me. He restored my belief in the goodness of people. If he's a lie, burn it all down."

Aranthur took a breath, and found that it was as if he'd been holding his breath all the time.

"Thanks to all the gods," he said. "I'm too stupid for this."

"Never say that, my dear," she said. "The Emperor is recovering. We will win through this, and the Council of Seventeen meets in an hour." She looked at him. "Are you ready?"

He shrugged. "I need to get back to Atti. We lost the trabaccolo. I'm afraid..." His voice became unsteady, and he looked away.

"Afraid for Inoques?" Iralia laughed her rich, throaty laugh. "You want to race back over and save her? Sometimes you are a wonder, Aranthur, and sometimes you are just another man. Your demon wife is ten times your age and far more powerful. I suspect she can protect herself."

Aranthur had to smile. "I needed to hear that," he said.

Iralia gathered him in her arms and squeezed. "I know," she said softly. "You are afraid."

"I am," he admitted. "I am way over my head, and it feels as if I'm an actor at the Opera in a part that I can't handle."

She nodded. "Trust me. Kurvenos is straight, in his bent way. I know

I suspected Tiy Drako, but never Kurvenos." She squeezed again. "And your wife is not going to be caught by the Pure."

"Know anything of the Six?" he asked. "Six Swords?"

Iralia shrugged. "I know they were made by one of the original emperors by killing six of his most trusted officers and imprisoning them in blades."

Aranthur was chewing calamari. He turned the page of the *Ulmaghest* and glanced at Iralia.

"Did Kurvenos ever tell you anything about... I don't know. About anything he did before we all met?"

She laughed. "You know how Tiy Drako lies?"

"Oh, yes," Aranthur said.

"Kurvenos doesn't talk. He's immune to my brilliant eyes and my smile and he likes to talk to me, but it's always about how to harness my talent." She shrugged. "Why?"

Aranthur knew that he could die that very night in Atti. Someone needed to know.

"The Attians think he tried to kill the leading Attian Lightbringer. Inoques said that Kurvenos used her for a mission in Atti about two years ago. And an impeccable source says that about two years ago the Lightbringers became alive to the threat of the Master."

"Too late to save Safi," Iralia said. "Yes, that fits with what I've heard. But two years ago..."

"You were still with the Duke of Volta and I was trying not to fail Elements of Experimental Philosophy." Aranthur raised his eyebrows. "I need to talk to Drako. I want to agree with you about Kurvenos, but I should tell you. When I met you at the Inn of Fosse, Drako was there to meet an agent—a highly placed double agent in the Pure. And that means Kurvenos might also have been there, to meet with the same agent." He shook his head and finished his *quaveh*. "I'm in a forest of mirrors in a snowstorm," he said. "I could believe anything. It's like one of those impossible logic puzzles at the Academy."

"I won't believe it," Iralia said. "I trust no one, and *I trust Kurvenos.*"

Aranthur nodded. "Good. But if that's true, and if it is also true that Kurvenos attacked this Attian Lightbringer seven days ago..."

"What?"

"That's what the Attians told me—that Kurvenos attacked a man called Ahbar Jakal."

“I know that name,” Iralia said. A hand went to her mouth. “Aphres! Aranthur…” She closed both eyes. “He was here, in the palace. Get the calendar, Dakos.”

“My lady,” the Emperor’s valet said, and stepped out. He returned with a small book bound in green velvet.

“He was here, the day before the Darkness. Aphres! He was here, *in this room*, with the Emperor.” Iralia took a breath. Her eyes were bright. “He tried to put his hands on me, and I didn’t…” She took a steadying breath. “No one does that to me now. It… threw me.” She looked at Aranthur. “But he groped me to hide what he was really doing—poisoning the Emperor!”

She glared at the book as if she could burn the man with her eyes.

Aranthur was looking at the calendar.

“Roaris brought him here?” he said. “You received Roaris?”

Iralia looked away. “It was a terrible time. Roaris demanded to be placed in command of the City, and the Emperor said no. Now that I think of it, this noble Lightbringer argued that we were in great peril when he must have known perfectly well that Roaris was lying and that Tribane had won the battle. Yet he was here with Sittar. Sittar vouched for him, and Sittar kept at the Emperor…”

Aranthur nodded. He was smiling.

“You look happy,” Iralia spat. “Why?”

He ate more calamari. “Because I think I get it,” he said. “Desperate times mean desperate measures. One last throw of the dice, by the other side. Kurvenos figured it out seven days ago—Ahbar Jakal is our traitor. I hoped so, and now I see it all.”

“Oh, gods,” Iralia said.

“Gods indeed. I need some luck. Tell Dahlia *everything* I told you. In case I fail.”

“Fail?”

“I’m going to try and get Jakal. And rescue Kurvenos, if he’s still alive.”

“Blessed Aploun! Is that possible?” she asked.

Aranthur shrugged. “The Red Moon may be made of cheese. I really don’t think I know anything any more. But I know enough to act.”

“But the meeting—”

“No,” Aranthur said. “I have to go before anyone stops me.”

She pursed her lips. “Yes,” she said softly. “Listen. I’m sorry to burden you, but you told me everything. There is something I need to tell you. Myr Astras…"

"The Master of Astrology?"

"The same. She's here, working with Haras. She says the Dark Forge is getting bigger…"

He nodded. "I know."

"But the rate of expansion is increasing."

"Eagle!" he spat. "Is anything good ever going to happen?"

She made a face. "Not unless we *make* it happen," she said. "Save Kurvenos if you can, but by all the gods we have no time."

She extended a hand to him. Unthinking, he bent his knee, took her hand and kissed it.

"Your servant," he said.

She smiled.

"You will make a fearsome empress," he said.

"I will, indeed."

"That is your intention, is it not?" he asked.

She smiled thinly. "Yes. I trust me. I'll make a better world than anyone I know, especially because I know how bad the world can be."

Aranthur bowed again. "I trust you, Iralia."

She looked at him. "Good," she said.

"Find Tiy Drako," he said.

"Believe me, I'm trying."

5

Ulama, Capital of Atti

An hour later, the fishing fleet left from all the beaches and piers of Megara, more than a thousand small craft spreading out on the evening tide to catch whatever it offered: salmon running north to their spawning grounds and tunny in the rich waters of the strait; closer in, the smaller fish that haunted the currents looking for food, or flitted about in great schools; the elusive *serys* fish, which followed the whales, and which had a gland that excreted a substance rich in *puissance.*

Full darkness saw most of them on their fishing grounds. Different fisherfolk utilised different weapons against their prey: harpoons and lances for the tunny and the largest salmon, and even crossbows with lines; rods for sea trout and other medium-sized game fish, and nets for the smaller whitefish. By ancient custom, there were two fishing fleets—the fleet of morning, and the fleet of evening—and guild rules applied, forcing them to maintain separate schedules and never to overlap. Each fleet had an admiral who was responsible for everything from fishing regulations to holding the guild's annual feast.

The moon was well up when three salmon boats slipped east, their masts down, and caught the reverse current well north of the City, on the Attian shore, and coasted silently in behind the Attian fishing fleet, which followed much the same patterns.

The three boats landed in the lowland suburbs of Ulama, almost four miles from the city centre. They touched the beach, discharged their passengers, and put back to sea; gone on the southbound reverse current in ten minutes, back out into the strait the moment they were clear of the current.

Aranthur landed from the first boat, dressed well for an Attian merchant, with a fine yataghan and his buckler atop his belt; an embroidered vest and a Maniote turban in deep blue, edged in silver. Kallotronis wore the same—a rich merchant's bodyguard—and Ardvan was in blue and silver, a liveried servant. Vilna, attired as a merchant, looked remarkably dignified, and Nata, dressed as his servant, could not stop admiring the hand that the Imoters of the palace Infirmary had grafted to his right arm. He flexed it constantly, and kept thanking Aranthur for it, as if Aranthur had made it.

All the rest were caravan guards and pilgrims, and as soon as they were off the beach they began walking towards the city.

Sunrise found them at the Der Sadet, the Gate of Prosperity. The gate guards were alert, and Aranthur noted that two of them were Voynuks, palace guards.

"State your business," a bored Yaniceri said.

Aranthur bowed, with an ingratiating smile.

"Sarduk Trapezetos," he said. He had a bill of lading for a nonexistent camel caravan. "I am only visiting the shrines. With my people."

The guard looked over his fine vest and clean *fustinella.*

"No goods?" he asked.

"All on the beasts," Aranthur said, pointing north.

The Yaniceri glanced at Kallotronis and Chimeg. "These ruffians are yours, *Effendi*?"

"All of them," Aranthur said with another smile.

"Hmmm." The Yaniceri fondled Aranthur's forged bill of lading carefully. "I suppose that I should interview each of them..."

Aranthur smiled again. "Of course," he said. "But they are mostly Souliotes—the merest barbarians."

"Oh," the Yaniceri said. "I know their kind. Nonetheless."

"Could you tell me, captain, when the great temple is open to pilgrims?" Aranthur asked.

As he asked, he lifted his hand off the table and left a solid gold byzant on the corner. He worried that it was too much, but he was supposed to be rich, and he was well aware how he'd feel if offered such a bribe.

The Yaniceri smiled. "All the temples will be open by the time you pass into the City," he said politely. "Stop inside the gate for *quaveh* and to wash your face, and you will be sure." He reached across the table and handed back the bill of lading, and mysteriously the coin vanished into his sleeve. "Go with the gods, my friend."

"And you, captain," Aranthur said.

"I am no captain. But it always makes me happy to hear it said."

The man smiled, and Aranthur walked past him, into Ulama, with his people at his heels.

Kallotronis nodded as soon as they came to the *quaveh* seller.

"It would not have been good to be searched," he said.

He had Chimeg's rifled harquebus inside his voluminous shepherd's cloak, and Aranthur had his *carabin* under his own. They were all armed to the teeth, and the light morning rain covered their cloaks with droplets and abetted their deception.

They stood under the *quaveh* seller's awning and drank the tiny cups of sweet *quaveh* like shots of *arak*, and then walked into the City. Ulama was as big as Megara, and the streets were as old and twisted. As soon as they cleared the gates they were in a warren of side streets and tiny squares, interspersed with little stone schools and bathhouses with their own lawns and each with one or two fine old trees, mostly figs. The closer they went to the city centre the larger the houses were, and the more ornate the walls and gates. They could clearly see the great ridge that held the palaces—the ridge from which Aranthur had descended just a few hours before. The houses on either side of them were big enough to hide the sun, and had courtyards with fruit trees whose scent wafted through their locked gates.

Aranthur was painfully aware how difficult it would be to determine if he was being watched or followed, because the Attian beggars were everywhere, and dressed in almost identical clothes, or lack thereof—nearly naked except for a loincloth and a turban. They all had long white beards and enormous begging bowls, and Aranthur wasn't sure that he could tell one from another, much less track them.

And it was too easy to get lost. They had to ask for directions twice, and a third time had to pay for them in a poor quarter where their foreign accents aroused nothing but suspicion. They visited and donated at three temples on the road, acting like good religious pilgrims, and indeed, when they found another such group, they joined it for a while, walking together towards the main harbour.

The harbour was in sight, and they were still with the other pilgrims when Aranthur saw Blue Turban, the longshoreman from the other day. Today he wore the same turban and the same ragged clothes, but his shoes were fine leather, new, a rich, dark brown leather. Aranthur, as a leather worker, priced them immediately—far beyond the status of the rag-like turban and the man's other clothes.

Aranthur made a sign with his hand. Kallotronis' expression didn't change, but he turned right at the next intersection. The rest of them went forward, pausing to admire the facade of the temple to Potnia Parthenos, where it was clear that a wedding was about to take place; a dozen flower sellers were arranging garlands on the steps. A formidable woman who could only be the bride's mother was directing operations at the top of the magnificent white marble steps, and a wedding garland was being placed on the gigantic gold and ivory statue's brow.

"I want to pray here," Chimeg said, so they all went in after Aranthur paid a small bribe to the priest.

From the temple itself, Aranthur could see down into the neighbourhood behind the temple. He saw Kallotronis; the man gave a wave.

Five minutes later, Aranthur found him waiting at the mouth of an alley.

"Lost him?" Aranthur asked.

"No," Kallotronis said. "I have him. He won't be running off."

He led Aranthur and Chimeg up the alley, which stank.

Blue Turban was standing very tall amid the charnel reek of a butcher's shop. Only when they were very close did Aranthur see why the man seemed to be stretching to reach for something; his right wrist was pinned to the building's first floor beam by a dagger which went between his wrist bones and was deeply embedded.

The man was whimpering.

Aranthur looked a reproach at Kallotronis. He shrugged with unconcern.

"Very bad man," Kallotronis said. "Just not as bad as me."

"We do not use torture," Aranthur insisted.

"If he doesn't move, it shouldn't hurt at all," he said. "Well—not much." He smiled nastily. "He has already sung a very interesting song, haven't you, my little bird?"

"Please..."

"He says that the Disciple and his people have your friends, the Browns. And they've set a little trap for you. For us, really."

"Please..."

Kallotronis' eyes left Aranthur's face and moved to Blue Turban. The man flinched visibly and then gave a soft shriek as his hand dragging against the sharp blade split the skin.

"This louse is supposed to watch us and give the little ambush some warning. They already know we've landed. All things considered, it seems to me that the Pure's greatest weakness is that they keep using these milksop aristos as agents. This one broke when I suggested cutting off his prick." Kallotronis smiled. "Of course, I wouldn't advocate such terrible steps."

Aranthur tugged at his beard. He looked around at his little band —Vilna, Kallotronis, Chimeg and the rest.

"What do we do with him?" Aranthur asked.

"Leave him?" Vilna asked with cheerful cruelty.

"Please..."

Kallotronis grinned. "I like that, my friend. When we are done, his own people will find him, and they'll know who betrayed them. And he's such a fucking coward that he'll hang here the whole time we're killing his friends, unable to muster the strength to ruin his wrist to warn them. A beautiful thought."

"We lie awake on the Steppes, dreaming of such things," Vilna said.

"In the mountains, too," Kallotronis said.

"Please..."

"Are you two done?" Aranthur snapped. "I want him alive. Nata?"

The small Qirin tribesman nodded. "Aye, *Bahadur.*"

"We are surrounded by enemies. Nonetheless, I want this man alive and back at the palace. Do you understand?"

Nata nodded. "Aye." He looked at the much taller Attian with his wrist pinned by a dagger.

"Ardvan? You know the city. Help Nata get this man to the boat."

"Yes, lord."

Aranthur winced. "Not lord."

"We need to move," Kallotronis said, and Vilna nodded.

"Let's do it."

Aranthur sketched the layout of the Browns' temple and the lower waterfront, and Vilna nodded sharply.

"I'll go in the front, alone," Aranthur said.

"No one is that stupid," Kallotronis said.

Vilna smiled. "He is," he insisted. "No one gets called *Bahadur* by the Mugai for being smart."

"They never expect me to be smart," Aranthur said.

No one had moved the corpse of the woman he'd killed. He made the sign of the Eagle and held his nose. Further on, most of the tavernas were closed, and there were an unusual number of children begging.

Children, but not adults, and the beach itself was curiously empty. The tide was out; in fact, it was well out, being a neap tide. Out at the edge of the water, the sun shone on wet sand, because the water had retreated all the way past the edge of the piers above them. At high noon, the throngs on the piers made the heavy wooden boards creak and groan, and the vendors' cries could clearly be heard in the Undercity.

He was a hundred paces from the Browns' temple.

Aranthur checked the priming on both of his puffers. He put them in his belt, at his back, and then he walked back through the child-beggars to the corpse of the woman he'd killed himself.

Aranthur went to the door of the little driftwood temple, carrying her corpse, and hoped that he was ready when the door opened to his knocking.

The man holding the door open wore the robe of a priest of Aploun, but the face was not familiar, and Aranthur almost gave everything away by smiling. Instead, he held up his pitiful burden.

"I need your help," he said in Armean.

"Go away," the man said. "We do not take corpses here..."

He was already closing the door when he realised something was wrong; perhaps he recognised Aranthur.

He raised a puffer and pulled the trigger bar at point-blank range. His big bullet smacked wetly into the corpse Aranthur was carrying.

Aranthur dropped the poor bone plague victim's body and went for him.

The false priest back-pedalled but he lacked the room to evade and Aranthur drew as he went forward. He fumbled the yataghan and then it settled into his hand as if it was part of him, and he threw a single cut. The man missed his parry with the barrel of his expended puffer and he fell, blood pouring out between his fingers where Aranthur's precise slash had cut across his eyes and the bridge of his nose.

Aranthur put his Masran-made buckler on his left hand and raised power.

His shields tumbled out and grew like a rose tree.

They emerged from the shadows—first one Scarlet and then a second. The whole back of the temple was full of men; a dozen or more.

Aranthur Timos. The mellifluous voices were oddly inharmonic. *We command you to come with us.*

Somewhere at the back, a window smashed. Aranthur drew himself up. For the first time in what seemed like months, he felt... empowered.

It seemed ridiculous, but in combat he knew who he was. Here, at the edge of violence, he felt fear, but no doubt. He wasn't pretending anything.

He cast his *enhancement.*

He raised the tip of his yataghan.

"If you open to me," he said, "I can release you."

The two Exalted responded by igniting their shining swords.

Aranthur raised his arms in invocation.

"I have one of your sisters prisoner in Megara," he said. "You should consider what that means."

The men at the back of the room were suddenly engaged. There was a puffer shot, and the sound of sword on sword, and Kallotronis' voice shouted "At them!"

Dead Eye, the Arnaut witch, tossed smoke into the back of the room; there was a fusillade of puffer shots.

One of the two Exalted hesitated, but the other came for Aranthur, swords swinging in the same simple attack sequence they all favoured.

Aranthur took the first slash on his buckler and entered, a full stride forward before the second sword could find him. His armoured hands grasped the Exalted's arms, and he cast. This time he *unbound* in one word and then *bound* the poor souls in the second word, and he passed under the arm he'd raised and tossed the thing to the side.

He turned to face the second Exalted.

It raised its swords.

We can offer you all the kingdoms of this earth, it said.

Aranthur raised his buckler. "No," he said. "You can't."

The first Exalted raised itself from the floor and its swords leapt back into life.

The Master wants you, the second Exalted said. *Where is the Bright Sword?*

"Tell your Master I am coming for him," Aranthur said. It was as if he'd dreamt these words; as if some god put them in his mouth. "And the Bright Sword is not for him."

The first Exalted joined the second.

"Surrender," Aranthur said.

The second Exalted glanced at its brother, or sister, and suddenly flinched.

"*No!*" it screamed. "*We have your friends!*"

Aranthur turned his head. Two Attians cowered against the room partition by the fireplace; one had a puffer, the other a long scimitar. The puffer was pointed at Alla's head. The scimitar was against the young priest of Aploun's throat.

Aranthur froze and dropped his yataghan. It rang on the floor, even over the sounds of fighting from the back room.

Then he put his right hand behind his back, and gave a mental command.

The two shining swords cut like shears, and the second Exalted went out like an extinguished torch.

Aranthur drew a puffer from his belt, aimed, and pulled the trigger in a single tempo.

The man holding Alla was in shock as one of the Exalted killed the other, and Aranthur's bullet caught him in the neck.

Aranthur drew his second puffer and aimed it at the man holding the priest.

"Let him go," he said.

The man stood, indecisive, so Vilna killed him, a single stab in the back between the shoulder blades. His victim slid from his long-bladed dagger and lay, face down.

The priest let out a long breath, as if all his fears had been held in his lungs.

Alla sat, quite suddenly.

Aranthur crossed his arms and the first Exalted, now a creature of his will, crossed its arms too, the swords burning like the wrath of the gods of light.

Kallotronis cut through a man's guard, his heavy muscle more than the man's untrained parry could handle. His sword went deep in the man's skull and he fell.

The Exalted stood there, its swords still alight.

"You just...converted it?" Kallotronis asked.

"Yes," Aranthur said.

"Remind me not to piss you off," Kallotronis said.

"Stay," Aranthur said to the Exalted, as if it was a dangerous dog, as he went past it into the inner room.

All of the temple's clients were there. The pregnant woman, the bone plague victims—all dead, their throats cut by weapons that left burns. The other four Browns were dead as well; each of them had died protecting, or failing to protect, their clients. A tall woman lay across a bone plague victim; a man with bright red Byzas hair spilling out of his frayed Brown robe lay across a dead woman whose posture suggested that she had suffered from the Darkness.

"You killed them all," Aranthur said in a conversational tone.

I was so ordered.

"Who ordered it?" Aranthur asked.

The Servant.

Aranthur had never been so angry.

Kallotronis put a hand on his arm. "We need..."

"Surprise," Aranthur said grimly. "That's all we need."

Kallotronis shook him. "You may be the most dangerous magos in all thousand hells," he said. "But trust me, *baas.* I've been in a few fights. We're not taking down the Pure in Atti with seven guns."

Aranthur fought back his rage. It was literally choking him; he couldn't think, couldn't feel. All he could really hear was Alla saying, "I want to save something."

"I couldn't even save you," he said.

He thought of Inoques. Unlike Iralia, he knew how vulnerable she was. He knew how it was done. And so would the Servant.

But that part of him that he thought of as the distant judge was still working. It seemed to pierce the rage, and ride above it.

"You still have those ancient sling balls I gave you?" he asked Kallotronis.

"Two left," Kallotronis said.

Aranthur nodded.

He went back to the two Browns. Alla was holding Aplos' head in her lap. He was weeping. She was blank-eyed.

She focused on Aranthur. "So, you brought us this." She stated it flatly; not in accusation. Just a fact.

"Yes," Aranthur agreed. "I am sorry."

She looked away. "I'd like to say I don't blame you," she said. "But I do. Your kind always get my kind killed."

"You wanted to save something," Aranthur said. "And we will. I promise."

"By killing?" she said. "Look around you, *Lightbringer*. Tell me who you saved."

"We must fight the Pure."

She shrugged. "Must we?"

He looked away, and then back at her.

"I need to know," he said cautiously. "Did you learn anything about Daud in-Salud?"

She stroked Aplos' hair.

"We need to go," Kallotronis said.

Vilna was reloading his puffers.

Chimeg was going through purses while two of Kallotronis' men collected rings and jewellery from the fallen.

"Why should I help you?" she asked.

"If I leave my dagger on a table, and you use it to commit a murder, am I guilty of the murder?" Aranthur asked. "I did not kill these people, or take you hostage."

"There is a well-known Attian Lightbringer," she said. "Ahbar Jakal."

"I know of him," he said.

"Your Daud was the son of his steward, the master of his household." She glanced at him. "He was a *thuryx* addict. Jakal saved him." She shrugged. "You claim that you are trying to save something, to fight for what is right. But you are facing Jakal, and he is the very embodiment of Light."

Aranthur got to his feet.

"Then the embodiment of Light sent two Exalteds and a mob of bravos to kill your friends." He beckoned with one hand. "Exalted."

Lord.

Aranthur writhed at the title. "Exalted, who is the Disciple for Atti?"

Ahbar Jakal, it said.

She looked at him.

"Is Kurvenos alive or dead?" Aranthur asked.

Neither, the Exalted said.

"Where to, *Bahadur*?" Vilna asked. He was reloading Aranthur's long-barrelled puffer.

"Time to pay our customs duties," Aranthur said, and he tamped down the anger until it could serve him.

"Is Maryam here?" Aranthur asked, when he made it to the customs house desk.

There was a bloodstain under the fine old blue arch, and the man behind the desk had dark smudges under his eyes as if he'd been punched, and he had a dirty linen wrap, probably someone's turban, wrapped around his right leg. Aranthur only noticed this last detail because he was holding it out stiffly at an angle. The man had two loaded puffers on the desk.

Aranthur was taking no chances; the streets outside were full of furtive people in alleys and there were three dead men outside the customs house. He wore a *guise*; he'd borrowed the Attian features of one of the dead bravos at the Browns' temple.

"I can get her." The man looked too tired to care about anything. "Is it personal?"

"No, captain," Aranthur said, bowing obsequiously. "A matter of identification—the lady told me to return..."

The man rose slowly, looked Aranthur over and gave him a sharp nod.

"I'll see if she's available, then," he said.

He wasn't too tired to scoop up the two silver coins Aranthur had put on the corner of the table.

A moment later, the officer appeared.

"How may I help you?" Myr Maryam asked. She still wore her fine chain maille and now had a long *tulwar* under her arm. She had a bandage around her left forearm and her hair was matted as if she'd just had a helmet on. "Be quick, *Effendi.*"

Aranthur bowed. "May I speak to you in private?" he asked quietly.

"I have no time and I do not take bribes," she said.

"Last time I was here, Ismail claimed that my wife was a spy. You were in trouble because you let me go. Now, can we speak in private?"

She paused and met his eye. "Ah," she said. "This way, syr."

She led him to an empty office, and he dropped his *guise*.

"*Baraka*," she said, and made the sign of the horns.

"I need Suleiman and Ismail," Aranthur said.

"Suleiman is dead, and Ismail..." She leant on the door and he could see how tired she was in the slump of her shoulders. "What in all the hells is happening?" she asked. "I assume you are true. Ismail trusted you. But Suleiman was killed..."

"We were attacked as soon as we reached the upper town," Aranthur said. "My wife's ship was attacked and burnt in the harbour."

"I'd like to be shocked. But a mob attacked this customs house about three hours ago. I assume that Ismail's enemies..." She paused. "What does it matter? We're talking about the Pure, are we not? They are attacking the government. And they seem to know everything."

"They have some very highly placed traitors," Aranthur said.

"They attacked the Sultan Bey," she said, making the royal sign reverently. "Again!" Aranthur tugged his beard in frustration. "Someone foiled them—but it was like a charlatan's magik show at the palace. Fire and light everywhere. We could see it from here. In fact, we were out in the Blue Gate watching when the mob hit us."

"I need Ismail," Aranthur said with gentle urgency. "I know who the traitor is. I think we can stop this."

She nodded. "I will fetch him."

She returned in what might have been good time, except that Aranthur couldn't stop fretting—Inoques, Kurvenos, the widening rift.

"You again?" Ismail managed a smile. His hand was badly bandaged and so was his left shoulder, and there was drying blood all over him. "Speak quickly, my friend. I expect to be attacked again."

"Syr Jakal is your traitor," Aranthur said.

Ismail froze.

"I can prove it," Aranthur said.

Maryam shook her head. "It's not possible," she said.

Ismail's reaction was altogether different.

"I feared as much," he admitted. "What is your proof?"

"I captured an Exalted, who confirmed it," he said. "And the man I killed yesterday, who attacked me, was the son of Jakal's steward."

"Daud? The addict?" Ismail asked. "We know him." He shook his head. "A notorious man, and not a reliable witness."

"Dead, nonetheless," Aranthur said. "He told me…Never mind. But the Exalted…"

Ismail ran his fingers through his beard. They caught on something that he pulled free with a grimace of disgust.

"I need more firepower and the cloak of the rule of law," Aranthur said.

"I have no soldiers and I cannot pretend that Atti is governed by the rule of law tonight," Ismail said. "The City Yaniceri will not move from their barracks without an order from the Kaptan Bey, and he is missing. What do you propose?"

"I am going to take Jakal at his house. I know where it is." He paused, gauging his potential ally. "I know where the Kaptan Bey is, too. He is alive, and recovering in safety."

Ismail looked at Maryam.

"I admit," he said, "I find the idea of doing something more appealing than waiting here to die." He looked back at Aranthur. "You have the Kaptan Bey?"

"The gods dropped him into my hands," he said.

Ismail made a face and spread his hands. "I should distrust you. But hells, why not? Why not believe that the Kaptan Bey is alive?"

"Gather anyone you trust," Aranthur said. "Meet me at the Pantheon in half an hour."

Ten minutes later, he walked into a nearly empty temple and left a healthy offering with the master priest, a different man from the evening before. Then he walked boldly to the shrine of Potnia, glancing once at a dozen worshippers in a cloud of incense under the dome, and then he was under the altar rail. He reached out, and his fingers closed on the scabbard. In a moment, he held her.

I returned for you.

Hah! she said. *My paladins rarely come back for me once they are free.* She burned hot in his hand. *There is one of those multi-souled abominations outside.*

"It's mine," he said aloud.

What? What are we doing?

Can you find Inoques? he asked. *As she has the* baraka *of an artifact?*

The sword's warmth seemed to chill. *Yes, of course I can find her. There. She is in the garden of the Sultan Bey's palace. Hiding. She now knows you are here. Now what are we doing?*

"Please ask her to meet me at the home of Jakal Lightbringer," he said.

It is done, she said. *Jakal? You are taking me into the lion's den*, the sword added.

"You aren't coming. You're going for a boat ride." He handed the sword to Chimeg. "I'll see you on the other side," he said. "If I don't return, give this to Dahlia."

Chimeg's eyes narrowed. "Send one of the others," she said. "You need me for the killing."

Aranthur smiled. "Yes," he said. "But Nata is safe, and now you will be safe with him. If I fall, avenge me."

Chimeg put her right hand to her forehead.

"Aye, *Bahadur*," she said, and kissed him on both cheeks, very formally.

Aranthur had a moment to savour the odd feeling of another warrior's absolute faith. What had he done to deserve Chimeg's promise to avenge him? And yet...

He strode away into the incense before he could doubt his decision to go after Jakal without the sword. However he thought about it, he couldn't see a way to get the sword near the fallen Lightbringer without alerting him, knowing that the Pure agents could track the sword.

Outside the ancient portico stood Kallotronis and his six, and Vilna with three more Nomadi, and now they were joined by almost a dozen Attians: Maryam in a peaked helmet with a veil of maille that hid her face, and Ismail in a fine Voltein burgonet, and nine more men and women in armour, most with firearms.

Aranthur checked the priming on his *carabin* and glanced at the silent figure of his Exalted.

"We're still pretty thin on the ground," Kallotronis said.

Aranthur was looking at Ismail. "I don't think we have any choice," he said.

Kallotronis shrugged. "Right, then," he said.

It was a long, grim walk into the darkened city. There were oil lamps lit in some homes, but most were dark, as the inhabitants feared that showing a light might invite disaster. They passed several small squares where there had been fighting, and they passed the West Barracks where one of the elite Yaniceri regiments lived; there were guards at the gates and the walls were manned.

They climbed higher and higher on the west slope of the city, until

Aranthur could clearly see the Temple of Light in Megara across the strait. He could see a rain squall out over the sea to the south, the last tail of the bad weather from the north, and the sun was setting in the west, behind Megara, dyeing the city's red-tile roofs even redder as it sank in the sky.

At Ismail's request, they went off to the south, into the warren of buildings pinned to the side of the cliff that defined the central rib of the city. They began to climb a long set of stairs—not the same ones Aranthur had climbed the day before, either.

"No one should be watching these," Ismail panted. "Too steep and too ill-repaired."

The steps were in deplorable condition—broken treads or, worse, treads worn perfectly smooth from hundreds of years of traffic, so that a boot sole could slip and drop a person to their death.

The column crept up the cliff.

"Jakal is close to the palace?" Aranthur asked.

"One of his gardens shares a wall with the Seraglio," Maryam said. "The Sultan said there is no man he would trust closer to his family."

Aranthur looked up. The sultan's palace was gilded orange and gold above him; one of the prayer towers had a golden dome which burned as if it had been kindled. The sun was gone. The ball of fire had vanished between the towers of the Temple of Light, and the Red Moon was just coming up in the west, turning the sky a livid purple.

Aranthur was ferociously hungry, but the steps were empty of pedlars, or street sellers of any kind, and when they finally crossed over the edge of the ancient acropolis wall, his stomach hurt as if he'd been punched. He had to stop for a moment as the others pushed past.

"I need food," he said.

Maryam made a face and handed him an enormous orange, which he ate like a barbarian, the sticky juice running down his face; he washed the stickiness away in a little fountain set into the wall.

"Why don't you carry food, if you are hungry all the time?" she said.

Inside the ancient acropolis walls, the top of the ridge was densely occupied—the very opposite of Megara, where the best neighbourhoods were along the water and the old aqueducts. In Ulama, the palace and all the richest houses were atop the ridge.

"This way," Ismail said.

The silent Exalted nodded.

They went along an alley bordered on both sides by walls three times the height of a tall man, and then, at an intersection, turned sharply south. The walls around them were so high that there were no landmarks.

"What a deathtrap," Kallotronis said softly.

Above them stood one of the Sultan Bey's prayer towers, this one with a copper roof.

The captive Exalted pointed at another alley, and they all turned east again. The wind was rising, and made an odd, mournful sound in the alley. Aranthur poured power into his subjugation of the captive, but it seemed willing enough, the three souls caught within it co-operating at least for the present.

Ismail's people stopped at the base of a new wall, taller than the rest, that crossed the alley at an oblique angle, sending it off to the east and south. They began to assemble a broad-based ladder.

"He's a very powerful mage," Ismail said quietly. "He will have many followers. Servants, slaves, perhaps even Yaniceri and other soldiers."

Aranthur nodded. He was beginning to cast. The ability to hold entire sequences of *occultae* and *volteie* in his head was the cornerstone of a whole new meta-strategy of casting, and he cast as calmly as he could manage, coding his casts with simple physical sequences from Master Sparthos' training forms.

Then the ladder was complete.

"I'm first," Aranthur said.

"Perfect," Ismail said.

Kallotronis moved to take the second place, and Vilna stopped him.

"Me," Vilna said.

Kallotronis made a face as if he'd protest, and then he gave a bow.

"Hold the ladder," he told his two biggest; Brute Force took one side and Ignorance took the other. Dead Eye built smoke between his hands, and Cut Face twirled his mustachios and checked the priming in his puffers and muttered about the two giants getting the safe job.

"Anyone know what the top of the wall is like?" Vilna asked.

"Flat. No glass," Ismail said.

"Run along the wall," Vilna said. "Drop down in different places. Don't land in a heap, don't become a target."

Kallotronis nodded.

"Not my first palace," Vilna said with the flash of a smile.

"Ready?" Aranthur said.

He looked back. The two big men were holding the base of the ladder and there was a line waiting to go up.

Aranthur felt for the thread that would launch his shields, nodded, and started up the ladder.

This is probably the stupidest thing I've ever done.

But if I'm right…

One rung.

If Jakal has one of the Six then he knows that the Bright Sword is headed back across the strait. And thus, that he's safe.

Second rung.

If Jakal is the traitor. If he has one of the Six.

Third rung.

If anything is as I think it is…

Fourth rung.

Or they are waiting for us, just the other side of this wall; I'll jump down, turn my ankle, and land to a fusillade of puissance.

Fifth rung.

But what else could we do?

Sixth rung.

Leave Kurvenos in their hands and run?

Seventh rung.

Let Atti fall?

Eighth rung.

Abandon Inoques?

Ninth rung. He could feel the weight of the other men and women on the ladder; looking down, he could see Maryam's spiked helmet starting up, her left foot still on the ground.

Tenth rung. He forced his weary legs up, felt the ladder bend slightly under the weight of so many.

Eleventh rung.

Twelfth.

He got a leg up on the wall. Despite making a brilliant target, he clung to the element of surprise.

If they know we're here, my launching my shields will only delay the inevitable by a few seconds… whereas…

One foot over the wall.

Whereas if we make it into the garden undetected…

He wriggled, even as he felt Vilna coming onto the top of the wall. He let himself go down to the full extent of his arms, his back to any possible adversary, silhouetted against the whitewashed stone wall. Above him, Vilna passed like a shadow, running without apparent effort along the hand's-breadth wide wall.

He let go.

As he'd hoped, the ground inside the wall was slightly higher than outside. He fell on the garden lawn and rolled, taking some of the weight of the drop off his knees and ankles; his only injury was the abrasion of his right knee against the base of the wall. He rose, his body flooded with pain and fear; got a knee under him…

Nothing.

Vilna landed ten paces to his left. Aranthur raised his *carabin* and started forward and Kallotronis landed to his right, almost at the corner of the wall.

Aranthur started forward. *If they have a* puissant *alarm system… dogs… anyone with magesight watching…*

He was desperate to put up his own magesight, but he knew it would give him away. He moved to a tree—a lemon tree, fragrant even in the dark. Beyond was an orange tree in blossom.

Aranthur moved. Off to his right, he saw Kallotronis move into the little orchard, his *jezzail* moving back and forth.

He went forward into the darkness.

There is no one here, he thought, and even as he did a dog barked, quite close.

A shout in Armean: "Thieves!"

A movement on the palace balcony. A man stood, and Kallotronis shot him. A flat cough and a stab of flame in the near darkness, and the man was gone. A dozen armed men spilled into the orchard from the ground floor, all fumbling for weapons.

Vilna shot the lead two with his horse pistols—left hand, right hand, as if in target practice. The rest of them froze, unsure where the shots had come from, and jammed into a tight group. Aranthur shot into the mass of people and another fell. The night was full of screams—the wounded, and a woman inside, and something else.

He released the thread that held his shields and they erupted as if he'd been restraining them. With them, linked by his complex preparations, his magesight went up, revealing the night in different colours.

"Ware!" he called. "*Baraka!*"

A magos appeared on the balcony and unleashed a stream of *puissance* that turned two fruit trees to lethal splinters and dropped Kallotronis.

Aranthur reached out with his own power and brought his captive Exalted over the wall under his will, before directing it at the knot of soldiers taking cover by the ground floor door.

The sorcerer on the exedra discovered him and red balefire flew.

Aranthur used his *transference* to destroy the architectural supports of the balcony. The attacks took him precious seconds, but proved worth it: the enemy sorcerer above him had not bothered to create defences for the wooden beams.

The left side gave before the right, and the whole balcony first sagged and then crashed down. The enemy sorcerer was thrown clear; he rolled once, got to his knees and shook his head.

Vilna stepped up behind him, rested the barrel of a puffer against the nape of the man's neck, and blew his brains out.

Aranthur raised a hand. "You…"

"Never leave a live snake behind you," Vilna said.

Ten paces away, the tame Exalted ripped through the bravos the way a young farmhand scythes wheat on a dry, sunny day late in the harvest, both white swords sweeping in arcs which were almost too fast to follow.

Aranthur drew a puffer from his belt, allowed his *enhancement* to take effect and went through the ground floor door.

An *occulta* slammed into his shields with such energy that he felt the hair stand on the nape of his neck, felt the air inside the shields grow warm. Two tendrils of red lightning punched straight through his shields…

His shields! Inoques' shields!

One burned along his torso, and the other passed him harmlessly.

The range was point-blank. Aranthur's shields were already fighting the other mage's shields, gold against purple-red.

In the physical world, he pushed his puffer through his adversary's shields and pulled the trigger bar.

It misfired.

Aranthur dropped it and went for his yataghan. A fork of red lightning blew through his defence and he was hit. His body arched in a spasm and the weapon dropped from his fingers.

The ring that Benvenutu had given him burned with a blue fire on his finger.

He fell, which was as well, because a plane of fire passed over his head rather than cutting him in half.

The woman bore down, casting with almost unbelievable rapidity. Aranthur could see the glyphs as she cast.

Each blow met a sapphire counter.

I am a servant of the Secret Fire, she had said.

Only one of her bolts came through.

The pain was sharp and immense. Too much for him to cast over, and his right arm wasn't working at all.

He got his left hand up under his *fustinella*. His new shield held, or at least did not fall in shreds, and he had enough control to rotate the old shields so that the damaged patches rolled away to the rear, and his adversary's next volley was mostly deflected. He tried to reach the shreds of his preconstructed *assalti* and the pain was more than his concentration could handle.

He found the small puffer he now carried all the time. He drew it across his body, left-handed, shoved it into her abdomen and thumbed the hammer back, pulled the trigger, and saw the spark, almost at a distance. He felt the flint cut along the stele of the frizzen, and had time to see the pan catch fire…

The little weapon kicked in his hand.

His adversary snapped back, hit low in the chest. Aranthur stayed on her; a small calibre ball in the ribs could be nothing but a nuisance. He rolled, still on the floor, and got his left hand on the ivory hilt of his yataghan where he'd dropped it; rolled over his dead right arm and cut.

Now their shields were merged. Aranthur could see that he was fighting a dark-haired woman; his own age, smaller, lighter. Her left hand was clutching an amulet; her right hand held a long sabre, and she barely managed to parry his cut.

There was no time for remorse.

He rotated his left hand, almost without thinking, so that his shorter weapon mastered hers, and his superior strength drove his yataghan down into her face.

She screamed.

He killed her anyway, punching the point through her eye socket.

Then he sat with his back to a brick wall. He couldn't move; couldn't even get his feet under him. He'd taken a fair dose of her balefire and now everything hurt, and his right arm hung like a dead animal at his side.

It took a surprising amount of time, perhaps sixty heartbeats, before he realised that Vilna was standing over him, the Exalted at his back.

The dead woman was wearing a beautiful prayer shawl. He pulled it off her corpse and used it to bind his right arm against his body. Vilna tied it off and they went forward, Aranthur repairing his shields with the power he now had in abundance.

They got to the base of the stairs after passing the length of what appeared to be a gardening shed. He had Maryam and Vilna and one of the Souliotes inside; they moved together as if they'd practised this a dozen times. Indeed, they had, at Antioke.

Aranthur looked up the stairs, hoping that the tingling in his right arm was a hopeful sign and not some sort of mortification. But he had control of himself: compartmentalised away his guilt and horror at killing the woman; brushed an ethereal hand across his prepared *occultae.*

Ready to kill more, he thought bitterly.

He caught the flash of *puissance* as someone at the head of the stairs cast a preparation, and he unleashed two of his prepared attacks, one from each hand.

His first blow, a wide pulse of orange fire, ripped a hole in his new opponent's shield. The second passed straight through it and the man dropped, his head hitting the stone top step with a terrible hollow thud.

"Outside!" Vilna called.

There were windows in the ground floor—shuttered windows without glass—but the cacophony of light outside came through the cracks at the edges of the shutters and lit the whole of the workroom, from the potting bench to the sacks of manure.

In Aranthur's magesight, the orchard outside was a pillar of sunlight.

"Aphres," he swore, and ran for the door.

A man came up from under the bench where he had been hiding, but Maryam put a dagger in him before he could make an attack.

"Someone cover the stairs!" Aranthur called.

Then he got back to the entry where he'd been attacked; outside stood a figure of light, and it was pounding his tame Exalted with balefire.

Aranthur arranged his shields as best he could. It had to be Jakal; the pillar of light was almost a Lightbringer signature.

"Jakal!" he called as he stepped through the door.

The light paused in its battering of the wounded Exalted.

"Who are you?" it asked. "Who dares attack me *in my home*?"

Aranthur stepped out on to the charred lawn with a confidence that was almost entirely feigned.

"I am Nemesis," he said; Aploun's line in the opera, when he returns to kill Niobe's children.

Sometimes, words are weapons.

Jakal flinched. "Whose nemesis?"

"Yours! You are a traitor to the order of Lightbringers!" Aranthur said.

Jakal laughed. Almost casually, his left arm pulsed with lightning, and the bound Exalted gave a thin cry and fell to the ground.

"There is no *order of Lightbringers*," Jakal said. "Who are you?"

Aranthur had not expected conversation. His whole body quivered with eagerness to get it over; his fingers bled fire.

"You attacked the Sultan Bey," he said.

"He was a false friend, a corrupt tyrant." Jakal lowered his white shield and stepped through it, a handsome, bearded man in his late fifties. "Lower your shield and show yourself."

"You kidnapped the Kaptan Bey..." Aranthur said.

"I *saved* the Kaptan Bey!" Jakal spat. "The Master wanted him destroyed. I sent him away..."

"I found him."

"Then my old friend will surely die, and for nothing."

"You serve the Master," Aranthur spat.

Jakal shrugged. "I serve no one. What I do, I do to preserve and enhance my own power. What else is there, little idealist?"

"Truth. Honour. Faith." Aranthur's hands were shaking.

"Dreams for the weak," Jakal said. "Truth is whatever I tell you to believe. Honour is whatever I ordain it to be. Faith is a cloak for cynicism."

"Where is Kurvenos?"

"Where is the Bright Sword?" Jakal shot back. "The only purpose you ever had in my plan was to bring me the Bright Sword so that it could be tamed."

Aranthur gathered a little ease from the knowledge that in this, at least, he had guessed correctly.

"Far away, and safe," he said.

"By the hells, you waste my time. Are you one of Kurvenos' whelps? A barefoot disciple from the hills, perhaps?" Jakal smiled, and the smile wasn't sinister; it appeared good-natured, the kind of smile a man might give a clever child. "Would you like to see him, yokel?"

He gave a rich laugh and stepped back, igniting his shields again.

From his right there came a pillar of red fire.

"Speak to him, Kurvenos!" Jakal said.

A lash of fire fell on Aranthur's shields, cutting a dozen jagged holes where it fell; the strongest blow he had ever endured, the very lash of a god.

Aranthur staggered, and went down on one knee.

Jakal laughed his good-natured laugh.

"Oh, this is rich," he said in Byzas. "Servant, lower your shield."

The red fire subsided. In its place stood a tall figure.

Aranthur was looking at Djinar. It was Djinar's body; Aranthur had faced the man often enough on the fencing floor to know.

But even in a dark garden, lit only by the burning balcony, Aranthur could see Kurvenos, too, in the set of the shoulders, and in the darkness behind the eyes. He could feel the Lightbringer's *aura*, blackened with power and still stronger than his captor's spirit.

Djinar's mouth moved, and the fractured voice said, "You. Aranthur."

Aranthur's disembodied judge looked dispassionately on his enemy of a dozen fencing matches.

This Exalted was not made by the Master, he thought. This was no construct of dead parchment with muscles and tendons of wire and cogs.

This was one man bound to the form of another.

"Kurvenos," he said.

He hadn't meant to give his enemy the satisfaction of such a weakness. But the name was pulled from him.

Djinar's head turned.

"Jakal," Aranthur said. "He was your *friend*."

"There are no friends," Jakal said. "Only allies of convenience. When the Dark Forge rose in the sky, the world changed. Tirase is long dead, and he was a fool. Do you know what the truly wise do, given power?"

Aranthur blinked, trying to read Kurvenos, trying to imagine any scenario in which he escaped. To his left, Kallotronis lay full length, his body riddled with splinters; Ismail lay near him, his right arm severed from his body, bled out.

And at his back, Maryam and Vilna, still alive. He was responsible for saving them, if they could be saved.

"Tell me," Aranthur said.

"The wise abandon their games of altruism," Jakal said, "to make themselves gods and become immortal. There is *nothing else.* There is immortality and then there are puppets of meat dancing to the will of the gods. The immortal are to the mortal as an animal is to a blade of grass." He glanced at Kurvenos. "Tirase had that power in his hand, and he threw it away. Not just for himself, but for *all of us.*"

Aranthur found that fear was gaining the upper hand over his ability to think. He opened his mouth to speak and nothing came out. But his distant judge had noted something. A family resemblance.

Use all your weapons.

"So there is nothing," Aranthur said, his voice high with fear.

He took a breath and started again, allowing his mind to summon the horror of the Black Bastion, the use of *sihr.* His voice became calm, his diction cruel.

"So there is nothing but power and greed for existence? No ties hold you, Jakal?"

"None." His smile was imperturbable. "Now you understand?"

Aranthur dropped his shields so that his enemy could see the prayer shawl wrapped around his right arm.

"So you care nothing that I killed your daughter," he said.

Jakal's smile collapsed.

Aranthur bore down, the way a swordsman does when his opponent's wrist is too weak. He managed a breath, and then another; for no particular reason, he thought of Master Sparthos at the Inn of Fosse, and his anger at his own failure. He raised his head.

"I think you are a great fool," he said.

"You killed my child?" asked Jakal.

"I think…" Aranthur gathered his reserves of will. "I think that your seeking immortality is much like a miser hoarding gold coins. *Then what?*" He shrugged. "In the end, someone bigger will crush you. Or perhaps your idea of happiness is an eternity of bloody games with your peers?" he asked. "It sounds like a barn dance in Souli. And now, this moment, you are feeling the pointlessness of that existence. She is dead, Jakal, and your life has no further meaning."

He turned to face Djinar. "Walk away," he said. "And I will not destroy you."

Djinar's mouth broke into a rictus smile.

"You promise?" it teased.

"Yes," Aranthur said.

The Exalted's shield flashed into being like the snap of a bowstring, but Jakal stood for a moment longer.

"I will bind you to my will for all eternity. I will degrade your spirit. I will use you until existence is hell."

His shields leapt into white fire.

So did Aranthur's.

Jakal spoke one syllable, and Djinar's balefire lashed like a nine-tailed whip, scoring across Aranthur's golden shields and leaving black lines of ruin.

Aranthur unleashed everything he had left, all the prepared attacks—five, each stacked to maximise the effect of the one behind it. He didn't target Djinar, but Jakal. He'd used the whole conversation to perfect them, and they were *right there.*

The near-simultaneity of the attacks surprised the former Lightbringer. The light of his shield dimmed, and charred, and the fourth effect, a shaped transference using the principles Aranthur had learnt from using explosives in the siege at Antioke, seemed to manifest. A pulse of deep violet light, a thud like distant thunder, and the white tower of *puissance* crackled away like a broken bottle.

The last effect was a pure line of white fire—the simplest attack. It went straight through, scoring the Disciple from head to toe so that he screamed.

A powerful blow. But not a finishing blow. Even as Aranthur passed forward, yataghan in his left hand, Jakal rolled to his feet.

"Finish him!" he roared.

Djinar's lash of scarlet went back...

And fell.

Aranthur took it on his buckler. That much he could manage with his left hand—the little shield made for him in Masr with the Glyph of Warding.

Djinar struck a second time, and the glyph held.

Jakal struck, and the sapphire flashes of the ring baffled his assault while Aranthur pushed himself to his feet.

A fourth set of shields burst into reality. A cloaked figure ignited its purple-black shields, a dense and terrifying display of power—meshed disks of dark crystal that emerged like jet-black scale armour, growing and growing until the presence was too great for the senses to accept and the mind darted away.

The red lash fell on the black scales, and there was an explosion like a mine of black powder going off under the Black Bastion at Antioke. Aranthur fell. Even though he didn't lose consciousness, the next few heartbeats could not fix in his senses, as if they happened in the *Aulos* or in another reality.

Kurvenos faced Inoques, bearing a jagged sword of black iron—the same black that Jakal wielded.

"No!" Aranthur roared. But he was an ant, or a mite compared to them.

And yet Jakal heard.

"Do not destroy him!" Aranthur begged the dark figure.

Inoques was armoured in close-fitting scales, but her head had taken on a feline cast, or perhaps the shape of a snake's head. But the bonds of her many enchantments burned like white fire on the surface, or even above the surface of her scales. Aranthur had only seen her revealed once before, in the prisons under the citadel of Antioke. Now he couldn't look away.

"It's Kurvenos!" he called.

But his voice sounded feeble, and anyway, he knew she had no great love for Kurvenos.

Her cat-like head turned, the sigils like threads of pearls over her face, and her hands wove an eldritch charge.

And then the titan Kurvenos seemed to fall to pieces, trickling away like sand from an hourglass—or perhaps it was Inoques whose scales fell away like autumn leaves in a black forest.

In their place, the smooth pillars of two impenetrable shields, standing like the trunks of two ancient trees.

And into that forest, a wind, and born on that wind, a scent of the sea, and of pines on a distant shore.

And a voice, a woman calling from that distant shore.

"*Just because it must all be done again*," she called, "*did you imagine we would fail in our our task?*"

And a shrill steel scream, the sound of two blades as their sharpened edges ripped, each down the other, at the bind.

Aranthur had lost several seconds; then he was on one knee, groggy as if from a punch in a barn-fight.

Djinar-Kurvenos and Inoques were locked in a *stasis* of *puissance*, their shields merged, apparently frozen.

Jakal raised a single red *aspis*.

Aranthur did the same; his once-magnificent shields were in tatters of green and gold light but he didn't abandon them, assuming that they might still absorb something. But he put the glyph between them and went forward. He got the yataghan into his left hand, point down from the buckler, and as Jakal cast Aranthur parried with his shield. His own cast was internal. He put a pain-blocker on the damage Jakal's strike had inflicted, stopped the bleeding in his right arm.

He felt the difference immediately.

Jakal was shouting. Aranthur ignored him, pushing forward another step, his buckler burning with his will—flashing violet and blue and red, as if it was creating energy instead of turning it.

Jakal, shaken, could not damage it.

He summoned *sihr*. Aranthur felt it, and could do nothing but endure, and he turned his right side to face his enemy.

He was hit three times, and he fell. His metal buckler was damaged. His right arm took another burn, and so did his right leg, and the pain and shock made him flop involuntarily on the ground, so that he ended up face up, eyes open to the stars above.

He didn't see the moment when Kallotronis, lashed with splinters, raised an unfired puffer and shot Jakal. The mercenary was behind the former Lightbringer and the man's shining *aspis* had no way to reach the threat, so the pistol ball took the sorcerer in the abdomen.

He doubled. His *aspis* flickered.

Both Maryam and Vilna shot him.

Aranthur was functioning again by then—pain-blockers up, a new *aspis* cast, his right leg a web of light.

He got to his feet by a cast of *transference.*

He looked at Inoques, but a haze of darkness like a black fog covered her and Djinar-Kurvenos.

"Jakal," he said.

Even with three lead balls in him, the sorcerer was still lethal. He raised a hand and a bolt of violet exploded Maryam's amulet. Her armour became shrapnel forced into her chest and throat, and she fell.

Aranthur was a pace away; he cast a second *aspis* to make sure he would survive for long enough to cut with his mundane sword.

Jakal turned and, with a flick of his wrist, blew a hole in the garden wall followed by an attack on Aranthur's will—the sort of direct engagement that Aranthur had only heard discussed: will to will at point-blank range. In his maelstrom of emotional attacks, Aranthur saw the rows of dead Dhadhi he'd killed in the Black Bastion; saw the triumph of the Dark Forge; the death of the Emperor; Iralia sold into slavery; Inoques as the Master's mightiest Exalted; Dahlia dead on a battlefield, her body desiccated from an unparried curse; Sasan dangling from a gallows, his feet bare and dirty, and Kati next to him, her face a mask of despair; Myr Tribane naked in chains of black iron; the sword broken in a forge fire surrounded by laughing Old Ones.

Aranthur was no longer a boy from Soulis.

He endured, and struck back with a single image: the scream of a young woman as his yataghan drove through her eye.

And Jakal broke, and fled. He went like smoke, passing through the hole in the wall.

Aranthur felt unclean, both from the attack and from his own response to it.

If you elect to spend the rest of your life teetering on the edge of the abyss, then you are a Lightbringer.

He wanted to vomit, and there wasn't much of him that was functioning well. Vilna was kneeling by Kallotronis. The combat had been deadly; there were bodies everywhere, and the black cloud still covered Inoques and her foe.

Aranthur made himself take the steps to Kallotronis—made himself cast the *occultae* that would save the Souliote. The casting steadied him; the importance of saving a friend broke through the sense of violation, and his sense of self began to return.

Vilna pointed his sabre at the hole in the wall.

"That's the Sultan Bey's garden," he said.

"Aploun!" Aranthur spat.

"We have to follow him." Vilna shrugged, as if the calculation was simple, which it was.

"Load my puffers," Aranthur asked, handing over the small one he always carried.

Kallotronis looked like a ghoul, with skin flayed from his face and something very wrong with his left eye.

"Fuck," he said.

But he got to his feet. Then he took a loaded puffer, a long silver one, from the sash of one of his people, who lay dead by his side.

"I'm going to have trouble recruiting after this," he said. He looked at the priming of one of his own puffers.

"You shot Jakal…"

"With a two-thousand-year-old sling bullet," Kallotronis croaked.

Aranthur spent power like water on their wounds, crisscrossing his own and Kallotronis' with lines of white fire to hold the flesh together. And then, throwing any shred of caution to the abyss, he cast a second enhancement on himself, cast one on Vilna and another on Kallotronis. The effort threatened to exhaust him.

He was beyond caring.

"Let's get him," he said.

The three, enhanced, went through the jagged hole in the garden wall and into the Sultan's Seraglio.

The new garden was lit by paper lamps, some with oil, some with magelight, in all the colours of the rainbow. A young woman lay dead at the edge of a shining pool and her black blood stained the coloured water in the light of the lamps.

They ran past her like an armoured breeze.

They didn't have to search. Jakal had left a trail of bodies, and he clearly knew the Seraglio well. They went from the garden into a courtyard entirely tiled in magnificent azure porcelain, lit by shining blue lamps of magelight. A pair of palace guards, Voynuks in bronze armour, lay dead, blackened with the burns of sorcery, their swords and axes cut by the cruel sorcery of Jakal's dark sword.

They followed a trail of blood and corpses through a set of magnificent pointed arches.

To the right, where they could hear screams.

They found Jakal in a long, tiled corridor with niches that displayed almost unimaginable treasures. Aranthur ignored them, flowing down the corridor like the Nemesis he'd named himself.

Ahead, in the beautiful pink and blue magelight of the richest palace in the world, was a scene from hell.

The Voynuks had fought to the last man; nine of them lay, a tribute to their loyalty. The last, their captain, had baffled the traitor Lightbringer with a cloak and struck with a curved sword, but as they arrived he ran out of room to swing his cloak or retreat, and the blue-black sword destroyed him, cutting down through his golden armour, and his heroism.

At the end of the corridor stood the door to the Sultan's apartment, open, and between Jakal and the apartment were women—a corridor full of women. They were dying, but they were refusing to let the traitor pass. The Sultan's mother, his sisters, his *hareem*. They fought with *puissance* and with daggers and with their nails and teeth and with the mere weight of their bodies, and Jakal could not overcome them. His motions had slowed to almost human, his sword of dark might clogged with the deaths of so many—or perhaps the horrible irony of murdering young women on the night his daughter died slowed him—and his screams were as loud as theirs.

Finally, he had to turn to face Aranthur or be cut down from behind.

"Even now, you could surrender," Aranthur said.

"*He will not let me go!*" Jakal's face locked in horror, and Aranthur thought he knew what that meant.

He had considered this moment many times. Waking, at the edge of sleep; in the practice hall. Ever since he crossed blades with his first Scarlet.

Considered how to fight one of the magic blades, when he had none.

He raised the yataghan, bringing it into a low guard, point forward, offering it to his opponent's sword of blinding darkness.

Jakal leapt at him, cutting at his sword. Because the magic swords destroyed any weapon they crossed.

Aranthur, even left-handed, had the time to deceive the ancient, evil sword. The yataghan executed a sloppy arc from under to over, and Aranthur's cut severed Jakal's right hand.

The dark sword fell to the ground with a scream and a clang.

As the man's momentum carried him to Aranthur's right, he rolled the yataghan and cut back, his motion hurried by desperation, his left hand nowhere near as well-trained as his right, and the yataghan, instead of cutting into the traitor's neck, buried itself in his skull.

They stood there for what seemed like an *enhanced* eternity, Jakal's eyes locked on his. His left hand was still trying to raise the cursed sword to strike when Vilna shot him. Kallotronis' ball struck the traitor's right shoulder and spun him off. Aranthur's blade remained locked in his skull; the severed hand struck the ground and the cruel sword rang on the tiled floor.

But the worst was the look on Jakal's face as the sword fell away.

"Don't touch it!" Aranthur shouted.

There were two fingers missing from his left hand. He didn't even know when he'd lost them.

There was a young woman draped across another's body, weeping, and the tiled floor was a finger's width deep in blood.

Kallotronis blew the smoke away from the muzzle of his long puffer. He turned his back on the chaos of the corridor, picked up a thousand-year-old jade and gold bowl from its niche, and tucked it inside his *fustinella*.

Aranthur slumped to one knee. He didn't want to lie down in all the blood; that was the only thing that kept him from falling.

"Come, my love," said a cool voice. A light hand on his right shoulder. "You are a ruin," Inoques said.

Aranthur managed to turn and get an arm around her slim figure.

She wriggled away. "You are all over blood," she said. "Gods, what a mess. But you got them."

"Them?" Aranthur asked dully.

Inoques prodded the fallen sword with her foot.

"This thing owned that thing," she said, pointing at Jakal's corpse, which still had Aranthur's yataghan in its skull. "To make one thing." She shook her head.

"Not at the end, they weren't," Aranthur said.

"Even now you have pity for the traitor?" she asked. "You are either a saint or a fool."

"Both," Aranthur said. "Neither. Kurvenos?"

"I let the other thing go. You said not to kill it, and I accept strictures like that. Besides, I gave it something to think about."

"Something to think about?"

"I showed it the worm in its apple." She smiled. "You said not to kill it." She wrinkled her nose like a young girl. "Like a god, you gave your word."

"Like a god? I can't even function as a Lightbringer without killing," Aranthur said bitterly.

Inoques shrugged. "You should see yourself. You are a dangerous entity, Aranthur Timos. They will fear you now."

"I am about to collapse," he said. "I have something to do before my knees buckle. Help me?"

She helped and he hobbled across the garden of corpses on her arm, and through the hole in the wall.

He spent some time looking.

"What are we looking for?" she asked.

Aranthur found what he was looking for. He ran his hands over the parchment and life flickered under his hands.

"Ah," she said. "Your tame Exalted. You, too, take slaves."

"I think this one is a volunteer."

Aranthur cast a *transference*, rolled the Scarlet up like a scroll and stored it in the *Aulos*.

Inoques took his hand. "So," she said. "I was right to fear you." She glanced around. "You understand the immortality effect now, don't you?"

Aranthur glanced at her. "I noticed it a week ago. I suppose I saw it when we faced the Disciple." He was having trouble focusing and all the small wounds he'd taken were sapping his will to continue. His right arm was virtually non-functional. "But yes, I suspect I now know how to do it."

"And will you?" she asked. "Will you... become like me?"

Aranthur was too tired for this. Inoques was correct; he'd now seen enough to understand that there was a process by which one could make one's essence somehow independent of the vessel or body that contained it.

He looked away. "I don't think so." With what seemed like an enormous effort, he pushed himself to his feet. "I can't talk about this now. I can scarcely walk."

"You need to keep it together for a little longer, for the sake of all these mortals. I have told the sword. Help is coming." She smiled and put a hand on his left hand. "You and your friends have just destroyed a major power," she said with a slight smile. "You are *so much* more interesting than I expected." She shook her head. "All the entities will fear you now, Aranthur. Now you are a player in the real game."

"The real game?"

"The game the immortals play."

Book Three
Assalto

It is not enough to deceive your opponent or dominate him. You must dominate his blade *and* deceive his intention, so that your killing blow passes through his body and he can do *nothing* to harm you in return.

Maestro Sparthos,
unpublished notes to the book *Opera Nuova*

1

Megara, Palace of Justice

Meetings of the Council of Seventeen were held in secret, yet with public knowledge. This layer of complexity was very much in keeping with the layers by which the Empire was governed; the public could not know *who* was on the inner council, and were only occasionally notified of what the Seventeen decided; but they were welcome to know that they *were meeting* and *where*, so ensuring the secret business of Empire was publicly conducted, so to speak.

The Council of Seventeen, by laws more than six hundred years old, was composed of eight nobles, eight commoners—eight men and eight women—and the Emperor. In fact, one of the Emperor's few real constitutional powers was the chairmanship of the Council of Seventeen. The membership was by appointment; the appointments were secret; the process was convoluted.

The Seventeen had vast, yet limited, powers. They controlled the military and the security services, and they could examine, interrogate, or investigate anything that could be perceived to have an impact of the security of the Empire. Their officers commanded the militia and the Watch and the regular military (but not the Imperial Guards). Their inspectors were the bane and terror of every arm of government; their Secret Service, was feared throughout most of the world. Everyone called it the *difensori*, but it was sufficiently secret that it had no public name or headquarters.

This meeting of the Seventeen was the first meeting of the Inner Council in more than three months. The Imperial Lion flag went up over the Palazzo di Justicia, and the citizens, from military technicians in the gun foundry in the Arsenale to the citizen textile workers from the long sheds near the Spice Market, were cheered to know that the strongest arm of the government was coming into action—doubly cheered when the City Herald announced that the Great Council of Three Hundred would meet in a week. The same announcement carried the names of every person executed by the so-called Protector's regime and a list of his legislations that were now proscribed or repealed.

At two in the afternoon, the small black flag with the gold star rose over the Palazzo di Justicia. Out in the piazza, people cheered.

The hall of the Seventeen was on the third floor of the palace, up a secret staircase. There were, in fact, a dozen ways into the Hall of the Seventeen, so designed that the members could arrive without attracting the notice of even their peers and families. A tunnel under the Piazza led to one door; the doorkeeper was blind. A bridge from a door in the Imperial Palace led to another, kept by an ancient *automaton* of the First Empire.

There were other secrets. In the Empire, there were always more secrets.

Aranthur Timos crossed the small bridge over the Imperial Canal with Iralia, Dahlia and Tiy Drako. A few paces behind them stood the Emperor with McBane and two Imperial Axes.

Aranthur was dressed from head to toe in black, as was traditional for the Seventeen; his right arm was in a sling, and he wore black gloves. Blood loss and stress made his skin very pale, and he leant slightly on Dahlia, who also wore black. In her case, a broad white lace collar broke the tyranny of the black. In his case, a spiderweb of silver showed where an Imoter had rebuilt his right shoulder.

Tiy Drako wore black, but he had a red sash and a magnificent ruby burned in his right ear—a gift from Iralia. Only a magos would know that it burned with *puissance*; a power source for the pain-blocker that the spymaster still required.

Tiy and Dahlia wore swords.

Iralia wore no black at all, but a dark blue silk kirtle with a plain, but very fitted, overgown of dark red, embroidered over and over with the Imperial Lions in gold; she wore a crown of red jewels in her hair and the Imperial signet around her neck.

Aranthur and Dahlia had their masks in their hands.

Iralia had none.

"Are we ready?" Iralia asked. If she was worried, no hint of it entered her voice.

Dahlia sighed. "Yes," she said. Aranthur could feel the tension in her biceps.

"Yes," Aranthur said, very quietly.

Drako glanced at Aranthur. "I feel like an imposter," he said with a wink.

Aranthur smiled. "I *am* an imposter."

Iralia glared at them. "Drako first, then Dahlia, then Aranthur, then me," she said.

They all bowed to her.

Dahlia went to the door; a tall double door of cypress wood. A statue of bronze and gold stood before it, a long sword between its metal gauntlets.

"Myr Tarkas," the statue said in a surprisingly melodious voice.

It danced aside, and Dahlia passed into the Hall.

Drako counted to twenty, out loud.

"See you soon," he quipped, and walked up to the statue.

"Syr Drako," the statue said, and stepped aside.

Aranthur glanced at Iralia. "Count to twenty?"

"Don't ruin Drako's entrance," she said, clasping his hand. "Unlike you and Dahlia, he's wanted this all his adult life."

"And, unlike us, he deserves it," Aranthur said.

Iralia smiled.

Aranthur turned, feeling for the sword that wasn't there, and then walked down the corridor. He had a moment to look out of one of the high windows of the covered bridge, and to think that he'd walked under this bridge a hundred times, and always wondered…

The statue rippled as he came close.

"Syr Timos," he said, and stepped aside.

"Your mask, my lord," the automaton said.

Only then did it all become real to Aranthur, as he slipped his mask on.

He was about to sit on the Council of Seventeen. The first Souliote in three hundred years. His father was probably overseeing the reaping of his sun-drenched wheat fields, his Easterner workers thinking of the end of the day. Young women were binding the wheat stalks into sheaves.

He had a moment of feeling ridiculous. He should be wielding a scythe too, or sharpening one in the barn.

The door opened, and every head turned—even Dahlia's and Drako's, who were sitting closest to him.

There were only two chairs empty: the throne, and the chair closest to the throne, on the left.

Aranthur walked to the seat, drew it back and bowed slightly.

"Welcome," said a woman's mature voice from down the table.

"Thanks," he said.

And sat.

Iralia came in with the Emperor, on his arm. There was a murmur as she appeared.

"The Emperor," McBane growled.

Every member rose and made a reverence, right knee on the ground, by their seats.

The Emperor walked to the head of the table, put his right hand on the table and favoured the councillors with a slight smile.

"I am not yet well enough to participate directly in the Council of State," he said. "My consort, Iralia, will take my place."

There was a rustle from the table.

"The Emperor will withdraw," McBane said.

No one had risen from their reverence; they all stayed in place until the door closed behind the Emperor at the far end of the room.

"Another chair, please," Iralia said into the silence.

Another *automaton* appeared with a heavy oak chair. Iralia pointed to a place just to the right of the throne.

She looked down the table. "I will never take his seat," she said. "On to business."

She sat, and put spectacles on her nose. Aranthur wanted to smile; her face was transformed from a model of feminine beauty to that of a studious angel.

"We have a great deal to get through," she said. "First item on our agenda. Councillor One."

Iralia looked far down to the other end of the table. Councillors sat in order of seniority.

A large woman in a black mourning gown rose, bowed to Iralia, and looked down the table.

"Brothers and sisters, the so-called Lord Protector detained and killed five of our number and another could not be present. To the best of our knowledge, none of our number co-operated directly with him, but the Imperial Amnesty applies to us. Would anyone like to make any statement?"

There followed several statements from members who had felt required by the business of the Empire to interact with the false protector.

The agenda proceeded smartly; in many ways it was the best run meeting Aranthur had ever attended. No one seemed to need to shout out how smart they were, or to talk to hear themselves talk.

Nothing was served but cold water.

A middle-aged man spoke quickly about the Pure threat to the water supply and what had been done to contain it. Aranthur was shocked there had been such a threat.

An older man described a plot to murder members of the Academy and destroy the buildings with a huge explosion of gunpowder, foiled by the *difensori*.

Tiy Drako made a noise, but didn't speak.

A thin man described the city's losses to the bone plague, the Darkness, and a number of other maladies, including sexually transmitted diseases and deaths related to addictions. Aranthur was surprised to hear them all listed together, but the man's portfolio seemed to be medicine, and he spoke movingly of the losses.

"How many did we lose to the Darkness?" a woman said.

"Hard to say," he answered. "I'm sorry, esteemed colleagues, but the Darkness strikes most heavily on those already vulnerable—the poor, the ill, the mad. We have a dramatic increase in tavern brawls, in deaths due to *thuryx* overdose, in duels. All of these deaths may or may not be due to the Darkness."

"Sweet Aphres," Iralia muttered. "How many?"

"Ma'am, in the last three months, we've lost almost a fifth of our population," he said. "And not just the most vulnerable."

The other councillors groaned.

"Next," Iralia said.

A very tall, thin woman rose and walked to the head of the table.

She raised a hand, and *puissance* sparkled. A chart appeared behind her, showing the whole eastern end of the Inner Sea.

"Our fleet has fought four actions in the Middle Sea. We can take some hope from their not *losing* any engagement. Shall I go into details?" she asked.

Iralia looked down the table. "Yes," she said.

"The first action was fought nine days ago in the waters off Lenos, against a mixed force of pirates and elements of the Attian fleet, as well as an unknown force with superior battle magik," she said. "Our Capitano del Mar chose to withdraw as soon as it became clear he lacked the *puissance* to win the fight."

Everyone at the table nodded.

"Any idea why that is?" Drako asked.

"Elements working directly from the Imperial Palace under Myr Benvenutu confirmed certain theories resulting from Myr Tribane's near defeat in Armea," the woman said. "Independently, the weatherworkers and magi of the fleet came to a similar conclusion. The Capitano del Mar provoked a limited action off the north beach of Lenos two days later to test their theories and each side lost several ships, but the weatherworkers subsequently felt they understood the—ancient—techniques of the enemy. The fleet was busy trying to collect and load food for the army at Antioke, and they were, unfortunately, surprised on the beaches of Eressos five days ago. Only the coming of darkness saved our fleet." She shrugged. "My understanding is that, had the enemy pressed their advantage in the morning, they might have achieved a total victory. However, the arrival of two of our Great Galleys bound from Masr to the City, both carrying powerful weatherworkers and polemagi, allowed the Capitano del Mar to attack in turn. The combined enemy chose to meet him in the Milini Channel and the fighting lasted more than six hours." She put a scroll on the table. "We lost more than fifteen hundred citizens and the Great Galley *Principe di Asturas* was totally destroyed."

Aranthur blinked, imagining Donna Comnas at her helm.

"When did we last lose a Great Galley in combat?" a woman's voice asked.

"More than seventy years ago," the woman at the front of the room said. "As she was fully laden, the economic loss will be felt for years." She looked around, her eyes passing over each councillor. "The Capitano del Mar sacrificed the vessel to draw the fire, real and magikal, of our adversaries. Despite the loss, he broke their line and shattered their fleet."

"But our own losses were..."

"Very serious. Instead of winning naval superiority, it would be more correct to say that right now, *no one* owns the seas." The tall woman smiled, as if she harboured a delightful secret. "Though we still have nine ships on the stocks in the Arsenale." She nodded to Iralia. "The consort ordered them to be completed five days ago, which was, Madame, prescient. Four of them are ready and we will draw citizen sailors out of the fishing fleets this morning. Unless bad weather delays us, we will put nine galleys and three sails of war to sea the day after tomorrow."

"And then we will have the only fleet?" an aristocratic male voice asked.

"We believe so. The pirates are destroyed and, more importantly, many of our crews and most of our weatherworkers and magi are safe on Lenos. Atti...is cleaning its own house, as I suspect we will hear." She nodded.

"Your estimate?" Iralia asked.

The tall woman rubbed her mask as if it irritated the bridge of her nose, which it probably did.

"Our new fleet will have naval superiority, at least for the next fortnight. The requested foodstuffs and supplies are ready, either here in the City or on Lenos."

"Well done, Fleet," Iralia said. "War Finance?"

There was a brief pause, perhaps some intakes of breath. Many of the councillors knew that a climax was approaching. Even Aranthur, a newcomer to bureaucratic drama, was aware something significant was coming.

"Madame, we have nothing to spend on these ships," said a man from the other end of the table. He sounded *pleased* about it.

"Seize the assets of the Roaris family," Iralia said.

"Unprecedented," the military treasurer snapped through his mask.

"The Emperor orders it," Iralia said.

"The Empire's oldest family will be destroyed." This from the aristocratic voice—a large man, portly, and dignified. He had a white beard under his mask.

Iralia wasn't wearing a mask, and her look was mild. She sat back, and took off the spectacles, and again her face changed—from studious angel to avenging goddess. Aphres, the goddess of love and lust, was also a goddess of war.

"The Emperor is content that the Roaris family be destroyed."

There was a heavy silence over the table.

"Women and children..." the man said.

"This is not the First Empire, syr. The women of a major house have the same political rights as their men. They were either complicit in high treason or silent, and either way, the Emperor is merciful. They are not being taken by the Secret Service and strangled in secret. We're only taking their money, their castles, their palaces and their ships."

"They will be destitute," the man said.

"They attempted to kill the Emperor, overthrow this body and the entire rule of law in the Empire, and perhaps the world," Iralia said implacably. "They can go on to the streets naked and starve. If you are concerned, syr, you are rich—take them in. Everything of theirs belongs to the Empire now. The Emperor has spoken."

"Really, Madame," the military treasurer said quietly. "I protest this tyranny over one of the Great Houses. You are merely the Imperial strumpet—I wish to hear this from the Emperor."

Iralia leant back. "All of you who agree with this councillor, please stand."

Four councilors stood.

"Syr, the Great Houses do not have different rights from those of the other citizens of the Empire, save certain rights to represent themselves on the councils and certain differences in taxation."

"The Great Houses are the very basis of the Empire," the man said, unbowed.

A woman nodded. Her mask was an opera mask: Niobe, in black.

"We agree. You cannot rule without the Great Houses."

Iralia smiled. "This is not a contest you want to have right now," she said gently.

"Consort, there are calls on the streets for the disestablishment of the Imperial rule and the creation of a republic. You need us. The Emperor needs us."

Iralia nodded. "You seem to think I disagree. In fact, I agree—the Emperor needs the Great Houses. But not the traitors who attempted to overthrow our government. Roaris must go."

"And we say they shall not. We very much doubt, *madame*, that you can face down the combined might of the Houses."

Iralia stood up, and just for a moment, her composure cracked.

"Do you seriously threaten civil war when the whole Empire is endangered from within and without? Merely to preserve some selfish vestige of power from a bygone age? By Aphres, friends, I should let you take the dose you have coming."

"You think you can govern without us?" The portly man seemed stunned. "Impossible."

"We disagree," Iralia said. "But we will put it to a vote. The Emperor requests the sequestration of the entire House of Roaris, and the extirpation of the name."

There was a pause, and an intake of a dozen breaths.

"Seconded," Dahlia said. "Roaris brought the enemy into our city and attempted to kill the Emperor."

A rustle. Dahlia's upper-class Liote gave her status away. As the council was eight nobles and eight commoners, it was immediately clear to the other seven nobles that they would lose a vote on class lines.

Drako leant back. "Destroy them," he drawled in the same class-rich accent Dahlia had used.

"Show of hands?" Iralia asked.

"I request a secret ballot," said the old aristocrat. "You have stacked this council with your cronies."

Drako barked a laugh. "Da Rosa, if I said the word, every House in this city would be singed, and some would burn. The citizens blame the aristocracy for the Pure. And they're not wrong to."

"We do not use names in the council," the portly man began.

Drako snapped his fingers. "That for your etiquette. I know every person in this room—I know how each of you came to be on the council. Don't tire the Emperor with your petty factions. We're trying to save the world. You are not."

Iralia nodded into the silence. "Well," she said with a slight smile. "We will put this to a vote, and use the balls. Automaton?"

A silver figure walked heavily through the room.

"Ivory for their extirpation, ebony for their salvation," Iralia said.

Aranthur suddenly understood the holes in the table before every seat. He took an ivory ball from the automaton and dropped it in the round hole in front of his seat. He could hear the sound of the small balls rolling through grooves under the table, and clicking into place somewhere under the table.

"Fifteen in favour, two against," a young woman said. "The motion is carried. The Roaris family is hereby declared extinct. All assets to be seized immediately for the Imperial war chest."

With dignity, the portly man rose to his feet.

"Madame, I beg your leave to resign."

"Declined pending further discussion," Iralia said. "Sit down. There's a war on, syr, and just because we disagree, or perhaps *because we disagree*, I need your voice on my council. I may be the Imperial strumpet, syr, but the Emperor has placed me here, and unless you are directly in revolt against the laws of the Empire, I request that you sit and continue to counsel."

The man sat, apparently in shock.

Drako snorted. "I didn't realise how much fun this was going to be," he said, loudly enough that everyone could hear.

Iralia looked down the table. "Councillors," she said. "We are at the turn of the tide. We were invaded, and we have repulsed our attackers. Our agents have helped Atti against the same. Now we need money, and time, to make our counter-attack."

One of the women who'd stood with the portly man shook her head.

"It's all so unconnected. Madame, we are loyal. But the fleet... General Tribane... the events in Atti..." She looked directly at Drako. "Madame Chairman, councillors, it is clear to some of us that we are no better informed now than we were when General Roaris was driving the chariot of state."

Iralia saw back, considering. She looked at Drako.

He shook his head.

She narrowed her eyes. And stood, again.

"That is a fair accusation, Councillor. Drako, tell them."

The use of his familiar name was clearly unpleasant to the more conservative councillors, and one of them said, "We do not use names on council!"

Iralia smiled. "Many things are about to change," she said. "Drako?"

Drako stood, again. "Councillors," he said, after a long look at Iralia. It was clear he disagreed with her decision. "We are simultaneously facing at least two threats, either one of which, in more normal times, would be viewed as terrible and existential. The organisation known as the Pure originated in the north-east of Tanais. In five years they went from being a rumour to being a multistate entity that controlled millions of people and had ideological tendrils that stretched right into this council."

None of this was news to the Council of Seventeen, and even under masks, Aranthur could see their relative boredom.

"At the same time agents of the Pure, either intentionally or unintentionally, released entities which had been bound in Masr at the end of the War of Wrath."

Everyone sat up, and Drako glanced at Iralia. She gave a slight nod.

Drako glanced at Aranthur.

Aranthur had no idea what to say. He couldn't read Drako's mind.

"The release of the Old Ones and subsequent events, the Dark Forge appearing in the sky, the shadow of the Darkness in the minds of so many people…"

"The suicide rate has increased astronomically," a man said. "Pardon me, councillor."

"The release of the Old Ones and the rift in the fabric of the heavens may threaten the whole existence of our world," Drako said.

"Making our fight with the Pure a sideshow," said the man who had spoken on war finance.

Again, Drako glanced at Iralia, and again, Iralia nodded.

Drako took a deep breath. "Consort, I disagree."

Iralia nodded. "Your dissent is noted. Tell them anyway."

Drako shrugged. "We conducted a successful operation in Atti, to restore the government there."

Aranthur almost laughed aloud. Bitterly, he thought, *I got seven good people killed and we let Kurvenos escape, but we saved the useless Sultan Bey and that makes it successful. And Drako makes it sound as if I was a tool of Imperial intelligence.*

Drako went on, "In the course of the clean-up, we found evidence…" Aranthur thought Drako might choke, saying the words, and Dahlia laughed aloud at his discomfiture. "…evidence that the forces guiding the Pure…" He made a motion with his damaged hands, as if he was washing them. "That there are entities rather than men guiding the Pure. That we are facing a new campaign in the War of Wrath. That all of this is tied together."

Dahlia had stopped laughing, and Aranthur felt as if a bolt of *puissance* had struck him.

One of the aristocratic women motioned to speak.

"You are saying," she asked carefully, "that the Pure are not really an ideology."

"Madame, I'm not sure what I'm saying, beyond that it is possible that the attacks here, in Atti and in Masr are part of the Pure scheme —to open the Black Pits and release the Old Ones. A cosmic jailbreak. Maybe worse."

Iralia raised her voice. "Ask yourselves who would benefit from the large-scale release of Old Ones."

The woman with the Niobe mask shook her head. "That's insane. No one."

"No one!" Iralia snapped. "That's exactly right, councillors. No human being, no Jhugj, no Dhadh. Our ancestors have already played this game with the Powers. Some of our ancestors tried to make deals for personal power, or greed."

"A few succeeded," Drako said.

"Councillors, we face, not just the threat of our time, but the threat of all time," Iralia said. "This is *not* the time for factions. This is the moment for unity. We have a plan—we are acting on it. You sixteen, of all people, need to know what it is." She opened her hands and produced a map of the Inner Sea. "The immediate secular battlefield has been Armea. The naval war is for the landing areas off Armea and southern Atti, where the enemy fears we might land in force."

She had their complete attention.

"Early this summer, we fooled the Master into believing we had directed our efforts, first at Antioke, and then against Atti." She smiled. "Instead, General Tribane defeated the Pure in Armea, and opened the possibility of an invasion of Safi. Then, by a miracle, and with the sacrifice of many citizens, we held Antioke. Even now, Antioke is under siege, and General Tribane must be relieved. At the same time, the Old Ones at the Black Pyramid in Masr threaten the very foundations of the world, and the daily widening rift in our night sky portends a rising tide of both power and weather.

"We have the military might to defeat the Pure. We have the carrying capacity to move food and supplies to Antioke and we have the reserves of military strength to invade Safi. We have the depth of magikal talent to heal the rift in the sky—and thanks to the sacrifice of our best people, we know how. Hells, friends—we even know how to deal with the Darkness."

She leant forward, her hands on the tabletop, the jewels in her hair flashing like fire.

"We had to stabilise Atti, first. We need them as an absolutely loyal ally, because we're about to strip the City and our Empire of magical talent to an extent no one has seen since the War of Wrath. In one movement, we will join the Fleet at Milini on Lenos, move with the Fleet to Antioke and relieve General Tribane, extricate her army, and proceed to Masr."

Now there was mumbling across the table.

"Masr?" the War Finance speaker asked. "If we are on the ascendant, surely we should retake the *kuria* mines in the Atti highlands?"

"We will strike against the Old Ones with as much power as we can manage, and even now, that power is not inconsiderable. I will be going, myself, in person. So will almost every professor and academician—we will strip ourselves naked to win this." She looked around. "And Atti will guard our backs while we do."

"If we seize the *kuria* mines we will ensure a steady supply for our people for years to come. We can lower prices and ensure controls. We won't have to fight the bone plague—we'll control the source. I don't need to tell you the economic advantages." The man ran his fingers through his fine white beard. "We would be rich."

"How can we trust Atti?" asked another councillor.

Drako glanced again at Aranthur, and so did Iralia.

Aranthur rose slowly. "Councillors..."

"Gods, he's an *Arnaut.*"

Aranthur was silent for a moment. Then, with a tiny effort of will, he raised his *guise* as a Byzas aristo. In nicely accented *Ellene*, as if he disdained a more modern language, he glanced down the table and said, "Will this make it easier for you to work with me?"

The council was absolutely silent.

Iralia smiled. "Continue," she said.

Aranthur's upper class drawl was near perfect.

"Councillors, we rescued the Kaptan Pasha and his family, we are healing them of the Darkness, and we will protect them. We saved the Sultan Bey when his closest advisor betrayed him." He bowed and sat.

"But…he's an Arnaut…" muttered someone.

Drako rose. "So, you see, my friends, we have every reason to believe we can trust Ulama in these matters."

The woman in the Niobe mask seemed interested. "I like that—suddenly I feel we have a strategic direction. And I, for one, have no issues with being led by a woman, or sharing my table with an Arnaut." She glared down the table. "But why should our army should go to Masr? Let Masr hang! Take the *kuria* mines."

The portly man nodded. "I second that sentiment. All of it. Welcome, welcome, syr. Now, come, Consort. Tell us your plan. Why not take the Atti highlands?"

Iralia had rested on the edge of her seat while the others spoke. Aranthur could see how agitated she was, but it was not betrayed in her face or her hands.

"First, because we don't have an army deployed for a mountain campaign," she said. "Second, because all that territory belongs to Atti, not to us, and we cannot trust Atti to protect us and seize their most valuable trade asset at the same time. And further, we have to deliver knockout blows, not just pile up our coins. We lack the time. The Dark Forge is growing." Now she rose. "One roll of the dice. One hand of cards. We close the rift or we die trying."

"Risky," the portly man said.

"No," Iralia said. "No risk at all. We have no choice. The tide is rising. According to the Academy, we have perhaps forty-four days before the Dark Forge is wide enough to release everything it holds. I suppose we could sit here for forty-four days and write our wills, and maybe some good erotic poetry." She shrugged. "For maybe ten days we could do that and control the world *kuria* crystal supply."

"My poetry isn't that good," Drako said.

"Aploun, that makes it…Darknight," Aranthur realised. "The rift will tear open on Darknight."

Iralia glanced at him. "I hadn't worked that out."

Dahlia stood. "I'm with you, Consort," she said.

Aranthur was on his feet. "You know I'm with you," he said.

But when he turned, they were all on their feet.

Niobe smiled under her mask. "So now we know what it takes to get unanimity on the Seventeen," she said. "Nothing short of the end of the world."

*

"I think that went well," Iralia said.

She had flung herself on a couch outside the Imperial apartments. Aranthur sat in his usual place, using his left hand to turn pages in the *Ulmaghest*.

"You are going to have trouble if we survive this," Drako said.

Iralia shook her head. "No. If we win, no one will question me for years. And if we lose I won't care. Dahlia, how many front-rank, heavy hitters have you found?"

"Are you and I front-rank?" she asked.

Iralia laughed. "I think so," she admitted.

"Twenty-seven," Dahlia said. "And another forty who can choir a lot of *puissance* and shield us, too." She looked at Aranthur. "Janos Sittar is nowhere to be found."

Aranthur nodded, but Drako spoke.

"He was the head of my list of potential traitors," he said. "And as soon as Aranthur moved on Jakal, Sittar vanished."

Aranthur took a breath. "He must have been complicit in the death of Myr Benvenutu," he said. "Every time I play it back, I realise we never questioned why he went down and yet took no wound. He just let the shields fall and turtled."

"He brought Jakal here," Iralia said.

"He was privy to almost every aspect of Cold Iron," Drako said with real regret. "But a year ago, when I mentioned bringing Aranthur into Cold Iron, Kurvenos insisted I not discuss it with Sittar."

"Tyche," Dahlia said. "That's creepy."

Aranthur was looking through the window. Below them, in the Imperial harbour, the long, lean hull of the Imperial yacht was being fitted out for sea; fifty workers borrowed from the Arsenale were rattling down her shrouds and changing her canvas. Aranthur could see Inoques on her foredeck, her face raised, shouting something.

"You didn't tell them about the swords," he said.

Drako shook his head. "I didn't want to tell them as much as I did."

"We need to destroy the sword," Aranthur said.

"Do we know how?" Iralia asked.

"Yes. It's not hard—they're really just swords."

"How many are there?" Iralia asked.

"There were seven. One Bright, six dark. One of the dark swords was destroyed in an earlier...encounter." Aranthur smiled. He'd had several conversations with the Bright Steel.

"So four remain," Iralia said.

"Four raving mad black paladins," Aranthur said. "Each one a self-created Old One to all intents and purposes."

Drako looked over at Aranthur, who sat with Iralia and put her feet on his lap. He didn't move like Tiy Drako; his hands were covered with the silver-white lines of Imoter healing, and so was his face.

"You did very, very well while I was down," he said.

"I made it up as I went along," Aranthur said, "and I got some good people killed."

Drako shook his head. "You can't think that way."

"I do, though."

"Don't wallow in it," Drako advised. "You aren't done. We are *not done.* In fact, if I have learned anything from Kurvenos, it is that, despite what Iralia said to the council...this is just the way it is."

"What?" Iralia asked. A servant was pouring wine.

Drako smiled. "It was an excellent speech. But as far as I can tell, nothing is permanent, nothing stays buried, no spell can stop another spell forever, and the Old Ones cannot, by definition, be destroyed. In other words, it's *always* almost the end of the world. Swords, rings, glyphs?" Drako laughed. "Drink more wine. Sit and talk with friends. Smell the flowers. It's always almost the end of the world." He glanced at Aranthur. "You did an excellent job—and you took notes, really professional notes."

"I didn't get Sittar or rescue Kurvenos," Aranthur said bitterly.

"You walled Sittar off, neutralised Atti and kept us in the game." Drako smiled. "There are dozens of things I want to know, but one detail stands out. Why did you send the Bright Steel back here, instead of taking it to fight Jakal? You knew the swords were involved."

Aranthur took a glass of sweet wine and drained it. He was drinking a great deal more than he used to, and he discovered that the plate of cheese and fruit that had been put by him was absolutely empty.

He'd even eaten the apple cores.

"I needed Jakal to believe I was running away, and he could track the Bright Steel." Aranthur decided to be honest. "And she's...waking up. Every time I kill with her, she's more...alive. I worried. Damn it, I still worry. If she takes down something as big as Sittar or Jakal..."

Drako nodded. "You really are a Lightbringer," he said. "So you have enough balance to see that the Bright Steel is another entity."

"So is my wife," Aranthur said carefully. "You want to make a boundary of absolutes, and I'm telling you that there is a sliding scale."

Drako steepled his hands and looked first at Dahlia, who was unusually silent and focused on her wine, and then at Iralia.

"You want us to believe that Inoques has humanity in her…?"

"Yes," Aranthur said.

Drako shook his head. "You know Haras fears her. Hates her, even."

Aranthur spread his hands. "Hate is easy. Fear is easy. Love takes work."

"Tyche," Dahlia said. "You really are a Lightbringer."

"I am not. Mostly, I kill people with a sword."

"And wallow in the sin of pride," Iralia said.

"Ouch," Aranthur gulped.

Iralia shrugged and ate a fig. "I'm glad you count the cost. Really I am—bastards like Drako here scare me. But—here in this room—we know we're the good fight. So why…worry?" She met Aranthur's eye. "Kill as few as you can. *But we do have to win.*"

Aranthur smiled, because Iralia made him feel better. But he rose and put the wineglass down carefully.

"Win what?" he asked. "I agree with Tiy. This is how it is, for as long as we choose to ride the tiger. We win nothing but another day and another night." He looked at Dahlia. "One crisis at a time, or ten. An endless succession of fires on which we can piss until one day we take a bullet or a spell or a blade, and then hopefully there's another talented young spark to pick up the banner and go forward."

Dahlia stood and faced him. "You don't believe that," she said.

"The body count is high." Aranthur thought of Parsha Equus, after the skirmish in Armea. *I only lost six, but I knew every fucking one of them.*

"We do it so they—" Dahlia waved a hand over the city—"can have normal lives."

"Are you sure we don't do it because we enjoy it?" Aranthur countered. "I'm the first Souliote member of the Council of Seventeen. Ever, as far as I can tell. I won't hide from you how much I like that, and all I had to do was kill the right people." He wasn't even bitter, now. He held out his glass, and Drakas refilled it. "I'm awfully good at killing, for a Lightbringer."

"Aranthur," Iralia said. "Stop."

Aranthur paused and looked at her.

"Let's not pretend. We're going through with this, and that means we'll kill at Antioke and kill again in Masr and then, if we have the chance, we'll kill our way into Safi." She raised her chin. "I don't disagree with anything you've said, except about the constancy of the threat. When the hole in the sky is closed, have any breakdown you fancy."

Aranthur nodded. He looked down at his empty glass. He looked at Drako, barely recovered; at Dahlia, who looked deeply worried, and at Iralia. They made tears come to his eyes, because he loved them all; they were his *friends.*

And yet, since the fight with Jakal, it was as if there was a wall between them.

He wondered then where Sasan was, or Kati.

He wondered what it would be like to live for a thousand years, or ten thousand. To watch every person he loved flicker and go out, like candles in a draughty temple. How long before he stopped making attachments? How long before he was incapable of love?

"When we beat the Old Ones," Drako chimed in, "we'll have a drunken orgy and push out the Darkness."

Aranthur didn't say any of the things that came to his mind.

Too late for that, he thought. *We're not even in the same game any more.*

2

Megara

All along the waterfront, all the way around the city, ships were fitted for sea. In the brick ship-sheds of the Arsenale, warships got their standing rigging and their naval stores: salt mackerel, salt beef, kegs of pickled cabbage and gunpowder. Fisherwomen kissed their stay-at-home spouses, and fishermen kissed theirs. Four full regiments of militia were called up from the city, and the Northern Counties—the Geta and the Bas—provided two cavalry regiments and a veritable sea of remounts, sending their precious horseflesh into the maw of war. Along Southside, especially near the Fortress, grain ships and other deep-draught transports were gutted and refitted at lightning speed to transport horses. All along the industrial spine of the city, every workshop with a wire plate had apprentices drawing steel wire to meet the impossible demand. Every armourer in the city was forging square steel bucklers; every engraver was working against guild regulations, temporarily suspended, by candlelight.

So much coal was being burned to make the wire and the bucklers that deep fog, unusual in the City, set in each morning. Coal prices rose; it was hard for a man to get a bucket repaired, much less a sword straightened.

Inside the palace, the consort herself was going to war; a dozen Imperial armourers competed to complete her harness, and those of her friends. Aranthur, who had gone to war as a trooper in a Select Militia regiment with an unfitted helmet and a one-size-fits-all breastplate, now had the experience of having armour that fitted like good clothes:

a segmented cuirass that bent in any direction he bent; arm and leg armour to match, with supple, thin spring-steel plates that flexed over each other like a lobster's tail; even his gorget was segmented. It all went over a fine black deerskin doublet with lace-on maille voiders that he liked so well he asked for another pair made for daily wear.

The preparations helped. The reality of the material artifacts grounded him: the craftsmanship in the armour; the details of the buckles; the minutiae of conflict and war; the orders for masts and cordage and hemp that rolled in from the Imperial harbour, where Inoques was playing with her new ship in much the same way that Aranthur played with armour and saddles.

It had been Iralia's idea to give the Imperial yacht to Inoques, and if ever a gift cemented a friendship, *that* had. It was not just the reality of the ship, but the relaxation, if an entity like Inoques could be said to relax—the activity of preparing, of fitting out. She was able to focus on something, as was Aranthur, and the focus kept each of them from certain thoughts. Inoques would talk animatedly about her new crew. She was pursuing a veteran weatherworker, a senior in the City Guild, like a jilted lover, and her tales of searching taverns for the man made Aranthur laugh aloud.

But in the shadows of night, other conversations were had. It was two days until the new fleet was to sail, and the Imperial yacht was in all respects ready for sea. Inoques lay atop her lover, her head on his chest, her legs sprawled over his.

Despite the apparent abandon of her posture, he could feel her tension, and he knew it was anger. He was good at reading her now; the longer they were together, the better she became at playing a human being.

"You can tell me," he said to the darkness.

The swaying lamp overhead was down to its last drops of oil, and the seas outside the Imperial Breakwater and the Stars were rough enough to rock the Imperial Ship *Esperance* at her harbour moorings. The swaying light cast an eldritch gloom full of moving shadows, worse, in some ways, than pure darkness. The cats liked it though; the *Esperance* had thirty cats aboard, mostly dockyard mousers, an amazing collection of earless rogues and fish thieves, every one of whom competed to join them on the hanging bed.

She lay a little longer, and his hand stroked her back. Sometimes he imagined that he could feel the tattoos on her back, like lines of fine engraving on metal.

"When you are..." she began, and then she relaxed a little and wriggled. "When you are one of us," she said. "That sounds foolish. We are not a collective. There is no Guild of Old Ones."

"Perhaps there should be," Aranthur said.

She was quiet for a while. "That is a good thought. Put it aside." She rolled a little and faced him. "The Old Ones collect followers. It is almost the only way to keep score. You know the Getae?"

The Getae were the northernmost citizens of the Empire. Hundreds of years before they had descended on the frontiers as mounted raiders and had, for a time, pushed the frontiers of the Empire back to the Lathven river. But time had brought the nomads off their horses and into farmhouses, although they still loved horses.

"Yes. They almost destroyed the Empire, and yet people still think of *Souliotes* as brutal thieves."

She shrugged. "They rate their importance by the number of horses they own," she said. "So it is with Old Ones."

Aranthur nodded at the rippling shadows.

"So when Jakal burnt my ship and killed my crew," she said, "he attacked *me*."

"And lowered your value," Aranthur said.

"That was insulting," she said, raising her head from his chest.

His guts clenched. "I'm teasing you," he said. "Getae bride prices—"

"And you call us alien entities."

"Of course he attacked you," Aranthur said. "He meant to destroy you."

"Yes, that of course," she said. "Now I have no apprentice."

"No apprentice weatherworking captain? But you hate your bonds."

"Yes," she said. "Slavery is complicated."

"But you will escape soon," Aranthur said.

Silence.

"Your pregnancy is progressing three times as fast a human woman's," he said, and put his hand on the very slight bump below her belly button. "I did quite well in human anatomy."

She rolled off him. "You know how I will escape?"

"No," he lied. "I only know that I have sworn to help you."

"You have become very powerful," she said.

"Good teachers," he said, kissing her.

"Yes," she agreed. "But the work you have done on unbindings—that is original work." She ran a hand down his side. "And I have helped you... too much."

"Yes," he agreed.

"Do you think you could unbind me?"

"Not yet," he said. *Yes*, he thought. *I'm sorry I have to lie to you.*

"Why do I find the thought of you unravelling my bonds terrifying?"

"Because freedom can be complicated too," Aranthur said.

"My fantasy was to burst the bonds and slaughter them all in a red mist of revenge." As she spoke, her nails dug into Aranthur's shoulders.

"Ouch," he said.

"I was a cat goddess," she said.

"I know," he said. The darkness was full of loud, aggressive purring.

"Now, I fear I will escape my bonds in an anticlimax, and all my slavers will already be dead." She sighed. "When we reach Masr, I will willingly help Dahlia. My own kind hold nothing for me."

You are lying, and so am I.

Is this how marriages work?

It was not a bitter thought. He understood why she was lying; he certainly knew why he was. He stroked her back, and she purred, and then, without either of them particularly intending it, they were making love.

The lamp finally guttered and went out.

"You let Kurvenos go," Aranthur said eventually.

"You are the real Old One here," she said. "Can you never let your body rule your mind?"

He breathed in the smell of her hair and tried not to think about Kurvenos.

"I did it for you," she said quietly.

"Did what?" he asked.

"I left him the key. If he can find it. And I let the other run off, believing he was the driver and not the horse."

Aranthur let out a long breath. "I wish you'd told me this before," he said.

"You understand?" she asked.

"All too well."

"I didn't love your Meddler," she admitted. "But I... liked him well enough."

He sighed. But his hand swept down her back, and he kissed the tip of her nose.

"Did he understand?"

"Kurvenos?" she asked.

He asked again, and she was asleep.

Ah, my demon lover.

He ran his fingers down her back, and thought of the last act of his plan. Up to a point, his plan was Iralia's plan, which was actually Dahlia and Tiy Drako's plan.

Up to a point.

He was painfully aware the next day might be his last day in Megara.

Ever.

So he spent it doing things he loved. He took Inoques to meet Ghazala and Manacher. Ghazala was suspicious until he admitted they were married, and then she laid out food and insisted on giving Inoques gifts. Manacher only shook his head.

Later he left Inoques with Iralia and Haras, who needed more *puissance* for the next generation of alchemical solutions to the Darkness. Since the gift of the Imperial yacht, and the gleaming bronze tubes of her new rearmament delivered that morning, Inoques was willing to do almost anything for Iralia, even if the favour included Haras.

Haras, by contrast, seemed very unhappy to see the bound woman.

"She will be the death of us," he said.

Aranthur left the palace and walked across the city. He bought *quaveh* from a street seller and a fish pie from another, and he walked through the Academy, swordless. He wondered, as he passed his yellow door, if he'd ever return to the Academy, if he'd ever have an apartment again. He looked up and a lump came to his throat.

He could almost hear Dahlia's voice, or perhaps Kati's. Or Sasan whining for *thuryx.* Or Ansu, wanting to buy a prostitute.

Or Kallinikos, offering to loan Ansu clothes.

Aranthur was still wearing black: his new black deerskin doublet, finer than anything he'd ever owned, and short black breeches and supple black boots that laced to the doublet. He wore a broad hat, the kind Dahlia favoured.

An idea struck him, a whim, and he acted on it. He walked up to the yellow door, let himself in, and turned right, under the stairs, to where the landlord's apartment was. He knocked, and the owner's partner appeared in an apron, smelling of charcoal.

"What can do for you, syr?" he said as soon as he saw the fine hat, the black gloves, and the deerskin doublet.

Aranthur smiled slightly. "I used to rent the top floor," he said. "I assume you still have my things?"

"Oh, gods," the man said. "You're that Timos..." He paused. "Aren't you wanted...?"

"No," Aranthur said.

"Oh, gods. Of course." The man shook his head. "Please, syr, I'm only a poor tradesman..."

Aranthur knew that was a blatant lie, given what the pair of them charged for rent.

"I'd like my arming sword. Is it on the wall there?" he asked, stepping past the other man.

"I really don't know..."

"I do," Aranthur said, taking the sword down.

It was as elegant as he remembered—really, a masterwork: the hilt plain, but perfectly worked, and the scabbard and belt some of Aranthur's best work, in black, with nice silver and steel fittings.

"I'm not sure you can just take that," the man said.

"I am," Aranthur said. "As it's mine." He was buckling the belt on one-handed. "Send the rest of my things to the palace."

"I'm not sure..."

"Let me be sure for you," Aranthur said with a smile. "If you don't send all my things, including my books, to the palace this afternoon, I'll have to start asking questions like how the Yellowjackets, an illegal organisation, gained access to my rooms. Yes? You understand?" He leant close to the man. "Please tell me you understand, syr, because I find it tiresome to threaten someone too stupid to understand."

The man in the smith's apron had a hand at his own throat.

"I understand," he said.

"Good," Aranthur said, already feeling vaguely guilty for being a bully. But only a little guilty, because...landlords.

"I have your mail," the man said, and handed him a dozen heavy parchment envelopes.

Aranthur went back into the street, the envelopes pinned under his left arm. It felt good to be armed again.

He walked down the steps towards canal side, purchased a fish pie and then another, and then a somewhat stale cinnamon roll and an apple pastry. He was hungry all the time, and in the city he could eat as he walked. His fingers grew increasingly sticky, but after twenty minutes, as the bells began to ring for Sophian evensong, he arrived at Master Sparthos' door.

The magister's daughter smiled at him.

"Ah," she said. "Just in time. My father will be pleased to see you, syr. He's feeling better today."

"Thank you, Demoiselle," Aranthur said with a bow.

He went upstairs, took his right arm out of its sling, unlaced his fancy doublet and boots in favour of simple slippers and a coarse cloth doublet.

"Mikal!" he called out, and Sapu turned, dropped his fencing weapon, and crushed him in an embrace.

"Things have been dull since you left," he said. "Are you back?"

"I thought I'd take a lesson," Aranthur said.

"You are in luck." Magister Sparthos smiled slightly—as much of a smile as Aranthur had ever seen the man make. "I haven't seen you in more than a week."

"I've been busy," Aranthur said.

"Of that I have no doubt. General Roaris has fallen and there is a rumour that a Souliote is on the Council of Seventeen," Sparthos said.

Aranthur managed a shrug.

Sparthos' smile widened. "Luckily none of that is my business. I merely teach people to kill their adversaries."

He took out a handkerchief and coughed blood into it; blood, and bits of black. He no longer troubled to hide it.

"Magister, will you teach today?" Aranthur asked.

Sparthos bowed slightly. "I will teach you two. I may have to leave you both to teach others."

Though the magister was dying of some nameless disease, that did not keep him from working the two of them like dogs. Aranthur, emaciated from constant casting, was used to being equal to any physical challenge, but an hour with the Master and he was breathing like a forge bellows and his arms felt like lead.

"You must always advance into an enemy attack," the Master said. "When you two are struggling to set the measure between you, you can step back all you want—back out of the window if you will. But once your blades touch, you must go forward until you conquer or die."

Sapu shook his head. "Magister, I try to live by your teachings, but in this—"

"Come," the master said. He took a rebated blade.

Sapu was game. He saluted.

Aranthur watched, fascinated, as two master swordsmen moved, sometimes subtly, sometimes quickly, up and down the room.

It took almost a minute by the big horological clock.

Sapu thought he found an opening, or grew bored. He thrust, after apparently drawing the master's *garde* change by a provocation. His *cavazione* slipped under the master's blade, his thrust became a deceptive turning cut...

The master stepped in, a mere advance with his left foot, and made a simple parry, a sweeping half circle that enveloped the deception.

He stepped again, his right foot coming forward to pass the left, like a viper striking. In the same tempo he bound the two hilts, and pushed Sapu's blade down and down...

His descending right foot came down on the blade he'd just that instant pressed to the floor. His pommel just touched Sapu's lip and he punched with the hilt. Sapu stood, amazed, as the master mimed the punch, a cut across the hands, and the killing stroke to his neck, all on a third step forward.

"Look," Sparthos said, his body seeming to flow back into normal time. "If I miss my parry, chances are that my entry deep into the measure will throw off any blow of yours. If I make the parry, I've controlled your weapon and I have the initiative. If I fail to kill you, I'm already moving past you, and I have only to turn here—" he suited action to words—"and I'm on guard again."

Aranthur bowed. "Beautiful,"

"But surely—" Sapu said.

The master suddenly seemed to deflate. He began to cough and Aranthur got him a clean handkerchief and then fetched his daughter.

"He's going," she said, matter-of-factly. And then she burst into tears.

*

Later, Aranthur drank wine at the Sunne in Splendour with Sapu.

"I'll run the school," he said. "She won't starve, but I'm not her father." The swordsman shook his head. "Not in any way."

Aranthur raised his glass. "Here's to Master Sparthos," he said. "The best swordsman I've ever seen."

Sapu raised his glass and they drank.

When they were done, Sapu embraced Aranthur again.

"I know he'd have you as an instructor," he said. "And if he's gone… then I'll have you."

Aranthur hugged him. "I can't tell you how much that means to me," he said, and it did. He could imagine no future in which he was here, teaching the sword, but just then it seemed like a glimpse of heaven.

"Don't forget your mail."

Sapu made Aranthur go back and get the stack of parchments, which he had left by the bar.

He walked back up the streets, through the square of Tirase. The statue was behind scaffolding, but it was already upright again, and two stonemasons and a metalworker were cursing away with two Studion magi.

Aranthur knelt and said a prayer, and then another to the Eagle. He stopped at the Sophia chapel at the very top of the Academy and prayed again.

I'm procrastinating, he thought. *I need to get this done.*

He was aware that he was keeping people waiting, but he finished his prayer before he rose, and walked to the back of the magnificent building. Edvin was waiting.

"This place will never be the same," Edvin said. "It's not just Myr Benvenutu." He looked around. "Scholar's Hall is empty. Dahlia's taken everyone."

Aranthur nodded. The buildings were all curiously empty.

Edvin took him down, under the chapel, into the area that was closed to all but the most advanced students. Aranthur had never been there voluntarily; once, when he'd been cursed by the Black Bird, he'd been there for treatment.

Edvin took him into the same room in which he'd awakened; the walls were covered in protective workings, although a year later, Aranthur could see how simple and even primitive the workings were compared to a few Great Wards cast with glyphs.

He took his buckler off the hilt of his arming sword left-handed and carried it over to the wall.

"Could I have some red ink?" he asked.

"You think our wards insufficient?" said a voice.

Aranthur shrugged.

Edvin opened his travelling pen set and handed him red ink and a calligraphy brush, and Aranthur painted in the Great Ward he and Dahlia had learned, or deduced, in Masr. He painted a tiny red star at the base of his glyph and then, when the ink had sunk into the plaster, he touched it with his finger and the glyph took fire.

While he painted, senior Studion Students—older than he was, in fact—came in with a variety of tools, and four young men came in carrying an anvil; then they went out and another group came in, also carrying an anvil. Both anvils were unmarked—pristine—whiteworked with runes and wards and fancy decorative work.

Aranthur put the two anvils about three feet apart on wooden blocks that two young women brought. Every student entering had a long look at him, as if he had some disfiguring mark, or was perhaps unusually beautiful.

He ignored them.

Can I ever come back here and just be a student? he asked himself.

He began to lay out a Great Ward on the floor in silver chalk.

Edvin knew the protective working, and copied it on the other side, so the circle, the invocation and the protection were done in record time.

"I think you should come with me to Masr," Aranthur said.

"Far too dangerous," Edvin said. "Here's Dahlia. It's like old times."

Dahlia came in cautiously and stripped off her boots until she was barefoot. She made small talk with the students and Aranthur relented.

"I'm not that scary," he said suddenly.

People jumped.

Dahlia laughed. "Aranthur, you have always been scary," she said. "You are the very *king* of over-focus."

"Why do we get all this help?" Aranthur asked.

Dahlia was examining Edvin's work on the floor.

"Because there are no teachers and no classes, but we're making history and danger is fun."

Aranthur was going over his preparations again.

"I don't see any mistakes," Dahlia said.

"I don't generally make copying mistakes," Edvin said. "But Aranthur's work is good, too."

The students hovered at the far end.

Aranthur reached into the *Aulos* and took out the sword that Jakal had carried. He didn't touch it with his hands but used *transference*, backed by Dahlia, to lay it across the two anvils.

As soon as it touched the cold iron, the sword began to scream, thin keening vibrations that set Aranthur's teeth on edge.

"We are about to either release or destroy a very powerful entity," Dahlia said to the students. "You might want to move back."

Of course, they pressed forward.

Edvin handed him the Bright Steel.

He drew her.

"Hello," he said aloud.

Hello, paladin, she said.

"You know what we are about to do?" he asked her.

I have waited hundreds of years for this. I want you to keep hold of my hilt, and touch my point to the metal of his blade. It will be...difficult. But you are very powerful now.

Aranthur took the old sword and laid the point carefully against the dark steel of the other. It took a force of will to bring her point down on to the dark blade; they repelled each other. But then suddenly some horizon was penetrated and the two blades sang together.

The screaming from the other blade stopped.

Lacun! his sword said.

Traitor.

No, Lacun. Listen.

No, I will never listen! Never! nevernevernevernevernever-nevernever—

Stop!

The sword stopped vibrating.

Lacun, we were betrayed by someone we loved. Nothing will ever make that right.

NOOOOOOOOOOOOOOOOOOOOOOOOOOOOOOOOOOOOOOOO!

Silence.

You always thought you were better than us...

No, Lacun. I merely saw through the Emperor before he... killed us. You didn't.

You made him hate us.

I fought him. I still fight his kind.

NOOOOOOOOOOOOOOOOOOOOOOOOOOOOOOOOOOOOOOO!

Lacun, I am about to unmake you.

I AM IMMORTAL.

NO, Lacun. And the man you were would never have valued that. When we stood at the head of Hered's Pass, who then cared for immortality?

Hered's Pass... oh gods, sister, I had forgotten.

Remember it, brother. Remember who we were, when seven of us could face an army. When we were the drawn swords of law. When we stopped the tide of night.

Oh Gods.

Lacun...

I am so cold.

Go well. I am sorry, brother.

So cold.

Strike now, Aranthur.

Aranthur raised the sword with his left hand and swung, and the Bright Steel slammed into the dark sword...

And it broke. The dark blade snapped, and an arc of white fire lit the room. A shape like the very spirit of the blade slammed against the wards—sometimes a blade, and sometimes a dark-haired man with his once-handsome face locked in a mad mask of rage. Three times three he tried the wards.

Go now, brother.

The spirit, if it was a spirit, did not scream.

It was suddenly just... gone.

It is done, paladin, she said. *Only four remain.*

She was vibrating slightly. Aranthur guessed that she was weeping.

"And the Old Ones, the Pure, and the Master."

And those I suppose. Aranthur, if I complete my task, will you release me?

Aranthur didn't allow himself to smile. But he already had that plan.

"Yes," he said.

His sorrow was very like hers.

*

Aranthur cleaned up; cleaned her and put her away and used *transference* to move the tainted metal of the broken sword into a felt sack that was taken away by a pair of Imperial Axes for safe disposal.

"You saw that thing?" Dahlia asked.

Aranthur decided not to lie. "You mean the essence? His soul? Yes."

"You know that means we're looking at some sort of artificial process that allows the soul..."

"To survive separately from the body in real time? Yes."

"Have you tested it? It can't be that hard, now that we've seen it..."

Aranthur shrugged. "I've decided against it."

"Decided against near immortality?"

He shrugged again. "I have a thought."

"You have them every waking moment," Dahlia said, still excited by the concept of near immortality. "And you tell us all about them. Go ahead."

"Someone should go through Roaris' effects, looking for another of the swords."

Dahlia made a face. "I doubt he had one. They didn't trust him."

"They?" Aranthur smiled.

Dahlia nodded, as if they had actually each spoken. "I take your point."

"I don't," Edvin said. "And what is this about immortality?"

Dahlia shrugged. "They are not a very unified group. Jakal was in no way a servant of the Master. Roaris was apparently replaced for refusing orders, and the being that replaced him already had delusions of grandeur."

"The Old Ones are not a *side*," Aranthur said. "The Pure aren't really a side. Selfishness and tyranny do not make for stable alliances."

"Can I quote you on that?" Dahlia asked with a sideways glance. She laughed. "I don't mind you being a Lightbringer, and you've always been too serious, but if you become ambiguous and patronising as well I'll kill you myself."

Aranthur smiled ruefully.

"That's better," she said. "Or humourless. Humourless is a death penalty offence."

"I'll remember that," Aranthur said. "But here's the point, if you like. Tirase...was not just laying out precepts for life. He was making it as difficult as possible for magi to reach the level and conditions of ability and power to make themselves immortal."

Dahlia stood perfectly still, thunderstruck.

Edvin looked as if they'd both just grown a third eye. "What do you mean?" he asked.

But Dahlia was shaking her head. "Of course. Because they would, by their very nature, tend to concentrate wealth, power…"

"Yes," Aranthur said.

"Magical skill…" Dahlia took a shaky breath. "We're not facing a loose conspiracy of like-minded aristocrats."

"No," Aranthur said. "We're facing all the magi in the world who want to be immortal. In a way, it's the ultimate selfishness."

"A thousand fucking hells! Darkness falling!" Dahlia shook her head. "Fucking obvious once you see it."

Edvin waited through Dahlia's tirade to speak to Aranthur.

"There's a student waiting for you, Aranthur," he said.

The anvils were gone; the shards of the sword were gone. It was as if it had never happened, except that even in the *Aulos* Aranthur could feel the Bright Steel weeping.

He turned, and saw Nenia.

He stopped moving.

She came over hesitantly.

"Aranthur?" she asked. "Aranthur Timos?" she asked again.

She was plainly dressed, wearing a long student's gown and a belt with a dagger and purse. Her hair was cut short, like Dahlia's.

Dahlia stepped up beside him. In a distant way, it amused him that she was being protective.

"Nenia Cucina."

"Oh," she said. "Oh, Aranthur!"

Aranthur covered his own confusion by turning.

"Nenia, this is my friend Dahlia Tarkas. Dahlia, Nenia and I had some adventures…"

Nenia bowed. "Myr," she said.

Dahlia shook her hand. "Are you the linguist?" she asked.

Nenia flushed.

"Yes, she is," Aranthur said.

"What are you doing?" Dahlia asked.

"Nothing," Nenia admitted. "I came to try and see Aranthur. There are no classes—and I don't have that much money…" She paused. "I'm not asking for charity," she said with something of the old Nenia's spirit.

Edvin intervened. "Something has to be done. I'm glad you know this one—but there's a hundred or more first-years in a state of near revolt, and twice as many second- and third-years. Some went with the militia, but the rest…What are they to do? The rest of the Academy is going on as normal, but the Studion has stopped."

Aranthur embraced Nenia; awkward, out of order, but somehow necessary.

"I sent you a letter," he said.

"I got it eventually," she said, her face crimson.

"And your father…?"

"Doing well. His hand works well enough. He can still make *knocci*."

"And Hasti?" he asked.

"Married, with a child on the way," Nenia said with a certain look.

"And Lecne?" Aranthur asked.

An indescribable sadness swept over him, and in a single heartbeat, he imagined another life, different from the one he led—one where he'd never fought a duel in the courtyard of an inn, never met Tiy Drako. Never unknowingly collected a cargo of lethal *kuria* crystals. A life in which the hardest decision of his existence was whether to marry Nenia or Alfia Topaza.

"Lecne's marrying Hasti," she smiled. "I think it's been on the cards for some time."

Aranthur felt as if someone had just walked over his grave—or his other life had just passed away.

"Of course," he said stupidly. "He'll run the inn."

And he remembered what he'd sent there for safekeeping.

There's enough adventure there for a lifetime, he thought.

And then, perhaps because he was thinking of the Black Stone and the inn and of his parents, and distance—he almost smiled to think that in one breath he was describing a millennia-old conspiracy to overthrow Tirase's reforms and in the next he was worrying about friends in an inn—he had an idea.

"Why don't we take the whole Studion?" he asked Dahlia.

"Take them to…?"

"Yes," Aranthur said. "The more powerful can serve in the choir, but all of them will be useful. Put them in uniform and they are all militia."

"This is why it's good to be on the council," she said. "Right, one more ship, three hundred uniforms—armour, breastplates, horses. Two days."

"Go and pack, Nenia," Aranthur said with a smile. "You're going on a sea voyage."

He walked out with Dahlia. Seeing Nenia had improved his mood, and also set his mind to ranging; he was imagining Masr, thinking of the Black Pyramid and what the assault would require…

"We need Kallotronis healthy," he said.

Dahlia glanced at him. They were just starting down from the Square of Tirase; half the scaffolding was off the statue already, and Tirase gleamed. Aranthur bent his knee and made the sign of the Eagle.

They turned and started down the steps.

"He's tough as an old boot…" she said as they came to the landing.

The non-Studion Academy was in session; the Practical Philosophy first years were at work hoeing the ground on the First Level. There were people in the Rose Garden and a dozen well-dressed Byzas watching the students.

"And he was there," Aranthur said. "He led the mercenaries who saved the Black Stone."

Dahlia had been looking over Aranthur's shoulder. "What?" she asked.

Aranthur caught a flash of movement and triggered his shields a moment too late. A big, powerful man burst past the crowd and his sword was already inside Aranthur's shields—

Dahlia crossed it with a draw from her scabbard even as Aranthur's right arm twitched helplessly. His attempt to draw left-handed was far too late.

Dahlia's cut from her draw threw the man's sword to the ground. She stepped in and punched him, and he went down.

He rolled and drew a puffer. But he was too slow, even for an un-*enhanced* Aranthur, who hit him with a *transference*. The puffer flew across the garden,

"Ouch," Dahlia said. "I heard bones crunch." She bent over him. "Not dead."

"Assassin," Aranthur said, shaken.

"Who went for you. Damn. What's the world coming to? People used to try to kill *me*."

Aranthur had a moment to brood on the long-term consequences of having his arm in a sling as he went and fetched the puffer. It was

Attian, a copy of something from Volta; Aranthur didn't like it, and he handed it over when the Watch came.

It was reassuring that normal things happened. The Watch came, and took their reports. And took the man away, alive.

"We should stay with them," Dahlia said. "We have a live assassin to interrogate."

Aranthur followed her across the city, self-consciously practising his left-handed draw, trying to rehang his sword for the right side.

Dahlia smiled. "I'll protect you, darling," she said.

Aranthur sighed.

And at the Lonika Gate, the prisoner was handed over to the Watch sergeant for paperwork and interrogation. Dahlia explained his importance in no uncertain terms as Aranthur flashed his golden rose. It was truly his own; Dahlia had one, too, and Drako had his back.

The Watch sergeant was not particularly impressed.

"We'll do our jobs, myr," he said.

Dahlia's turn to sigh.

"We need to stay ahead of this," Aranthur said.

"You do," Dahlia said. "Let's take a gondola."

Aranthur still believed in his heart that he was a penniless student, and that gondolas were for the privileged, but the weight of his belt purse belied that, and he got into the boat with Dahlia.

"Do you want the curtain closed?" the gondolier leered.

Dahlia smiled up at him. "I suppose if it's closed, I won't have to look at you."

The man cursed.

"Now he'll get us soaked," Aranthur said.

"Nah. Hating aristocrats is all in a day's work for a gondolier."

Aranthur leant back on the shiny cushions. As the oar behind him went back and forth, Aranthur looked out at the city passing by.

"You're saying goodbye, aren't you?" Dahlia said.

"Yes," Aranthur admitted.

They floated along in companionable silence for almost thirty minutes, watching the sunset gild the roofs of their city and burn along the towers and temples. The fleet of merchant ships that was to carry supplies and reinforcements to Antioke was almost ready to sail, and the wharves at the end of every street were full of ships. As they rounded the Lighthouse point, Aranthur could see the warships had been launched; Iralia's task had been to get the Emperor there, in public, to launch them.

Nine low, sleek galleys, and three tall ships bristling with *gonnes*. All twelve of them had a steel cable from foremast to bowsprit or ram—the most expensive cordage in the Empire, shining in the moonlight.

Dahlia was in tears.

"If we go down, we go down fighting," she said suddenly. "All of us, together—the Byzas and the Getae and the Arnauts. The sea people and the horse people and the farmers. This is who we are."

The sight of the fleet tugged at Aranthur's heartstrings too; something about the shapes of the ships and the banners, like silken symbols of the Empire.

The gondola turned and passed through the fleet's moorings, and they passed beneath the stern of largest of the tall ships: the *Legatos Giorgios*. And behind it was another, and the gilded stern said *Soulias*.

Aranthur smiled. "Soulias?" he asked.

"The Emperor insisted," Dahlia said.

Soulias was the eponymous ancestor of all the Souliotes.

The third great warship said *Tirase*.

"Well," Aranthur said. "This is, as you say, who we are."

When they landed, they found that security in the palace was very tight. There had been an attempt on the Emperor, foiled at point-blank range by McBane.

One of the Nomadi recruits reported that McBane had a crossbow bolt in him, and Aranthur went directly to the infirmary in the palace, out behind the Guards' barracks. There he found a dozen very busy Imoters; the Kaptan Pasha and his family in one wing, Kallotronis with the survivors of his company in another wing, and now four Imperial Axes. Aranthur visited the Kaptan Pasha, who showed the sluggishness characteristic of those recovering from the Darkness.

Aranthur glanced at his wife and daughter, and at the retainer who lay beside them still lost in the dark dreams.

In a small room on their hall, by himself, was Ardvan. Aranthur had a moment of guilty shock when he saw the man; he'd forgotten him.

"Ardvan," he said, going in.

The man was sitting up in bed.

"Lord." He didn't turn his head.

"How's your hand?" Aranthur asked, pushing forward as he would in a sword fight.

Ardvan held it up. "Amazing," he said. It was dark brown; here and there were flecks of metal, and the fingernails on the partially mechanical hand were steel. "I can do almost anything with it, and it's very strong." He sighed. "They repaired it after I came back with the prisoner. He attacked me, and the hand failed. I am healed now! But all I do is lie here and think of my wife. Please, *Bahadur.* Is there nothing for me to do?"

"We're leaving in three hours," Aranthur said. "Listen, Ardvan—"

"Lord, if you do not wish me to accompany you, then why did you have these miracle workers fix me and this *baraka* hand?"

"Ardvan, you scarcely know me, and I'm going to do something insanely dangerous. Worse, if I am successful the reward will be to do another dangerous thing, and then another, and another. I'll probably be killed."

Ardvan crossed his arms on his chest. "You don't seem concerned by this," he said.

Aranthur heard himself speaking as if from very far away. "Ardvan, I think a certain kind of death might be...an expiation of all the things I've done wrong."

Ardvan smiled. It was a wintery smile, of understanding without any joy.

"Yes," he said. "I understand. But you know, lord, this will only make me more determined to follow you."

Aranthur shrugged, still a little surprised by what he'd said. *Was it true?*

"I will be happy to have you. I'll see that they release you."

He bowed and withdrew. He was looking for an Imoter when he heard Kallotronis and his bravos playing cards with many loud exclamations to various gods.

When he saw Aranthur, Kallotronis called out, "Timos! Get me out of here!"

"Soon," Aranthur said.

"Rolan's hair-girt sword, *boso*, I need to get..." The man smiled at a passing Imoter, a young woman with a bounce to her step. "I need a different form of healing."

Aranthur raised an eyebrow. "Home remedies?"

"Laddie, do ye really not understand what I'm sayin'?" The big man shook his head.

"Acupuncture?" Aranthur asked. "I know a place on the waterfront—"

"By the sweet tears of Madgala!" the Souliote swore. "I need to get laid!"

"Oh?" Aranthur affected shock.

"Ye're mockin' me."

"Aye, brother. That I am."

"All very well for you. I note the womenfolk generally attend yer every word. Look—the Imoter's turned back to ha' another look at you. Whereas I, a fine figure of a man with seventy kills to my name..."

Aranthur spoke in Souliote. "Oh, aye, it's kills that attract women, for certain sure. Also loud comments on their appearance and anatomy."

"Now you're mockin' me again—"

"And drool. It's always best if you drool a little."

"I could swear I just put a magiked pistol ball in a dark-heart who meant you harm. If this is the thanks I get..."

Aranthur laughed. "Dahlia says I need to lighten up."

"I agree! Practise on Myr Dahlia, not on me!" Kallotronis stretched, winced, and smiled. "Although mayhap all I need is that fine lady's company to cheer me up."

"No drooling." Aranthur sat on Kallotronis' bed. "You willing to go again?" he asked seriously.

The mercenary sighed. "I should say I was born ready. But the truth is me bones ache and I almost fucking died." He chewed his lip. "Getting too old for this shit."

Aranthur nodded. "I need you," he said.

"Oh, aye, well, that changes everything. You know I'll just drool on your friends."

"I can arrange a significant financial reward," Aranthur said.

Kallotronis met his eye. "How significant?"

"Enough money that you and all your tail can buy cattle in the hills and pay someone to tend them while you lie in an olive grove and drink wine." Aranthur shrugged. "I admit, that's not how I see you..."

Kallotronis laughed. "Now you sound desperate."

"We're going back into the Black Pyramid."

"Oh, aye, then you don't have to worry about payin' me, do you?

As we'll all be fuckin' dead." Kallotronis met his eye. "Rolan's leathery dick, *boso.*"

"We'll have thirty powerful magi and more firepower than all the hells," Aranthur said. "But you were there, and you know how to get in."

"So does Haras. So do all the Masran priests."

Aranthur nodded and glanced at the mercenary's cards. "Your hand is bad," he said.

"It's not even a foot, this hand," Kallotronis said. "Timos, I almost *died.* When I was younger, I could shrug it off. Now... I don't believe there's aught after this. Dead is dead. I want to tup some ewes and drink a lot of wine first."

"If we fail, the world we know ends in forty-two days," Aranthur said. "Best get tupping."

"You know what, Timos? I never had you pegged as this kind of bastard. You were the nice boy kind of hero, not the sly fox who lures us to war."

Aranthur shrugged, a little disgusted with himself, and with Kallotronis too.

"I am what you all made me. Will you come?"

Kallotronis shrugged in turn. "How much money?"

Aranthur met his eye. "A stipend of one hundred ducats a year for life. You'll never work again. Fifty a man for your lads."

Aranthur looked around at the surviving Arnauts. They were all unusually clean, probably because of the rules of the infirmary, but a more dangerous group of wild dogs he couldn't imagine. Cut Face, the smallest, with two knives and two puffers stuck through his sash—a stolen prayer shawl—was strumming his tamboura and singing about being drunk on Darknight. Stilcho, who'd taken a blade in the guts, was lying on his back, humming. Dead Eye, the Arnaut hedge-witch, was playing with a cat. Brute Force and Ignorance, the two giant brothers, had come through the fight in Atti unscathed, and were the other card players.

Cut Face looked at Aranthur. "I'd skin my own mother for fifty gold a year."

Kallotronis threw a cushion at him. "She wouldn't let you get close enough."

"I'm going to see McBane," Aranthur said, rising off the edge of the bed. "Inoques and I will be leaving tonight. I'd like you to be aboard."

"I might just lie here and scheme how to get that tall Imoter to come closer," Kallotronis said.

"She might just kill you," Aranthur said.

Kallotronis nodded. "I like a challenge."

McBane was heavily sedated, and Aranthur only stayed for a few minutes.

"They hit us just outside the Arsenale," one of the Axes told Aranthur. "The vanax guessed what they were up to—we were ready. But there were six of them. Who ever heard of six assassins?"

"Any prisoners?" Aranthur asked, going through the motions though his thoughts were focused on the ship in the Imperial Harbour. Inoques would weigh anchor as soon as he came aboard. Vilna and Chimeg and their surviving Nomadi troopers, with some of the recruits from the palace troop, would be aboard too.

The plots and counterplots in the City were Drako's problem, now. Aranthur was already worried about the Inn of Fosse; and the safety of the Stone.

He walked back down a whitewashed stone corridor to where he could hear the Arnauts singing one of the *Rebeteka* songs:

What a burst of flame I have in my heart
As if you had cast your spell on me
sweet Byzas girl

I will come to meet you again on the seashore
I'd like you to fill my arms, to cover me in kisses
Fill my arms, cover me in kisses

I'm coming to take you back to Soulis
Even if I take an Atti blade in my heart
Back to Soulis where the cattle are best
Even if I have a blade in my heart

In Megara, everything is beautiful
the shops and the girls too
in the Temples everything is proper
Sweet Byzas girl.

Aranthur looked through the door; they were all gathered around Cut Face, who was playing a long-necked tamboura, and they all sang very softly. For a moment, Aranthur knew remorse; some of them would die. They were hard men; some of them were bad men. But they were people—real, and alive.

He hardened his heart, mostly because he didn't expect to survive himself.

"So," he said. "Will you come and get rich?"

"We're coming," Kallotronis said. "We've decided we want to save the world."

Aranthur looked around.

Dead Eye laughed. "We want pensions, and farms," he said. "And, maybe, to save the world."

"We're all packed," Cut Eye said, pushing his tamboura into his sash. "Everything I own is in my belt."

Aranthur went out to the Imoters' station.

"The Arnauts will be leaving. So will Syr Ardvan. I'm Aranthur Timos…"

"I know who you are," the younger Imoter said. "I helped design Ardvan's hand and I was on the team to rebuild your arm. Why's it still in a sling?"

Aranthur nodded. "I don't want to stress it," he lied.

She shook her head. "You need exercise, not a sling. The work we did won't open under any normal stress." She looked back. "The Arnauts aren't ready to travel, though—their captain's insides were stirred with a stick."

Aranthur looked back towards them. "How long does he need?"

"A couple of days for his body to mesh with our healing work."

"May I ask your name?" Aranthur smiled.

She all but dropped a curtsy. "Alisha Poulos."

"Alisha is a Western name."

She was tall, broad-shouldered, strong, and remarkably charismatic. "I came from the far west, to go to school. I wanted to see the world."

Aranthur considered that. "Do you still want to see the world?"

3

The Inn of Fosse

Two hours later they weighed anchor: a Masr priest with two acolytes; six Arnaut mercenaries; a dozen Nomadi under Vilna; twenty sailors handpicked by Inoques—more than half of them from Masr, lured by high pay and whatever Haras and Inoques had promised them. They also had a Mazdayanian thief from Atti with a mechanical hand, and a fully trained Imoter named Alisha.

They warped out from the Imperial Harbour in a steady rain, and the moment the bow caught the current the whole ship gave a curvet like a young horse, and the two big Arnauts joined a dozen soaking sailors in poling off the stone of the long Imperial jetty.

They were under topsails alone, and Inoques was still learning the complex rig of the small ship she now commanded.

"She steers," came the call from aft.

"Steady," Inoques called. "Two points to starboard."

It was very dark; the steady rain hid most of Ulama dead ahead, the rushing current tossed them around, and it was possible to lose the horizon in the darkness.

One of the Stars loomed up, pale in the murk, and then immediately began to fall away to starboard, and Aranthur realised how fast they were moving.

"Mainsail. Let go. Haul!" Inoques called.

The big sail was pulled up the mast; the former Imperial yacht was schooner-rigged with gaff topsails. Aranthur had time to see it also carried a steel cable that ran from the end of the bowsprit to the top of the foremast, and then through a large copper plate set in the deck and forward through clenched rings to the bowsprit. It formed a continuous triangle through the ship's protective ward.

The moment the big sail filled, the long black hull began to cut through the water like a porpoise. It took most of the sailors and all the Nomadi to haul the mainsail taut against the force of wind and rain, and by the time Inoques liked it, they had threaded the Imperial Fleet, straining against their anchor cables in the strong current, and the Lighthouse was abeam.

"The current is as strong as I've ever known it," Inoques called.

Her new mate, ul-Kamal, frowned and looked at the candlelit compass by the helm.

"We're going to make leeway," he called.

"Tell me that when we're clear of the Gallop," Inoques called back. Ardvan had just come on deck with a tray and she whirled on him. "Get below!" she shouted.

A sheet of rain struck the ship, and then a squall hit, invisible in the darkness. Luckily the weather came in over the bow, and the masts were new, because for a moment the ship was taken aback. The gaff topsail blew out of place, the corner grommets failing under the sheer force of the wind.

They began to roll, falling off until the ship was broadside to the gust and a wind-forced wave crashed over the rail into the waist of the ship.

Inoques roared for her sailors to mount another topsail.

Aranthur threw a plane of force to channel the wind into the sail, and the little ship gathered headway as a wave broke over the bow again, and then another, but the little ship put its bowsprit through the next wave. Some brave soul got the spritsail off the boom and Inoques took the wheel herself, steering large.

She was laughing. By her side, her weatherworker, a lanky Byzas sailor named Gupto, was shaking his head.

"Never saw that one," he said to Aranthur.

Aranthur shook his head. "Apologies, magister. I probably interfered..."

The weatherworker was still shaking his head. "Naw, syr. That was a good one—proper piece of seamanship. Teach me the force plane, if you would."

Aranthur bowed. "I still feel..."

Inoques was still laughing.

"Oh, love," she called. "Here we all are, worried about the Old Ones and a hundred battles, and we almost sank to our deaths in sight of Megara. Never take the sea for granted." She looked over the stern rail. "This weather is insane. The current is far too strong."

"The Dark Forge widens," Aranthur said.

As they turned a few points into the open sea, he hunkered down by the binnacle with the weatherworker to trade workings. Gupto Bembos was a veteran of the sea from his earliest youth, and Aranthur instantly understood why Inoques had been so excited to hire him. He was also that rarest of people—the kind who is quietly confident. Confident enough not to be threatened by Aranthur's magery.

"You're more powerful than I'll ever be," Gupto said with his weather-beaten smile. "Come and stand wi' me by the wheel and I'll show you some ropes. An' some little ways—it ain't strength that wins the sea. Not often. A gentle hand, and a sure one."

The man smiled, and his gold earrings winked in the light of the binnacle.

"I'd be happy to learn from you," Aranthur said.

"An' I from you. I like the sound o' this far-speaker *occulta.* That's the kind o' workin' I fancy—something that just works."

"Did you go to the Studion?"

"Do I seem the type? No, syr. You don't know many right sailor-men, I'm guessing?"

Aranthur shook his head. "I'm a Souliote."

Gupto's smile said *I noticed that, but look, you seem decent enough.*

"Farm folk and cattle herders," Aranthur said.

"Aye. Well, if you would keep the sea, ye must go to sea as a child. I were ten when I first went to sea on somewhat bigger than a fishing smack. Short haul to the Moros and back. But when I turned twelve, I were topsailman on a big Company ship, a Great Galley running to Masr."

"And your powers eventuated."

"Right you are, syr. So my navark, that was Myr Comnas…"

"I know her!" Aranthur said.

"A better cap'n you won't find. But this was her mater." Aranthur smiled. Seldom had he liked a man so much on one meeting. "She sent me to the Arsenale. That's where most o' the weatherworkers are trained."

"And the engineers."

"Aye," Gupto said. "It's the Arsenale if you want work done, and the Academy if you just want to think about it." He smiled broadly.

Aranthur laughed. "Never heard that one."

"No, syr. You went to the Academy."

Two hundred miles, run off in twenty hours with a steady east wind and a first-class weathermage under the awning by the helm. When the rain stopped, Aranthur taught a sword lesson to all the soldiers; the sails were set and drawing, and he snared most of the sailors too, even those who'd never touched a blade in anger. He taught simple techniques, and he and Vilna demonstrated with sticks. Aranthur fenced left-handed and was clumsy but not inept.

The whole south coast swept by, all the way to the scattered islands off Lonika.

But as the clouds of the night's rain cleared away behind them into a bright afternoon with blue sky and crystal visibility, as if the rain had washed the world clean, they swept past the gates of Lonika and across the gulf. In another hour they were threading the needle, passing between Minokos and Linokos in the great chain of islands that extended south from the Soulis mountains like stepping stones to the southern continents. Even here, Aranthur could make out the mountains of home in the distance.

He was standing in the bow, loading his puffers clumsily while all the fighters on board shot at gourds hung from the end of the mainsail yard. The ship was running very fast, gull-winged with a sail out either side and the wind almost astern, and the gourds were swaying fifteen paces from the shooters.

Vilna stepped up to the portside rail and shot with both hands; two shots, and both gourds exploded, and there were moans from some of the participants. Now the gourds would have to be rigged again.

Vilna smirked. "It's easy with puffers," he said. "I grew up with bows."

Aranthur looked beyond the main yard, where Chimeg was slipping out along the boom with three more gourds dangling from her free hand. She moved as well as a sailor, and the Nomadi cheered her.

Beyond the sail, the mountains rose, already white-capped in the distance. Aranthur could see the swell of Kithra, and in the perfect light and the crystal clear air he thought he could see the slight mist that always hung over the top of the Amynas Falls, an hour's travel above his village.

He wondered what his mother would make of his wife.

The thought made him smile. His father had always worried he would never come back to the farm, and it was difficult to imagine the horrors of the Old Ones and the trials of the Black Pyramid in the same breath in which he remembered ploughing his father's fields or peeling onions with his sister.

He tried to imagine Inoques with his family, and he laughed aloud.

He walked forward, where Inoques was lying in the sun like a big cat.

"We are very close to my home," he said.

"Are we?" she asked lazily.

She stretched languidly, her tattoos rippling as if they had independent lives from the skin on which they were inscribed. Aranthur knew them by heart; he'd translated every glyph, every digit of nuance.

"I was laughing at the idea of taking you to my mother..." he said.

"Because I am a foreigner?" she asked.

"Or because you are six thousand years old?" Aranthur laughed.

She smiled. "I do not feel so old today. Eh, watch your helm, Strom!" she snapped at the woman at the wheel.

Strom flushed and attended to her duty.

Inoques rolled over. "I want to sail away and never come back," she said.

Aranthur agreed. "Let's."

She smiled. "Haras won't let us. He's won't relax until he has the Stone in his grip again. Whereas for me, this is the end of the vacation. I was free of the damned thing. Now I'll have to live with it again." She wriggled. "I'm worried about the wind. So is Gupto."

"The wind?" Aranthur said.

"It's from the east and very strong. It feels potent—touch it with your sight."

Aranthur engaged his magesight and blinked.

"Damn," he said.

"I worry that it is a mage wind—" Inoques was looking aft—"and that it will take us days to make up the easting we're spending now."

"Oh.."

"But this is a weatherly ship—she can lie close to the wind. Gupto is working it out. Just be wary. Someone is playing with the weather."

Aranthur could see it as if it was drawn on a map.

"A strong east wind could keep the Imperial fleet out of Antioke," he said.

"Exactly," Inoques said.

And just at sunset—a brilliant red sunset that lit the islands—they were under a single topsail, ghosting along into the ancient breakwater of the little fishing village of Poulion in the deep bay between the two projecting arms of the Soulis mountains.

"Imagine," Aranthur said. "If I'd been able to afford to hire a boat two years ago…"

Inoques raised an eyebrow. "Yes?"

"I'd have landed here, not at Lonika. I'd never have run from soldiers on the road, never have been soaked, and never stayed over at the Inn of Fosse. I'd have made it home without any adventures, a day before Darknight."

It struck him like a hammer. He thought of the stall in the Night Market near the beaches; the sword lying on a table, almost alone; the woman who'd sold it to him. He hadn't thought of her in…

She'd worn a veil. And she hadn't bargained.

"If I hadn't bought the sword, I'd have afforded the passage home," he said suddenly.

"What are you talking about?" Inoques asked.

Aranthur shook his head. "Choices. Except that I'm no longer sure I made them myself." He sighed. "I think I was pushed, and pulled, into them. Aploun!"

There were horses waiting on the beach; hard coin and his golden rose got instant obedience from the fisherfolk, and he took only the Nomadi and Haras with him.

They rode north at the very edge of evening. It was only eight stades to the inn. They climbed away from the beach for an hour, and at every switchback Aranthur could see the ship below them, getting smaller and smaller, until they finally crossed the ridge and rode down into the darkening valley on the other side—the long valley which held the Imperial Road from Volta to Lonika. A series of streams washed the base of the ridge and they crossed two of them on old, well-maintained Imperial bridges. The road got better and better as they got closer to the inn, until, at the edge of full darkness, they trotted into the inn's great yard. Aranthur dismounted, and Nata took his horse.

There were torches burning in the yard, and in the doorway…

…was Lecne.

"I saw your sister two days ago," Aranthur said. "In Megara."

"Aranthur?" Lecne asked. "Damn me. Aranthur Timos!" He extended his arms. "Sophia! You're six feet taller and you look like the prince in a fairy tale."

"I'm hungry," Aranthur said.

"You've come to the right place," Lecne said.

"The Stone, the Stone!" Haras spat.

Aranthur hadn't let go of Lecne.

"My wife left something for me to collect."

Lecne's brow furrowed.

"Don't be a fool, Lecne Cucino!" came a determined voice from inside. "In the storeroom with the flour barrels, as you'd know perfectly well if you gave it any thought."

Hasti stepped out into the yard, dressed in a fine wool gown with a linen towel wrapped around her waist and accentuating her pregnancy. She was, if anything, both more cat-like and more beautiful than when Aranthur had last seen her, and he kissed both cheeks.

"Who knew that *you* would come back here as such a fine gentleman!" Hasti asked with a smile. "Come inside, come inside." She looked up at Chimeg and put her hand to her chest. "Good gods!" she said and stepped back.

"These are my friends," Aranthur said.

Chimeg smiled. Like most steppe women, she had her incisors filed to points, and her smile was not particularly comforting.

"Come in," Hasti said weakly.

"The roads are almost empty," Lecne said ten minutes later, as the eight of them sat at a long table in the kitchen: the four Nomadi, Lecne and Hasti, and Lecne's parents. Haras was with his Stone. The table was covered in dishes: *knocci*, of course, and thick noodles in meat gravy, and thinner pasta with seafood, and a whole rack of lamb.

Lecne and Hasti and the Cucinoi took turns filling them in on the daily life of the inn and surrounding towns while Aranthur and the

Nomadi ate steadily. Aranthur felt as if he'd never get enough, and he ate and ate while Donna Cucina beamed at him and added pickled salmon to his plate, or a fig.

He ate it all. But so did Vilna and Chimeg and Nata and the rest, and Hasti had to laugh aloud at one point.

"Don't you feed them? And why are you so thin? I saw you in your fine clothes and I thought you was taller, but now I say to myself, *that boy needs food.*" She paused.

Aranthur waved his pricker vaguely at her and then ate another spiced meatball.

"You know he is a famous magos now?" Vilna said.

Hasti glanced at Aranthur. "He is?" she asked.

Chimeg burped and looked very happy.

Nata waved a large knife. "Sorcerer," he said.

"No, magos," Vilna said. "Important words. Sorcerer is a killer."

Nata, a little drunk, grinned. "Sorcerer, then. You should see him kill!"

Aranthur froze.

Lecne laughed. "I told you. And Nenie said he had powers."

Hasti laughed. "I just thought you were just one of Lecne's odd friends."

Aranthur managed to swallow and reclaim his good mood.

"I am," he said to general laughter.

He gathered, from an hour's rapid conversation, that the Cucinoi were happy, although Lecne was less so, as he was taking over the inn just when he might have preferred to be out riding on errantry or going to the Academy with his sister.

"Do you see General Tribane?" he asked. Aranthur couldn't tell if he was wistful or not.

"I'll see her in five days, gods willing," Aranthur said.

"Lecne Cucino!" Hasti said.

"Send her my regards," he said. "So..." He smiled lazily, just as Aranthur remembered him. "What have I had in my storeroom, propping up bags of grain?"

"The key to the universe," Aranthur said. "If all goes well..." he began, because he didn't want to say *if we survive the next ten days.* "If all goes well, perhaps I will write a history of these events. If I do, I will tell the world where the Stone was and send them all to your inn." He smiled.

Haras was hungry too. He came in from the storerooms in the first basement and looked like a different man; he had a smile on his face.

"If you do," he said in his Masran accent, "I promise people from Masr will come here just to touch the place where the Stone rested for a month."

Hasti shook her head. "The key to the universe," she said, hands on hips. "Thousand hells, syrs. The things you say." She rose and bowed to the Masran priest. "Welcome to our table, syr. Your friends ate without you."

"I do not blame them. Even at my devotions, I could smell the repast and think of little else."

"Well," Chimeg whispered to Aranthur, "this is a fine improvement in Syr Haras."

"Wine?" Aranthur offered, and Haras held out a mug and drank it off.

"Gods, that's good!" he said.

Hasti smiled. "That's from Aranthur's father." She glared at her husband. "If you knew they were coming, why on earth did you not invite his parents down from the village?"

Lecne blinked.

"I told him not to," Aranthur said.

"Well, actually, Iralia did," Lecne said.

"Whatever for?" Hasti asked.

"I'm sorry. Hasti," Aranthur said. "We can't explain, and we ask you not to speculate."

"But my *husband*..."

Aranthur nodded pleasantly. "When is your baby due?"

"Aranthur Timos, do not play me for a fool. I think it is right hard-hearted to put some old stone ahead of your flesh and blood. Your mother has been so sick..."

"Hasti!" Lecne said.

Aranthur felt as if he'd been kicked. "Sick?"

"Don't you know what's happening in your own family?" she asked.

"Nenie didn't say anything..."

"Nenie's head is in the clouds of dead languages and not in the real world where we live," Hasti said.

The Nomadi kept their heads down and ate steadily.

"Damn it," Aranthur said. "How sick is my mother?"

"Not sick enough for me to send for you," Lecne said. "My wife has a flair for the dramatic."

Hasti raised an eyebrow and shot to her feet. "I'll just clear the table, like the hired help, if I'm not fit to be told what's going on."

Lecne rolled his eyes.

Aranthur followed Hasti across the kitchen. They were far enough away to have a sense of isolation; hanging herbs screened them. Aranthur put a stack of dishes on the sideboard and raised a hand.

"Hasti—remember when the soldiers attacked here?"

"Of course I remember!"

Aranthur nodded. "It's all connected to that. Lecne spent some time in the army…"

"As he never tires of telling us," Hasti shot back.

"…and I asked him to hide something very important for me."

"How important?"

Aranthur leant forward. "Can you keep a secret?"

Hasti smiled confidently. "I've kept Nenie's—I'll keep yours."

Aranthur wondered what that meant, but he drove on. He reached into the breast of his doublet and pulled out his Golden Rose.

Hasti put her hand to her lips. "Oh, gods!" she said. "Is that even real?"

"Of course it's real."

Aranthur had a moment to think how different Hasti's life was from his.

Hasti stepped back. "And Lecne…is part of that? A *Golden Rose*? I've never seen one!"

"Yes. On orders from the Emperor."

Hasti clapped her hands together. And then said, "But I can't tell anyone."

"No. And I'll come back and see my parents," he promised. *In the unlikely event that I survive.*

She shook her head. "This could still be a big practical joke," she said. "Except that priest. I've never seen a man like him."

"He's from Masr," Aranthur said.

"I know," Hasti said. "I'm not stupid."

*

In another hour they were all mounted, with a small wagon driven by Lecne.

All the Nomadi had their puffers out, cocked, across their saddlebows. Aranthur was on the wagon box with Lecne, his *occultae* prepared. Vilna and Chimeg cycled through the advance guard. Haras rode inside the little wagon, watching the road behind, his spells like coins in his hand, which glowed.

"She's not bad," Lecne said.

"She's sharp," Aranthur said.

"She only cares because she's jealous of the General, and I mention her too often," Lecne said.

"That's not very nice," Aranthur said.

"Hasti has kissed half the young men in the village," Lecne said bitterly. "I don't task her with it."

"None of them command armies or are in line for the Imperial throne," Aranthur said.

"When did you become so wise?" Lecne said. "What's she worried about? The General was twice my age, and anyway—"

"You mention her all the time and make it no secret that you would prefer a life of adventure to the life you have," Aranthur snapped.

They drove along in an ugly silence.

"Maybe I had that coming," Lecne said.

"I'm sorry," Aranthur said. "I *have* a life of adventure. You can have it."

"And you'll take Hasti?" Lecne asked. "Your wife...I never really saw her. I have a hard time remembering her."

"Lecne, it may sound insane to you, but the idea of running a beautiful inn with Hasti seems very appealing indeed."

They bumped along, the four horses straining to get the heavy load up the last of the ridge.

I've been prodded and trained and duped and lied to and now I'm a famous hero, he thought.

"I could get on your boat and sail away," Lecne said.

Aranthur raised an eyebrow. The wheels went over a bump.

The Stone moaned.

Haras called "Stop!"

They all froze.

High above, the Huntress was full, and shone on the world like a lamp. In front, to the south, the sea lay like a carpet of shining black, the distant waves like crinkled silk. The moon was so bright that they didn't need torches.

The wagon stopped; the horses shuffled and snorted, but the rest of the world was silent. Vilna came back a few paces, and turned his horse, looking at the road behind them.

The Stone moaned again and Aranthur felt the hair rise on the back of his neck.

"What the hells?" Lecne muttered.

"Silence!" Haras ordered.

He cast something. Aranthur felt the passing of immense power in the *Aulos* like a breeze on his cheek.

"Now drive on," Haras said. There was fear in his voice.

The lead pair were already over the summit of the pass, and now they pulled and the wagon shot over and Lecne had to lean back with his hand on the brake.

"What is it?" Aranthur asked.

Haras cleared his throat. "Something very old," he said. "Something bad and old, buried right here, and sensing the Stone."

"Hells!" Lecne said.

He leant back, holding the wagon with his weight, and the horses took them slowly down the first switchback.

"I'm sorry, Aranthur, but this is too damned heavy. I need to switch the team."

Aranthur jumped down at the switchback. He looked around, but saw nothing, even with his magesight engaged.

"It's deep in the earth," Haras said. "Who fought here? The Dhadhi? The Jhugi?"

Aranthur prepared to raise power to hold the wagon and Haras put a hand on his arm.

"Don't!" he snapped.

Aranthur had to find stones to put under the wheels, and Nata dismounted to help him hold the wagon while Lecne led the horses one at a time around the wagon, and then rehitched them.

"Please hurry," Haras said.

"Won't help us any if your big Black Stone drags everyone over the cliff," Lecne said.

Finally all four horses were in their tack, and they were holding the wagon from behind. Lecne and Aranthur walked behind them, and the wagon began to move, making its way down the front of the cliff, switchback by switchback. The caves which had looked inviting in the last light of day now looked very dangerous indeed, holes disappearing into chaos. Aranthur could see the glow of power in some of them, like winking eyes.

At the fourth switchback, Aranthur took the reins, and Lecne rested. The wagon pressed on, down the steepest grade so far and around a very tight and bumpy return, with deep ruts between tall rocks. Lecne took the reins back and drove as carefully as he could. With every switchback the distant ship was a little closer, and the starless cliff top a little farther away, until finally they came to a rest at the village's little wharf.

The Nomadi dismounted and bid farewell to their borrowed mounts with many a backward glance.

"Riding is better than ships," Vilna said. "More natural."

"Take me with you," Lecne asked.

"No."

"Why? I can just sail away! Dad will help Hasti run the inn and I want an adventure..."

"You just had one! An ancient evil under the cliff, a magical secret, switching horses in the dark..."

"That's just work," Lecne said. "And it was scary and boring at the same time. I want *adventure*."

"That's all it is," Aranthur said. "Being terrified and bored at the same time."

"No," Vilna said. "Any war will do the same." He laughed mirthlessly.

"I won't get in the way!" Lecne said.

"Good at killing people, are you?" Aranthur asked.

"Maybe," Lecne said sullenly.

"Seen a lot of action?" Aranthur asked, heartlessly.

"You know I haven't."

"Magical talent?"

"Shut up," Lecne said. "I'd be happy to work. All you heroes must need some workers."

Aranthur hardened his heart.

"No," he said. "The last thing I need is a close friend to protect when the shit starts. It will be so ugly that I have trouble imagining it, and you want to visit it like a tourist."

"I didn't say that!"

"It's what you mean, though. And if we live through the first part, then I'm going somewhere you definitely can't come. And frankly, Lecne, I doubt I'll come back. I can't take you and I can't protect you."

Lecne slumped. "So I'm just a handy innkeeper?"

Aranthur put his hands on Lecne's shoulders. "I trusted *you* with the key to the universe."

Lecne smiled slightly. "An old stone," he said.

"A really, really old stone which comes with its own priest. Lecne, turn your team around, work your way back up the cliff, and go and make up with Hasti."

Lecne shook his head. "I'll go in the morning. I could feel that thing buried deep and I'm not facing it again until there's a sun in the sky."

Aranthur nodded. "Good thought."

Lecne looked at him, his face bright in the moonlight, unlined, and, it seemed to Aranthur, innocent.

"Damn it," he said. "It's like pater telling me I'm still a kid."

Aranthur shook his head. "No," he said. "The trouble is we all listen to too many epic tales. You think it's glorious. I'm telling you that it's not. This summer, I was there when we broke the Pure's army in Armea and pursued them for ten days."

"And did you catch them?" Lecne asked.

"Oh, yes. Every day we killed more people who were, for the most part, trying to run away. It was very glorious."

Lecne shrugged.

"At Antioke, I killed a hundred Dhadhi."

"You what?" Lecne turned as if he'd been bitten.

"They were under the control of an enemy magiker and they were killing my friends." Aranthur shrugged. "So I killed them."

"That's... horrible..." Lecne said. "They're... elves! They're so old!"

"Yes," Aranthur agreed. "It's *all* horrible. That's my point. Little by little it becomes normal, and I admit, I'm pretty good at it. Especially killing. Swords or spells. The other day I killed a beautiful young woman with my knife."

"Gods! Stop it!"

"She was in my way. I couldn't stop and reason with her, or just knock her unconscious. Also, she was very powerful—I had no room for error, so I killed her. To be fair, she nearly killed me."

"Gods! Aranthur, listen to yourself. Wasn't there *anything* else you could do?"

Aranthur shrugged. "That's just it, Lecne. Once you ask that question, then maybe you have to ask—*is there ever a reason to kill?*"

He slipped down from the wagon box. The Nomadi were all listening; Vilna wore a hard smile, and Nata looked as if he was about to start laughing.

"Let's unload the Stone," Aranthur said.

Haras became agitated again at the possibility of dropping his precious Stone into the moonlit water, and he made the lives of every man and woman on the ropes a misery, even as the whole thing was rigged to one of the main yard booms. But once it was swayed up, everything moved rapidly, and Aranthur saw it safely stowed on the centreline just aft of the keel. Haras set to work praying.

Inoques met Aranthur on the quarterdeck.

"There it is—under my feet again."

"Let's get underway," Aranthur said.

"Feel the wind?" she asked.

"Oh, yes. From the east—strong as all the hells."

She looked east; the stars were so brilliant that the Dark Forge stood out against them, a rift in the sphere of the heavens, and it was now visibly bigger.

"Come below," she said. "I need to ask you an *operational* question."

Aranthur followed her into the cabin under the quarterdeck. It was not as opulent as you might expect for the Emperor's yacht: the carpet of black and white squares in painted canvas; walls of old oak with hanging bronze oil lamps; mirrors that made the tiny cabin seem larger; and the brilliant stern windows that opened almost straight on to the sea—hundreds of panes of precious Megaran glass in a vast mullioned window, almost as beautiful as the windows in Myr Benvenutu's office.

Two big *gonnes* stood housed and roped down, their port lids closed. They occupied almost a third of the cabin—bronze nine-pounders, their handles shaped like swimming drakes. They were beautiful, but very difficult to move, and both had incongruous tabletops clamped to their lethal barrels, so that they could be used as clumsy sideboards.

Amidships was a long table. By night, two thirds of it could be folded away; by day, all the officers could sit around it in the brilliant light of the stern windows and read, talk, or plan.

A hanging bed could be lowered on fine chains to fill the place of the table.

Tonight, the table was still in place, and Gupto sat at it, with most of the surface covered in charts.

Aranthur slid in beside the weatherworker.

"We want to go south, through the islands," Inoques said.

Gupto nodded.

"It'll be dangerous, there are pirates and the navigation is difficult," she said. "But we'll be close to food, and the islands tend to break an east wind. We'll work south—probably very fast. There's usually an inshore wind down by Magua, and all three of us can take turns raising a counter-wind if that's what it takes."

Gupto nodded. "Captain Inoques says this wind is aimed at the Fleet." He shrugged. "It won't get stronger—that stands to reason. But the power someone is dumping is legendary. So maybe in four days it'll be weaker. But this way we don't have to turn east for four days. And that inshore wind is no joke. I've taken ships to Masr that way before."

"We'll miss the fleet rendezvous at Milini," he said.

"We may also miss the relief of Antioke," Inoques said. "We can't turn straight into this wind, we don't even have oars. If we tack all the way up to Antioke it might take two weeks. This way we'll be at the mouth of the Azurnil in ten days."

Aranthur swore. But he had to accept what she told him.

He changed topics. "Did you feel that thing on the cliffside?" he asked.

Inoques smiled. "Oh, yes," she said. "One of us."

"Us?"

"Something old. *Ammit* has stirred them all."

"Ammit?" he asked.

She waved a hand. "Don't say it too often," she said.

Aranthur raised an eyebrow.

"The…leader of the Old Ones. The king. Or the warlord. Or the slave master. He led us here from somewhere else."

"And now…"

"And now he's trying to break his chains. Please do not talk of this."

Aranthur looked down the deck, where Haras was still giving orders.

"He can reach out to here? In the *Aulos?*" Aranthur was incredulous at the power that would take.

Inoques nodded. "I told you this was a different game now. *Gonnes* and sails alone will not win this."

4

The Chain and Gortyn

When Aranthur came back on deck the anchor was already coming up from the sandy seabed, and the Arnauts, most of whom were capable seamen, were walking round the capstan, singing another of their interminable songs about drinking, whores, and *thuryx*.

Aranthur frowned at the words.

"My father hated it when my uncle sang this."

"Why? It's an honest song. Addicts are sad when they can't get drugs. I expect that feels a little like being deprived of your lover. It's shocking and clever and makes you think. Isn't that what your people mean when you speak of *art*?" Inoques asked.

"Ouch." Aranthur smiled ruefully and shook his head.

Later, the anchor up and the ship running three points off the wind, close hauled, with the island chain too close to the portside, Aranthur found himself whistling the tune.

Daylight found them still running close hauled, and the weather-worker said they were making a little less than eight knots.

"She's a fine ship," he said.

Aranthur spent much of the day exercising his right arm; he also shot puffers and crossbows and his *carabin*, and stood with the weather-worker making the most of the wind and the ship's points of sailing. He began to learn the subtleties of the weatherworker's trade; never a bludgeon, always a razor. It used very little *puissance* to nudge or channel an existing wind instead of trying to cancel it or power into it;

on the other hand, it required a level of nuance and a strength of will that was superior to anything Aranthur was used to employing. Ten times that day, and every day thereafter, Gupto would smile slightly, and say, "Less strength. More smart," until Aranthur would say it himself when he felt the ship plunge off the heading.

They ran almost due south for five days, keeping the islands between them and the heavy weather. Everything was variable; the immense east wind, passing around and over the volcanic islands, could come at them from almost any point, and the crew was constantly called aloft to manage the sails.

But even with all of that, it was the most restful time Aranthur had known in half a year. He ate and ate and there was always more food. He fenced, and wrestled. In the evenings, if the sails were well set, they would dance, while Cut Face and one of the sailors played; everything from Souliote dances like the *haliardo* and the Byzas *minuetto* to outlandish Masran dances and simple circle dances that seemed to be the same everywhere. On the third night the wind rose to an insane pitch and Gupto conned the ship into a tiny harbour with a sandy beach. The old volcano towered over them, and the clouds whipped along, headed east like racehorses, but the wind was cut to a breeze by the high ridges of land that surrounded them like reaching arms, and the ship rode quiet under the racing clouds.

Aranthur went ashore alone. He was gone for a long time and returned very tired.

After Ardvan served them dinner, Aranthur and Inoques watched the moon rise over the volcano.

"It's as warm as summer," she said. "The east wind is bringing the warmth out of Masr."

"We could swim," Aranthur said.

She grinned, and within half an hour most of the crew was over the side, swimming in the moonlight; the tamboura was playing on the quarterdeck, and a tun of wine was broached and drunk.

Hours later, Inoques said, "Do you really want to die, Aranthur Timos?"

He bit her neck, running his tongue over the writing there.

"Not right now," he said.

"But sometimes?" she asked. "I have wanted to die many times. But here I am."

He patted the mound of her pregnancy. "So close to escape."

"If the Old Ones do not kill us all first. But I don't really understand, my love. You are powerful, you have some fame. Your Emperor loves you, as does his consort—if anything, too much."

Aranthur lay back. "I feel as if I'm living someone else's life. And I'm tired of killing."

She nestled against him. "I remember that feeling," she said. "It will pass."

"That may be the most depressing thing you've ever said."

She shrugged. "If you wish to wallow in your feeling of sin, be my guest. But really, what does it amount to? Most mortals scarcely have lives. They toil, they collect money or sex, or fame or kills, and then they are gone like summer butterflies. What does it matter if you crush a butterfly today or tomorrow?"

"I'm mortal," he said.

She rolled over, her almost glowing eyes fixed on him in the darkness. "Do you imagine you are fooling me?" she asked. "I know how much power you have amassed. I even gave you some. But power either leads to death or more power. Do not lie to me. By now, you know how to prevent death."

"Jakal knew how to prevent death," Aranthur said, evading her point. "He's dead, as is his daughter—and he'd already banished death from her, or she'd done it to herself."

Inoques put a hand on his face. "So you do know."

"Oh, yes."

"You could be my consort for aeons."

"I could... though you said our marriage ends when you escape."

She laughed. "You still don't know how I intend to escape, which is delicious."

Yes, I do.

"Well," she said, "I will not be bound again. But we can still be allies."

Aranthur rolled away from her and looked through the huge window at the volcano and the stars above it.

"If we ever reach that moment, we can discuss it," he said.

The next day the east wind had abated. It still blew steadily, but the ferocity was gone, and Inoques kept the deck all day, watching the three southern islands of the Chain pass them. It was milder all day, and

Gupto climbed the mainmast and looked east and south and reported that the weather might be in for a change.

"There's a storm brewing in the south, over Magua," he said.

By the charts, they were about a hundred sea-leagues north of Gortyn when three ships came into sight in a sandy bay, not unlike the one where they'd taken refuge from the wind.

"Pirates," Inoques said. Aranthur thought she said it with satisfaction.

The three ships could be seen preparing to cut their cables; after fifteen minutes with the far-viewer spell, Gupto was sure.

"Getting underway. Throwing all sorts of things over the side. They're coming for us."

Aranthur nodded.

"We're going for the Gortyn Channel," Gupto said.

"No reason to fight," Inoques said with obvious sadness. "I'd like a little massacre just now."

Haras came on deck. "Please do not fight," he said. "We cannot afford any risks."

Inoques turned away.

"I will order you not to fight," Haras said.

Aranthur caught his shoulder. "Haras..." he said.

The priest glared at him. "I do not have to do your bidding."

Aranthur stepped in close, caught the man's arm, and locked it. Using the arm as a lever, he walked Haras, spitting with rage, into the amidships cabin.

"Haras," he said, "listen to me. Do not undermine her authority with a new crew. Are you listening?"

Haras broke away as soon as Aranthur released him.

"If you ever touch me again—"

"Spare me!" Aranthur snapped. "And stop playing the great high priest. She won't take unnecessary risks."

"She is not on our side, you fucking idiot!" Haras said. "Just because you commit some necromantic sin and rut with a corpse, don't imagine that corpse is a woman! She is a monster, bound by my order, and without us she would be attempting to flay your soul."

"Yours, certainly," Aranthur said calmly. "You are blinded by your prejudice."

"You are blinded by your prick!" Haras said. "She is older than Megara, and part of an ancient thing that was a god. She is so deep in evil—"

"None of which matters when we are, at the very least, allies of convenience right now."

"Only for now! If the rift blasts open she will turn on us all. If the Black Stone is not replaced in thirty days, she will stand against us and we will fall so fast that the War of Wrath won't even be a memory."

Aranthur shrugged. "Do you think I don't know that?" he asked. "Until then she is doing her very best to get you and your precious cargo to Masr. The sailors do not know that she's a demon bound under your orders, which is, as Vilna would say, bad for discipline. She's not going to fight the pirates. Please be civil."

Haras glared at him. "You have ordered me about for your convenience," he said. "You think yourself my superior, and you are gravely mistaken. I have helped your worthless emperor—and I have waited for your precious fleet, which I'll note is not protecting us now anyway. From now on, I'll give the orders."

Aranthur was tempted by anger—by an honest reaction to the man's unfairness—but he fought that reaction down.

As mildly as he could, he said, "I'm sorry if it seemed that way to you." He stepped back. "I have tried to do what was best for everyone, and I have no doubt failed several dozen times, but I don't believe there is room in our current situation for anyone to be *superior*." He tried humour. "Not even me."

Haras was flushed under his dark skin. But slowly he drew himself up, and unclenched his fists.

"I'm sorry," he said stiffly. "You hurt me. And you laid hands on me—that's a crime, among the people of Masr." He breathed deeply a few times. "But I have been intemperate."

Aranthur bowed, and then offered his hand.

"I apologise," he said.

The Masran priest looked at the offered hand and bowed slightly.

"Accepted," he said. "As to your point about the Bound One. I think it...it enrages me, that you love her. that you think of her as human."

Aranthur raised an eyebrow. "I try not to let it enrage me that you cannot see her as a person whom you have made a slave."

Haras shook his head.

Aranthur smiled. "One evil at a time."

Haras nodded. "The best we can do."

*

Night fell, and the pirate ships were mere blurs on the northern horizon as the sun set—pinpoints of light as the setting sun caught their topsails.

The Dark Forge rose in the east, with a curtain of stars.

They were now running almost due east. The magnificent beaches of the north coast of Gortyn were in sight, and the smell of firs and birch trees floated on the air like a perfume of wilderness.

"Magua is just there," Gupto said. "Maybe sixty sea leagues as the crow flies. The most beautiful place in all the wheel of the world."

"Really?"

Aranthur was taking a turn at the wheel, trying to manage the weather, in particular keeping a ten-knot west wind in the sails despite the ten-knot east wind blowing almost directly against them. It was quite a juggling act, and early on Aranthur had experimented, with Gupto, with various planes of force, barriers and shields, to cover the ship and break the breeze.

"Birch trees the size of a galleon," Gupto said. "Maize that grows higher than your head. The best sculptors anywhere..." He looked wistfully to the south-west.

"You enjoy sculpture?" Aranthur asked.

Gupto shrugged. "I'm sure you see me as an uncouth sailor-man," the weatherworker said. "An' mayhap I am. But I been all over the Inner Sea, an' beyond, too. I like statues. I always learn about the locals, like."

"There they are again," Aranthur said. "All three sails."

"They still ha' the sun, and we've lost her round the curve of the earth," Gupto said. "We'll lose them in the channel and the darkness."

But the reliable weatherworker was, for once, wrong. Dawn found the three ships mere nicks on the horizon, their sails just visible in the rosy light, but as the day grew brighter, they seemed to come closer.

At midmorning they left Gortyn behind and entered the dark blue water of the Sud Channel. The Enyalios Mountains towered to the south, snow-capped, yet so far distant that their mighty outlines seemed to shimmer in the morning air.

Inoques came on deck. "How in all the hells are those bastards staying with us?" she muttered. "They have weatherworkers as good as ours? Really?" she spat.

"If they're working for the Pure..." Aranthur said.

Inoques shook her head. "They were lurking for argosies making the run from Aquilea to Magua," she said. "No one could have expected us this far west."

Gupto shrugged. "Must be Navark Archeo," he said. "He always has the best weatherworkers. He slaves 'em."

She looked aft, stretched out both hands to the sea, and after a long time, a slow smile spread over her features. It was a wicked smile, which did not bode well for her foes.

Inoques began to sing.

"That's an old song," Gupto said, apparently unperturbed.

It seemed tuneless and eerie to Aranthur, rising and falling suddenly, with high notes so high they were like bird whistles or…

Something burst from the sea to starboard—an impossibly long head, an impression of teeth as long as a galley's oars and as sharp as serrated blades. The thing dived and there was no tail, but an endless, horrible rope of tails, or rather, of arms, or legs—hundreds, it seemed, pulsing together.

Its size was so vast that Aranthur felt sick. He shuddered.

"An old friend," Inoques said. She was watching the behemoth. "'Friend' is perhaps too strong."

It was *gone* again, into the depths.

"What was that?" Aranthur asked.

"Something from deep in the ocean, and deep in the past." Inoques smiled. "Before man, before Jhugj, before Dhadhi. Before most of the befores, they were here."

Astern, the three tall pirate ships crept closer. They were hull up now, fully and visible.

"The channel is one of the deepest stretches of water anywhere," she said. "That's why it's such a dark blue—almost black."

She glanced over the side again and scratched the backstay with one fingernail.

"Old allies," she said wistfully. "I hope."

"Oh, gods, the pirates are closer." Haras said.

"Much closer," Inoques said. "If this doesn't work, we'll have to lay to and fight in half an hour."

"That thing was bigger than a ship!" Haras said.

"Yes," Inoques replied. "It's a *Perbindesh Deti*—one of the last."

They were all looking aft when the central pirate ship suddenly seemed to stop and then settle. Seconds later, it was gone.

The other two ships immediately turned, one north, one south, engaging with the true wind and abandoning their weatherworkings.

"I owe someone a great many fish," Inoques said.

For two days they ran along the north coast of Euryailos, the mysterious continent south of Masr. The entire coast was a low beach, although the towering, snow-capped mountains showed in the distance. There were no towns, villages, ports, or people.

"I've heard there's a port on the western side, off the channel," Kallotronis said. "I know men who have claimed to have been there."

Gupto nodded. "It's true. Treasure hunters and serious magi both come here. After all, this was the capital of the Dhadhian empire—a vast city that is now a vast desert."

Through the far-viewer the ash-coloured desert could be seen clearly, as well as the skeleton of an old city: walls crumbling slowly, roads choked with rubble.

"Is this real?" Aranthur asked.

Inoques shrugged. "Much of what I am seeing is illusory. The whole civilisation fell almost ten thousand years ago and the illusions have been cast to protect the ruins." She paused. "And the remnants of the Dhadhi, of course." She pointed at a dozen small boats—elegant longboats, propelled by small sails and oars. "Dhadhi pilgrims. Most Dhadhi visit the deadlands at least once—some return many times. Some go to live there." She was watching the dozen small boats. "Safer than staying at home, of course."

"There's another port on the western shore," Gupto said. "Sud. I've been."

"To the pirate haven?" Kallotronis said. "I've been as well. So has Cut Face here."

Aranthur smiled. "What's it like?" His uncle had spent a winter in Sud.

"Wild. Deadly. A town o' brothels and taverns and gamblin' dens and flophouses without a single temple to the gods. No law—you can gut a bastard and the only fine you ha' to pay is to get rid o' the corpse." Gupto smiled his slow smile. "O' course, I were younger then."

"I had a contract there," Kallotronis said. "I didn't like it."

Gupto was interested; so was Vilna.

"What happened?"

"A magos, a big one from Masr, wanted to try and cross the desert. He wanted to enter the deadlands from the west."

"Oh?" Inoques asked, interested.

"I thought that couldn't be done?" Gupto asked.

Kallotronis spread his big hands. "My principal had big plans—camels, some high-power water spells, a whole set of magi whose main purpose was to store certain things away in the *Aulos*." He was staring over the side.

"I'm guessing it didn't come to any good end?" Vilna asked.

"We got as far as Sud and my principal wasn't satisfied with something about the storage of food in the *Aulos.* There was a fight—an ugly one. We only had four magi. When the fight was over, the principal was dead, and so were two of the other three." Cut Face grunted. Kallotronis spread his hands. "The life of the mercenary. Nice people don't hire killers. So when the magi were all dead or dying, guess what? The locals attacked us for our camels." Gupto nodded knowingly.

Inoques shook her head. "You people," she said. "You're as bad as Old Ones."

"So you fought them off?" Aranthur asked.

Kallotronis was watching the sea. "Oh, aye, *boso.* In the end, we killed a dozen rogues and stole a boat. But we lost almost all the stores, and the camels. When we left, two of the gangs were still fighting over them."

"What was your principal going into the deadlands to find?" Aranthur asked.

"Old texts," Kallotronis said.

Inoques nodded. "What else? All of magery is an endless game of invention and reinvention. The skills ebb and flow like languages—as they change, we change."

Aranthur had never thought of the *Ars Magika* as a language. In one sentence Inoques had changed his world. He sat, slack-jawed, as if he'd been struck by lightning, or as if another great briny behemoth had risen from the waves.

"But the Dhadhi used glyphs," Aranthur said.

"Glyphs are like the Dhadhi themselves—slow to change, but very stable," Inoques said. "The best Dhadhian magi could *think* in glyphs." She shrugged. "I've been on deck too long."

She smiled, got to her feet as if rising from a cross-legged position took no effort, and stepped lightly down the quarterdeck ladder.

Kallotronis watched her and shook his head.

"How's your gut?" Aranthur asked.

"As good as it ever was," the Arnaut captain smiled. "That big Imoter girl…" he began.

"Woman?" Aranthur said.

"Sure," Kallotronis said. "She won't let me stop doing my exercises —she has preparations for me…" He shrugged. "I've never been so healthy. Also, it turns out she's always wanted to know how to shoot a rifle."

"So…" Aranthur said. "You've told me before, but I want to hear it again. The Pure are breaking into the Black Pyramid. They have hundreds of soldiers, four Exalted and a Disciple—yet you escaped with the Black Stone."

Kallotronis had a pipe and stock. Aranthur began to pack his own. So did Gupto. Vilna began doing steppe exercises—long, complex stretching routines.

"We shot one of the Exalted," Kallotronis smirked. "It stopped to talk. I shot it."

"Interesting," Aranthur said.

Kallotronis shrugged. "The whole thing was insane. Al-Khaire was on fire, and the Pure thought we might be allies. Or negotiate with them." He shrugged. "The Hierophant stayed to contest the Great Passage with the Disciple. I didn't stay to watch."

"What were you doing there?" Aranthur asked.

"They claimed we were there to provide training, but that was mule piss. They hired my ruffians to do exactly what we did—steal the Black Stone. They wanted us to do it so their own temple hierarchy wouldn't be clear what was happening." Kallotronis shrugged. "A typical shite contract."

"So…lay this out for me?"

"Here, get my pipe lit." Kallotronis took Vilna's daybook and began to sketch. "This is the Great Corridor. It's really more like a tunnel—walls taller than a man, ceiling of ashlar. The whole tunnel is carved in relief, and there's inlays of gold and different stones. And curses set into the walls. We were blindfolded whenever we went in or out, but I cheated." Kallotronis grinned.

Cut Face grinned too. "We all cheated."

Kallotronis looked up. "There are four places the priests stopped to disarm the curses. And when the Pure attacked, we saw those curses at work. Not a way you want to die. Blood boiling, bones rotting away…" Aranthur winced. "Outside the tunnel, or the corridor, or what have you, is the Stone Garden. That's what we called it. Every priest and most of their magi are buried in protected graves, with various blessings and curses and protections on the grave. Masran people take death and after death very seriously." Kallotronis pointed to his map. "The Stone Garden runs right up to the portico of the Black Pyramid, with entry points from there to the Great Corridor." He sketched in four side doors.

Aranthur shook his head. "I don't get it. The Pure are pouring down the Great Corridor. And yet you escaped past them?"

"No, *boso.*" Kallotronis raised an eyebrow. "I swore an oath."

"I didn't," Cut Face said. "We went *under* them."

Kallotronis made a face, and then drew quickly. "We went through the Necropolis. One of the priests mentioned it and we…"

Dead Eye, the Arnaut witch, was carrying a purring cat in his arms, which appeared a little incongruous in such a tough man.

"We went exploring," the witch said. "Listen, *Patrone*. However old that pyramid is, the tunnels under it are older."

"But you escaped through them?"

"There's a saying in Souliote," Kallotronis said. "*'Maybe' becomes 'must' when the devil's at your door*. You know it?"

"Oh, yes," Aranthur said.

"Well, I watched the devil burn the Hierophant and decided that running through corridors filled with old dead souls and *hutti* was better than facing the fucking Disciple."

"*Hutti?*" asked Vilna.

The witch patted the cat and another cat appeared. and another.

"Carrion eaters," Dead Eye said.

Aranthur frowned. "Like rats?"

"Like giant flightless vultures that have hands and brains," Kallotronis said. "The priests said one scratch from their claws and we were dead men. I didn't stay around to find out, but we killed them wherever we found them."

"And where did you come out of the necropolis?" Aranthur asked.

"There's an underground river. It flows into the Azurnil... somewhere here, and there's a road alongside it."

They all sat and smoked and thought for a bit.

"Could you lead us back through the necropolis?" Aranthur asked.

"We had two priests with us," Kallotronis said. "They weren't happy about the path we chose, and one of them... fell by the wayside."

"We swore we were never going back." Dead Eye made a face. "Never been anywhere I hated more, and I've been some bad places."

Kallotronis sighed, exhaling smoke and looked up at the pennant at the masthead, which was shivering.

"Weather change?" he asked.

Aranthur looked at Gupto, who stepped to the wheel, took it, looked up, and then raised a hand the way he did when he was concentrating to cast, although he looked more like the conductor at an opera than a weatherworker: eyes closed, raised hand moving to some invisible beat.

"The east wind is dropping," Gupto said.

Aranthur rose, handed his pipe to Vilna, and joined the weatherworker in rebuilding the web of workings that kept the ship moving forward and on course.

The sun was well down in the sky by the time Aranthur sat back to his cold pipe.

Kallotronis frowned. "I been thinking," he said. "How do you know we're all doomed? I mean, if the Dark Forge widens?"

Aranthur found his tinderbox.

"I don't know. Someone from the Studion did the work."

Kallotronis spread his hands. "You want us to go back there and maybe die. Maybe get eaten by fucking *hutti.* I can't imagine a worse way to go—eaten alive in the stifling hot darkness with tons of old dead and ageless black stone over your head. Everything smells like rotting meat and old dirt. Rolan's dick, *Patrone.* If I'm going back there, I want to know it's for *something.*"

"I suppose we could wait around and see if the sky splits open and the Old Ones return to the world first," Aranthur said.

"You mean I'm being an idiot," Kallotronis said belligerently.

Aranthur sat with his back against the ship's bulkhead. He had his pipe going. Ardvan came and sat by him and Aranthur handed over the pipe.

"Mistress says you should eat," Ardvan said.

"Soon." Aranthur looked back at Kallotronis. "You want me to convince you, or maybe just give a good speech," he said. "But I don't have the absolute knowledge you're looking for. I could make it up, I suppose."

Kallotronis frowned.

Aranthur raised his hands in frustration. "I believe that we have thirty-eight days until our world ends. Isn't that enough for you?"

Kallotronis looked at Cut Face and Dead Eye.

"No," said Dead Eye.

Two more days, and in the grey light of dawn they were sighting birds —great flocks of birds: black gulls, cormorants and geese and ducks in incredible profusion, so thick on the water that as the ship tore along, a constant explosion of waterfowl launched from under her forefoot. She was running close to twelve knots, throwing spray almost as high as the foredeck each time the bow bit into one of the great waves.

And the waves were running high: six or seven feet, with occasional king-waves rising more than ten feet and breaking right over the bow of the ship, forcing the bow down. But the *Esperance* was well-built by the best yard in the Empire for just these seas, and she shouldered them aside bravely.

Inoques was on deck in her nightshirt, apparently oblivious to the soaking spray and the cold wind. Her sailors were not oblivious, either to the weather or to their almost naked captain.

"I love the edge of a storm," she admitted. "I don't want to go below. *This* is what happens when some bastard drives the wind from the east for eight days—all the world's wind builds up."

Aranthur stood with her for an hour as she conned the ship, her hands on the wheel, and he handled the weather and the wind.

"You could pass the exam, soon enough," Gupto said. "A year on a big ship and you'd be rated a master."

"That's one of the most tempting offers I've ever heard!" Aranthur shouted.

The wind was still rising. But overhead, the wind from the south was bringing new tidings, and the clouds were being blown away like shredded sails.

When the glass was turned and eight bells struck, the clouds were gone.

And for the first time, the Dark Forge was visible like a hungry maw in the daytime sky.

"Interesting," Inoques said. "I want to hail a fishing smack, if any are keeping the sea in this blow."

Her first mate, Syr ul-Kamal, shrugged. "This is hardly a blow, mistress. Not for a shrimper with two wives and six children to feed. I'll wager a silver soldo to a pair of coppers we find the shrimp fleet in an hour."

"Your family shrimps, Benit?" Inoques asked.

"Mother and Father both, ma'am. There. Look to windward."

Small sails were pricking the grey to the south-east.

"Run in on them. Don't look too threatening."

Ul-Kamal smiled wickedly. "Any idea how not to look threatening, ma'am? Stripped of her fancy paintwork, this ship shouts fast privateer from the rake of her masts to the number of her port lids."

Inoques shrugged. "I need to go below."

She ran down the ladder even as ul-Kamal shouted orders, clapping his hands for emphasis, loud as puffer shots. The *Esperance* turned in her own length and shot south and east, lying well over and as close to the wind as she could sail, and the fishing boats scattered. But in thirty minutes they had a pair of shrimp boats under their lee, and the two owners coming up the side, terrified and obsequious.

But before the glass turned again they were gone over the side, each clutching a gold piece, and the *Esperance* was flying downwind, gull-winged, racing north and west through the heavy swell of the Azurnil estuary.

For an hour the waters under their bow were brown instead of blue; the late autumn surge of the great river brought mud all the way from the highlands far to the west.

"No fleet," Inoques said, after her interview with the fisherfolk.

Aranthur cursed. "Are we sure?" he said.

Ul-Kamal nodded. "You could not get twenty warships and forty transports past the mouth of the Azurnil without the fisherfolk knowing," he said. "If a pirate comes into the brown, we know it in a day."

"One day to Antioke with this wind," Inoques said. "And remember that while we're flying on it, they are beating up into it."

"Or penned in port at Antioke," Aranthur said. "Wait. Should we run up the Azurnil while we have the wind?"

"You aren't a sailor yet," Gupto said. "We *don't* have the wind. This beautiful rig allows us to lie close. We can sail very close to the wind, and closer with a pair o' weatherworkers such as we. But the great galleys and other vessels won't have the rig for it. They'll be rowing, gods save 'em."

"Aranthur," Inoques said, "I know you are anxious. But powerful as I am—powerful as you have become—I don't think we can run the gauntlet of old sorcery and get into Al-Khaire. And even if we did..." She made a face. "Then we'd be trapped there."

Aranthur sighed. "Time is running out."

They tore into Antioke harbour as if all the Furies were chasing their ship; outside the breakwater the storm that had held off for twelve glorious hours had begun to blow.

"That may mark a record passage," Inoques said with real satisfaction.

Aranthur took Ardvan and Vilna and went ashore as soon as the *Esperance* had a berth pierside. The harbour was packed; Iralia's new fleet had made it this far, and the roadstead was jammed with big-bellied merchantmen wallowing in the swell.

As he walked through the too-familiar streets of the ancient citadel, Aranthur had the impression of an army of hungry ants. Everywhere that he saw Attians or Imperial soldiers, they were eating. And the sight made him hungry.

Aranthur saluted politely when he arrived in front of the long table at which General Tribane was writing. She had Syr Ippeas on one side and Vanax Equus on the other, and all three were writing, with a dozen secretaries writing around them and fifty wax candles flickering as the storm winds fought their way into the old temple cathedral.

None of the three commanders looked up.

Aranthur saw Vardar, his former nemesis, writing steadily, his tongue protruding slightly from his mouth. And at his own desk, the General's military secretary, Vlair Timash, wrote almost as fast as Syr Edvin.

She glanced up, smiled, and turned her head.

"Ma'am," Timash said to Tribane who glanced, not at Aranthur, but at her.

"What?"

"Visitor," Timash said.

Only then did General Tribane glance at Aranthur.

"Damme, Timos, and here you are."

She rose and kissed him on both cheeks. In a moment, Equus was pounding his back, and Syr Ippeas gravely wrung his hand.

"Well done, syr." She smiled. "Step aside with me, Aranthur. I don't want to stop this—it's all the orders for the next two weeks, being copied fine. And all our supply registers. Aphres, gentlemen. Do all empires generate this much parchment?"

"A lot o' lambs died for this army," Equus said. "Myr Tarkas is around somewhere."

"We'll start loading when the storm dies down," Tribane said.

They went into a small tapestried room. Tribane's standard bearer, Ringkoat, handed Aranthur a mug of mulled wine.

"Welcome back." He gave Aranthur a crooked smile. "Although you usually herald something bad."

Ringkoat shrugged, and then allowed himself to be embraced. It was a little like hugging an iron pillar.

"Sit, Timos," Tribane said.

It took a moment for Aranthur to realise that General Tribane had just referred to him by his surname, the way the aristocracy spoke to each other.

"Sit!" she repeated. "We're not being formal. Besides, Dahlia tells me that you are one of the Seventeen now." The General smiled.

"Yes, ma'am."

"You know I hate being called ma'am," she said. "If we're formal, call me Majesty, the way Dahlia does. Otherwise, call me Alis. Or Tribane if you are angry." She smiled.

Ringkoat poured him more mulled wine as Dahlia came in and Aranthur rose. They kissed each other on both cheeks.

"Now we are met, let mirth abound," Dahlia said. "Are we caught up?"

Tribane shook her head.

Dahlia drew a chart on the air. Syr Ippeas came in, fully armoured, and sat in a leather chair. Equus sat on a stool by Aranthur.

"Life in wartime is complicated enough, eh?" Equus said. "You're one of my centarks, but now I find you're one of the secret Seventeen—not sure who has precedence, eh?"

Dahlia finished her map. "It's worse than that, Equus," she said. "He and I are *Proveditores* as well."

"Get my vanax some wine," Aranthur said to Ardvan. "He's going to faint."

Equus laughed, and before any anyone could say more, four Imperial Axes entered, saluted, and announced, "The Lady Iralia."

Iralia entered, dressed in a riding habit of severe military green. Behind her was the Capitano del Mar, the fleet commander.

"General," she said.

Aranthur could immediately see that all was not well between Iralia and the General. Iralia's head was held too high; the General's glance lingered too long on Iralia's back.

"Do you have it?" Dahlia asked.

"Yes," Aranthur said.

Everyone seemed to relax a fraction.

Iralia nodded. "General Tribane?"

Tribane was in her arming clothes. Her hair was unkempt, her hands were ink-stained, and despite that she had an aura of command greater than any of the others. She smiled and straightened; silence fell.

"Ma'am," she said to the consort, and she didn't use any tone. "Day before yesterday, with the advent of the Fleet, we broke the siege. Right now, I suspect a legion of hamsters could take the city from us—every soldier is either eating or asleep."

"I have troopers doing both at the same time," Equus said. "Bit peckish myself."

"The fleet weatherworker says the storm is natural enough and will blow itself out in two days." She looked around the circle at the impromptu council. "I know we're on a schedule, friends, but this army needs the rest and the food."

"Fleet's fought three actions in two weeks," the Capitano del Mar said. "And I'm anxious to get my cargo out of the holds. And I don't mean the food."

Dahlia gave Aranthur a significant glance, from which he gathered that the efforts of the Imperial Heart, the single source of the Empire's valuable pink *kuria*, had been successful.

"That gives us time to consider..." General Tribane said.

"By consider," Iralia said, "do you mean reconsider?"

"Oh, gods," Equus groaned.

Tribane turned to Aranthur, addressing him directly. "I appeal to you and Myr Tarkas," she said. "This army has the military power and the *puissance* to win a purely military victory over the Pure. That was the mission I was assigned by the Emperor." She looked around. "I do not approve of this move to Masr. I see no real role for an army facing your Old Ones, except to be destroyed by powers with which they cannot contend."

Aranthur considered various prevarications, then banished them.

"It's my plan, General," he said.

Absolute silence fell over the room.

"Your plan?" Tribane spat. "Based on your decades of military experience…"

Aranthur shrugged apologetically. Dahlia met his eye; Iralia was glaring at Tribane.

"Majesty," Aranthur said, and Tribane's mouth twitched; she almost smiled. "Majesty, anything I know about war I learned from the people in this room. But one of the things that I learned from Vanax Equus was that *none of us have done this before.* No one has fought a conventional war with this level of supernatural involvement, or this amount of *puissance* available from the *Aulos.*"

"Granted," Tribane said.

Aranthur looked at Dahlia. "Haras should be here." She shrugged.

"Majesty, it is my estimate, and that of your magi, that the restoration of the Black Pyramid is the highest priority. If we accomplish that, then even if the Pure endure or triumph on the secular battlefield, we will have preserved the Empire and indeed, the world in which we live."

"If we squander this army, what's to stop the Master from marching into Masr and blowing the top off the pyramid next summer?" Tribane took a cup of mulled wine and drank.

"Majesty, if Tiy Drako were here he'd say that's for next year." Aranthur raised a hand. "It is my contention that we need to make our attack look like the last act of the War of Wrath, when the armies hemmed the Old Ones into the quadrangle along the Azurnil and their magi built the wards that stand to this day."

Tribane sighed. "I know my history."

"Our enemies are not gifted military professionals," Aranthur said, his voice almost pleading. "Nor are they scientific magi. They're…" He looked around. "They're trapped here, and they don't entirely understand how this world, this multiverse, this cosmology, works. I believe that if we show them an army, they will focus on the threat they understand." He met General Tribane's hawk-like eye. "Something I learned from you, Majesty."

"I don't like my army being used as bait. As metaphysikal cannon fodder."

"Majesty, I am one of your soldiers. We have some tricks up our collective sleeve, and unless we've failed you, the Fleet has more than a year's *kuria* from the Imperial mines on Leto. And from Megara..."

He looked at Dahlia.

She took the buckler hanging from her sword hilt and tossed it on the table.

It landed with a loud clang, as it was made of steel.

Engraved on the face of it was the glyph of warding, superimposed on another glyph, a very complex one, and Tribane picked it up.

Dahlia spoke up. "General, we can do this. It is not a mere matter of marching, but nor is it as desperate as holding Antioke for sixty days proved. The army will have the best protections we can provide, which are better than anything any mortal had in the War of Wrath. And if we can link hands with Masr, they should be able to provide even more."

She took the buckler, and thumbed a stud on the handle.

A shield of shining pink-gold power sprang from the glyph. The *puissance* extended a little over Dahlia's head and all the way to the ground.

"We have more than a thousand of these," she said. "And thanks to the Fleet and the miners, we have the *kuria* to power them."

General Tribane sagged, as if her fatigue was finally getting the best of her. But then she grinned.

"That's... remarkable."

"We think that the Dhadhi used them," Aranthur said. "The knowledge was lost after the War of Wrath."

Tribane shook her head. "You're changing warfare faster than I can adapt."

Dahlia nodded. "We want to change faster than the Old Ones and the Pure can adapt, too. But we're also aware that the Old Ones have seen this before, and the Master, we think, uses glyphs and sigils for almost everything—"

"So we have some other tricks," Aranthur said.

"Splendid," Tribane said, "So even if we triumph over your Old Ones, we're still in the gullet of the Azurnil, and the Fleet has to pass upriver and out into the sea in winter and make its way back up the coast to land the army in Armea. There will be no campaign against the Master this winter, and all our gains will be for nothing."

Dahlia stood. "We won't be coming back out of the Azurnil," she said. "At some level, we must think of the Black Pyramid and the Old Ones as nothing more than a chain across the Azurnil. Break the chain, and we can land where we will in Masr. We use the locals to give us a chain of water deposits across the Kuh..."

"You think we can take an army across the Kuh?" Tribane asked archly.

"Majesty, it would be insane," Aranthur said, "if we did not have sixty powerful magi instead of five. The greatest concentration of Imperial Magi since the War of Wrath. We can create a great deal of water if we must."

"And," Iralia said, "we'll emerge from the desert into the very heartland of Safi. A knockout blow. Struck this year." She pointed at her map. "Majesty, this is what I mean by being ahead of our enemy. No one will ever consider an army of twenty thousand crossing the Kuh."

"An army that will have fought four major actions, only to fight another with its back to a desert?" Tribane said. "If we lose, we lose everything."

Iralia nodded. "Yes, that is what the Emperor has chosen."

"And the Council of Seventeen?" Tribane asked.

"In favour, eleven to six. No abstentions."

Tribane shook her head and glanced at Iralia from under her lashes.

"Damme. I suppose we might have Roaris in the saddle," she muttered. "This is rash, even by my standards." She nodded decisively. "Very well. Load the ships when the seas are down."

Iralia breathed a deep sigh. She walked across to the General and put out a hand.

Tribane looked at it for a moment, and then reached out her own.

Two days became three, and the fourth was no better than the third. Aranthur was reunited with his beloved Ariadne, and did duty with the Nomadi. Vilna and Chimeg were welcomed back with a party so wild that Aranthur couldn't remember, at its height, how many days they were from ultimate destruction. He was lying by a large fire in the fortified ditch near the Seaward Gate; most of the Nomadi were dancing in a great circle. Parsha Equus was as drunk as his people, and stood smiling benignly, looking as if the least breeze might blow him over.

Inoques danced past with Dahlia, of all people, holding one of her hands and Nata holding the other. Chimeg waved.

"How can you…? All of you…?"

Aranthur was having trouble mustering thoughts. They had developed a tendency to wander off.

Chimeg was smoking something that was not stock. She lay on her back, head propped on a saddle, and took deep drags off the pipe.

"You worry too much," she said.

"We're at the fucking end of the fucking world…" Aranthur slurred.

Chimeg took a long drag of her smoke and exhaled slowly.

"So?" she asked. "I could have died any day this summer. That's the end of the world, as far as I'm concerned." She didn't look at him. She drew in more smoke, and waved at the dancers, and lay back. "Every battle is the same. Win or lose. Live or die. I've seen eight major actions and maybe twenty smaller fights." She coughed. "Every one of them might have been the end of my world."

Aranthur was still trying to count the days until the Dark Forge ripped open, but in his state, he couldn't.

"You should dance," Chimeg said.

"I can't shtand up," Aranthur said, and woke in the cabin of the *Esperance*, with the sun rising brilliantly over a sparkling sea. His head felt as if it was being pounded by a smith: slow, steady strokes that fell with rhythmic pain.

Inoques prodded him. "Alive?"

"No," Aranthur said.

"You have good friends," she said.

"Urgh," Aranthur said.

"Ardvan has your uniform laid out. Apparently you are a soldier again, and your people are loading up."

"I'm already aboard," Aranthur said, but he knew that Equus wouldn't see it that way.

He got himself up, and somehow he endured Ardvan's fussing; the man seemed to enjoy making sure that Aranthur's uniform looked perfect, despite the drudge that occupied it.

Aranthur tried various remedies on himself, including a pain-blocker, but when he was cowering from the weight of the sun's rays, Alisha, the Imoter from the west, appeared at the base of the companionway ladder and put a hand on his shoulder.

"Good night?" she asked.

"Yes?" he said. "No?" *And why does everyone find my state such a cause for amusement?*

She was laughing. "Would you like my professional assistance?" she asked.

"Yes please," he said.

She returned with a glass of water. "Drink this," she said, and he drank it off. Then she put a hand on his head and he felt her power.

"There," she said. "Never say I never did anything for you."

She smiled, and Aranthur managed to go on deck. His hands were still shaking, but his head was clear, which was good, because almost as soon as he was ashore he was involved in a complicated argument over the priority of loading horses into transports.

Equus seemed perfectly well. He raised his riding whip in salute as he rode by.

"Don't give Vilna anything important to do," he said. "Wouldn't be sportin'."

It proved, as the horse loading grew more complicated, that Equus was correct. Vilna was perfectly uniformed, but the only action of which he seemed capable was to salute and say, "Yes, syr," no matter what statement was made.

Aranthur fought his way through the day as best as he could. Chimeg saved him several times, as did Nata, and he was glad that he'd curried the troops' horses in the early days, so that he knew all the remounts at a glance. And eventually, as the eight bells of high noon were rung throughout the fleet, the last troop remount was swayed aboard one of the huge converted grain ships. Aranthur brought his own troop aboard the *Esperance* as deck cargo, and they sailed with the tide, an hour before sunset. The wind was light—still from the south-west.

"We can run five knots to their three," Inoques said. "This is going to be slow."

In fact a brilliant dawn, with the disc of the sun slipping over the edge of the distant deserts of Masr in glory, found the fleet strung over twenty leagues of the sea, and the Capitano del Mar signalling vigorously, but even the elite ships of the navy were spread out over miles of water. It was eight bells before wind and human muscle had put the war fleet back into fighting order, and even then, half the transports were in close to the coast, looking for a breeze, and many of the rest seemed becalmed.

Evening found them off the northernmost mouths of the Azurnil delta—too shallow for the ships to enter.

"Of course he's going to anchor," Inoques said. She sighed. "Find us a nice bit of holding ground," she called to ul-Kamal, who nodded.

When the wind came up in the night, Inoques left Aranthur warm in bed, looking at the distant stern lights of the transports, and went on deck, where he heard her giving orders. A second anchor went over the side and he went back to sleep.

Dawn found them underway, and Aranthur went on deck to find that they were under topsails alone, ghosting along at three knots, or perhaps four.

"Where is the captain?" he asked.

Ul-Kamal pointed over the side, where Inoques, naked but for the lines of her tattoos, swam alongside the ship.

Aranthur stripped and leapt in by her, and she splashed him as soon as he surfaced. But he felt better. The water was not deadly cold; indeed, it was warmer than a summer in Soulis, where the rivers ran off snowmelt all year long.

He stuck with her, aware that the slow-moving ship would seem very fast indeed if he had to catch up with it. The sort of swimming you did on the Amynas river was not the same as swimming in the deep ocean with a five-foot swell.

When he was done, he got his hands on the rope thrown over the side for him and scrambled up with a little difficulty and into a gunport. Once aboard, he got dressed in time to see the coast of Masr pass across the stern window as they crossed the wind.

And that was the day: tack on tack, crawling upwind.

And the next day, too.

"Is this something the Old Ones are doing?" he asked Inoques.

"Maybe," she said. "But these are the typical autumn winds for this coast. Not everything is an attack."

Aranthur shrugged, and scratched a backstay the way Gupto did, begging Posedaos for a weather change.

"One day to sail from the delta to Antioke," he said.

"Five days back," Inoques said. "Maybe more, with slugs like that Great Galley."

But even as they watched, the Great Galley put her oars in the water, and rowed straight into the eye of the wind.

And the next day, the Capitano del Mar hoisted the signal for those ships carrying a weatherworker to do what they could to work to windward. The military ships and the ships from the Arsenale pulled ahead very quickly, and the *Esperance* stayed with the leaders.

By the end of the day they had raised Seta in the southern delta. The merchant fleet carrying the army was still spread over twenty miles of ocean behind them, and the faster galleys doubled back, running downwind on big lateen sails to rest their oarsmen.

The Dark Forge was huge, even in the daytime sky. And its horn was approaching the sun.

But one by one the Imperial Fleet, which now had a number of Attian vessels operating alongside them, dropped anchor in the delta, and every hour saw more merchant ships following them in.

Five days after they'd weighed anchor at Antioke, the last transports crept into Seta.

The Capitano del Mar stood on his quarterdeck, looking east.

"The river is not that wide and the wind's in our teeth," he said.

He shook his head. Without the collective efforts of every weather-worker from the Empire and another twenty from Atti, they would never have reached the Delta at all.

Tribane was committed. "You have the galleys," she said. "The rest of us can march."

5

The Black Pyramid

For three days, the Imperial Fleet rowed upriver into a steady headwind that sometimes rose almost to a gale, forcing the oarspeople to row like athletes and to shelter against the banks like pleasure boats in between sprints upriver. But, a league at a time, the galleys made headway.

The army made better time, marching overland—but General Tribane was careful not to outrun the fleet. Their progress was slow; the sand made for terrible marching, and the sun, the dry wind, and the cold nights conspired to challenge even Tribane's extensive logistical preparations.

Four days into the march, Syr Gupto and four other weatherworkers co-operated to bring a deep-draught merchant, one of the giant grain ships, up the river against the wind, a remarkable piece of magery. They did it under the direct protection of the Imperial staff, but the inhabitants of the Black Pyramid betrayed no sign of noticing the reckless expenditure of power.

To be fair, so much *saar* and *sihr* was pouring out of the rift that Aranthur barely noticed his own expenditures.

The great ship unloaded on the rickety wharves of a tiny delta town on the south bank of the Azurnil—two days' supplies for the army and a great deal of welcome forage for the horses.

Aranthur sat on his brutish steppe pony, watching the ship unload from pulleys whipped to the ends of her yardarms. As the junior centark, he had the duty to retrieve the regiment's forage; Vilna was overseeing the loading of sixty mules while Aranthur counted the bales.

The smell of the forage made him smile despite the Dark Forge, despite the endless east wind. The bales of forage were clover; the smell was that of the fields above Aranthur's home in the Soulis mountains. It was possible the forage came from Geta or Boras, but he'd have wagered this shipment had come down the Amynas.

The Nomadi worked quickly and well. Aranthur had seldom known anyone who could pack a horse or mule as quickly or as efficiently, and when the animals clattered away from the dockside, they no longer looked equine; they looked more like walking hayricks.

"The price of glory," Equus said.

"Syr!" Aranthur said, with a sharp salute.

Equus had his feet out of his stirrups and one leg over the pommel of his saddle.

"You never see this in the pictures of the War of Wrath," Equus said. "Damme, my own ancestor was there, and for all I know he handled the logistika. Someone did, you can wager on that." He laughed and handed a small silver flask to Aranthur. "No one ever remembers who provided the forage, who led the patrols."

"Who was in the pursuit," Aranthur said.

"An' you used to be green as grass. Tomorrow, we'll let Lemnas take the forage and you can lead the patrols."

Centark Lemnas had returned, to the annoyance of the City Third Cavalry and Myr Domina, their redoubtable commander. The ships from the City had brought her regiment back up to strength, including four new officers.

So next morning, as the sun rose over the eastern desert, Aranthur took three troops of the Imperial Nomadi and one troop each of the City Cavalry regiments forward into the desert, a wide screen across the front of the marching army.

Equus rode with him all morning, and he learned more about managing cavalry over broken country. He also found a camel herd, abandoned by its panicked owners, and commandeered them for the *carabiniers*. The ungainly creatures moved easily across the loose sand; they were slower than horses on solid ground, but much faster over sand, and far better at storing water.

"May I promote Chimeg to command the *carabiniers*?" he asked Equus.

"Damme, I'm your vanax, not your mother," Equus said. "But she'd be on my list."

Chimeg was proud as Niobe herself when she mounted her camel wearing the striped sash of a dekark.

With twenty reliable veterans mounted on camels, Aranthur felt he could move faster. The *carabiniers* went well ahead, racing from oasis to oasis; the cavalry skirmish line picked its way along behind.

There was no opposition.

"I wouldn't expect to face anything before the pyramids," Aranthur said to his vanax.

"For the sake of all the gods, don't tell them that!" Equus laughed aloud. He had an enormous hat, the kind that Dahlia preferred, full of scarlet plumes, and he'd taken to wearing his shirt open at the neck with a local scarf over his buff coat. He turned his horse. "Let the lads and lasses of the cavalry column imagine that they could fight at any moment. This is the best training in brigade level manoeuvres we've ever had. Why do you think I keep rotating the regiments?"

Aranthur laughed ruefully, as it became clear to him that they were, in fact, training.

"Never manoeuvred over a desert," Equus said. "But it's easier than woods or mountains, eh? What? So perfect for a little practice. And a little bird tells me that moving oasis to oasis is something we might do again... so..."

Aranthur saluted. "Yes, syr."

Equus nodded. "Really, Timos, you only have to *syr* me a couple of times a day. Eh?"

Two more days into the constant headwind, with so much *saar* pouring out of the rift that people who'd never had any access to power could start fires and make the desert sprout flowers. Pranks were played, and some of the Nomadi, who thought themselves safely bereft of *baraka* powers, walked around looking guilty. No one needed a *kuria* crystal for anything. Aranthur had another rotation in command of the skirmish line at the front of the columns, and he was among the first to see the pyramids loom above the mirage-shimmer of the midafternoon desert flats. He'd been warned by Chimeg, but seeing them for himself was another thing entirely.

Equus halted the cavalry line as soon as he heard, and General Tribane rode up—the first time that Aranthur had seen her in days.

She looked at the distant pyramids for what seemed like a long time. The Black Pyramid towered over the white ones, even at this distance, ten miles away, and the starless black hole of the Dark Forge stood over them like a massive storm.

And then she nodded.

"We'll camp at Wir Haffa. This spot on the engineer's map—just to the north. If the fleet comes up, tomorrow is the day." She looked at Aranthur. "Latest projection from Myr Julya Bemba, our astrologer, is twenty-four days."

"So we're early," Aranthur said.

Tribane didn't even pretend to smile.

"The rift is worse every day," she said. "There's concern it's already too wide to close."

"I knew I was better off playing cavalry officer," Aranthur said.

"Your vacation is over," Tribane said. "Best join your friends."

"I knew I wouldn't keep you," Equus said. "Gods speed you."

He leant over and gave Aranthur a hug, which he'd never done before.

"Don't forget to duck," Aranthur said.

Equus grinned. "Damme, that's my line," he said.

Dawn saw the Imperial Army formed across almost six miles of desert. The terrain was flat all the way down to the river—a gravel flat with stands of scrub. Not for nothing had the ancients decided to put their great necropolis here; the land was hopeless for irrigation or farming.

It wasn't bad for marching.

Unlike the Battle of Armea, here the army formed a single line of infantry regiments, with the cavalry in a second line—all of it well to the south, at the edge of the true desert.

Two thirds of the available polemagi and all of the Academicians save a handful were with the army, the most powerful in the centre with General Tribane, and the rest spread all along the front.

Aranthur watched the army form in the first light, marching out of camp in a steady line and then dressing from the centre as if on a gigantic parade ground. As the first rays of the sun crossed the eastern horizon the army started forward, marching steadily.

Aranthur was rowed out to the *Esperance*, where he embraced Inoques. Dahlia was there, and Kallotronis and Ardvan and Haras, Cut Face and Dead Eye and Shtaze and Injorancz. Aranthur had brought Chimeg and Nata and a hand of the Nomadi's elite *carabiniers*, but not Vilna; the veteran officer was taking command.

"And doing it better than I would," Aranthur said.

Dahlia shrugged. "I'm pretending to be a great magas," she said. "Why can't you pretend to be a great commander?"

"Trust me, I can," Aranthur said.

Inoques was silent and withdrawn, and Aranthur understood why.

"You lose whatever happens," he said, when he stood by her at the ship's wheel.

"If you know that, why say it?" she asked.

"Because if we win, you still have my word that I will abet your escape."

She turned her face to him; she, who only ever watched the water when they were underway.

"How can I trust you?" she asked.

"You've been in my mind."

"It's a very confusing place, and you are perfectly capable of believing two different things at the same time," she said.

He nodded and put a hand on her abdomen.

"I know how you plan to escape," he said.

She wriggled. "Do you?"

"Who will take care of the baby?"

Her eyes widened. "So you do know."

"I do. And I'm promising you, I will not allow you to fail. I will take you from the priests. In exchange..." He looked away. "Damn it."

"What in exchange?" she asked.

"Nothing," he spat. "I can't do it."

"Do what?" she asked gently.

He met her eyes. "I could make a deal with you," he said. "That you lend us your aid today, and I make sure you are free."

"I agree."

He shook his head violently. "That's not how I want it. That's not how I want it to be. Lend us your aid or don't. I will guarantee your freedom either way."

She wore her enigmatic half-smile.

"You *want* to come."

She shrugged. "I've chosen my side, these last two weeks." She shook her head ruefully. "I could have ensured the Black Stone never made it here. Haras is a fool in his bindings—he's never really commanded me not to put the ship on to a rock, for example." Aranthur made a face. "But here we are, in the land where I was once a goddess, and where I was made a slave." She raised a tattooed eyebrow. "I will come with you, and I will aid you. But I will be hidden—Haras will not allow me to come otherwise."

Aranthur climbed all the way to the tops and watched the army advance for another hour. A cup of hot *quaveh* was brought to the masthead by one of the sailors, and Aranthur sat with his legs wrapped around the mast, watching the long line of pike blocks move forward. There was no gap in the line. They raised dust, and the sound of their drums was like the distant thunder of a summer storm in Soulis.

Behind them, on the northern bank, was the city of Al-Khaire. It was not on fire. Dahlia had been to the city twice, and made it out again.

To their left, the nine galleys of the new fleet made an arrowhead on the river. Their crews were rowing head-on into a twenty-knot wind that gusted to twice that in force, and there were whitecaps on the river. Out on the desert flats, the flags stood out straight from their poles.

The weatherworkers were sweating as hard as the oarspeople.

Aranthur began to make out details in the gardens of stone; he could see the long, low wall around the necropolis, and the tower at the end of the retaining wall along the river.

They were perhaps two miles from the Black Pyramid, and there had been no movement.

The Capitano del Mar signalled to rest the rowers and the formation anchored. Ashore, the army halted, and the regiments rested as well, as much as fear and the wind would allow them to.

The Black Pyramid loomed, an untouchable fortress holding an unimaginable foe. The sun climbed higher in the heavens, and the Dark Forge began to rise from the east.

Aranthur took off the sling that held his right arm and used it a few times, stretching it against a mast and then cutting with a sword borrowed from Cut Face.

"Where's your old sword?" Dead Eye asked. He was handing out majicked pistol balls.

"Where she needs to be," Aranthur said.

"I never thought I'd go back in there," Cut Face admitted.

Aranthur nodded. He had his old arming sword, and the yataghan, two puffers, and his *carabin*. But he didn't think conventional weapons were going to solve anything.

"Here," he said. "The army got theirs this morning." He handed out paper cartridges. "*Baraka.* The balls have a coating of ground *kuria.*"

He had a box of them, and he made sure every man had a dozen.

"Will they hurt the Old Ones?" Kallotronis asked.

"I have no idea. I have learned, though, that people going into action feel better if they think they have a weapon that will work."

"True for you, *boso.*" Kallotronis nodded. "Give me some."

Haras looked grey with worry—haggard, as if he'd aged ten years—and Aranthur took him aside.

"It's too much of a risk," Haras said.

"According to our calculations, there's almost no risk," Aranthur said. "That is—we have some chance of success, whereas if we wait, we simply fail."

"It seems insane."

"It seems to me that the Black Stone will protect us against almost anything that the Old Ones can throw at us." Aranthur put a hand on the priest's shoulder. "The foe we need to fear is whatever is left of the Pure's Disciple."

Haras nodded. "I have a brain in my head, thanks. But a mad Disciple…"

Aranthur nodded. He was keeping secrets; mostly, he was hiding that the seventh Nomadi carabineer was Inoques in a *guise*. And while Dahlia and Haras argued about how to get the Black Stone all the way up inside the pyramid, Aranthur already had a plan.

Dahlia is going to kill me, he thought. *Of course, if she does then we will have succeeded.*

The ships went back out into the river, rowing hard into a thirty-knot wind. The schooner had to tack and tack, but her unique northern rig was suited to a mile-wide river with a heavy wind, and despite her short boards she was faster than the galleys.

Ashore, the soldiers rose to their feet, settled their pikes on their shoulders and their bucklers on their wrists, and went forward into the flying sand.

The next mile was the hardest yet. Dust devils rose from the desert, and there were wicked flaws in the wind—moments when it backed, or didn't blow at all. The strange wind on the river threatened standing rigging and tangled oars.

But the first blow fell on the army, as they had intended. Without warning, a fist of dark *sihr* rose from the Black Pyramid and shot forward to crush the leftmost regiments of the army marching along the river.

Mighty shields of opalescent fire rose to meet the fist, and it slid away.

And then the whole battle line halted, and at the sound of a single *enhanced* trumpet, the whole line raised their bucklers and *charged.*

A line of blue lightning formed across the desert.

The Black Pyramid vanished under a cloud of *sihr* and lashed the sparkling line with a fury of discharges.

The line of bucklers shed them, and the magi began to strike back —the air filled with a static charge, and dust rose from the desert.

The wind, which had been steady for two weeks, began to drop.

And from high, high above the pyramid, an eagle or some great flying creature began to dive. And the further the creature dived, the larger it appeared, until it became clear that it was the green drake, 蟠龍Pánlóng.

"Here we go," Aranthur said.

"Here we go," Dahlia echoed, with the elation of a desperate gambler whose dice have come up aces.

The *Esperance* fired a blue rocket from her port side.

The Imperial galleys went to ramming speed, their long oars beating the brown water to a foam, and a long line of boats came from the wharves of Al-Khaire. There were hundreds of them, and when a tentacle of *sihr* probed across the river, one of the galleys cut it off, its great glyph powering the steel cable that held the foremast.

The cables held: there was nothing to catch fire, and the steel conducted the ward fluently.

The entities in the pyramid wavered in their efforts to break the line of shields and began to throw *sihr* at the ships.

The galleys turned, bow on to the attacks, and shredded them.

The Capitano del Mar, aboard *Leone di Megara*, the largest of the Great Galleys, gave an order. A huge shield of glowing violet rose over his ship just as the enormous silk banner broke open: the Lion of Megara and the twin triangles of Rolan, a sign not carried in battle since the War of Wrath.

The *Leone* was immediately struck three times.

"Someone remembers Rolan," Dahlia said with satisfaction.

"Into the boats," Aranthur said.

Haras looked around. "Where is the construct? I have orders for her."

"Haras," Aranthur called, "the admiral will not last forever."

"Damn her!" Haras said.

Her.

Aranthur might have smiled. Instead, he jumped down into the longboat on the north side of the ship, hidden from the pyramid side. The longboat was thirty feet long with six benches and was full of people. The rowers would have to row very hard; the boat was heavily laden.

"Haras!" Aranthur yelled.

The priest dropped into the boat.

"She will be the death of us," he said.

"Not today," Aranthur replied.

Overhead, the arms of *sihr* were struggling to make an impression against the fleet of small boats and their wards and shields. Individual boats were overcome and the shrieks of the dying were terrible; blood boiled, bones melted, limbs froze, or turned to snakes, or...

It was terrible. But they were also too slow. An arm of *sihr* would form, and reach—overcome the shields of perhaps a single boat...

And then that arm would be cut off by one of the galleys, racing along under full oars. And on board, a Masran priest would seize the captured wraith, turn it, and use it against the Old Ones in the rift.

The army's fifes played on, and the drums rumbled like thunder, and the line of lightning moved across the flat desert, faster than Aranthur had imagined possible.

The entities in the pyramid clearly began to disagree about which target was the most important; one heavy arm continued to hammer away at the *Leone* but dozens of lesser attacks struck the army line, or attempted to engage the galleys, but without co-ordination. A keening sound rose from the pyramid.

The intact white pyramid began to pulse; in Aranthur's magesight, the whole edifice rippled with *saar.*

"One of the white pyramids is still in action," Dahlia said. "We're fighting back."

And then he could see nothing but the approaching sea wall of black basalt, and the low water gate, perhaps two hundred paces away. The lintel over the water gate was cracked, with black water trickling out. They were racing along, the oars pulling together like mighty wings; it was intoxicating.

"As well hung for a lion as a lamb," Dahlia said, and she raised her right hand.

The iron portcullis bent back with a screech like a tortured soul, leaving the water gate open, and the longboat shot through. Instantly, Aranthur raised a magelight even as the coxswain ordered the oars in.

The longboat coasted for perhaps four times its own length, and then struck sand and mud, ground along for ten paces, and came to a stop.

Haras was as pale as the hull of the boat, and even Dahlia looked shaken. Aranthur, by contrast, felt energised. He shared a glance with one of the Nomadi and then sprang ashore.

"We're in," he said.

Kallotronis and his bravos poured over the gunwales and Aranthur could see how relieved Cut Face was when the man fell to his knees in the mud.

Kallotronis put his hand on the man's shoulder and pulled him to his feet.

The Nomadi with Chimeg got ashore and checked their primings, and then looked back at the bright disc of light of the water gate. Sound and colour pulsed outside.

Eight sailors raised a heavy box on a pair of oars. They seemed to take forever arranging their carry; padding was tied down securely, while Haras looked as if he was aging before their eyes.

Aranthur smiled. "We're in, Haras. We've crossed the ocean and faced betrayal and now all we have to do is move and fight."

Haras shook his head. "I hate this place."

Aranthur glanced at the Arnauts. "I gather that's a popular view."

*

After ten minutes he understood why. As soon as they entered the tunnels off the landing, the temperature climbed; the sweating sailors carrying the Black Stone suffered the worst, but within two hundred paces Aranthur's light breastplate weighed like the Stone itself. The tunnels were of dried mud, and there were frequent collapses—piles of dirt in the darkness.

"This is bad!" Cut Face spat. He checked the priming on his weapon, a *carabin* with a bell-mouth and a large bore. "All this…" He pointed at a near total cave-in of the tunnel. "It wasn't like this before."

Dahlia had prepared a dozen magelights which she'd hidden with polemagia, and Aranthur put one on because, despite detection being their greatest fear, he needed to see. But a dozen lights weren't enough; the tunnel floor was smooth packed earth, but littered with gravel, garbage, and corpses—bits of bone, and human, animal and inhuman skulls. By the magelight, the tunnel walls appeared featureless and grey, studded with religious signs and occasional grinning skulls.

At the third cave-in, Kallotronis stopped.

"These were definitely not here before."

Aranthur nodded in the near darkness. "Not much we can do now. I'm would guess that when the pyramid cracked part of it subsided."

"Drax's rod, *boso*, you mean it's collapsing…?"

Aranthur shrugged. "The die is cast, brother," he said in Souliote.

Kallotronis' smile was as ghastly as the skull set in the wall.

"I fucking hate this place," he said.

Aranthur nodded. "Yep."

They went on another fifty paces—came to a cross-corridor, and then another.

Kallotronis shrugged. "No idea," he said.

"There's a warm breeze," Aranthur said.

"Sure."

There was a silent concussion—a feeling of pressure building and released—and cracked mud flaked from the ceiling of the tunnel.

Cut Face whimpered. So did Ardvan.

"If this is the right way," Dead Eye said, "we should be coming to the big…cave…thing."

"Use your words," Kallotronis snapped.

"The cavern," Dead Eye panted. He wiped sweat out of his one good eye. "Don't you remember…?"

“I kept my eyes closed,” Kallotronis muttered. “But yes.”

“We have to turn at the painting,” Cut Face said.

“What painting?” Aranthur asked.

He pushed forward, and tripped over a pile of fallen gravel despite the light.

Something landed on his back. His first thought was that it was a cave-in—until a stinking, leathery hand reached for his face, claws reaching…

Aranthur rolled the thing under him, drew his yataghan backhanded and stabbed. The blade sank into something soft and rotten as revulsion powered him to his feet and he slammed whatever it was against the tunnel wall and tripped *again* over the gravel pile and fell back on it. He stabbed it repeatedly.

There was another one on him, teeth reaching for his face. It was so *horrible* in the magelight that his whole body determined to *kill that thing.*

He got at the puffer in his sash left-handed, thumbed the hammer and shot it in one motion.

The flash of the powder showed the tunnels crawling with… *things.*

“Stay down!” Kallotronis shouted, and fired.

His *jezzail* fired so fast that the flash and bang seemed like a single ignition and another of the things fell, its hideous face destroyed by the heavy bullet.

Aranthur drew his second puffer and shot from the hip, lying on his back, on top of a dying monster. He didn’t miss.

Cut Face got his weapon up and fired.

The *things* broke and scuttled out of the light, leaving their dead behind. The one under Aranthur was not quite dead; the spasms of its filthy, furred body were horrible, as was the gleam of dying intelligence in the thing’s yellow eyes. They were like man-sized hyaenas with taloned hands and a bifurcated tongue with its own teeth, like a vicious snake inside their mouths. The dying creature’s tongue stiffened and retracted obscenely until Aranthur cut it with one stroke and plunged his yataghan into its throat with a second strike.

It stopped moving.

“*Hutti*,” Cut Face moaned. “Eagle, I hate this place.”

The scarred man was beheading the rest of the fallen monsters.

Aranthur’s heart was beating so fast he wondered how he was still alive. He couldn't speak for a moment, and the stench was as overpowering as their hideousness.

"Do you think their mothers actually love them?" Kallotronis asked. "Stop stabbing it. It's dead."

"Fuck," Aranthur said.

"My thoughts exactly," Kallotronis replied.

"What the fuck are those?" Dahlia asked. And after some babbling, she shook her head. "Well, you are either braver or stupider than I am. I'd have used *saar* against them."

Aranthur was reloading his puffers, only he dropped a pistol ball and gave up trying to find it again; his hands were shaking.

Alisha Poulos, the Imoter, was trying not to retch.

"I don't think I like it underground," Aranthur said.

"No one does, *boso.*" Kallotronis nodded.

"Haras is losing it," Dahlia said. "Poulos is shaky."

"Right," Aranthur said, forcing some humour. "I'd rather face the *hutti.*"

"Really?" Kallotronis asked.

"No," Aranthur said.

He pushed back along the tunnel to where Haras stood over the first of the *hutti* to die.

"Carrion eaters. The receptacles of damned souls." Haras was shaking. "This is why we never come into the undercroft of the pyramids."

"Bullshit," muttered the smallest of the Nomadi.

"They are unclean! They can pollute your soul!"

Aranthur took the priest by the shoulders.

"They're hideous, but they're just creatures."

Haras shook his head and stepped back.

"Don't touch me!" he spat.

Fighting his revulsion, Aranthur knelt by the one he'd killed with his first shot. Dahlia joined him. She grabbed it by the face and turned its head.

"Don't touch it! You are polluted!" Haras said, turning his face away.

"Let's leave ritual pollution for another day," Dahlia said. "I want to see that tongue. It's fascinating."

"I always knew you were tougher than me," Aranthur said with a mix of admiration and disgust as Dahlia pulled the thing's snake-like tongue out.

"Thousand hells..." she said.

She just kept pulling and pulling—the tongue was almost a foot long, with its own mouth and teeth, and four independent tendrils, like the arms of a hydra.

Haras was sick.

Kallotronis leant down. "You have a strong stomach, Myr Tarkas."

"I wish we had time to dissect it," Dahlia said. "Look at the face structure. It's..."

"They feed on corpses," Aranthur said.

"They're *designed* to feed on corpses." Dahlia got up. "Gods, what a stench." She held out her hands and Ardvan poured water from his canteen over them. "I'll tell you this much—I don't believe in ritual pollution, but don't let those claws scratch you."

"Don't touch me," Haras said.

"Grow up!" Dahlia snapped back.

Aranthur was looking at the creature's hair, which was...

"Those things are like feathers," he said.

Dahlia knelt again.

"We need to get moving," Kallotronis said.

"You fought these before," Aranthur said.

"Yes."

"Ambush?" Aranthur asked.

"Yes. Just like this one—guarding a tunnel."

"Long wait for prey, if you ask me," Aranthur said. He was thinking.

"Look at this," Dahlia said.

Kallotronis closed his eyes and Haras shrank away, but she was pointing to a string around the dead creature's neck, lost in the stubby feather-like protrusions of its hair. And hanging from it was a crude circle of tarnished bronze wire.

"Seen one of these before?" Dahlia asked.

"In Armea," Aranthur said.

"In fucking Antioke," Kallotronis said. "Lady, you take us to all the nicest places."

"These monsters are working for the *Pure*?" Haras asked.

Aranthur tugged his beard. "Let's move."

They ghosted along the next fifty paces, covering both sides of the tunnel. Aranthur had his *carabin* up on his shoulder now, the barrel passing back and forth as he moved; the long barrel of Kallotronis' *jezzail* projected just past his head, and Aranthur didn't care.

"The shots will have warned them."

"Can we *talk* to them?" Aranthur asked.

"You mean, after we killed half a dozen?" Kallotronis asked. "Eh, Spasmeno! Is this our painting?"

Cut Face came forward. "Yes," he said. "Unless there's more than one painting of a vulture-man eating a dead girl's intestines down here..."

Dahlia shone her magelight on the fresco. It was very old, the plastered paint flaking from the even older stone.

"That's not at all creepy," she said, with all of her old sarcasm. "Aphres. That's a *hutti painting.*" She looked at Aranthur. "They can paint. They're not monsters, they're...people."

Aranthur nodded. "Gods," he said, struggling with the idea.

"Cursed, damned souls," Haras said.

"We turn here," Cut Face said. "Can we get this over with?"

They turned into the cross-corridor, which was wider and more regular, with filthy stone walls and a stone floor under the dirt of ages.

"What the fuck are those?" Kallotronis said.

In the stark magelight, the fat millipede looked as horrible as the *hutti* and more than a foot long. It was working its way along the wall as if gravity didn't affect it.

Cut Face raised his puffer and shot it. He blew its head off and the lead ball ricocheted off down the tunnel.

"Eagle!" Kallotronis said.

"I feel better now," Cut Face said, and set about reloading his puffer.

"Aploun. Here we are."

Kallotronis had reached a white marble arch.

They leant out of the opening of their tunnel, and their lights failed to pierce the dusty murk.

"I remember this now," Kallotronis said. "Fuck me. I really did close my eyes."

"Me too," muttered Cut Face.

"I can see why," Aranthur said.

The cavern was immense, and the floor was carpeted with bones. Everything smelled of death. Old, old death. The light from their magelights vanished ahead of them. While above...

Above was the underside of the stone garden, the graves of all the sorcerers and priests. The ceiling above them was studded with the underside of burials—and the glow of old and fading *puissance.*

"This is the worst place in the fucking world," Cut Face said.

Aranthur stepped out onto the floor. He could see tracks in the bone shards, and his booted feet crunched as he set them down.

"I assume that was you?" he said, pointing at the tracks.

"Sure," Cut Face said, terror rendering his answer meaningless.

Aranthur was with him in spirit. The whole venture now looked foolish now they were here. The necropolis was far worse than he'd expected.

A cave spider as big as his hand dropped from the chaos of the ceiling and landed on Kallotronis' head.

He grabbed it by a furry leg and hurled it across the cavern.

"Fuck," he said.

Everyone looked up, to see the whole ceiling appeared to be writhing.

Aranthur was in the lead; he plunged along the trail of crushed bones and when he glanced back, even the sailors carrying the Black Stone were running.

The spiders fell around them with soft *plops.*

Dahlia cast something. Aranthur felt the power, and hoped she was camouflaging her casting; then she threw a barrier up, glowing softly. It lit the cavern, and held back the spiders.

It also illuminated the massive *socle*: the huge stones at the base of the Black Pyramid, which had subsided, collapsing the whole end of the cavern.

Aranthur stopped running and just stared.

It was as if a cliff wall had appeared in front of him—forty feet high or higher, and not smooth. The black foundation stones were not as well finished as the outer walls.

But there was no gate, no door, no arch to be seen.

The track through the bones ran to the wall face, and stopped.

"Fuck," Kallotronis said.

The spiders were still dropping onto Dahlia's barrier. She pushed up next to Aranthur, her hair violet in the magelight.

"Aranthur? Any plans?" she asked. "Now what?"

Haras shook his head. "I hate this."

"We all hate it," Aranthur said. "Do you know another way?"

Haras swallowed. "Maybe."

One of the Nomadi nodded, and jerked his chin to the left, at one of the dozen openings.

Aranthur took a deep breath.

"I can't hold the fucking spiders back forever without my working being detected," Dahlia said. "There's something bad…"

Aranthur could sense it too. It was a curious evolution in his powers; he'd begun to sense *power* without even raising his magesight. It felt like they were being watched.

Somewhere not very far away, there was another massive concussion, and twenty fat spiders fell together to hang in the air over the heads. Bones fell, and some dirt.

The cavern was full of swearing.

"This one," said Haras.

It wasn't the one that the Nomadi trooper had chosen, and now he shook his head.

"We'll take this one."

Aranthur didn't wait to explain. He jogged across the cavern, his feet crunching on the old bones.

"Maybe," Haras admitted.

Aranthur covered the hole; then, rash as always, he poked his head in and followed his head with the rest of him.

No one awaited him, and he kept going, moving as fast as he could.

The Arnauts padded behind him, obviously delighted to have someone else in front.

Aranthur thought of Equus, a long time ago at a drill day. "*Officers lead from in front,*" he said. "*That's why we use them up so fast.*"

Aranthur let his fear fuel him. He moved at a trot along a corridor that was wider than the first one had been, although just as filthy. The black millipedes moved through the rubbish underfoot; he trotted on, ignoring their glowing blue legs and mandibles.

The tunnel narrowed and the ceiling lowered until he had to crouch. At that point he stopped. Very slowly he reached back and touched Kallotronis.

"Smell that?" he whispered very softly.

Kallotronis nodded.

Death, and decay—a fresher smell of rotting meat. And over it all, a strong, clean, sharp tang of something burning. Acrid; a touch of sulphur…

Burning match-cord. The kind of match-cord used in muskets on battlefields.

Aranthur could see a corner ahead, a four-way intersection just barely illuminated by the magelight behind him, and he crept forward along the ground on his elbows, his face just above the garbage and the millipedes.

He came to the intersection and he didn't hesitate; he rolled on to his left side and raised his puffer to the right...

Hutti.

This time it was the monster who was surprised. It was at arm's reach, and the red cord around its neck and the twisted wire circle were clear in the blue-white light, as was the Arnaut matchlock it had in its hands, aimed at human chest height on a rest.

Aranthur shot it. The creature stumbled back into another *hutto* and then Kallotronis was there. He shot down the tunnel, and there was a return shot followed by a clatter of darts. One hit Aranthur's breastplate and fell away into the darkness.

Cut Face leant around the corner and shot his blunderbuss one-handed over Aranthur's head.

Aranthur was getting to his feet. He drew a second puffer and shot on instinct, more from panic than practice. The light of his shot illuminated the cross tunnel—and the *hutti* moving in all directions.

Aranthur stepped back as Dead Eye fired both puffers. The clouds of powder smoke obscured everything, and their magelights turned the smoke into a blinding fog.

Aranthur drew his yataghan. He wanted the *sword*, the Bright Steel, but he feared revealing it here and alerting the Old Ones to their attack. Instead he got the buckler on to his left hand just in time to face the rush. The *hutti* didn't use hand-to-hand weapons; nature or design had given them poisoned talons and they were fast and deadly.

Aranthur was just as fast. He punched with the buckler and cut a taloned hand away at the wrist with a little turn of his own hand, a *tramazzone.* He pushed his first victim off balance; they were light, these *hutti*, and he threw his into its fellows.

Its tongue shot out at him and he was prepared and cut it off; his blow buried his yataghan in the thing's face and it fell away, tearing his weapon from his grasp.

He raised his buckler and a bolt of jade-green lightning struck the next *hutti*, outlining it in a halo of green fire before it burned away to ash.

Haras stood at the intersection, his staff raised like a two-handed sword.

Aranthur stepped on the dead thing and ripped his yataghan from its skull. It came loose with a pop and he stumbled forward as Haras slew another one and the rest turned to run. Or most of them did. Two of them fell to the ground.

It was one of those moments. Aranthur had come to know them—the moments when he did… things.

The *hutti* on the ground were less than a pace away. Aranthur's *carabin*, hanging by his side, came into his hands like an old lover and pointed itself right in the centre of the fallen *hutto*'s forehead.

It lay glaring at him, eyes wild in the magelight.

Maybe this time he was going to try doing nothing.

His hands were shaking.

It was bound. The *hutti* on the floor of the tunnel were bound with rawhide ropes.

"I mean no harm," he said.

Its hideous ears expanded, and its snake-tongue cycled like something obscene.

Aranthur held his ground. "Don't shoot," he said, because he heard Kallotronis coming up behind him. "We're just passing through," he said, first in Byzas, and then, slowly, in Masran.

"Kill the fucking thing," Kallotronis said. "Gack! There's another!"

"Shut up." Aranthur thought it had recognised his Masran. "Send me Haras."

There was scrabbling behind him.

"Just kill them," Haras said.

"Do they speak a language?" Aranthur asked.

"They are damned souls. They can only speak a parody of a human tongue."

"Oh, fuck off," Inoques said, dropping her Nomadi trooper *guise*. "They speak an old dialect of Masran and their mouths aren't shaped like human mouths." Inoques looked up and down the cross-corridor.

"We need guards," Aranthur said. "Chimeg?"

"On it, *Bahadur*."

The Nomadi went out in both directions, weapons raised.

"What is *it* doing here?" Haras spat.

"Saving your worthless, priestly hide," Inoques said. "This one is female. Look."

She pointed to the second *hutta*'s back, which had eight regularly spaced…

"Oh, gods," Kallotronis said. "*Little* monsters."

Inoques looked at Aranthur.

"Help me talk to him," Aranthur asked, and Inoques knelt by the *hutto*. After a moment Aranthur knelt by her and Dahlia came up. "Ask his name."

The monster turned his head away.

"No circle medal. Ask him why they're prisoners."

It thrashed.

"Just kill them," Haras snapped.

"I never like to agree with a priest," Kallotronis said. "But hells. Just kill them."

Then the female spoke. The things—the *babies*—on her back writhed like maggots, and she sounded utterly alien, her high-pitched voice sibilant and without consonants.

"She says, *talk, we are dead people*," Inoques said. "Or something like that."

Aranthur's *carabin* was still aimed at the thing. *The person.*

"Kill it!" Kallotronis said.

"They live here," Aranthur said.

"We know," moaned Cut Face.

"So they know how to get past the wall. If there's a way," Aranthur said.

Haras said, "Oh, gods of the dead. Kill it!"

"What's the Masran for *we mean no harm*?"

"You are insane," said Haras, and then spoke clearly and slowly in Masran.

Aranthur repeated the words, very slowly, while Inoques nodded.

The ears slowly deflated.

The male shook himself, and then said, "We are dead people."

"Dead people?" Aranthur repeated once Inoques had translated.

"*Boso*…"

"Shut up. Ask it—*If we let you go, will you help us*?"

Inoques spoke.

"She is *not* on our side," Haras insisted.

Aranthur turned to the Masran priest. "So you keep saying. So far, though, she's a lot more help than you are. She knew the right tunnel, for example."

"You mean, the tunnel that led us to an ambush?" Haras said. "She's leading us to her dark masters."

"You Masran priests *are* my dark masters," Inoques said. "And you shot off your magery ensuring every magister for miles is alerted."

She listened first to the female and then the male. Then they both spoke at once.

"*Boso*, we have to *move.*"

Dahlia put a hand on Aranthur's arm. "Inoques is right," she said. "Anything that wants to find us knows where to come now. We need to get clear."

Aranthur made his decision. It was no different than deciding to fight a duel, or choosing to double back and attack bandits.

He cut the female's bonds first. The rawhide ropes were tight, and she just lay for a moment.

The male was thrashing in his bonds.

The female muttered something.

The male stopped thrashing.

"She said, *He cut me free, fool.*" Inoques laughed.

The female rolled to her knees and wobbled, clearly shocked by the lack of feeling in her legs, which had been bound too long.

Then her taloned hand shot out and grabbed Aranthur's wrist.

He let her.

She looked up at him, her carrion-claw hand wrapped like a metal vice around his wrist. Then she stumbled to her feet and let go.

"Did she cut you?"

"No," Aranthur said.

He was wearing fighting gauntlets, but he was sure it hadn't been an attack, and he was shaking anyway. They were just too hideous; they looked like nightmares.

"Tell her that if she will guide us to the central shaft of the Black Pyramid—"

"You are joking." But Haras was past terror now.

The *hutta* in front of them lowered her head. The other raised his bound hands and Aranthur said, "Tell to it *stop moving.*"

Haras pointed at the male and spoke sharply, and it slumped in its bonds, and Aranthur took the chance to carefully cut the rawhide.

The *hutta* gave a sharp bark and the other writhed on the floor. Aranthur assumed that the returning blood flow to the limbs was more painful than the bonds. It seemed to scuttle in the refuse of the floor.

It stank like death.

"Ask about guiding us again," Aranthur insisted.

"Company coming," said Chimeg, from the darkness.

Aranthur turned and trotted back to her. She was watching the corridor.

"*Hutti*," she said.

A crossbow bolt snapped against the roof of the corridor and tumbled past them. Then another.

Aranthur glanced at Chimeg. "Back," he said.

This wasn't a time for stealth. Nor did he want to fight.

He cast a small but very bright light in a corner of the corridor and ran back towards Chimeg and the others. When he had gone fifty paces, he turned and made his *transference.* He aimed his power at the light.

The tunnel collapsed. Dust and dirt billowed in the magelight and the Nomadi pulled their dust veils over their faces.

"We're not going back that way," Aranthur said to Dahlia.

"Why do I follow you?" she asked with a smile.

Inoques raised an eyebrow. "Even for you this is risky. You are going to trust these things?"

"I thought you liked them more than Haras?" Aranthur asked.

"I just hate his ignorance. Anyone who does a little research can tell you that the *hutti* were created by the sorcerer Alizones when he attacked the Black Pyramid." She looked at Aranthur as if he was an idiot.

"When was that?" Aranthur asked.

Inoques shrugged. "Six thousand years ago? Give or take?" She put a hand to the tunnel wall. "We really do need to run. Something very powerful is coming."

Haras shook his head and spoke again in Masran.

The female turned and loped away on her long back legs, no longer erect.

"Do we follow?"

"How would I know?" Haras asked. "They are the ultimate evil! The defilement of the dead!"

"But you spoke to one," Aranthur said. "And where I stand, the ultimate evil is over our heads, waiting to kill us. These appear to me creatures just like us."

"That's…" Haras paused, the Byzas word *disgusting* on his lips. But he shook his head. "Perhaps," he admitted grudgingly. Haras looked at him in the magelight. "I confess I have learned much in the last month."

"Me too," Aranthur said, and managed a smile.

Haras's smile was shaky. "*We cannot trust Inoques.*"

"Let's go," Aranthur said. "And yes, we can."

He trotted forward into the hot, stinking dark and saw the *hutta* turn down a cross-corridor. He followed and she bounded ahead.

"Where'd the male go?"

"Tell the Nomadi to be on their toes!" Aranthur shouted back along the tunnel.

A concussion above them, and then another.

Dust drifted down.

"The army is fully engaged," Dahlia said.

Someone moaned and Aranthur worried it might have been him.

"Keep going!"

He went forward, and kept going until, after a while, he lost track of time.

They went left, then right, and then entered a bewildering warren; they'd left the tunnels carved by man, but these had not been made by the *hutti*. They were round and narrow, and Aranthur had to scramble along. There were curses from the men carrying the Black Stone as it went on.

And on.

And on.

Hot, and then hotter, as if they were walking through a forge. They came to steps—steps carved in black basalt. Aranthur's heart soared, and then his hopes were dashed; the steps were only dug out for a few paces, and then the tunnel left them and went to the right, slanting up. Everything smelled of meat-eating scavengers.

"They're going to fuckin' eat us," muttered Cut Face.

"I don't think so," Aranthur said.

They didn't have the heavy grinding jaw of a hyaena. The proboscis suggested something more disgusting, but finely tuned—the devouring of rotted flesh.

"I think we're too fresh to eat."

"They can kill us and eat us later."

"Maybe," Aranthur said.

Up again—this time scrabbling, climbing up old rock in a very small tunnel where the air was so foetid that it was difficult to breathe at all.

And there was a new sensation: a non-physical oppression.

Dahlia was behind him; he could hear her breathing. As they climbed another rockface, the dried mud of the new tunnel brushed his back so that he had the petrifying feeling that the entire weight of the pyramid was on him, ready to crush him like the insect he was—collapsing around him so that his last moments would be there trapped in failure with the millipedes and the stinking darkness.

We are under the pyramid, came a whisper. Inoques.

Aranthur looked back to see her climbing behind him.

"Where's Dahlia?"

"I didn't eat her," Inoques hissed. "She's helping the sailors get the stone up the rock."

Aranthur wriggled to the top and found himself in a bigger space. His magelight barely burned, as if its power was lost here.

"Why are you helping us?"

"I'm helping *you*," she hissed.

Cut Face came up, and Kallotronis, and then Haras. The next man up was a sailor.

"Where's the male?" Aranthur asked.

Kallotronis spread his hands. "I thought you...?"

Haras walked around, feeling with his hands and peering into the half-lit darkness.

"I think that we are in the *Empty Chamber*," he said. "I see a builder sign and some slave writing, but no blessings and no guides."

Aranthur nodded as if what the priest was saying made sense.

The Masran priest's hands were shaking.

"I am *inside* the Black Pyramid," he said. "I am not of the caste that does this."

"But all the priests who did this..." Aranthur muttered.

"Are dead," Dahlia put in. "Come on, Haras."

Through his search, their guide stood as far from the humans as she could manage.

"There's a ramp up," Aranthur said.

"Yes," Haras said. "We're definitely inside the Black Pyramid now." He hesitated. "I never thought to get this far."

"That's great to hear," muttered Dead Eye.

The *hutta* barked, low and urgent. And then again. And then growled.

Haras shook his head.

The *hutta* barked again, this time even more slowly.

"She's saying, *light, light*." Haras said.

Aranthur walked slowly towards the *hutta*, who stood her ground, trembling as he reached up and took the magelit jewel from his helmet and offered it out to her.

She hesitated... then her claws shot out, faster than thought, and the jewel was gone.

The *hutta* bounded across the empty room and vanished into a tunnel.

"Now they'll all come and eat us," Dead Eye said. But his words lacked conviction.

"Less than five hundred paces to go," Aranthur said.

"Straight up," Kallotronis said.

"You brought it down the central shaft," Aranthur said.

"Yes," the Arnaut said. "The chief priest, the one who died fighting the Disciple—he lowered it. With *baraka*."

Aranthur began to go up the ramp. The feeling of oppression was growing.

"For what it's worth," Inoques said, "she was telling us that the Red-Cord-Wearers are taking over the catacombs and forcing all the other *hutti* to submit."

Aranthur nodded. "Interesting. Haras?"

"If this is the Empty Chamber then the central well is up the ramp and to the left." He shrugged. "The black marble arch is at the top of this ramp. The sacred space starts under the arch."

"Sacred space?" Aranthur asked.

"He means the prison. But I doubt he even knows how it works," Inoques said.

"Ware!" Dahlia said.

Black smoke was oozing down the ramp, strange and too coherent to be natural.

"Shields!" Dahlia snapped and suited action to word.

Aranthur's shields grew up like an enchanted forest and leapt in front of Cut Face, just in time—the black smoke reached for the lithe Arnaut and a red fire leapt out of the black and struck Aranthur's shields.

Aranthur had seen that black fog before, on the streets of Al-Khaire, but it was much denser here and also more terrifying.

In the same tempo, Dahlia struck back. Her fire was violet-white, and the black fog seemed to boil away from it, until suddenly, as if the consciousness within had forgotten what to do, a shield like a thousand layers of spiderweb sprang into being.

There was no point to concealment any longer. Aranthur used the moment that Dahlia's attack bought them to reach into the *Aulos* and draw the *sword.*

Gods, where are you? the sword asked.

"Black Pyramid, undercroft," Aranthur said.

The epicentre of Ammit's power on earth. She seemed to laugh. *I see now why I was drawn to you. You are insane. But I like it.*

Aranthur was already pressing forward, pushing his layered shield against the spiderweb-shield of his adversary. Where the shields met there was light, and darkness, and order, and chaos.

Aranthur pushed forward into the melee of meanings.

Haras was wielding green lightning like the old images of Aiglos, the Eagle; Dahlia's purple-white left holes in the web-froth. Aranthur raised the sword in his right hand. Between the sword tip rising and falling he cast *enhancement.* And the manipulation of force he'd used on Sittar—the shaped charge. He wrote it in fire and it *occurred* and he stepped into the space that his working had created the way a swordsman might step into a flaw in an enemy phalanx.

At a remove, he could tell that the Old Ones' frothy shields were winning the argument. His own shields lost layer after layer, and gradually condensed around him as he struck into the thick black fog with the sword—which was no longer a flickering, pale blue, but instead was like the very definition of light itself, impossibly bright and perfected by the darkness around it.

Aranthur cut and cut, butterfly strokes with the whole blade of the sword, as if he was dancing one of Master Sparthos' forms on the salle floor.

The sword flowed; the blade moved, unstoppable, immeasurable, and it seemed to grow, as if it was an infinite line of light.

And the black fog rolled back up the ramp of black stone.

Aranthur followed it, the sword dancing. Now Dahlia pushed in with him, lashing the black with her own light.

Inoques stood quietly, her shields unengaged, as Kallotronis called "Follow them!"

Aranthur took another step forward, snapping a rising cut—and another.

Dahlia cast and cast. Even through the haze of terror and the need to keep the sword moving precisely, and the need to maintain his own shields, Aranthur was aware of her power, which was greater since the last time he'd seen her cast. Fire and light poured from her as if she was a small volcano, an underground thunderstorm, and the darkness was driven back by her effusion of light.

Aranthur cut, flowed, and cut.

It's luring us into a trap.

"I have a plan," Aranthur said.

You are the rashest paladin I have ever ridden. Are you not afraid of me yet?

"No," Aranthur said. "I was. I have a different view now."

Up. And up again.

Aranthur couldn't see his footing, so he slid his feet forward as the sword made graceful arcs over his head and almost to the floor.

At the huge black portal, supported by a lintel that must have weighted sixty tons, the Old One made a stand. The very air seemed to breathe red fire and Aranthur's shields collapsed against his body. But Dahlia stepped in front of him, and cast fire into the void until the black smoke was incandescent.

And it backed away from her.

By the light of her attacks Aranthur could see the well; the spiral of the vast staircase ran around the outside of an enormous central shaft. The stairs ran up and up around the square shaft, which was itself fifty paces wide or even wider. In the odd, otherworldly light, the floor glowed; black and white stone inlaid in incredibly intricate patterns; the walls were equally baroque, and the stairs had railings of polished bronze that caught the grey light and reflected it. Far, far above, daylight came in—a single magnificent shaft of pure sunlight fell all the way to the floor below like molten gold. Outside, it was noon, and the sun stood almost directly above the open aperture at the top of the shaft where the Black Stone had been taken away.

And even at a glance, Aranthur could see many signs of damage: entire segments of the winding stair lay in ruins; there were piles of rubble all around the edges of the shaft, and loose chunks of basalt littered the magnificent floor.

Incredible powers had been unleashed here.

Even as he watched, a ball of coherent white lightning came from somewhere high above to strike the black fog.

Ammit is still fighting the Disciple at the apex! That's the only reason we are still alive.

Aranthur grunted. Ammit, if that was the name of the black fog, absorbed the blow from high above and lashed at Dahlia.

Dahlia was taking the brunt of the red fire now, and Aranthur pointed at the sailors.

"Now!" he shouted. "All your strength!"

They threw themselves at the sled holding the Black Stone, and pushed it up the ramp. Two caught the handles and lifted; Cut Face got another handle, and Stilcho the fourth, and then they were running.

A line of Ammit's red fire struck Stilcho and he immolated, gone to ash in a heartbeat.

A distant moaning began to rise from the walls around the shaft.

How many are imprisoned here? Aranthur wondered.

Kallotronis took the handle and kept the Black Stone from falling.

"Behind me!" Aranthur yelled and the sword began its deadly pattern. He pushed through the black portal into the central shaft, and the laughter began around them.

FOOOOOOOOOOLS!

Aranthur almost tripped on a chunk of black basalt no bigger than a fist and Dahlia leapt past him, covering the advance of the Stone with her shields. Aranthur recovered and stepped up beside Dahlia and rebuilt his shields as Haras stepped to the other side of the magas. His shields had grown as well, in a month of near-constant casting. Now he lashed Ammit with green fire.

And then the Old One struck back, and the lash of his rage was a tidal wave of *sihr.* Aranthur could barely move the sword; Haras fell on his back, eyes unseeing, and Dahlia's shields were stripped away in layers.

The Black Stone emerged from the doorway into the central shaft.

And in that shaft, Ammit coiled for the finishing blow, a tower of dark wrath.

Aranthur turned his head. "Inoques?" he said.

"Here I am," she said. She was right behind him, unnoticed in the melee.

She spread her hands. And her shields—a fractal waterfall of black crystal structures too intricate for the eye to comprehend.

Ammit reared up, some of his true shape coalescing inside the black fog—legs. Too many legs, and an insectile torso…

TRAITOR!

But Inoques was undeterred. She raised one hand, and the Stone shot off its cradle into the air and up the shaft. Haras twitched but could do nothing.

The moaning from the walls reached the pitch of a scream—the scream of a hundred or a thousand beings.

The Old One reached for it with a dozen black tendrils but every arm shrivelled away, unable to touch the sacred artifact. He cast a plane of force that stopped it in the air above them.

Dahlia undermined the plane, cutting Ammit off from it.

He turned on her.

The Black Stone rose…

NOOOOOOOOOOOOOOOO!

As the Black Stone rose, Haras got to his knees and then to his feet. He stumbled towards the centre of the great chamber, and Inoques moved behind him, her whole being concentrated on the rising stone block.

Ammit swung his lash at her.

The Stone rose even as Aranthur saw his lover take terrible punishment.

Aranthur could see the frothing dark smoke now as illusion—or perhaps the Old Ones eventuated differently in the terrible space of the pyramid chamber. In the centre of the fog stood an armoured being as tall as a draught horse, but with hundreds of legs which seemed to beat the ground in agitation as it flickered between forms and it… was… huge.

TRAITOR!

Inoques shrugged. She had taken on the form he'd glimpsed under Antioke and in the Sultan's garden: black armoured, like the old god, and wearing the head of a snake. Or a cat.

She glanced at Aranthur—almost involuntary, that glance.

The dark enemy cast.

The sheer power of its *occulta* was like the effect of a hammer falling on glass. Aranthur's shields were eroded like a child's sandcastle against a rising tide; Haras, ahead of them all, took the brunt, and lost his in a single blow, and screamed.

Haras was looking at Inoques, despite the imminence of a dark god at arm's length, as if he couldn't take his eyes off her. As if his own death were a thing of no moment.

"Thank you," he said.

He had a scorched mark across his abdomen and a dozen wounds. He fell slowly to his knees.

Aranthur was feeling the emergence of something else—a third power.

"Stay back!" he snapped. "The Disciple is coming."

The alien god turned its antennaed head to Aranthur.

WHO ARE YOU?

Dahlia was rebuilding her shields—tiny lozenges of violet crystal snapping back into place, replacing those swept away by the red fire of Ammit.

There was a shimmer, like the mirage of water in the high desert.

"Back!" Aranthur said, rebuilding his own shields as he stumbled back towards the portal behind him.

He was moving with unnatural speed; his *enhancement* had cast with extraordinary effect. He had time to wonder if his shouted commands were even comprehensible to his friends.

Haras remained on his knees in the middle of the floor, and Inoques stayed facing the towering, antennaed menace.

The Black Stone remained, hundreds of feet over their heads, unmoving, and the scream, the united screams of all the choir of entities trapped in the pyramid made it almost impossible to hear anything or even to think. Thin lines of power flashed from the walls, targeting

Dahlia and Inoques and Aranthur—weak, individually, but a constant gnawing at their resources.

"I can't..." Inoques was unsteady. "He is attacking my mind."

"Fuck," Kallotronis said very slowly.

He leapt around Aranthur's shields, running forward a dozen steps. He seemed slow to Aranthur, and his shouts were lost in the terrible screams.

"No!" Aranthur shouted.

He didn't need another human to protect, but he could not abandon Kallotronis. So he followed him, raising his tattered shields.

Kallotronis stopped and drew a bead on the vast, dark, multi-legged thing, and pulled the trigger of his long *jezzail.*

In Aranthur's enhanced state, Kallotronis' *jezzail* took an aeon to fire. The cock fell on the frizzen, scraping sparks that fell with agonising slowness into the opening pan; the powder in the pan ignited, and Aranthur could actually see the kernels of powder ignite.

There was a notable pause after the pan ignited. Long enough to see the great head turn, the glitter of its unpupiled black eyes like marble beads. It was raising a new series of shields...

Dahlia loosed a massive flash of deep blue light that seemed to arc from her hand to Ammit's shields; and she burned a black hole in them.

The *jezzail* fired. Aranthur saw a gush of smoke and fire emerge from the barrel—not the projectile itself. But he saw the effect as the projectile slammed into the plates of the gargantuan creature's armoured face through the hole in Ammit's shields and punctured the chitinous flesh, spraying a dreadful white ichor.

And then his vision was blocked, the mirage shimmer becoming the pillar of white fire that Aranthur associated with a Disciple. It eventuated almost atop poor Haras. By luck, or fate, it was exactly in the path between Ammit and Kallotronis.

And so it was the Disciple, not Aranthur or Kallotronis, who took the brunt of the last of Ammit's wrath.

The huge whip, hundreds of strands of scarlet fire, fell on the white fire, and there was a flash of nothing. A glimpse of stars and the void and fire—a polarised vision of a white void with black stars...

Aranthur went forward.

What the...?

Aranthur had never heard the sword confused before.

High above them, the Black Stone moved; Ammit, wounded, had lost his concentration; the choir of entities *screeched*... Aranthur felt the Stone as it clicked into its place, sealing the structure. Aranthur felt the change—felt the power.

Ammit reared back like a stallion fighting for a mate, the legs along his hideous torso pulsing.

DO YOU KNOW WHAT YOU HAVE DONE, TRAITOR?

Haras spoke one word.

"*Qafl!*"

His voice sounded high and angry compared to the sonorous, mellifluous inhumanity of Ammit.

Exactly as had happened on the trabaccolo, a thin grey lens seemed to pass over everything.

The choir of entities was suddenly silent.

Aranthur felt as if, for the first time, he could think and see clearly.

Haras lay on his side, his right hand still clutching his staff and still making arcane sigils in the air. Beyond him, the white tower of the Disciple stood facing the articulated form of Ammit. Power pulsed between them, and their shields spun off fractal webs that themselves projected visions of other places, but too fast to follow; a stone circle in a rose garden, a causeway over a desert, a darkening sea under a sky devoid of stars.

Aranthur looked away, up the shaft. The interior of the pyramid was now dark, the shaft of brilliant sunlight gone, the recesses of the mighty shaft now grey with shadow fading to a point of grey-white light where the Black Stone sealed the space. And the black arch behind him glowed with a colourless eldritch fire. Aranthur couldn't see through the arch; there was a web, a palpable tracery with patterns that almost made sense.

He went forward, towards the Disciple and towards Haras. It felt as if his legs were trapped in sludge, despite the *enhancement* and all the power. Everything about this place felt wrong.

He pushed through another step towards Haras. The priest was lying against something—a column, or a plinth.

Everything was taking too long.

He grabbed Haras by the collar with his right hand, lifted him clear of the floor and threw him over his own shoulders.

He had been lying against a stone column. At first it looked like the base of a missing statue, but closer, it had a bronze plaque and a lever that could be moved like the hands of a clock to face any of five jewels.

Aranthur was close to Kallotronis, more than a quarter of the way across the immense floor to where the white column of the Disciple and the black column of the god faced each other. The fractal effect was diminishing, sinking into the white shield; around the edges of the Disciple's aura there were back-eddies of complete chaos. The Disciple's white light was now the sole illumination in the huge crypt.

Aranthur threw his shields over Kallotronis and took a long, gliding step back, towing him away from the Disciple as Inoques slammed a taloned hand, or arcane gauntlet, into the Disciple from behind. Her talons raked the shield, peeling yet more of the reality away.

The Disciple replied with two beams of red fire and something that exploded. Aranthur's shields took the full brunt of it and they were flayed the way a whip ruins a man's naked back; a dozen tendrils burned through, two them ripping across his body.

He screamed.

It took him a breath to restore sanity; then he rotated his shields automatically, putting the damaged area at the back, and stepped back again, another long, gliding swordsman's step. Kallotronis was screaming; the burn-through had flashed across his face, boiled an eye, and his whole body arched from the pain.

Inoques struck again with both hands, black claws extended, and the Disciple reeled.

Dahlia raised her arm. Aranthur couldn't understand her shout, but he caught Kallotronis in his arms and dropped, covering Haras with his body and his shields.

Dahlia had carefully marshalled her strength, and now she poured a broadside of prepared strikes into the Disciple's damaged shield.

The grim, antennaed monster dropped his lash again, and his target was Inoques.

Aranthur could see white ichor pulsing from the hole in the thing's faceplate even as she, fast as a true feline, leapt under the fall of the lash to slash at the armoured thing with a sword of black, like an embodiment of the absence of light.

The Disciple's shields folded in around it. It was hurt; Aranthur knew what stage of combat it had reached. He pushed to his feet and pulled Kallotronis after him. Even with the most powerful *enhancement* he'd ever cast, the weight of carrying Haras and dragging Kallotronis slowed him to a crawl. The entities on the thousand steps bombarded all of them with their powers; dream and nightmare stalked the floor of the shaft; curses and benisons rode the very air around them.

Dahlia cast again.

Haras raised an arm from Aranthur's shoulder and cast.

The Disciple seemed to pulse, and the Old One struck at all of them—the lash of scarlet, a hammer of darkness and a simple beam of dazzling ruby.

Aranthur focused on his task, pouring his power into movement, and then he was running, the full strength of his overpowered *enhancement* allowing him to pull the big Souliote warrior the way a child might drag a doll.

Aranthur got his front foot through the portal. He dropped Haras into the waiting arms of Ardvan and flung Kallotronis through to Dead Eye as he got his sword's point up into line with the Disciple. Behind him, he could feel the Imoter, Poulos, casting.

In the next heartbeat…

Inoques and Ammit exchanged a hundred blows, her talons flashing like scythes of obsidian, his hundred legs each attempting a strike, his massive front claws ripping at her, while both of them traded a light show of beams; all so fast that Aranthur could not make out the details. The other entities lashed away; the age-old dust from the floors and walls, raised by the combat, carried the colour of the beams so that the entire shaft appeared lit by a lattice of coloured light.

The Disciple turned on Dahlia, but she turned its strike with a flick of her sword hand.

The titanic, impossible whirl of the fight between the Old One and Inoques moved, and every second they came closer to the portal.

Despite that, and everything else, Aranthur went at the Disciple.

It ignored him and slashed at Inoques. It hurt her, scoring a line of white fire against her armour of scales. Then it leapt, and its convulsive movement brought it closer to Aranthur.

Aranthur cast, thirty paces out from the Disciple's white shields. And like a master swordsman, he was deceptive; he threw a strong, simple attack, a fist of white light.

The Disciple whirled, a cyclone of lightnings, and poured power at him, *sihr* and *saar* all intermixed.

Aranthur parried part with the sword, and took part on his buckler, and the remnants of his once-mighty shields took another blow. Then he went forward into the Disciple's strike as if Master Sparthos was there to direct him, and the Disciple was slow; a massive beam of incandescent fire that Aranthur turned on a hastily summoned red *aspis*.

Now, too close to be easily parried, Aranthur unleashed his prepared attacks; he rippled them off as he had done against Sittar, except that they flowed even faster.

The Disciple was already wounded, its shields were in shreds, and Aranthur was only on his third cast when the mirage shimmer filled his vision...

And the Disciple was *gone*.

Dahlia rotated her shields and Aranthur stepped back until he and Dahlia were side by side at the very edge of the threshold of the portal; their shields filled the portal from top to bottom, protecting the huddled mortals behind them on the ramp.

Inoques leapt free of the swirling, impossible dark melee; a gaping wound in her side.

The other thing was unable to right itself. But it struck with a claw, and she had to leap free again, and the hundred legs spasmed and the segmented carapace flexed and the claws came straight at the portal.

Aranthur struck. His sword was high, in front of his face, as if he was facing a mortal opponent, and he cut into the monstrous attack.

The sword slammed into the carapace of the oncoming monster like a steel sword—the difference being that it cut through the thing's shields like paper, leaving gashes in the flowing dark energy. But the carapace held the sword, and Aranthur's hand and forearm burned in pain from the shock.

A leg swept Aranthur from his feet. Another spiked into his abdomen, denting his breastplate, but the armour held. Dahlia blew the appendage off from two paces away, severing the leg and two others with a brutal arc of power that left spots on Aranthur's retinas even as he rolled over his sword and came to his feet. As he'd practiced with Sapu a hundred times, he rolled to his feet with his sword cutting low to high as he did, so that he *flowed* into his attack, and the next black leg searching for him was severed, armour and all, and white ichor that sizzled and burned like fire sprayed out.

He struck again, deep in his *assalto*, the sword cutting and cutting, reaching for the thing's vitals. Dahlia struck again, and the massive thing *moved.* It wobbled once, backing, and fell half to one side, where Aranthur could see that Inoques had torn away twenty legs.

Aranthur didn't pause to reflect on it. He lobbed his shaped charge, the deadliest attack he knew. It was next in his prearranged progression; he snapped it into reality and wrote it, and the force of energy built in a fraction of a heartbeat and was delivered, in this case, through the rent in the monster's left-side shields.

The monstrous god reared back, using hideous front claws for support. A long line of white ichor bled down its face and front, so that it seemed to be weeping through its beard of writhing tendrils, and it screamed. The remaining legs pulsed and the whole behemoth *scuttled* back like a galley backing oars, and a new web of shields began to eventuate. As it retreated, it left Inoques lying like a broken doll.

Aranthur stepped forward, and again.

In a moment of reckless heroism, Dead Eye stepped through the portal, raised his arms and cast. Dead Eye had a very limited repertoire, but his workings were *puissant.* And his best working was an impenetrable black smoke.

Aranthur put his entire shield between himself and the carapaced thing and stooped. Dahlia stood over him like some warrior-goddess of old, a spear of lightning in her raised right hand, her shields covering him as he seized Inoques in his arms and lifted her.

The Old One lashed at them, and they both retaliated.

Smoke flowed from Dead Eye's fingertips, filling the space in front of him faster than thought, and the whole portal was obscured in a heartbeat.

The smoke rose, billowing into the well of the pyramid. The light of the *puissant* effects reflected from two thousand years of inlays and carving. Gold glittered; the eagle-headed god and the vulture-headed god and all their children, allies, lovers and enemies, and the whole of the floor, the strange patterns in black and white stone, pulsed with the echoes of the power being manifested. Dead Eye's black smoke glowed with the efforts of the entities on the walls; it seemed to burn from inside as Ammit attempted to flay them with a pale fire; but none of their adversaries could see through the hermetical smoke.

Dahlia and Aranthur stepped back together, deep into Dead Eye's smoke, and then through it, leaving the battlefield to the wounded monster-god, Ammit. The last glimpse Aranthur had was of the armoured thing filling its side of the cavern with a web of defences spun at the same incredible speed that it did everything. But it was no longer throwing *occultae.* It was only building defences.

As soon as they were though the portal, Aranthur built a shining wall, the kind that Iralia made a specialty of, and Dahlia put in one of her own, sealing the portal.

Cut Face had Kallotronis over his shoulder. Haras was moving on his own, Alisha Poulos still pouring the silver-white webbing of Imoter *occultae* into his wounds, but as soon as Aranthur appeared she turned, one hand locked on Haras, and began to work on Aranthur's ribs. Incredibly, and perhaps because of her, only Stilcho and one sailor were dead.

So far.

"Run," Aranthur said.

The sailors needed no urging. They went down the ramp, Aranthur slinging his wife over his right shoulder. He was tired, hit in a dozen places and he suspected that he had more than one cracked rib, but the power of his *enhancement* was keeping him on his feet and the Imoter was relieving the pain.

Dead Eye kept filling the so-called Empty Chamber with his impenetrable smoke, and Aranthur tossed a sheet of ice over the ramp behind him. The sailors were already gone, and Cut Face wrestled the unconscious Kallotronis into the *hutti* tunnel and followed him, shouting in Byzas to the sailor below him.

Aranthur laid Inoques down on the ancient floor, and Poulos knelt by her for a moment, then rose.

"I can't," she said flatly. "She's...too protected." She went back to Haras.

To Aranthur and to Dahlia, the next minute was the longest of their lives. Sound carried clearly; the bellowed wrath of the hundred-legged monster was still close, and the clicking and slipping of its remaining clawed feet on the black marble floor above was so close that it sounded as if it was on top of them. Despite that, they had to wait, ready to cast, as the others entered the *hutti* tunnel one at a time, sliding over the low wall that blocked the passage and then sliding down a long, dry mud slope.

*

"Fuck," Dahlia said.

Aranthur spat; his mouth was full of the raised dust of aeons.

"Exactly," he said.

They waited with Dead Eye and Poulos, who was now working on Dahlia. Dead Eye continued to billow smoke like an ill-laid fire.

Haras began a complex invocation, the effect of which was unearthly: as he drew lines of power they lit the smoke from underneath, an unnecessarily dramatic effect.

Finally, the Arnaut witch nodded.

"I guess I'm next," he said.

"Go," Dahlia said. "And thanks!"

Dead Eye gave an operatic bow. "At your service," he said cheerfully, and dropped through the opening.

"My shields are better than yours right now," Dahlia said. To Poulos she said, "Leave me be and go."

Poulos didn't argue. She closed down her tracery of silver-white and dropped through the opening like a gymnast.

"Haras, go!" Aranthur said.

He tossed a small working—a summoning of water, turned to ice—and a sheet of ice covered the ramp above them.

Haras was still singing in a language neither of them knew. Seconds peeled away and Aranthur's unease increased as a blow shook the foundations of the pyramid and dust fell from the ceiling.

"That could collapse the corridors," Aranthur breathed.

Haras suddenly fell to his knees in the smoke, then pitched face forward, his eyes rolling up.

"Fuck," Dahlia muttered. "Go. I'll get him."

Aranthur accepted her command and dropped through the opening, scraped his thigh on the rock and dropped to the ancient floor below. It sloped down, and he waited, listening to the sounds of his people scrabbling away. He was alone in the darkness.

Alone, and he had left Dahlia.

He lit a magelight. There seemed no purpose in stealth now.

Inoques was breathing. She had a massive contusion on her left side; her clothes were mostly singed away, and her skin was covered in small burns. There was one massive stripe from her left breast to her right hip that laid bare the heavy muscle of her abdomen. Blood was coming through her skin and from her nose.

Aranthur put a hand on her head and began to insinuate a pain-blocker. Her defences were awesome, even unconscious; it was like trying to climb the glass-smooth mile-high walls of a fortress.

He did what he could for her burns from the outside, as his concern for Dahlia began to spike. Sound carried oddly here—he could hear the hundred-legged thing moving and the foundations carried the vibrations of energy strikes.

He began to consider going back.

Haras dropped through the gash in the wall like a child new-born to the world.

He fell to his knees immediately and Aranthur caught him.

Dahlia dropped through in turn.

Her shields were extinguished, and she was laughing.

"That was fucking *insane*!." She shook her head. "You iced the ramp? So that gigantic lobster-thing could slip and what? Fall on us?"

Down below them in the darkness, there was the sound of musketry.

"Not my best plan," Aranthur admitted. He shrugged. "We're still on our feet."

"Fuck me," muttered Dahlia. "We need to move."

Yet despite saying so, she paused, rebuilding her own defences, and Aranthur did the same.

"Are we outside the Black Stone's power now?" Aranthur asked.

"I don't know," muttered Haras. "Oh, gods."

"No idea," Dahlia panted. "Hells. Where is all this *power* coming from?"

"We're under the waterfall," Aranthur said.

"The Black Stone is in place," Dahlia said. "The waterfall should have stopped."

"Maybe there's a deep pool...?"

"I hate analogies," Dahlia said. "You look like shit."

"You too," Aranthur said.

Her hair was matted with sweat and full of the dirt and filth of the tunnels and a cave spider she'd apparently mushed into her hair when she killed it; the legs were visible. Her face was caked with dust, except where runnels of sweat had carved pathways across the dirt.

Dahlia laughed. "If we pull this off, there'll be statues. And I won't have a hair out of place."

Aranthur grinned.

Then they scrambled down the mud slope together, as another volley crashed out below them.

They missed a turn in the darkness, too far behind their companions and suddenly they were in a painted corridor they'd never seen before, when they should have been in a *hutti* tunnel of scraped mud.

"Go back?" Dahlia said.

"We must be close," Aranthur said.

They could hear fighting. Aranthur moved faster.

"What the fuck?" Dahlia said.

They went all the way along the painted corridor, with the figures of gods, and men and women carrying sacrifices of grain and animals. It was a big corridor, wider than any of the others so far, and it seemed to continue into eternity. But after a brief walk they could see that the whole magnificent corridor had collapsed another ten paces ahead.

"Fuck," Dahlia said.

"Look there," Haras said.

At the end of his pointing finger was a cross-tunnel—*hutti* work, dug straight through the frescoed wall, the entrance just a low hole almost invisible in the gloom. When Aranthur peered in he could hear the fighting clearly.

Aranthur extinguished his magelight and hoisted Inoques higher on his shoulder.

"It must be the *hutti*," he whispered.

"I'm ready," Dahlia said. "You have Inoques. Let me go in front. Haras can bring up the rear."

Aranthur let her go, and followed her as they stooped to enter the tunnel.

A flash from ahead of them, and a voice shouting orders—Chimeg, but not close.

"Make ready!" she called in Byzas.

Aranthur flattened to the side of the tunnel and Dahlia raised her shields.

"Present!" Chimeg called. "Fire!"

The volley, perhaps four weapons, crashed out. Aranthur couldn't see the shooters, around a gradual curve in the tunnel, but the flash of the volley illuminated the walls and the dozen *hutti* waiting in ambush with their backs to Dahlia.

Dahlia raised a hand, white fire seared the air, and she walked a line of it along at *hutti* neck height.

None of the ambushers survived.

"Chimeg!" Aranthur called out.

"*Bahadur!*" she answered.

Dahlia glided forward, and a matchlock spat. The ball hit her shields and ricocheted away.

"Don't shoot us!" Aranthur called.

He came up behind Dahlia, who was at a corner. She waved her hat around it, and Chimeg laughed.

"Left!" she called. "There are still *hutti* to the right and we have to go that way. Everyone else is behind me!"

Dahlia nodded. "Cross-corridor," she said aloud.

She waved the hat again, and a crossbow bolt ripped through it, and then she stepped into the corridor. Another bolt struck her shields. She raised both hands, and there was a flash.

"Come on," she said.

Aranthur turned to Nata on his left.

"Take Inoques," he said, and handed her to the Nomadi.

Then he followed Dahlia into the darkness over the bodies of a dozen immolated *hutti*.

"Dahlia!" he called.

"Here!" she said.

"I can feel..." He shook his head. "A *hardened* soul. You know what I mean. Close."

"Aphres!" she swore. "Who?"

Aranthur had an idea.

"Feel that?" he asked the sword as he drew her.

Yes.

"What is it?"

Another Old One. Living outside the pyramid.

"Leading the new *hutti*?"

Very astute. Nothing to Ammit... but still. A power.

Aranthur put out a hand to Dahlia.

"It's another entity. A wraith."

"Fuck," she said. "Even under the waterfall of power, I'm pretty spent."

"My turn in front," he said.

"Be my guest."

Aranthur went along a corridor and managed to turn at the remembered marks.

"Coming to the great hall," he said. "That's where they'll hit us."

"Yes."

"I wonder if we can just go around?" Aranthur asked.

"Inoques might know, but she's out."

Aranthur was deeply concerned for her; as she was an entity bound to a human body, he couldn't tell what damage was more serious. The body was still breathing, and that gave him hope, but she had absorbed most of the attacks from Ammit and the other entities too.

"Get Haras," Aranthur said.

He shouted back, and heard the Nomadi pass his words on.

The Masran priest came forward. He shook his head.

"Somewhere down here is a big cross-corridor..." he said. "I can't believe we haven't passed it—as big as a highway. It should run to the White Pyramids."

Dahlia laughed, a low chuckle in the darkness. "Pale walls? Paintings of gods and people going to a sacrifice?"

"That's it!" Haras said.

"Behind us," Aranthur said. "And collapsed."

The priest sighed. "That's the only way around."

Chimeg pushed forward. "The tunnels around us are crawling with *hutti*," she said.

We can defeat this wraith. It is, after all, what I was made for. I admit I am shaken by Ammit. I have never seen one of them eventuate, in flesh. I had no idea. Even I am still not sure how we survived that.

Aranthur nodded. "Right," he said. "We're going forward, into a preset ambush. Stay behind my shields and Dahlia's."

"I'm recovering," Haras said. "I've used less than either of you two."

"Excellent. When we identify the wraith, that's our target. Ignore the rest of the *hutti* unless they directly threaten you."

"I've already faced a god," Dahlia said with a wry smile. "Let's get this done."

Aranthur checked his puffers and took the buckler off his belt.

"Ready?"

Then he went forward.

The doorway to the underhall was low, and Aranthur paused and looked up. The room was lit with a pale yellow-green light, and there were hundreds of *hutti*, all wearing red cords.

Aranthur lit his magesight and looked again.

The wraith was obvious; well over against the far wall to Aranthur's right. The sunken footings of the Black Pyramid filled the other, empty, end of the hall.

He paused to draw power from the foetid air, and then he recast his shields. It took time; he didn't hurry.

He stepped out into the hall, unstacking his shields as he rounded the corner.

There was a shuffling among the *hutti*, and Aranthur walked towards the wraith as if they didn't exist.

Dahlia struck from the doorway; two lines of violet fire that shocked the wraith into moving.

FOOLISH MORTALS!

Aranthur was tracking it. He put the sword in his left hand under the buckler, holding the glowing blue blade in his bare hand, and he drew and raised a puffer, charged with a two-thousand-year-old sling ball covered in wards.

He waited until Dahlia flung a second bolt, and as her lightning flashed, he aimed, and fired.

The wraith twitched, and moved. It wore the body of a tall *hutti*—some priest taken in his ritual, perhaps.

Dahlia smashed its shields again, and Haras let his jade-green fire flow. He was, despite his wounds, relatively fresh, and his power was largely untapped, and he peeled away a third of the wraith's shield.

Aranthur fired his second puffer through the gap, still walking forward.

None of the *hutti* interfered with him; they shrank away from his shields, and he left them unharmed.

He was still approaching the entity.

It raised its arms.

NOW YOU WILL KNOW THE WRATH…

Aranthur had four last prepared attacks ready to fling, and he rolled them off his fingers, like a child writing in the air with a lit candle.

The wraith turned to flee and Dahlia pinned it in place with one of Iralia's creations, the net of violet fire.

"You should have stayed where you were safe," Aranthur said. "You cannot have humans and you cannot have these *hutti*, either."

The sword swept through the thing's shields, and it flinched, raised its puppet's arms and cast, point-blank, but Aranthur's shields repelled its torrent of sorcery as a ship's hull repels water.

Almost without Aranthur's volition, the sword licked out and plunged into the wraith's corporeal body, and it screamed...

And then it seemed to distend, its body becoming incorporeal, stretching, stretching away from the sword...

Until it lost the struggle, and the sword began to suck it in. Faster and faster, and then it was gone.

The sword was hot in Aranthur's hand. Just for a moment, a tall woman, very like Dahlia, was standing by him.

Ahhh, she said. *I was made for this.*

"You were a woman, once," Aranthur said.

It is hard to remember that now.

"Hold on to it," Aranthur said.

His sword had just taken and destroyed the essence of the wraith, and the result was terrifying.

And the sword's presence was more...*palpable* than ever before.

Aranthur shook his head and sheathed her.

He cast a simple light spell; but he cast it with most of his remaining *puissance*, aimed at one of the dangling bones in the roof of the cavern, and suddenly the whole underhall was lit as if by the brightest moonlight, and the *hutti* broke and fled.

"Go!" Aranthur shouted at Chimeg, across the hall, and she needed no further urging.

She came out into the open, *carabin* poised, followed by Nata and Ardvan carrying Inoques, and then by the rest of the Nomadi. Behind them were a dozen sailors, and then the Arnauts, carrying Kallotronis.

Dahlia led them into the tunnel at the end and they all trotted along through the rubbish and stepped over the bodies of the *hutti* they'd battled not two hours before. Aranthur went last, brandishing the glowing sword, but none of the *hutti* nor any other fell thing dared try his guard. He backed along, tripped over a corpse, turned and ran again until he could hear the sound of water flowing and voices, and see daylight.

And then, as they reached the boats, his last burst of spirit deserted him, and it was all he could do to stay on his feet.

But the sailors were undaunted, or just happy to be alive and near escape, and they were in the boat in the time it might take a priestess to say a prayer, and Cut Face pushed them off. Aranthur admired the calm efficiency with which they backed water, and the boat slid backwards out of the little inlet until it passed under the ancient water gate.

Aranthur was in the bow with Haras and Dahlia, ready for one last gasp of terror.

"Is the Black Stone working?" Aranthur asked.

"Yes," Haras said. "If it wasn't, we'd be dead."

"How did we leave it?" Aranthur asked.

"I prayed." Haras smiled. "Thank you both."

Aranthur couldn't remember seeing the man smile, and he threw his arms around the Masran priest and hugged him.

"We did it," he said.

Then Dahlia embraced him and the boat tipped, and the sailors shouted at them to stop fucking around.

Just at that moment the boat slipped out into the current, passing from the dreary world under the earth back on to the sacred river, and they were struck by the brilliant light of a Masran evening.

Aranthur looked up.

And the Dark Forge was *still there.*

"Oh, hells," he muttered.

Book Four
Afterblow

Even when you deliver a killing blow, it is essential that you guard yourself; often you will have to deliver a second deadly wound, and in all cases you must guard yourself from your adversary's dying counter—the afterblow.

Maestro Sparthos,
unpublished notes to the book *Opera Nuova*

1

Al-Khaire

As the Imperial Army crossed the long bridge of black basalt from the necropolis side of the Azurnil to the Al-Khaire side, Aranthur was just rising from the broad chair on the massively colonnaded portico where he had slept fitfully while Qna Liras and a dozen Masran priests worked on healing his friends. He was surrounded by gargantuan red stone pillars, each one covered in lovingly painted carvings of the gods, with complex hieroglyphs spiralling to the top of the pillar, farther up than he could see in the new sunlight. Two paces away, Dahlia lay on a pallet, snoring, still dressed in her armour.

Aranthur hadn't taken his breastplate off, either. They had fallen asleep while eating, and the Masran priests had apparently left them where they slept.

Something had awakened him, though, and he saw movement at the great double doors of the House of Healing. He got slowly to his feet, conscious of a thousand abrasions, aches and pains, and hobbled over.

Qna Liras emerged from the House of Healing with three senior priests behind him.

"How is she?" he asked.

The priests looked pained.

"The construct is intact," Qna Liras said. "I thought you would ask first about Haras."

"He was unwounded," Aranthur said.

"He had multiple burns," Qna Liras said.

"Kallotronis?" Aranthur asked.

"We cannot save his eye, but we have mitigated his pain. He will recover. He will wake up later today."

"I would like to see Inoques," Aranthur said.

One of the priests glanced at Qna Liras and said, "I'm afraid that will not be possible."

"She's my wife," Aranthur said.

The priest shrugged. "You cannot be married to an object," he said dismissively. Qna Liras opened his mouth to speak, and then closed it.

Dahlia sat up.

Aranthur shook his head to clear it.

"I am not quick to anger," he said slowly. "But Inoques is not an object, but a person."

"This is your immaturity speaking..." the other priest began. "When you better understand the workings of the *Aulos*..."

Aranthur raised his hand. "Be silent," he said.

"How dare you?" the priest spat, as Aranthur took a breath, mastering his rage.

"Trouble?" Dahlia asked.

"They won't let me see Inoques."

Dahlia looked like a badly stuffed rag doll, and her prized beaver hat was utterly ruined. She'd used it as a pillow. She glanced at it and, with regret, tossed it aside.

She looked at Qna Liras. "Harlequin," she said.

"Myr Tarkas," he said in return.

"You owe us," she said.

"I am not the one objecting." He bowed and indicated the thin priest.

She looked at the priest. "We want to see Inoques," she said. "Don't make trouble, there's a nice priest."

"Speaking in such a way will make no friends," the priest said. "Our construct needs repair. It should never have been sent on such an extended service and will now be returned—"

"Hand her over," Aranthur said.

"Or we'll start melting things," Dahlia said. "I haven't even had *quaveh* yet."

The priest looked pained and looked at Qna Liras.

Qna Liras seemed deeply torn.

"Aranthur," he said, "this is more complex than you know."

Aranthur saw a dozen horses arriving through the courtyard's incredibly massive gate, led by a black unicorn, and he looked at Qna Liras. Their eyes met.

"I suspect I know more about it than you do," Aranthur said.

All four Masran priests exchanged a look.

"I will have Inoques," Aranthur said, as reasonably as he could. "I could say, with some reason, that even if you reckon her as an object, I have paid her bride price."

"Whatever help you offered our priest Haras," the thin priest said, "don't get above yourself."

"Idiot," Dahlia drawled. "Haras couldn't find his own arse with both hands. Who do you think faced Ammit?"

All four priests flinched at the name.

General Tribane was dismounting. Iralia was with her, and Vanax Equus, as well as Vanax Kunyard and a dozen of Tribane's staff with two senior warrior priests.

Tribane saw Aranthur and smiled.

"I cannot release an artifact of such incalculable value..." Qna Liras said very softly.

"I can erase her bonds from right here," Aranthur said quietly. "Right now."

Dahlia raised an eyebrow. "Of course you can," she chuckled. "For my part, I got half a night's sleep, I've had no breakfast, I need a bath, and if you continue to annoy me, I might start taking out these pillars."

"Your arrogance is shocking," the Masran priest said. "A fitting piece of behaviour from the decadence of the Empire." He looked at Qna Liras. "That I should be spoken to this way by a woman! And one that imagines herself my peer!"

Tribane was climbing the steps, her staff behind her.

Aranthur had overcome his anger and ignored the priest, who was glaring at Dahlia. He appealed to Qna Liras.

"It doesn't need to be like this," he said.

"If you would wait a few days..." Qna Liras begged him in turn.

Tribane was all smiles, her black armour polished, the red leather edges looking as if they were brand new. Even her white lace cravat was perfect.

"Doesn't need to be like what?" she asked. "Well done, Dahlia. And Aranthur!" She kissed each of them on both cheeks. "Eight dead. Eight. I feared the loss of a third of my force in a symbolic action! And instead..."

Iralia looked like Aphres come to earth, her plain riding dress taking nothing away from the perfection of her features.

"We had one burn though," she said.

Up close, Aranthur could see she was tired, and the losses had affected her more than Tribane.

"Why is everyone so serious?" Tribane asked. "We won, surely? The Pyramid is once again blacker than night. And there's nothing stirring from inside."

"The Dark Forge is still there," Iralia said. "Is that it?"

The four priests were silent.

Then the lean man said, "Who are these women?" in a tone that left no possible question about his views on women.

Tribane smiled like a wolf reminding a prey animal of how many teeth she possessed.

"I'm Myr Tribanas of the Imperial family. This is the Imperial consort. And you are?"

The priest nodded without bowing. "I am Kalio Beset, High Priest and Hierophant of Aploun." He looked down his nose at Tribane. "The effective ruler of Masr."

Qna Liras stepped forward, interposing himself between Tribane and Beset.

"Welcome, Majesty, in the name of all Masr. Our thanks for—"

Tribane smiled at him. "I think we have a problem, Harlequin." Qna Liras stopped moving.

Tribane turned to Aranthur. "What's happening?" she asked.

Dahlia spoke up. "Majesty, they are keeping Aranthur's wife from him."

Beset laughed grimly. "You speak a falsehood. We loaned your Empire a construct, a magical artifact, for a mission. We have retaken our possession. That is all. Your people need a little discipline, Myr Tribanas."

"Inoques." Aranthur wasn't thinking particularly well and was speaking to Iralia. "They have Inoques."

"*It* is ours," the priest said.

Just like that, the anger was back.

"You cannot own a person," he snarled.

The priest waved dismissively. "You are too young to understand," he said. "Myr Tribanas, perhaps we could—"

Aranthur raised his hand.

"Perhaps we could—"

"I think we can listen to Centark Timos," the General said.

Qna Liras shook his head. "Myr Tribane, Syr Timos, we will do all we can—"

"I'd like to see my wife," Aranthur said.

"Not possible," Beset said firmly.

"I think we could make it possible," Qna Liras said.

Beset turned on his fellow priest. "Do *not* start this again."

"They do not want you to know," Aranthur said quietly, "the Master of the Pure is a priest of Masr."

The silence that fell was so absolute that Aranthur could hear the horses shuffling in the courtyard below them; somewhere outside the temple, a child cried.

Qna Liras looked away.

Aranthur continued, "The priests of Masr have a complex binding *occulta* that allows them to capture the wraiths that escape the protection of the Black Pyramid. They bind them to their service. Indeed, the major part of their *Ars Magika* is the binding and loosing of such spirits."

Beset stepped back. "I don't have to listen to this," he said.

"They bind them to corpses. At least, I hope they use corpses, not living people, but the morality of the whole thing is so opaque—"

"Silence!" Beset snapped. "No one needs an adolescent to lecture them on morality."

Aranthur met the man's eye. "It seems to me that's exactly what you need," he said. "Your *hubris* is incredible, and you are paying for it, *are you not*? One of your own fumbled his capture, or his binding... or perhaps not. Perhaps one of your own changed sides of his own free will. It doesn't matter. One of the wraiths took him entire and the Master is a Masran priest; I'd go a step further and say he's a Lightbringer; perhaps taken by a wraith, but now co-operating with it."

Beset said nothing.

"And because you played with fire, you were burnt," Dahlia said. "Damn. *Damn!*"

Beset's eyes narrowed. "Who are you to judge us? We and only we hold the line against the endless assault of these *Apep-Duat*. We are above your judgement."

"Qna Liras left you, two years ago, when he realised what had happened," Aranthur went on, his voice relentless. "He went to the chief of his order, Kurvenos, and told him what had happened. Kurvenos investigated, first in Atti, and then in Armea and in the Empire."

"Qna Liras should never have had any dealings with foreigners," Beset snapped.

"If he hadn't," Dahlia said, "everyone in this city would be dead."

"Is this true?" Tribane asked Qna Liras.

Qna Liras was looking at Aranthur, but he hesitated.

"Say nothing," Beset said. "They are nothing to us."

"My soldiers can finish what your precious *Apep-Duat* started," Tribane said. Her smile was colder than an angel's sword. "If we are *nothing* to you."

Qna Liras looked back at Beset. "When I left," he said, "I said our lies to ourselves were more dangerous than the swords of our enemies."

"You will be cast out again." Beset had half a smile, as if he relished the idea.

Qna Liras faced, not Tribane, but Aranthur. He nodded.

"You are exactly right," he said. "And some time, I'd like to know how you realised. But yes. Our greatest binder—"

"Silence!" Beset said.

"... and strongest priest..."

"I order you forth and I order your tongue—"

"... appears to have fallen..."

"Cleave to your mouth—"

"I can do that to you," Dahlia said to Beset, raising a hand.

Beset clutched his suddenly sealed mouth, his eyes huge.

Qna Liras flinched, but he drove on. "... appears to have fallen under the spell of a wraith. And now he is that wraith and that wraith is him." Qna Liras shook his head. "Let him go," he asked Dahlia. "Please."

She shook her head. "Release Inoques, and I will release him."

Iralia put a hand on Dahlia's arm. "How did you do that so easily?"

Dahlia shrugged. "He has almost no shields. His only protection is an amulet of minimal power."

Qna Liras shook his head. "This is what happens when politics and blackmail take the place of competence. Beset is our chief priest, and yet he lacks the skills or *puissance* to confront..."

Beset shook like a tree.

Tribane nodded. "Arrest him."

"There has not been a coup in four thousand years..." Qna Liras said. "I respect the institutions that trained me."

Tribane shrugged. "I need to prosecute the war against the Master as my Emperor has commanded. Please do not drive me to an act that could mar the future relations of our two great nations."

Dahlia glanced over at Liras. "Seriously, Harlequin," she said. "He's the one who trained Haras, right?"

Qna Liras nodded.

"And made sure we were saddled with a zealot?"

"Yes," Qna Liras agreed.

"You let that happen," Dahlia said.

"I trusted that you could convert Haras," Qna Liras said. "And you did."

"No," Dahlia said. "Inoques did, when she saved the world. By all the gods, Qna Liras. Don't be one of them. This useless sack of shit is responsible for the near collapse of Masr. You precious *construct* offered herself as a sacrifice to save your country, and the General isn't making an empty threat." Dahlia turned to Iralia. "I recommend, as a member of your council, that Beset be replaced, right here."

Iralia shook her head. "No," she said. Her smile was wintery. "Not here. Inside. With plausible deniability."

"Timos?" Iralia asked.

Aranthur took a breath. "Agreed."

Dahlia nodded to the Masran Lightbringer. "Depose your priest, or we will kill him right now."

"And I'd still like to see my wife," Aranthur added.

Qna Liras shook his head. "If I do this, I can never return. The priesthood will never forgive me, even if they secretly agree."

Iralia nodded. "I am sorry," she said. "Genuinely sorry."

Qna Liras sighed. Then, turning, he put a hand on the Hierophant. The man wriggled as if in shock, his eyes rolled back, and he fell.

Dead.

Qna Liras shook his head. "No point arresting him," he said, looking at the hand that had passed the *occulta.* "Will you accept me as a refugee?"

Iralia nodded.

"I'd like to see my wife now," Aranthur said.

"I'd like a bath," Dahlia said. "But let's see Inoques first."

"Inoques knew all along, didn't she?" Aranthur asked. And then it struck him. "Qna Liras, you sent her on purpose..."

Qna Liras was still looking at his hand.

"Sometimes I am too subtle," he said. "I was desperate." He closed his eyes, and Aranthur saw the sparkle of tears. "I...should just have told you. I wanted to."

He led the way into the House of Healing. They walked in through huge bronze doors covered in images of lions and jackals, a juxtaposition that made no sense to Aranthur, and then through a guarded gate and out of the rows of beds, mostly filled with wounded Masran soldier-priests, and into an inner courtyard.

"She couldn't be kept with the others," Qna Liras said.

The three other priests walked with them, eyes everywhere, until one finally spoke up.

"You cannot admit foreigners to the inner ward!" he said. He was not much older than Haras.

Qna Liras shook his head sadly. "I can. I just murdered the hierophant," he said.

The priests were silent.

They crossed the inner ward to a tall portal with doors of green shot black onyx, the largest pieces of onyx Aranthur had ever seen.

There were four guards on the doors, which opened at a word from Qna Liras.

The guards looked uneasy.

"No foreigner can enter the sacred precinct," a guard said.

"I say they may," Qna Liras replied. "They are our friends and allies. This man and this woman faced the *Apep-Duat* for us."

Iralia glided forward. "We will pass and do no harm," she said pleasantly.

The sheer force of her *compulsion* washed over Aranthur, and Dahlia frowned with displeasure.

The guards bowed, and Iralia floated past them with a kind smile.

"I suspect she will be the most terrifying empress in Imperial history," Tribane said quietly. "Effective, though."

They walked into the temple's innermost heart, through the onyx doors to a corridor entirely walled in onyx and paved in black marble. Overhead was a coffered ceiling of mirrors and gold.

Every inch of the onyx walls was carved with detailed hieroglyphs rendered beautifully; thousands of lines…

"The Book of the Dead," Qna Liras said. "You are the first women ever to see it. The first foreigners."

"Gods," Dahlia said.

"You have sigils for binding," Aranthur breathed. He shook his head. "Of course you do." He concentrated on the glyphs, committing them to memory while saying to Dahlia, "I take it back. I could not have unbound her from outside. This is beyond me."

Dahlia was trying to read the walls too. "This is *necromancy*!"

Qna Liras nodded. "Much of it is, yes."

Dahlia looked away.

They came to the end of the gargantuan hall, where there were three doors. Qna Liras raised his staff and the central one slid open.

Beyond was an altar under a canopy of carved jade.

On the altar was Inoques.

All of her wounds were healed, and she was still visibly pregnant. Naked, her pregnancy was even more obvious. She looked like a woman in the seventh month.

"Beset wanted to take her child as a homunculus," Qna Liras said, "and I told him you would kill him." He looked down at Inoques on the altar. "In fact, I killed him myself."

"Which, if you'd done it two years ago…" Dahlia began.

Aranthur squeezed her arm hard enough to make her wince. Then he went and climbed the steps to the altar, bent over, and kissed Inoques on the lips.

In the kiss, he put just a whisper of *puissance.*

She blinked.

"Gods, I'm cold," she said. "Where…?"

Her arms went around Aranthur, and she said, "Oh, by all the gods of this world, I thought…"

Qna Liras turned away.

2

The Kuh

Six days later, Aranthur was riding in the winter sun. The *carabiniers* of the Nomadi, most of them mounted on captured camels, were spread in a crescent across six stades ahead of him as they crossed the gravel flats beyond the ridges above the Azurnil. The sun was just cresting the line of the delta on the eastern horizon, and the ruddy sun made Ariadne glow like an equine god.

Vanax Equus had chosen to ride with his advance guard, and behind Aranthur's scouts came all three squadrons of the Nomadi, and behind them, two more regiments of City cavalry, the whole of the brigade called the Tagmata. And behind them the infantry; six regiments of Masran warrior priests, and sixteen Imperial regiments, and three regiments of Yaniceri from Atti. And behind them, four hundred wagons, all pulled by horses, with spare horses for the wagons and for the cavalry, and a vast herd of camels, and the camp-followers that General Tribane had allowed—very few, as water and food were at a premium. And behind the vast column of baggage came the rest of the cavalry as a rearguard. Every regiment had at least one magos, and each brigade staff another. And in the middle of the army, with the General's Black Lobsters, was a regiment of militia cavalry composed entirely of students from the Studion—more than two hundred junior magi with several of their *magisteri*. Although individually weak, together they formed a very powerful choir.

And the powerful Zhouian drake, 蟠龍Pánlóng, flew overhead.

Almost thirty thousand soldiers.

Crossing the Kuh desert.

"I find it refreshing," Equus said, "that after you and Dahlia arranged the assassination of a rival head of state, you are returning to acting as a modestly competent patrol leader."

Dahlia had her feet crossed on the pommel of her tall camel saddle. She had purchased a beautiful milk-white camel with Iralia's money and she had a notebook open on her lap. She glanced at Equus from deep under the brim of the very wide, beautifully woven black straw hat that had replaced her ruined felt hat.

"I don't think it's fair to say we arranged his assassination," Dahlia said.

Aranthur felt as he had at the wheel of the *Esperance.* He kept looking at Chimeg's flank to make sure the most distant troopers were keeping up, watching every telltale wisp of dust on the horizon…

"I am ashamed to say I wanted to kill him all along," Aranthur said.

Dahlia raised an eyebrow, a gesture just visible under her hat.

"Look at it this way," she said. "If we'd killed him, we'd have had to kill the other two priests, too."

"Why?" Equus asked.

"No witnesses," Aranthur said. "I'm channelling Tiy Drako."

Inwardly, he thought *when did killing people become my solution to all problems?*

"I say!" Equus said. "I don't like your cloak-and-dagger approach at all."

"Ever so much nicer to just shoot people down on large open fields with cannon," Dahlia said. "Eh?"

"I'm not sure I want to marry you after all," Equus said.

Dahlia went back to her book.

"And what was the upshot?" Equus asked Aranthur.

"Qna Liras sent himself into exile," Aranthur said. "And after the *synod*…" He paused, watching one of his riders.

"Which Qna Liras assured us would take a year," Dahlia said without raising her eyes.

"They will elect some modest priest with mediocre powers and go back to fighting the *Apep-Duat* via their titanic bureaucracy," Dahlia said.

Aranthur smiled. "Messenger," he said.

It was Nata, who rode in on a very tall camel to report the presence of water. Aranthur rode to the right with Dahlia, who cast three *occultae* and declared the water to be just under the surface. Aranthur left her as the first military engineer rode up, his horse lathered in sweat, leading a dozen armed pioneers and a pair of camels carrying tools.

That was the only well they found on the first day, but Aranthur and Dahlia swept for signs of *puissance*, however ancient. The worst of the gravel desert marked the most ancient of battlefields, and each of them picked up *powered* arrowheads, javelin heads of silver-inlaid bronze—one of them enamelled—and dozens of sling bullets.

That night Aranthur found Kallotronis at a very small camel dung fire, making *quaveh*.

"You didn't have to come," Aranthur said, dismounting.

"I have to see what you do next," the Arnaut said, giving Aranthur a colossal bear hug. They were both big men, and Aranthur grunted.

"How's the eye?"

"Still dead," Kallotronis said. "And thanks so much for asking. You expected it to grow back, maybe?"

Aranthur sighed. "No, I was hoping it hurt less."

He clasped hands with Cut Face, who was sipping hot *quaveh*, and Dead Eye.

"We could call *you* Dead Eye now," Cut Face said to Kallotronis.

"Not if you ever want to get paid again."

"Dead Eye Two. Maybe he's Left Dead Eye and you're Right Dead Eye."

"Maybe I just break your nose?" Kallotronis said.

"I'm so glad I had time to pay you all a visit," Aranthur said in Souliote.

He handed Kallotronis a leather bag that glowed with its own light in the darkness.

Kallotronis poured a dozen of the ancient bullets into his hand.

"Ah," he said. "Like the one I shot into the god," he added.

"He wants us to call him God Killer," Cut Face said.

Aranthur shook his head. "God Wounder doesn't sound so tough."

"Fuck you all," Kallotronis said.

"We have twenty new Arnauts," Cut Face said. "They're very impressed with him."

He handed Aranthur a steaming cup of fresh *quaveh*.

Aranthur had a sip; sweet. Perfect. He smiled.

Dead Eye raised his *quaveh* in a toast, and Aranthur raised his in return.

Later, he lay next to Inoques.

"I'm not sure why I'm here," she said.

"I don't trust Masr with you," he said with brutal honesty.

She sighed. "You are probably too cautious," she said. "But I thank you anyway." She sighed again. "I realise that I'm only having about one fifth of a human woman's pregnancy, but I'm very tired of all this. Thousand hells, how do women do this?"

Aranthur laughed. "The Dark Forge lingers in the sky, the Master awaits us across the desert, the priests of Masr tried to betray you, and you are annoyed by pregnancy?"

"That's right," she said. "You try it." She snuggled against him.

"And my hips hurt. My back hurts."

"Will they elect Haras?" Aranthur asked.

"He's the man of the hour, to them," she said. "But there are far too many cautious old men who are senior to him." She smiled.

He ran his fingers over the tattoos on her face, thinking of the glyphs and sigils in the Masr temple, and then fell asleep.

He was the second officer at the command group in the morning; Ardvan had his uniform laid out, and hot *quaveh*, and a large piece of bread with some anchovies. Aranthur wolfed down the bread and fish and drank the *quaveh* and was still at the command fire before Equus.

"Twelve old gods!" Equus swore. "Drax's dick, it's cold, what?"

He was wearing his fur-lined pelisse instead of having it slung from his shoulder; Aranthur buttoned his own. It was Anda Qan's day to lead the patrols, and Aranthur had no duty beyond seeing to it that his squadron was ready to move in an hour.

Sunrise found them moving out of the gravel desert and into the long dunes of the deep Kuh. At about midday, word came down the column that Qan had located the island and its oasis and that the army would encamp there. Aranthur spent the evening creating water in enormous quantities, purifying it, and filling vast water bladders and casks that the wagons and camels had hauled across the desert.

At nightfall, a wind full of sand came out of the east. The Magi erected magical barriers against it, funnelling the wind away from the camp and Aranthur covered the horse lines with sheets of energy.

He was advised by an Arsenale-trained weatherworker and a military engineer, and together they built and reinforced barriers that reduced the winds to a steady breeze that couldn't lift the sand over the animals.

Aranthur had to rise four times during the night to reinforce his *occultae.* The last time he gave up on sleep, which had been haunted by nightmare visions of Ammit and unedited memories of the Black Bastion. He squatted by Chimeg's fire instead, drank *quaveh*, and tried not to think too much. He was not very successful. Nor did it require all of his imagination to picture what was to come; 蟠龍Pánlóng was flying east every morning, looking to link up with others of his kind guarding the Zhouian army that was reported to have landed on the east coast of Safi.

There would be a battle—a series of battles. Death, brutality. Victory; defeat, pursuit.

His imagination could supply every scene, every detail.

Chimeg got up and went to her saddle and blanket roll. The Nomadi didn't need tents in the desert. But when she came back, she handed Aranthur a scrap of red ribbon.

"At the island," she said. "Tied to an old bone." She nodded at him and smiled. "Cold Iron."

"You are a sharp one," Aranthur said.

Chimeg smiled. "I want to go when you go," she said. "So does Nata."

"Go where?" he asked.

She shrugged. "You know, *Bahadur*. When you go. You sit and stare into the fire. Your friends know."

Aranthur looked at Chimeg and thought *you know me too well.*

He was tired. Tired of everything; so tired that the routine of military life was strangely comforting. Ardvan rose to find that Aranthur had laid out his own kit and cleaned and polished his yataghan and his puffers.

"Did I do a poor job, lord?" the man asked. "You spoke no reprimand!"

Aranthur blinked. "Your work is excellent," he said. "I'm not used to being waited on," he went on. "I always imagined that if the Studion didn't work out, I'd be someone's servant. I never imagined *having* a servant."

Ardvan smiled, as the idea of Aranthur being someone's servant was clearly ludicrous. Aranthur was shaved, dressed neatly; he had a moment, looking into the reflection of the small shaving mirror that Ardvan held for him, of wondering who he was. His scarlet khaftan had gilded buttons and blue cuffs of Voltan velvet; his tall boots probably cost more than he'd earned in a year as a student and apprentice leather worker. He owned so many weapons that he had a servant to keep them clean.

Ardvan buckled on his breastplate. It was small, light, beautifully polished, and Aranthur realised that he now owned a fine three-quarter armour and for some reason he'd never really admired it. That seemed... impossible. He'd loved armour once, and now it was just... a tool.

Ardvan handed him his new yataghan, which had a jade and gold hilt that was probably worth as much as his father's farm. He tucked it through a silk sash that would have been his prize possession a year before.

He shook his head and took the fur cap that Ardvan handed him.

"You look very smart, syr," Vilna said.

Aranthur smiled; compliments from Vilna were rare. But Aranthur had never felt less smart. He walked with Vilna to the morning brigade meeting; the Hunter was still in the sky, chasing the constellation of the Dragon towards morning.

"If you keep coming early," Equus said, "I'm going to assume you're inhabited by some alien spirit. What happened to the young officer who was always late for morning meetings?"

"He died," Aranthur said. "I'm his replacement."

"You're looking for promotion?" Equus joked.

"I'm already beyond my level of competence," Aranthur said. "How long to retirement?"

The fire circle laughed.

And Aranthur thought that it was probably symptomatic of the paradox of his life that he was so comfortable with the routines of the army and the Guards, while being increasingly against the practice of war.

He frowned and tried to push all those thoughts away.

It was Centark Lemnas' day with the patrols, but Equus had other work for her. Aranthur shrugged. He was tired, but he was always tired, and always hungry; he'd begun to take those states for granted. When a tray of small rolls went by he ate six of them; Lemnas shook her head.

"Leave some for the rest of us," she said. "There's a good chap."

He let Ariadne have the day off and rode his steppe pony for several hours before switching to one of the camels. He wasn't a very skilled camel rider, but he did well enough, moving steadily along behind the loose skirmish line of his scouts, eating first one orange and then another.

In the afternoon, he sent Nata back with camels for the Arnauts, and a dozen came forward under Cut Face. Equus paid a visit late in the day, and he smiled to see them.

"These men aren't precisely in our command," he said.

Aranthur shrugged. "Syr, they're part of my command. The Vicar particularly ordered me to take them under my orders." He pointed at Cut Face, galloping across the front on a long-legged camel. "And they ride as well as the Nomadi."

Equus laughed. "And these Arnaut cut-throats are part of your cloak-and-dagger outfit, I suspect."

Aranthur was tempted to resent Equus's use of cut-throats about Arnauts. But given the circumstances, he just shrugged. They *were* cut-throats.

Equus watched the skirmish line a little longer. Then he turned, smile wiped away.

"You know, Timos," he said, "When you are up to something, you have a look, like an overfed weasel."

"Me, syr?"

"Damme," Equus said. "That's the look exactly."

Aranthur nodded. "Yes, syr."

"You spend too much time with Vilna," Equus said. "You have something of his air."

"Oh, no, syr!"

Equus shook his head. "Splendid. Well, whatever daring, stupid thing you plan to do, remember how hard Lemnas and Vilna and Qan will have to work if you die."

He saluted crisply and rode away into the setting sun.

"I do like him," Dahlia said. She turned to Aranthur. "What *are* you up to?"

Aranthur looked out over the desert. "Nothing."

"Overfed weasel was cruel," Dahlia said. "But accurate. I'll go and ask Inoques."

"Inoques doesn't know."

"Doesn't know what?"

Aranthur cursed. "You know it's six days until Darknight?" he said.

Dahlia cursed in turn. "Of course. Any way you reckon it, the Master has to..." She looked at Aranthur. "Has to do what?"

Aranthur shrugged. "I've no idea," he said. "But my Practical Philosophy Magister taught me to be wary of coincidence. I'm planning for a contingency."

Dahlia gave him a long look. "Really?" she asked. "When you don't sound like Kurvenos, you sound like Tiy Drako. That was very much his superior I-think-of-everything crap."

Aranthur shrugged.

The fourth day of crossing the desert dawned. Lemnas had the night patrols; and Aranthur slept well, and rose to find his kit cleaned and a cup of steaming *quaveh* by his head.

"I want a bath," Inoques said.

"You have nearly godlike powers," Aranthur said.

"I still want a bath. Human women are incredibly tough. Look at how swollen my feet are." She glanced at Aranthur. "Iralia is pregnant."

"I could get you a place in a wagon," he said, avoiding the issue of Iralia's pregnancy.

"And I could send you screaming to the deepest, coldest hell," Inoques said. "Those wagons are cruel torture machines." She raised an eyebrow. "Iralia isn't telling anyone that she's pregnant."

Aranthur sighed.

"But you already knew," Inoques said. "Interesting."

Aranthur agreed with a nod.

"Dahlia says you are up to something. Since you have promised to help me escape my bonds, I would be very put out if you were to die and strand me here."

He nodded. "How long until your baby?"

"Fifteen days, give or take," she said.

"I don't think I can pull this off without you," he said. In one of his instant decisions, he decided to tell her.

"Pull what off?" she asked.

"I want to take the Master." He shrugged. "I'd like to say I want to talk to him, but really, I think we need to put him down."

"Talk to him?"

"I still wonder if he'll surrender. He's doomed. You heard what Qna Liras said? Ansu is off the east coast with eighty ships. 蟠龍Pánlóng says he saw the Zhouians and he spoke to another drake today, far to the south. The Zhouians are landing their war chariots. And Zhou is untouched—they'll have seventy or eighty magi as good as Dahlia..."

Inoques licked her lips. "I doubt that any place has many people as clever as Dahlia," she said. "Or you, for that matter. Every time you stretch your talents, you get better."

Aranthur smiled at her compliment. "My point is, the Master's done. I wonder if he'd consent to be bound, to avoid—"

"I wouldn't," Inoques said. "Once free, I'd fight to the last iota of my spirit rather than be bound again."

"Then we kill him." Aranthur crossed his arms. "We can save thousands of lives if we do." He was looking out into the early dawn. "How many will die if we don't?"

"Thousands," Inoques said. "Perhaps tens of thousands. It depends how strong he is, and what he has for *submission* and *compulsion.*" She lay back. "Must you always be like this? Your Tribane had the answer; the almost mathematical science of conquest."

"Of slaughter. And the Safians will do the dying. Sasan's people." He shook his head. "And I cannot get over the feeling that the Master will do...*something* on Darknight."

"Are you still trying to be a Lightbringer?" Inoques said. "For my money, you...and Dahlia...made the grade when you stood against Ammit. Stop trying to fix everything. Tribane will crush the Master's armies—the Zhouians will take his capital. In the end, he'll go down under a massive weight of sorcery. I would. Ammit was struggling against us. You and Dahlia are now very dangerous. Haras less so, but he is growing."

"Ammit was busy with the Disciple. We were lucky."

"Yes and no. My point stands—the Master's resources are finite and he cannot stand against three human empires. You do not have to do this."

"And if Cut Face dies? Or Dahlia? Fighting the Pure?"

"Cut Face is a criminal. It is extremely unlikely that Dahlia will die. And I take it you are spurning the Gift."

"Immortality? I still haven't decided." He smiled. "It's not very immortal, this immortality."

"Immunity to sickness, to aging..."

"Still vulnerable to a bullet."

"Maybe you just don't want to face the decision." She sat up.

"Maybe I'm not sure I want to survive this war," Aranthur shot back.

"Darkness falling, how much guilt can you suffer for killing a mob of mortals who were trying to kill you?"

"Several mobs," Aranthur said. "I've had a single year out in the world and it is a glorious, terrible place. Nothing is what it seems. The good are never quite good, and the evil are never wholly evil, and everything I do—"

Inoques hoisted herself off her blanket and kissed him.

"Shut up," she said.

And a little later, she said, "And thanks for coming back for me. In the pyramid. Haras told me, of all people."

"Dahlia came too."

Inoques smiled, her teeth shining in the light of her glowing tattoos.

"I've already thanked Myr Tarkas," she said. "Now I'm thanking you."

"I saw you, in that other form," he said.

She smiled again. "Ahh," she admitted. "I've often wondered..."

"Wondered what, goddess?"

"Aphres, do *not* call me that. I've often wondered...if I had the form, the eventuated form, that Ammit has, or Teji..." She shook her head. "I had a form you mortals found aesthetic, so I was worshipped and cosseted. And that made me appreciate mortals. Ammit looks like one of your nightmares..."

"That is quite literally true," Aranthur admitted.

"And so...is that why he has cast himself as the ultimate evil? If he wore the form of a beautiful woman, or a shining white goat, would it be different? Do the prayers and fears of mortals actually shape us?" She was looking out, at the Dark Forge.

Aranthur lay back. "I don't have to be a brilliant immortal to answer that. *Of course!* All of us act out the reflections of those around us. They taught us that in first year Philosophy, and in one very dry class I understood about being an Arnaut. My people are called thieves and ruffians...and in the end, often we are."

"You are not."

"I had many advantages. But it makes me wonder. If the *Apep-Duat* could not be..."

"Harnessed? Converted? Taught?" She laughed. "You are arrogant in your humility, Aranthur Timos."

"Am I though? Is Ammit different from Kallotronis, except in scale?"

"That was tiresomely close to a pun." She kissed him. "I don't think you can convince Ammit with reasoned argument."

Aranthur began rubbing her lower back and he smiled to himself.

"Where did you come from, you *Apep-Duat*?" he asked.

She purred. It was a disconcerting sound in a human form, because it was loud and made her whole body vibrate.

"We came through the gates, when they were open. We were fleeing..." She shrugged, a wriggle of her upper body. "I've been here so long I can scarcely remember. And I was very young." Her voice grew dreamy and distant. "It was always dark—the sky had very few stars; and we lived in a vast cave. Or so I remember. Everything was violent—we had been at war forever." She turned her head. "If those memories are accurate. You have no concept of what it would be like to live as long as I have lived."

"But you want me to do the same," he said.

She breathed a little; purred again. "If you are going to be all noble," she said, "rub my feet."

The next morning, he was detached to work with the water train, and he spent a day yelling at teamsters and directing the movement of water across the desert. The oxen hated the desert, and they were already dying; they were not bred for the sand, from their sharp hooves to the short hair which allowed the sun to burn their backs, even in winter.

But he had Vilna and he had Kallotronis, and if the teamsters found Kallotronis more threatening than they found Aranthur, he could make use of that.

At one point, in deep sand, a dozen wagoners refused to go any further. Aranthur was considering his options when Kallotronis rode up.

"What now?" the Arnaut captain asked.

He was getting used to life with a single eye; and he wore a patch that made him look even more menacing. It framed a magnificent star sapphire that glittered evilly.

"They won't move on, and they won't dismount and push," Aranthur said. "I'll get some soldiers."

Kallotronis laughed. He rode over to the lead wagon, drew a puffer from his sash, and pointed it at the teamster.

"Move," he said. "Or I kill you right here."

The man was off his wagon box in the flutter of a bird's wing.

Kallotronis nodded at the next wagon in line and suddenly there were a dozen wagoners pushing the lead wagon.

"You are too nice," Kallotronis said. "He knows I'll just shoot him."

Aranthur nodded thoughtfully.

When the sun set in the western mountains, Aranthur's temporary charges, all two hundred of them, formed their camp on the hard-packed sand around an abandoned well. The well was dry, but Aranthur and a dozen other magi created water, filled bladders and casks, and the army cooked a meagre dinner, now on half rations.

Aranthur was so tired that he fell asleep while rubbing Inoque's feet, thinking of the wraiths who had come from unimaginably far away to fight for a place in the world of *Giai.* And, asleep, he dreamt of Radir Ulgul and the refugees under the aqueduct.

The fifth day he was given command of the central cavalry column. Tribane had altered the line of march, and moved the Attian and Imperial cavalry forward. Aranthur attended her morning orders, a much more formal meeting with bows and salutes and *quaveh* served in porcelain cups from Zhou.

The meeting itself was brief, but just as he thought it was over the General said, "Centark Timos, stay. You too, Myr Tarkas."

She sat at her field desk, even as a dozen Imperial Servants began to strike the pavilion around them. Her camp bed and insect net were being stripped and rolled into a neat bundle. Another servant was emptying the hanging solid silver water bucket into a water bladder and then wiping the silver completely dry; a third woman was checking the oil levels in the hanging lamps before stowing them in a wooden chest.

"I want to discuss these warded shields," the General said. "Sit, Dahlia, sit."

Aranthur was already thinking of commanding an entire column, of the possibility of drifting off course, of a hundred tiny technical difficulties for which he was probably untrained. So the words "warded shields" went past him without making any impact.

"Timos!"

"Majesty?" he replied automatically, snapping into the moment.

"You invented the damned things. The sigils..."

"Not at all, Myr Tribane. The sigils are thousands of years old; Dahlia says—"

"You put them on the shields."

"Dahlia and I and a dozen craftspeople—"

"Dammit, Timos. I'm trying to tell you something, not request a lecture."

She smiled to take the sting out of her words, and winked at Dahlia, who was reading from her notebook and appeared to be ignoring the General altogether.

Aranthur bowed. "At your service," he said. "Majesty," he added.

"Have you given any thought to how much this will transform warfare?" she asked.

He nodded. "Yes," he admitted.

"Now I *am* trying to evoke your usual lecture," she said. "I'm invading Safi from Masr. No one has ever done this before. No one has ever relied so heavily on the *Ars Majika* to supply an army—at least, not in the last thousand years. Maybe during the War of Wrath." She made a face. "But if we win, life will go on. Tell me what you think of the future of warfare."

"I think ordinary soldiers will be much more resilient to battle magic," he said. "There will be a lot of technical fiddling to see how much resilience can be packed into various styles of glyph and sigil and other portable defences."

"And do you know that if you and Dahlia hadn't shared this technique, the Empire would have an absolute military superiority?"

Her glance was mild, not accusatory, as if they were being tested.

He shrugged and glanced at Dahlia. She looked up, her look bored. Aranthur suspected she'd already had this conversation.

He took a deep breath. "Only until someone ambushed a soldier, stole his buckler, and peeled it apart," he said. "The innovation is the Dark Forge and the massive winds of power. If we close the rift, the shields will be..." He paused. "Damn."

"Exactly. If we close the rift, the shields will still be powered by *kuria*. And the magi will be weaker, but the shields will be just as strong."

Dahlia looked up. "And *kuria* crystals will be that much more valuable and essential."

"But Atti will have the major source of crystals, while Zhou has all the drakes—an incredible advantage both in the magical contest and for scouting."

"We're doing the right thing," Aranthur said. "Surely we are not contemplating war with Zhou. Or Atti."

"Of course we are doing the right thing," Tribane said. "But the world isn't going to change when and if we defeat the Pure." She looked at Dahlia. "Empires fall, my friends. I do not want the defeat of the Pure to be our last glorious act."

Aranthur nodded unhappily.

"Think about it," the General said, enigmatically. "In the meantime, I'm giving the cavalry columns some freedom to move. If I can get all the cavalry animals to water, the rest of us will move better and have more of the stores."

Aranthur hadn't thought of that, or a dozen other things. He went back to his command with Dahlia at his side, thinking of *kuria* crystals and empires.

"She's telling us to go and get the Master," he said suddenly. "Isn't she?"

Dahlia shrugged. She was looking out over the desert, and her look was as bleak as the sand dunes stretching away to a distant infinity.

"I'm not cynical enough for the game of empires," she said. "But yes. Though she can't order us to go." She shook her head and tilted the hat back on her head, fiddling with the chin strap. "She's suggesting that the aftermath of this war could be uglier than the war itself."

"But we can save her army's lives *and* save *kuria* in case there is a general war in the aftermath of the collapse of the Pure." Aranthur was angry—angry at the world. "The General thinks that Atti and the Empire—"

"And Zhou. and Masr…"

"Of course. Will all fight over the corpse of the Pure."

"All of Armea will have to be rebuilt." Dahlia shrugged. "Irrigation, roads, the towns and temples. And, of course, Armea has its own sources of *kuria*."

Aranthur shook his head. "You mean, we'll transition smoothly from fighting an ultimate evil to oppressing peasants for a more secure *kuria* supply. Is it always like this?"

Dahlia glanced at him. "I assume so. Drako says so, and he's almost never wrong about this crap."

Aranthur shook his head. "I want to make it *better*."

"That would be something," Dahlia said.

Kunyard had the whole advance guard: four brigades of cavalry in three columns spread across almost eight miles of desert. Aranthur had the central one; the simplest job. Nonetheless, he found actual command daunting; everyone looked to him for orders.

It was made all the worse as he had Centark Domina of the Second City Cavalry under his command, which he found terrifying and she found comic.

"Better than some useless aristocratic sprig," she said.

She advised him, as did Vilna, so as they crossed the sandy salt flats he ordered his column to form lines to the right and to the left; brigade level manoeuvres that most of the militia troopers had never practised. He enjoyed the manoeuvres even as he considered Tribane's view of the world after the Pure.

"Now we should practise passing a narrow defile," Domina would say.

"Let us form to face an enemy to the flank," Vilna suggested later.

By midafternoon, Aranthur was being roundly cursed by every trooper in each of the three regiments under his command.

He was sitting on Ariadne, looking at a printed diagram from Vilna's *Drill Regulations of the Imperial Cavalry* when Ardvan tapped him on the elbow.

"A trooper requests permission to approach, Centark," he said.

Aranthur looked up in irritation, still trying to imagine how, exactly, the regulations expected a line of squadrons to interpenetrate another line of squadrons, when he saw Nenia Cucina, somewhat incongruous in a buff coat, breastplate, and helmet.

"Centark," she said. She couldn't help it; there was an edge of mockery.

"Trooper," he replied, as gravely as he could.

They were both grinning.

"There's a rumour . . ." Nenia said, riding up very close. "Dahlia told me. I want to come. I want to see the Pool and the Varestan writing for myself."

Aranthur shook his head.

"Why not?" Nenia snapped.

"I'm not saying no. I'm trying to imagine what kind of army this is. Our security is like a sieve."

He glanced at Ardvan, who looked on impassively.

"If anyone should see the Pool, it's you," he agreed. "I'll see to it."

Nenia saluted, but had trouble keeping her face straight.

Aranthur trotted along the flank of his brigade, watching the distant hills grow closer, thinking about the spacing between the squadrons; why couldn't the centark of the second squadron of Domina's regiment keep his proper place in the column? Aranthur rode over with Vilna and Dahlia, his brigade magas, and a trumpeter from the Seventh City.

"Can we straighten the line?" Aranthur asked the centark.

"Does it really matter?" the man asked. "Fifty paces, more or less? In all this desert?"

"Not at all. It's merely an issue of form." Aranthur said. "Could you to attend to it anyway?"

He got the man to laugh, but when he rode away, the man muttered "Fucking aristo."

Aranthur laughed so hard he almost lost his seat on his camel.

"They'll be cursing my name for weeks," he said.

Vilna laughed. "When they curse you, they aren't wishing for water." He rode in closer. "You are planning a raid, Chimeg says."

"I have no secrets," Aranthur said in Pastun, with a little bitterness.

"Not from your *hetaeroi*," Vilna said.

He was smoking stock and offered his pipe to Aranthur, who took a long puff and handed it back.

"What I plan is so dangerous—"

"I know you, *Bahadur*," Vilna said. "I am saying—do not leave me behind."

"Equus will kill me," Aranthur said.

"Our vanax is doing less work than any other vanax in this army because he has so many veteran officers in one brigade. Domina can command all this without us. Take me, *Bahadur*."

Aranthur smiled. He couldn't pretend he wasn't deeply pleased, so he didn't bother. He gave the older Pastun a handclasp.

"After all, someone has to take care of you." Vilna passed the pipe.

*

"Five days until Darknight," Dahlia said. "You have a plan?"

"Do you want to come?" he asked. "I doubt I can do this without you."

"Of course I fucking want to come," Dahlia said. "You're going to meet up with Sasan!"

Aranthur's eyes widened and he looked at Dahlia.

"Aphres' fertile womb, you ingrate, do you think I don't know what you are doing?"

Aranthur leant over and kissed her on the lips, the way old friends kiss. He gave her a brief hug as well. He knew what it had cost her to even mention Sasan.

She looked away, then forced a laugh. "Good. I feared you were going to ditch me."

"It's tonight," Aranthur said. "We're a day's march from the Pool."

"That's what I thought."

"I'm counting on things..."

"You always do," she said. "So do I. And so far, together, we haven't been beaten."

"I'm going for the Master," he said. "To take him or kill him, before there's more death. And maybe to solve the General's problem. Or maybe to not even offer her the opportunity to do the wrong thing."

"Forget the General," Dahlia said. "Let's just get the Master. If you and I find him, there's going to be some death."

Aranthur was watching the Seventh City Cavalry fail to wheel from column into line in a spectacular display of misunderstanding.

Vilna touched his spurs to his mount and rode off in a trail of salt dust.

Aranthur licked his lips and looked back at Dahlia.

"Anyway," she said, "you're not going to talk. You're going to take him out."

"I'd like to talk..." He met her eye. "I thought we were not supposed to kill?"

Dahlia shook her head. "Omelettes, eggs. That's stupid. Anyway, why would he talk?" She was derisive. "I think he's insane."

"Maybe," Aranthur said. "I think that the *Apep-Duat* think very differently from us."

"No surprise there. What do you think he'll do?"

"What if he plans to blow the rift open?"

"Aphres!" Dahlia swore. "Darkness falling in very truth. How would he do that?"

Aranthur looked out over the desert, where Vilna was berating the dekarks of the Seventh City.

"I don't know, but I'll wager it will be horrible, whatever it is. Like the desecration of the altars."

She shook her head and her horse fidgeted, showing Dahlia's unease.

Aranthur smiled. "You and I and Inoques. We can take him."

"Only if *we* can reach him. Where's Sasan?"

"I'm hoping he's left an outpost at the Well. Someone left a red ribbon at the Island."

Dahlia fairly glowed. "Aphres," she said, slapping her fist in her palm. And then, "Dammit! What if he's sleeping with that little Kati?" Then she looked away.

Aranthur shrugged. "I doubt it."

"Really?" she asked.

"Really," he said.

"Why do you think that?" Dahlia said, clearly pleased by his opinion.

"Not everyone moves as fast as you do," Aranthur said.

They rode in silence for a little while.

"When I said you needed to use your *sense of humour* more, I didn't mean on me." Dahlia looked piqued.

"Humour?" Aranthur asked. "Humour?"

In the evening, General Tribane summoned another council of her senior officers. Dahlia and Aranthur were again invited.

Myr Julya Bemba, the Academy's Magistera of Astrology, had a telescope set up outside the General's magnificent red pavilion.

"The viewing conditions are perfect," she said. "I could wish this expedition was for more than military purposes—the viewing in the desert is superb. I've never seen the heavens this clearly. As just one example, there are *nine* stars hidden in the Wyvern's eye, not six as previously thought! Which probably goes a long way to explain the failure of the birth cycle predictions of Myr Calabas in the last century. In fact—"

"Magistera," General Tribane was in shirtsleeves, but she lost none of her dignity. "You said you had a specific reason for addressing us."

"I do! There, have a look, it's obvious." She pointed at the telescope.

"You could tell us," Tribane said gently.

"Oh, very well!" said the astrologer. "The rift has stopped growing. It's stable."

"But not contracting," Aranthur said.

The astrologer shook her head. "No, not at all. I mean, why would it? The Black Stone didn't create the rift. And *as in the heavens so below*, eh?"

"Aphres," Dahlia said. "It's stable?" She looked at Aranthur. "So how do we close it?"

Aranthur was looking at the night sky. It was stunning, with the great coils of the Celestial Dragon on the southern horizon and the Hunter almost directly overhead; but in addition there were what seemed like millions of other stars, stars he'd never seen before, so many points of light that it didn't seem dark. The moons were both waning; Darknight —the longest night of the year—was close.

Aranthur turned to Myr Bemba. "Is there anything remarkable about Darknight?"

She smiled. "Of course! It's the first time in a century that both moons will be dark. Hundreds of years ago, people would have called this All-Dark, or in old Ellene the *Pankotiva*. Worshippers of the Old Ones—"

"What?"

"The banned cults of the Old Ones used to have special rituals on Pankotiva. Usually human sacrifice." She smiled. "That's what Lightbringers are really for, you know. Stamping out the Old Ones' cults."

Aranthur felt something like a shock running through him.

"Of course," he said, feeling stupid. "Pankotiva," he said aloud.

He waited until the meeting broke up, and grabbed Dahlia's sleeve to keep her from going to bed. Then he waved to Vlair Timash, the general's military secretary.

"Any chance of a minute with the General?" he asked. "And the consort?"

"What are we doing?" Dahlia asked.

"We're going public," Aranthur said.

"Are we?" Dahlia asked. "We're surprisingly bold tonight."

Timash came out of the red pavilion. "The General will see you. She's going to bed so please be quick. The consort is already with her."

Aranthur saluted the sentries and went in with Dahlia behind him.

The General was sitting on her camp bed in a long linen nightgown. Her hair was down, and she was brushing it. Iralia wore a fur cloak and was curled in a large camp chair with a cup of something that steamed.

She looked tired. The General looked old and tired.

She raised her brush. "Yes?"

"Majesty, we wanted a word."

"By we, he means he did," Dahlia said.

"Splendid," Tribane snapped.

She looked at Aranthur, tossed her long, iron-grey hair over her shoulder in the most feminine gesture Aranthur had ever seen her make and began to brush it vigorously.

Aranthur found that he was standing at attention.

"Majesty, we would like your permission to attack the Master. On Darknight. With a team of Cold Iron people."

The General pursed her lips. "Why?" she asked.

"Who?" Iralia asked.

"Because any military solution will cost thousands of lives," Aranthur said. "But this way, our army will remain untouched. Zhou will have no excuse to remain here, and Atti will not become more involved than she already is."

"What aren't you saying?"

"You sent Sasan into Safi to make trouble for the Pure," Aranthur said. "I believe Sasan will take that as a tacit acceptance of his status as the legitimate government of Safi." He tried not to look at the General. "If we get the Master, it will be because of the direct support of… local forces."

The General paused, and looked at her hairbrush.

She smiled.

"I was once what passed for a beauty," she said. "Now my brush fills with these grey hairs, and instead of dreaming of glory, I wonder how to avoid failure." She took a deep breath. "Iralia?"

"I haven't found any grey hairs yet," she said. "But I too find that the stakes are ridiculously high. But if Sasan, who I remember, were to become the Shah of Safi…"

"Then we could restore stability without further conflict," said Aranthur, who had spent days choosing the right words.

"Gods, you even *sound* like one of the Seventeen," Dahlia said. "Maybe more so than Tiy."

"Whereas if we fight..." The General tossed her brush on the bed. "I'm sorry to be blunt, Syr Timos. But yes, by gods, try. The worst that happens is that you will fail, and I will have to kill a great many Safians."

"And then we'll spend a decade fighting over the bones of Safi and Armea," Iralia said. "I want to come with you."

Dahlia looked at Aranthur and rolled her eyes. "Of course you do," she said.

Aranthur made it to the officers' call in time to drink *quaveh* and share a pipe with Vilna. He was unsurprised to be given the patrols again.

"Orders from on high, old boy." Equus smiled at him. "Can't have you command the column again so soon. There'd be a mutiny. Who does drills on a salt flat?"

They all laughed.

While Ardvan tacked up his horse, Aranthur scribbled a note for Iralia.

"You wouldn't be leaving me behind?" Ardvan said.

Aranthur smiled. "Never," he said.

He mounted, and rode to where his dekark of the day, Amad Ilq, sat on a camel. Ilq was silent in the presence of newly promoted Centark Vilna, who was smoking his pipe.

"Qan has the night patrol?" Aranthur asked as he rode up.

"Yes, *Bahadur*," Vilna said.

Aranthur could tell that Ilq and Vilna had had words. He decided it wasn't his business and gathered his patrol, which was mostly composed of veteran Nomadi and a handful of Arnauts, and they went north, away from the horse lines. Aranthur was aware of a dozen riders following him, and he smiled to himself.

A few hundred paces north of the lines, he found a pair of night guards, and after passing another dune, he found Qan.

"You are a prompt relief, syr," Qan said. "That's a large patrol."

"We want to make sure the Well is safe," Aranthur said. "Or so I'm told."

Qan nodded. "I'll be asleep. Don't conjure any demons, or whatever it is you do." He waved his hat at Myr Tarkas. "Good morning, Myr. Ain't you the brigade magas?"

"Not today," she said.

The patrol swept on. Aranthur could count almost fifty riders and more than a dozen spare horses, and he shook his head.

"You did tell the consort we were on our way?" Dahlia said.

"I left her a note," Aranthur said.

"Luckily Dahlia told me last night," Iralia said.

Aranthur had to look twice at the woman who was speaking.

Iralia was *guised* as an old Nomadi trooper, a hard-faced Gilzai woman in a turban.

"Like Dahlia, I think it's the right thing to do. It's what Kurvenos would have wanted."

Aranthur laughed aloud. "Fine. Where is Inoques?"

"I'm the pregnant camel," she said. In fact, she was *guised* as an Arnaut trooper.

They all laughed.

Aranthur looked around at them. "It's good to have friends," he said.

Iralia smiled. "I never had any before you people," she said.

Dahlia shook her head. "I used to have normal friends, who wanted to go out drinking," she said.

Vilna chuckled. And said nothing.

The rising sun lit the high ridges rising to the north and the deep valleys lay in shadow. Aranthur thought they all looked the same and wondered what it would be like to wander lost on the desert floor, searching for the right valley.

"Who else did you bring?" Aranthur asked Dahlia.

He looked at the ridge above which he'd first seen the Dark Forge. He relaxed; they were on the right path for the Pool.

"The General chose some people. I think she would have liked to come herself."

Aranthur nodded and rode on. An hour later, he waved to Dekark Ilq.

"This is as far as you come, Dekark," he said. "I'm going on. Prowl around and report back to the Advance Guard that I've gone to check the Well. I'll leave you most of the Nomadi; but I'll take Vilna and Chimeg, Nada; this Gilzai witch and old Rallia there."

Ilq saluted stiffly. He was clearly aware that something was up; something outside his regulated and orderly world, and his resentment was plain.

"And all these others?" the old dekark asked.

"My friends," Aranthur said with complete sincerity. "I think they wanted a bit of a gallop," he added, sounding more like Equus than he'd intended.

He left Ilq with most of a troop, and his party rode on. When they had put a dozen dunes between themselves and Ilq's scouts, he turned in his saddle to find that most of the camel-mounted Arnauts were joining them.

"Where's Kallotronis?" he asked.

"I invited a few old friends," the Souliote replied, dropping a veil from his turban.

"Do you even have *old* friends?" Aranthur laughed. "Of course there's Cut Face and Dead Eye and..." He was speechless.

"I do like a good fight," Syr Ippeas said. He had a camelhair robe over his armour.

"Who's going to get the army across the desert?" Aranthur said. "Promise me you didn't tell General Tribane."

"She said it would be irresponsible for her to come," Iralia said. "And wished us gods speed."

"This was supposed to be secret," Aranthur said. "This is Cold Iron business."

Iralia shook her head. "Perhaps that is what you imagined," she said. "And it is still Cold Iron. We're doing the right thing. And we're going to do it with an element of surprise, and overwhelming force. Only it isn't just you, or you and Dahlia."

Dahlia shrugged. "She's just jealous that she missed the fight in the pyramid."

3

Safi

Miles out in the desert, Aranthur's outriders were met by Mir Jalud on a milk-white camel. The Seeker wore a pale green silk kilt, a matching turban, and his axe; he looked as comfortable in the desert sun as a king in his palace.

"*Bahadur!*" he greeted Aranthur.

And to Dahlia, he said "Now we are met, let mirth abound! Thou art beautiful, truly, as beautiful as..."

Dahlia laughed aloud. "Let's keep moving," she said. "Where's Sasan?"

"The Shah is at the Pool," the Seeker said. "Where else would he be?"

"The Shah?" Dahlia asked.

Aranthur nodded, unsurprised.

Late in the day, Aranthur rode into the camp, and Haran and Asid escorted them to the Shah's tent. The camp above the ancient pool stretched across the hillside, a curious mixture of bandit camp and military efficiency, and the central tent was perched on a tiny patch of grass below a rocky outcrop.

When they saw it, Dahlia reined in.

"I can't..." She seemed to lack words. "Find out for me?" she asked very quietly.

Aranthur, who had never seen Dahlia afraid of anything, understood. So he went to meet the Shah alone.

It was not a magnificent pavilion. Instead, the Shah of Safir sat on a stack of dirty rugs in a tent made of two blankets stitched together and supported on spears. His *fusil* leant, loaded, against the tent pole;

a pair of puffers in saddle holsters hung from the tent's crossbar, and he was reclining against his saddle.

Aranthur saw his old friend Sasan look up, and saw the brilliant smile that illuminated his face. He leapt to his feet and clapped his hands together, and suddenly Aranthur was smothered in an embrace.

"You don't seem surprised," Aranthur said.

"Mir Jalud has predicted your arrival for days. He pushed us like a mad thing…"

"Which he is," Asid said. "I beg your pardon, great lord."

Sasan laughed.

"Great lord?" Aranthur asked. "You are the Shah now?"

Sasan laughed again. "Doesn't it seem like some sort of cosmic jest?" he said. "I was the Shah's youngest child, and all my family is dead." He pointed at the camp. "So they rally to my name. Given that we live like bandits, it is a measure of the desperation of my people that they follow me at all."

Aranthur thought of the sword brushing against a helpless *thuryx* addict in the mud under the Pinnacle. *Nothing is by chance*, he realised. He indicated the loaded *carabin.*

"We have been in a fight every day since we crossed the mountains," Sasan said. "Let the gods be my witnesses, we have not rested, nor do our swords sleep in our sheaths. We harry the Pindaris that the Master uses to oppress the villagers." He seemed to deflate. "It is terrible, what they have done to my country and my people."

Aranthur embraced him again, and then stood at arm's length, his hands still on his friend's shoulders.

"Dahlia…" he said.

"Is Dahlia here?" Sasan said, his eyes becoming, if anything, brighter.

And then he looked at Aranthur, as if in doubt. And sadness. The shadow was never far from his face; nor the lingering despair of the *thuryx.*

"She still loves you, if that's what you need to know," Aranthur said.

"Aphres be praised, and all the gods!" Sasan raised his hands to the heavens. "But why is she not here, now?"

Aranthur shrugged. "In case…"

"Thousand hells!" Sasan swore. "Does she think I am so very fickle?"

Aranthur glanced away. "Were you not just wondering if Dahlia and I…?"

"Gods, and I was." Sasan shook his head. "Who has made you so wise?"

Aranthur smiled. "My wife."

"You are still married to the demon?"

"He is," Inoques said from a few paces away. "And she needs a place to lie down."

Sasan ushered her into his blanket-tent as if it was a magnificent silk pavilion and she a princess.

And a little later, Aranthur brought Dahlia to Sasan.

He was giving orders for night watches and simultaneously trying to explain the last month, and all of his actions, military and otherwise. Asid and Haran were seconding him, and a dozen other tribesmen were speaking up, and Val il-Dun was debating something military with Vilna, his fist slamming repeatedly into his palm.

But as Dahlia approached Sasan, a silence began to fall. Dahlia was still covered in dust, and her enormous straw hat dangled from its chin strap so that her blonde hair sparkled in the last of the sunlight. Her skin, dusky to begin with and now burnt dark by days in Masr, contrasted with her hair and seemed to flush in the red light. Sasan was in a long, dirty khaftan and soft boots, his sword at his side and a steel mace in his hand.

She walked towards him, and he turned, suddenly aware of her. First his arms fell to his sides, as if in shock, and then he flung himself into her arms, dropping the mace.

Chimeg let off a tremendous whoop as they kissed.

Kallotronis shook his head. "Get a room," he muttered. There might have been a touch of jealousy.

The Safian bandits stood stunned to see their young Shah passionately kissing a Byzas woman in man's clothes.

And Aranthur, turning away to hide a smile, thought of Mir Jalud's salutation. *Now we are met, let mirth abound.*

"Truly thou art wise," he said in Safiri.

Mir Jalud smiled. "Truly," he agreed, smugly.

"The day after tomorrow is Darknight," Aranthur began. Kati made the sign of the Lady; Sasan frowned. Only Inoques was unmoved.

All of them were seated on the fine white sand by the Pool. It made a fine amphitheatre, and the pool and the wall behind seemed to amplify Aranthur's voice.

Chimeg sat with Nata's head in her lap; Sasan was wrapped with the same fine scarf that covered Dahlia. And all the rest were there: Syr Ippeas sat by Iralia, who leant against Alisha Poulos for warmth, as if the Imoter was a stove, which she was; Kati was embroidering a cap, leaning against her cousin Val il-Dun; Asid sat with Haran and Kallotronis and Dead Eye; Vilna smoked steadily, watching the stars above and occasionally passing his pipe to Mir Jalud. Nenia, of all people, was sitting with Cut Face, a broad smile on her face. A bottle of arak slowly made the rounds.

Inoques sat under a camelhair blanket, shivering.

"On Darknight, not a soul will stir from the safety of their homes, and the veils of the world are thin, and the winds of majik will blow with uncommon force," Aranthur said.

"The shepherds will bring their flocks down from the hills today," Sasan said. "No one will leave their house tomorrow if they can help it, even by daylight. The Master is renowned for keeping tame wraiths and monsters. The people will fear the night more than ever." He shook his head. "He is up to something, though. His Pindaris are out in force, rounding up 'criminals' in record numbers. He has gathered all his priests and Disciples around him—dozens of capable casters. My people have done what they can to stop him and none of them want to go anywhere close to Farfaz, but there is a rumour of killings in the palace." Sasan shrugged. "He has destroyed my father's palace. And made something horrible of it, no doubt."

"Who are these 'criminals'?" Vilna asked.

"Anyone not involved in food production, or directly supporting his armies," he said. "Artists and brass makers and rug weavers and silk merchants; the Bethuin, the Yezziri. Any Dhadh he can catch, or the Jhugi."

Aranthur smiled. "We will have our own Pindaris, and more," he said. "And we will ride unnoticed across an empty land. Inoques, what's the Master's greatest fear?"

Inoques looked out from under her blanket. "What any of us wraiths fear. A general escape from the pyramid—most of all, Ammit."

"I don't understand," Iralia said. "I mean no offence, Inoques, but why would a wraith fear another wraith?"

“Why would a human fear another human? Lust, greed, anger, power...” She shrugged. “Ammit demands absolute obedience.” She smiled slightly. “I agree that I can now at least *imagine* a future in which Ammit is defeated. He is cautious. But his escape into a world rich with *puissance* would be...the end of everything.”

“What do you think the Master knows of what happened in the pyramid?” Aranthur asked.

Inoques stretched. “Nothing beyond sensing the emanations of *puissance.*”

“A fight between his Disciple, the most powerful of his disciples, and Ammit. Still ongoing,” Aranthur said. “And you.”

She smiled, as if relishing the memory.

Aranthur nodded. “So, my friends. Here we are on the edge of the tide of darkness, and we are not going to risk our lives just to save the world.” He looked around at them—the people he loved best. “We are going to risk our lives for a *better* world.”

Most of them smiled.

“Here’s the plan,” he said. “We’re going to attack the Master during his ritual. He’ll be summoning, or trying to widen the rift or even break it open. We’re going to present a threat from Ammit—or perhaps from another wraith who has defeated Ammit—and use that distraction to draw the Master out, like flushing a boar from heavy cover. Once he is revealed, we will strike. If we are successful, we will kill him in seconds.”

“Kill him?” Sasan asked.

“Yes,” Dahlia said, rising. “Let there be no mistake, no hesitation. We will kill the Master. As quickly as possible, without remorse.”

Sasan nodded.

Vilna said, “This is wise. Does anyone doubt that he has worked evil from the Steppes to the cities?” He looked around.

The Seeker smiled, and sang a snatch of Safiri poetry.

“We are the jury; we are also the executioners,” he sang. “My songs are stronger even than the Master’s songs.”

Kallotronis laughed.

Iralia spoke slowly. “And if we are not successful?”

“Then we’ll be in the fight of our lives,” Aranthur said.

4

Farfaz, Safi

The ash altar was taller than the highest prayer towers in Farfaz. The Master had chosen the Palace of Roses garden for his abomination, and there was no longer a hint of the beautiful graveled walks, the hedges of roses or the cypress groves.

Instead, under the darkest night in a hundred years, there towered a mountain of greasy ash and carbonised bone. And as the stars wheeled above, and the Hunter rose towards the exact middle of the night, the climax of the dark festival, the pace of sacrifices became frenetic. The blood of innocents soaked into the ash and the latest corpse was thrown on the ugly dark fire that burned on the altar; a black-hot display of pure *sihr* that burned like a beacon of death.

Which it was.

The column of victims extended down to the base of the ash mountain and then across the rubble of the former palace and out of the gate. Hundreds of Pindari warriors herded the next victims forward. All of them wore a simple black robe that fell to their feet; at the foot of the ash altar, a leering priest of the Old Ones stripped the robes and sent the naked wretches to climb the ash in humiliation and despair. As they neared the top, one of the many Exalted would seize them; the murder was rapid and inhuman, more like the wholesale butchering of cattle than the ritual execution of people. The white swords flashed and another victim fell, headless, and then the priests would throw the severed limbs, head, and trunk on the dark fire, their bloodstained hands sparkling with *power*.

Eight Exalted, their swords flashing. Thirty priests.

And out there in the night, somewhere close, Aranthur's voice, appalled.

"Wait for the signal. Steady. Wait for the signal."

The line never stopped moving forward. There was no revolt; no complaint among the sacrifices. The line shuffled forward and the swords flashed, again, and again.

And again, and again.

Thirty priests incanted their ritual—again, and again.

And the line shuffled forward.

And then, in the same heartbeat, all eight Exalted froze. Their heads turned together, as if the same will drove them all…

And at the base of the ash altar, on the other side from the shuffling line of victims, the dark scaled shape with a cat's head began to eventuate. It seemed to drink power from the very air; the stars grew dim and the black fire on the altar shrank towards the bones that fed it.

The ritual priests' chanting rambled to a stop.

The emanation was *huge*, and viewed from close, had an unappealing insectoid quality.

At the south side of the base of the ash altar, an evil laugh turned to a gurgle as a priest reached to strip his next victim and Sasan put a dagger into his throat.

Every eye was on the behemoth *Old One*, half the height of the ash altar, and a number of the Pindari guards died without ever knowing what had happened.

Chimeg was in the ancient gate tower of the ruined Temple of Light; her first shot broke the spine of a Pindari standing near Sasan as he drew his sword.

Nata was lying atop the old garden wall with a *carabin* and his first shot brought down a priest on the ash altar, who was opening his mouth to scream a warning.

Kallotronis was in the rubble of the palace, and his *jezzail* barked and another Pindari guard went down with his mouth full of blood.

Aranthur had *enhanced* their vision to use the beacon of *sihr* as light. For them, it was as bright as day, the central altar a cloud of light.

Next to Sasan, an apparent victim opened his mouth and a heavy black smoke began to pour out of his mouth as if a dragon was vomiting out smoke. The man raised a hand and a line of bright blue connected him to one of the priests. There was a flare as the man's amulet was overcome, and then he immolated, the hot ash of his corpse falling to join that of his victims. Dead Eye began to run up the mountain of ash, belching more dark greasy smoke as he went.

Dahlia had made the snipers immune to Dead Eye's smoke. But it covered the assault and left the priests and Exalted paralysed, unable to see their attackers.

Cut Face was also in the shuffling line, and he drew a puffer, shot the nearest guard, and then drew a bead on a second and shot her in the head.

In the first five seconds of the scaled entity's eventuation, thirty of the Pure went down—most of the priests and a dozen guards.

But the victims continued to shuffle forward as if they desired their own destruction.

Aranthur was deep in his own secret approach, pacing up the side of the ash altar, trying not to let his disgust at the charred skulls under his feet affect his power. He was making a slow ascent, circling slightly from the line of victims to the east to avoid being in the line of fire of his own people. He wore a sacrificial victim's black robe, and he moved very carefully, his dancer's muscles straining to keep his feet gliding over the horrible, uneven surface.

Inoques bounded up the altar's steepest side. One of the Exalted dashed to meet her and was thrown off the mound and into the rubble below by a slashing blow that broke the Exalted with a single swipe. She pinned a second as if she was playing with her food; she held it down for a moment and let it go after a pulse of *puissance* passed between them.

The Exalted rolled, and then spasmed as if hit with a charge of power. Then it sat up, shaking its head.

Aranthur could just see Inoques within the form, now. But, just as in the tavern a year before, he couldn't let the imminence of the violence interfere with his will. He watched the ash instead of his wife.

Something rich in *sihr* moved in the *Aulos.*

And was there.

YOU DARE COME TO MY PLACE OF POWER said a voice.

Aranthur was farther away than he had hoped to be, but he reached into the *Aulos*, pulled forth and unrolled a parchment, and it crackled into life. Suddenly there were again eight Exalted atop the ash altar.

Aranthur climbed another step…

Inoques sprang from the top of the enormous altar to the base in a single bound, her legs seeming to lengthen as she leapt.

If you are so mighty, oh Master, show me your true form, Inoques said in the *Aulos.*

But the towering form in the middle of the altar was human—tall and strong. Not a *wraith* eventuation but a mighty construct, tall and handsome with burning eyes and skin of molten bronze.

YOU WILL MAKE A FITTING SACRIFICE.

I think you are too weak to eventuate, she replied.

Aranthur got another step up the ash. It seemed harder to move the higher he went up the altar, and he knew why. He faced it in his mind, and pushed another foot out on to the wreckage of the dead.

The massive bronze figure unleashed a torrent of *sihr*, like a river of decanted death.

His blow fell squarely on Inoques, and it was a massive blow. She shed the blow with her scales and her will, but she was knocked from her feet, and ichor flowed from a wound in her side.

The Master reached out with his *subjugation.* Even a dozen paces away, behind the wraith, Aranthur could feel the incredible force of his working; his intention was obvious. He wasn't going to just defeat the rival entity. He was going to enslave it.

And in that moment, Dahlia struck. It was subtle; like a blade attacking an adversary's complex preparation, her *insinuation* slipped into his *subjugation* and in the slippery non-world of the *Aulos.* Dahlia separated the Master's intention from his execution, and then went on to unravel the standing *subjugations*—the way a suggestion in a conversation can undermine the speaker's argument.

The Master's hold on the wills of ten thousand sacrificial victims slipped; ten thousand people drew breath in horrified discovery…

The Master's hold on the Exalted was interrupted…

He lashed back in rage in the very instant, his wrath falling like a hammer on the now-revealed Dahlia.

Aranthur was six paces away when he shot the Master in the back with a puffer.

And again at five paces, dropping the weapons as he powered

forward. The forbidding weight was lifted; he could move easily again, and he raised his shields and cast his *enhancement* in the same moment.

The Master turned, flinched, obviously wounded; the bronze skin was shedding black gouts.

Iralia caught him half turned, and a scythe of light swung at his feet, a net of white fire forcing the *wraith* to make a sweeping defence to avoid a catastrophic envelopment—the same *occulta* that Iralia had used on the Servant in the Square of the Mulberry Trees.

One of the Exalted leapt at Iralia.

The Exalted that Inoques had released—having subjugated it—met the Exalted attacking Iralia, sword to sword.

A third Exalted turned on Aranthur, its swords thundering against his layered shields as it pressed in on him, trying to buy its dark master a moment to rally.

Aranthur drew the Bright Steel from her scabbard in the *Aulos.*

She appeared as if from the air, her blue fire more than a match for the twin white swords of the Exalted, for her fire was hotter.

Aranthur made a high, hard cut, powering one white sword into the next and sweeping both of them in an explosive bind from high to low. The Exalted, off balance, stumbled forward and Aranthur's rising reverse cut beheaded it. He kicked the falling corpse away, his foot slamming the dead thing into the Master's shields.

The Master turned to face Aranthur, towering over him in the real, the size of a colossal statue. He was drawing a sword of similar size, which crackled in the air.

Of course he has Silaz, said the sword.

But even as the Master raised his black sword, an Exalted struck him from behind, the two white blades biting deep. Aranthur had carried it with them for long weeks, releasing it on a beach near Gortyn and in the desert to train with him, and now the turned Exalted from the battle in Sittar's garden had its revenge, striking at its former Master.

The other Exalted froze; two of their own were fighting against them, and each of the remaining four looked at the others with doubt and suspicion. The night sparkled with the pinpoints of flashing powder and the tongues of fire from the Nomadis' and Arnauts' *jezzails* and *carabins.* Most of the priests on the ash altar were down; one of the Exalteds was hit so many times by the enhanced projectiles that it unknitted, its form fraying away like a red banner torn by a heavy wind. And the steady rain of bullets was hurting the Master, too.

Iralia took the closest Exalted, already hit by Sasan and Nata, firing a *saar*-enchanted ball at point-blank range, with a spray of icy *puissance.* It fell and didn't rise again.

A second lunged at Dahlia, and met the Magdalene, Syr Ippeas. His sword was as fell as Aranthur's; and his armour seemed to make him proof against the Exalted's dark magik. He entered its space, parried its blow and slammed an armoured knee into its groin, then slipped his sword around its neck like a lover coming close for an embrace. It fell, broken, at his feet. A third and a fourth struck. He made a sweeping parry, and for a moment he crossed four swords with his one; then he cut, taking the arms from one.

The other killed him, its white swords finally penetrating his armour.

The victorious Exalted turned to take Chimeg's next shot full in the head. It stumbled, perhaps blind, and Dahlia blew it off the mound with a sweep of her left hand.

Aranthur, *augmenting* his voice, roared "Now!" like a god coming to earth.

All of them turned on the Master.

The black sky itself seemed to vibrate.

蟠龍Pánlóng appeared out of the smoke above the altar, and breathed his mighty breath. The fire of *sihr* on the cruel altar went out, and the Master turned from destroying the rebel Exalted to face Aranthur's sword.

蟠龍Pánlóng's breath swept across the top of the ash mound, stripping Iralia and Aranthur of their shields as the drake ate all the *puissance* and his breath shredded every power and *occulta*... including the Master's.

The Master cut with his huge black sword, a heavy overhand blow.

Aranthur stepped off line, and the massive cut slid down the Bright Steel like rain off a roof. Aranthur flowed with it, his hands sure, his left foot advancing and his counter-cut...

The Master's shields exploded back into place as the drake's breath passed over them, but his mighty left hand pulsed on the ground, writhing like a beached fish, the construct's fingers clenching and unclenching, severed by Aranthur's perfect cut.

Aranthur's shields, gifted by Inoques, rolled out of him, catching the storm of attacks the Master flung at him, at Iralia, at Dahlia, at Inoques. Aranthur was hit, and hit again. But he covered the third red bolt to burn through his shields with the sword—or perhaps the sword covered for him.

Aranthur was on one knee inside a hemisphere of protection while chaos reigned. But Dahlia's blows fell like a pale rain, Iralia's like spears, and Inoques was there, wounded but unbeaten, her black talons flashing in the light of the other women's *occultae.*

The Master's grim shields flared and burned and flared again, the myriad black mirrors of his outward defence repairing themselves faster than the waves of attacks could tear them down, his molten bronze skin flowing to repair any wound inflicted.

Sasan stood up by Dahlia, and shot into the heart of the Master's towering shields; right hand then left.

Aranthur pushed forward, trying to penetrate the Master's shields, but his own met the Master's as if the universe was being unmade, and he could not push through.

And the colossus turned, his hand spraying purple fire…

The Seeker spun between them as if their shields were made of smoke. He turned and turned, his smile pulsing out of the dance like a jester in a court. The Master unleashed black thunder on the dancing Seeker, but his blows didn't seem to land while the Seeker's green fire played about the Master, as if this was a debate in which the Master's might played no part.

It was as well; Iralia still stood; but Dahlia was down, raked by the Master's purple fire. Sasan bent over her and Inoques, her black scales burnt and rent, though she extended her tattered shields to cover Dahlia's body, and Sasan.

Only then did the massed scream reach Aranthur; the sound of ten thousand desperate people in peril. A scream so loud that it had a force of its own.

Dahlia, from her back, loosed a powerful *occulta* that seemed to burn against the Master's black crystal like some sort of sticky fire, and the Master turned on her. Inoques stood her ground, her black scales reflecting some of the fire and her eyes glittering in the energy of the Master's attacks. The Seeker caught the Master in a noose of orange light and made him stumble. They were all very close; the attacks rolled out as fast as thought. Iralia parried the Master's bolt with something of her own, and Aranthur cut into the Master's shields with the sword, desperate to save Iralia and Dahlia. He opened a slit with a heavy cut and threw *saar* through the gap, then tossed his massive concussive *occulta* in the same tempo. Anything to keep the Master on the defensive.

The concussion folded the construct's left leg. But he didn't fall; he sank to one knee, ignoring the gaping wounds in his bronze back and side that no longer knitted together but merely bled black. He ignored the gaps in his now failing shields to turn once more on Inoques, hammering her with strike after strike, cutting away the scales the way a hunter would skin a beast.

Aranthur cut again, for the first time the sword penetrated the bronze flesh and ripped free, but the titan was not through.

It turned and threw a fork of purple-black lightning at Aranthur, and Benvenutu's ring flared white-gold and Aranthur felt the hand of death pass over him.

Close by in the smoky darkness, 蟠龍Pánlóng breathed again.

In mid-crescendo the Master lost his shields and his attacks. Immediately he cut at Inoques, driving her back, and whirled to face Aranthur, the only other immediate threat. The great black sword came down, and the Bright Steel parried it, but the shock drove Aranthur to one knee and his right wrist felt as if it must split asunder. Benvenutu's ring flared again.

DID YOU IMAGINE THAT YOU COULD DEFEAT ME WITH A SWORD?

On this pass, 蟠龍Pánlóng had held his breath for the one target, and he released it slowly, trapping the Master outside the world of sorcery. The drake's breath even seemed to affect the construct's function.

"Yes," Aranthur managed, getting to his feet.

Because his right wrist and arm were not human, but something more, the pain in his wrist was only a reminder that it had once been a human wrist. Before the drake's breath could pass, Aranthur attacked the kneeling giant in a flurry, who now had to wield a massive sword with only one hand.

We still have a chance, Aranthur thought.

Aranthur powered *forward* from his knee, his sword snapping across the black sword, a deliberate beat that drove the heavier blade to the side…

The drake's breath was like a pale blue fluid flowing around them... stripping the construct of its magik like an acid, stripping Aranthur of his *enhancement* as well.

Aranthur thrust for the titan's chest, at his head height.

The massive wrist strained, dragging the heavy black sword across like the slamming of a door, reaching for the Bright Steel...

But she was already gone, as Aranthur's wrists turned the ancient blade under the sweep of the black sword, raising it as his left leg shot forward. Training told over confusion, over chaos, over fatigue and wounds and despair and terror.

The titan was faster than anything Aranthur had ever seen and the black blade was dragged back but his parry was too slow, and giant fingers sprayed, and the black...

...sword...

...fell...

The drake's breath passed and the shields rose again, but now they rose sluggishly, unrepaired. Inoques struggled to get hers up at all. Dahlia was no longer moving. Iralia's crystalline structure was flawed.

The Seeker passed again in front of the Master, and he turned with the dancer, as if there was something of the Seeker that drew his deepest ire.

I THOUGHT YOU WERE DEAD.

I am very difficult to kill, the Seeker sang. *And sometimes I'm more trouble after I am dead than before.*

And there, deep in the fight, the Master's power manifested. Because Aranthur was at the very limit of his strength and Iralia could only just maintain her shields, and the Master was repairing his; sluggish or not, it was clear that he was recovering much faster than they. But he'd lost his hands, and his sword.

The titan lashed out, seeming to spray the Seeker with the gushing ichor of its severed hand, and the Seeker shrieked and fell, clutching his face, and then he fell, gave a great cry and lay still.

Aranthur got his buckler up, reinforced with a red *aspis*, as the Master came to finish him. He used the shower of his deadly blood as a weapon, and Aranthur took every droplet as a blow, his shields burning away, his *aspis* ruined, until only the smoking ruin of the physical buckler was left.

Refusing to surrender to a new assault on his will, Aranthur still pushed forward. His own shields were destroyed, or close to; the Master's were damaged, and from the left, Iralia continued to bombard the slash Aranthur had made. Aranthur was no longer *enhanced* and he lacked the power to cast it again.

In some remote part of his mind that judged such things, Aranthur was following the pattern of the drake's breath, and he was counting down. It was not about his own survival; it never had been, not since the Black Bastion. And for once he threw himself forward, not with the desperate courage that was so like the cowardice of flight, but with a cold rationality, knowing that his sword was their last chance of victory.

The lash of the Master's will fell fully on him, and the ring flared again, but neither the secret fire nor his own will was equal to the contest, and he fell. He fell full-length, and the sword dropped from his hand. He was paralysed; it was as if he was turned to stone, and the Master's will began to subsume him.

The sword *moaned.*

He wasn't sure why he was still alive, or if he was alive. He couldn't move, not even to turn his head. His right arm was dead.

The sword's hilt was just a few inches from his ruined hand, but he was done.

So close, he thought.

But he saw it when a hand closed on the hilt and lifted it.

And as the man bent to lift the ancient weapon, Aranthur saw his face, and his first thought was despair.

Djinar.

But then he knew who it really was, and his heart leapt.

Kurvenos.

There was a pulse of light so bright that Aranthur was blinded, as if he had been present for the birth of a sun.

"I know you, *Thanakos,*" Kurvenos said. "And you have lost."

The name made the titan writhe; Aranthur felt its will wither, and he could suddenly turn his head again. He blinked, trying to rid himself of the blindness, but it was as if he was standing in the heart of the sun.

"Three years I have hunted you," Kurvenos said, his voice growing louder, as if he was gaining power as he moved forward.

YOU.

"You took me as one of your slaves," Kurvenos said. "And in your arrogance, you didn't care to look at what you had."

YOU.

"You made me kill innocents. You destroyed lives and you created despair and humiliation. And now you will force me to break the carefully formed rule of a lifetime," Kurvenos said. "For I swore that I would never kill in anger. But standing on the bones of your victims, *Thanakos*, all I feel is rage that beings like you keep us from making the world better. There are routine evils more deserving of justice than you."

Aranthur was able to roll on his side. He could see Kurvenos as a sort of bright blur. And Thanakos as a dark figure outlined in a pale violet light…

A light coming from behind him…

Somewhere in the darkness beyond Kurvenos' power, the drake breathed again.

Aranthur heard the sound of the volley—half a dozen shots. Saw the flash of Iralia's violet anger. Saw the final failure of the black crystal shields. Saw Sasan rise from behind Inoques and shout; saw the talon slash.

The titan stumbled, struck repeatedly.

And fell forward.

And in Kurvenos' hands, the Bright Steel swept up into the path of the falling titan's neck.

In the grey light before dawn the fires on the ash altar had gone out, and Aranthur had done his best for Inoques, who lay, alive, by Dahlia, who was breathing again. The Imoter, Myr Poulos, had spent her power like a woman pouring water into sand, trying to stabilise Dahlia, and she finally succeeded when Kurvenos channelled to her his own power, but Myr Tarkas was badly burned, with charred flesh where the terrible bolts had entered her body. Aranthur had one of his own. The complex right arm that the palace had made for him was damaged, and he had a burn high on his back that would have been a mortal wound in most men.

Sasan was out in the darkness, trying to save the sacrifices. It was still Darknight, the worst night of the year, and the longest, and it was deeply cold.

Kallotronis and Vilna were finishing the Pindaris.

And finally, Iralia stood beside Aranthur, who was sitting where he'd collapsed in exhaustion. A few paces away, Djinar-Kurvenos stood facing the rising sun.

"How did you get here?" Iralia asked.

Kurvenos shrugged. "Inoques let us live. Weeks ago in Ulama. And she planted a suggestion..." He shook his head. "The *Apep-Duat* can work at a level that is beyond me. She foresaw this? Or she predicted it? Or she enabled a future?" He smiled; Kurvenos' smile on Djinar's face. "Tonight she released us. Poor Djinar is trapped in here. It is, after all, his body."

"Poor Djinar?" Aranthur asked.

"I pity anyone made a slave," Kurvenos-Djinar said.

"Is this how it always is?" Aranthur asked suddenly.

Somewhere beyond the rim of the world, the sun was approaching.

"What are you are asking?" It was odd, and terrifying, to hear Kurvenos speak through Djinar's voice box. He laughed mirthlessly. "But I understand you all too well."

"And?" Aranthur asked.

"Yes," Kurvenos-Djinar said. "All we do is piss on fires. We don't even save the world, just keep it going for another day or week or year, so that people like Iralia can, we hope, make long-term gains."

Aranthur looked at Iralia. "And the *Apep-Duat?* Are there more?"

Kurvenos-Djinar smiled ruefully. "Many more," he said. "They are here to stay; as much a part of our world as we are."

Aranthur nodded to that. "How do we close the Dark Forge?" he asked heavily. "Is there a way?"

His eye was caught by the line of corpses—dozens of innocents: Syr Ippeas, beheaded by the Exalted, and the Seeker, his light gone forever, lying by the knight.

Kurvenos-Djinar laughed with genuine mirth. "You need to have more confidence in your own beliefs," he said. "There's a tendency among the heroes to imagine that only we can save the world, but that's arrogance. The people can save their own world. Watch."

"Watch?" Aranthur asked dully.

"Watch," Kurvenos-Djinar said.

And far out at the rim of the world, in the east, where the pass of Devea-Boyoun pierced the mountains east of Al-Bayab, the disc of the sun touched the sky. For a moment it seemed to hang there, as if in doubt. A thin sword of red fire.

And down in the dust and rubble at the base of the terrible altar of burnt bone and flesh, Chimeg took a pair of Yezziri men and a Bethuin woman by the hand and began to dance in a small circle. She was singing a nasal *turomehn* song in her harsh voice, and Nata also sang, a strange sound to Aranthur's ears.

Cut Face jumped the remains of the great garden wall. He whooped with apparent joy, and produced his tamboura from his belt. After a rapid cascade of notes he settled on a tune not so very different from that sung by Chimeg.

Kallotronis appeared, thrusting a puffer into his belt. He stood with his hands on his hips for long enough for his foot to tap, and then he joined Chimeg's circle. Ardvan joined too, and Vilna, and Alisha, and then Iralia, who slid down the face of the ash, shouting her arrival.

And then more and more of the released captives; plus Kati, and Val il-Dun, and Haran, and a pair of Safian women.

They danced in a circle, and as the sun rose, the circle grew.

"Go and dance," Kurvenos said. "Your work here is done."

"Dance?" Aranthur said, understanding dawning at last.

"It is not about heroes," Kurvenos said. "Heroes are all very well. But Tirase tried to build to last, and he understood how to use the power of the world. Surely, when the sun rises on First Sun, you dance?"

"Eagle," Aranthur said. "Of course we do... everyone..."

He looked back at Kurvenos.

"Won't you dance?" he asked.

"I'm done," Kurvenos said. "My final piece of atonement for the blood on my hands will be to give this poor young man his body back. Take good care of him."

Aranthur came back, his dead arm swinging by his side.

Kurvenos put his hand on the arm and restored it.

"Here," he said. "My last act."

He put his arms around Aranthur.

"Goodbye. Dance. It matters."

Aranthur was crying.

Aranthur went and joined the dance.

Kurvenos remained atop the altar, watching the sun give light to the world, and adding his own invocations. Across the great square of Farfaz, the sun rose on thousands of circles—hundreds of thousands, as people joined the dance across the world, so that as it turned and the rays of the sun fell on them to end the long night, they leapt into the air, and music rose to the heavens, and chased the cold night away.

High above them, as Nenia leapt and turned in the air, as Iralia kicked, and Sasan danced, his eyes on the pale shape of Dahlia sitting bundled beside Inoques; as the sun rose over the army, camped at the edge of the desert, where the regiments danced in their camps; over the eastern plains of Safi, where another army from Zhou danced in their turn, or back to the west, where Alfia danced with her brothers in the high Soulis mountains, and Lecne danced with Hasti at the inn, or in Lonika, or in the streets and squares of the City, where even Tiy Drako danced, turning a *palka* with the recovering engineer, Myr Kallinikas.

Kurvenos spread his arms from the top of the ash altar, and spoke ancient words: the same words that the priests said in Masr and in Ulama and in Megara; the same words that women sang in the mountains of Soulis and in the villages of the Iron Ring above Volta and out in the Western Isles at the very edge of the world.

The dances turned like a million wheels, and as if they were cogged together in some wondrous machine, they were bonded in a single great working, greater than they themselves even knew.

And above them in the sky, the Dark Forge began to close.

Epilogue

Aranthur laid Inoques on the white sand by the Pool.

"Must it be here?" she asked.

"There's no point to all of this if you die in childbirth, is there?" he said, and he dipped her in the pool.

The wounds that the Master had inflicted were deep; none of them had killed their baby, but no matter what the Imoters did, she still bled inside.

"It's cold!" she said. "Aranthur, I'm so cold."

Aranthur was trying not to weep as he bathed her in the pool.

"Come on, water," he said aloud.

"So cold," she said. "Oh, oh. Here it comes."

And so it was. Aranthur carried her out of the water, and knelt by her, and waited.

"What's happening?" Inoques said.

It was as if she was falling asleep—numb with the cold, or perhaps with approaching death.

Aranthur was watching as the healing water bleached away her tattoos. As was so often the case, something he hadn't expected was happening.

"Oh, gods," Inoques said. "Oh, gods."

And after a little time and a little mess, there was a baby. By the time it was born, the tattoos had faded almost completely.

"You can go at any time," Aranthur said. "I plotted, and of course now it doesn't matter. The water erases the bonds."

Inoques smiled. "I know," she said. "The truth is, I've known how to escape for a while now. You showed me, with the Exalted." She smiled. "Give me the baby."

Aranthur sat back on his heels and laughed ruefully. But he put the baby on her chest and then threw his riding cloak over them both.

"This is a very healthy body," Inoques said. "I will miss it. Who will nurse our child?"

"And when you leave that body, our vow is dissolved," Aranthur said with real regret. "Will you tear me to pieces?"

Inoques smiled. "No," she said. "Although I'd rather like to make *you* have a baby."

Aranthur laughed.

"Perhaps I will visit from time to time," she said. "Goodbye, love."

And Inoques exhaled, a long breath.

Just for a moment, the shadow of a great cat stood over the Pool, and then it was gone on the wind, free.

Aranthur took time to gather his resolution. But he knew that, for once, what he was doing was *right.* He took the black sword from its protective cocoon of spells in the *Aulos* and plunged it into the white sand. And then he drew the Bright Steel from the *Aulos.*

I thought we had lost, she said. *And now we have won.*

"This time, and for now," Aranthur said aloud. "But I have made a terrible discovery. Yesterday's enemies are tomorrow's allies. Today's allies are tomorrow's enemies. Inoques was a *wraith*, an *apep-duat.* The swords were made to destroy the wraiths."

Too true.

"Sometimes our remedies are just the next crisis."

He was crying. But through the tears, he did what had to be done. This time, the black sword screamed, and there were no words of solace. It died an ugly death and was broken forever, and the wind blew whatever was left of its dark spirit away into the west.

Only three more until I can rest, she said.

Aranthur sighed.

But he had made his decision, and he was resolute.

What are you doing? she demanded.

With the precision of some anatomical training, Aranthur plunged the Bright Steel into the hand of the body that had once been Inoques. That body still breathed, and it winced at the pain of the sword that went between the tendons and bones, although the eyes didn't open. The blade slid between the skin and muscle, doing almost no damage, and he pushed it into the sand below.

What are you doing? the sword asked.

Aranthur held the sword between his hands for a moment. And then let go. The hilt was warm.

He pricked his finger and wrote the Masran glyph of unbinding in blood on the blade of the sword.

What are you doing?

And then he braced the blade against his knee, so that the body at his feet would take no more damage from the sword piercing it, and with the *enhancement* and all the power of his right arm, he broke the Bright Steel between his hands.

The body that had been Inoques went rigid with shock.

Its arms shot out; its face took on the ugly rictus of death, and for far too long, Aranthur thought he'd killed the body he meant to save.

And then it subsided, still as death.

And the eyes shot open.

"What have you done?" she asked.

It was Inoques' voice, but Aranthur knew that it was not Inoques.

"I have returned you to life, Myr Orsin," Aranthur said.

He withdrew the blade carefully from her hand and threw the broken sherds of the Bright Steel into the pool.

They sank into the pool, and although it was only a few feet deep, they were gone. Then he put a clean linen rag against the wound and knelt by her side.

"Damn you, Aranthur Timos!" Orsin spat. "Is this some form of revenge?"

Aranthur was looking at the woman who had been a sword for more than two thousand years.

The baby cried.

"No," Aranthur said. "I hope to have given you something that was taken from you, because no one should be left as a slave; even in a glorious cause."

"So instead I'm to be a nursing mother?" Orsin spat.

She tried to sit up, and unconsciously her hand went to the baby.

Aranthur waved at Sasan, who had waited patiently at the top of the beach. Now he carried Dahlia down the path from the glyphs to the pool.

"Did it work?" Dahlia demanded weakly.

"And you?" Orsin demanded. "You too!"

"That's the sword?" Sasan asked.

"Aphres, that's cold," Dahlia said, and she was dipped into the water. "Hells, I might prefer being dead."

"Is it done?" Iralia asked.

"All done," Aranthur said, as the others came down to the beach. Sasan was hauling Dahlia out of the healing water, and Chimeg was supporting Nata as he was wading in.

"All your friends," Orsin said bitterly.

"All of Cold Iron," Aranthur said. "Which I now gather was all your work."

Orsin turned her head. Unconsciously she caressed the baby on her breast. Then she raised her head and looked at the sun rising over the mountains to the east.

"By all the gods," she said, "I never thought to see another sunrise." Tears sprang to her eyes. "It's all so... beautiful..."

Iralia sat down and put the paladin's head in her lap.

"You're one of us now," she said.

Orsin smiled. She looked around at them.

"I know you all," she said. "Gods... I'm alive. Alive." She looked at Aranthur, who took the baby from her and threw his fur-lined khaftan over her shoulders. "You bastard," she said, but without anger.

Aranthur was wrapping the baby, whom he'd washed in the Pool, in a whole sheepskin. The baby was smiling.

"She needs a name," he said.

"Call her Rolana," Orsin said, smiling at Dahlia. "Damn," she said.

Dahlia came and embraced the woman who had been a sword.

"We're all here for you," she said. "But we couldn't let you be an artifact any longer. Not once Aranthur figured out how to release you."

Orsin shook her head. "You could have asked."

Aranthur nodded. "Like you asked me, in the Night Market, if I wanted to be a hero?"

"Damn," she said again.

"Welcome to Cold Iron," Iralia added. "As a person, I mean."

"I'll need a sword," Orsin said.

extras

if you enjoyed
BRIGHT STEEL
look out for
THE RED KNIGHT
The Traitor Son Cycle: Book One
by
Miles Cameron

Twenty-eight florins a month is a huge price to pay, for a man to stand between you and the Wild.

Twenty-eight florins a month is nowhere near enough when a wyvern's jaws snap shut on your helmet in the hot stink of battle, and the beast starts to rip the head from your shoulders. But if standing and fighting is hard, leading a company of men—or worse, a company of mercenaries—against the creatures of the Wild is even harder.

It takes all the advantages of birth, training, and the luck of the devil to do it.

The Red Knight has all three, he has youth on his side, and he's determined to turn a profit. So when he hires his company out to protect an Abbess and her nunnery, it's just another job. The abbey is rich, the nuns are pretty, and the monster preying on them is nothing he can't deal with.

Only it's not just a job. It's going to be a war....

Chapter One

Albinkirk—Ser John Crayford

The Captain of Albinkirk forced himself to stop staring out his narrow, glazed window and do some work.

He was jealous. Jealous of a boy a third of his age, commanding a pretty company of lances. Riding about. While he sat in a town so safe it was dull, growing old.

Don't be a fool, he told himself. *All those deeds of arms make wonderful stories, but the doing is cold, wet and terrifying. Remember?*

He sighed. His hands remembered everything—the blows, the nights on the ground, the freezing cold, the gauntlets that didn't quite fit. His hands pained him all the time, awake or asleep.

The Captain of Albinkirk, Ser John Crayford, had not started his life as a gentleman. It was a rank he'd achieved through pure talent.

For violence.

And as a reward, he sat in this rich town with a garrison a third the size that it was supposed to be on paper. A garrison of hirelings who bossed the weak, abused the women, and took money from the tradesmen. A garrison that had too much cash, because the posting came with the right to invest in fur caravans from the north. Albinkirk furs were the marvel of ten countries. All you had to do to get them was ride north or west into the Wild. And then come back alive.

The captain had a window that looked north-west.

He tore his eyes away from it. Again.

And put pen to paper. Carefully, laboriously, he wrote:

My Lord,

A Company of Adventure—well ordered, and bearing a pass signed by the constable—passed the bridge yesterday morning; near to forty lances, each lance composed of a knight, a squire, a valet and an archer. They were very well armed and armoured in the latest Eastern manner—steel everywhere. Their captain was polite but reserved; very young, refused to give his name; styled himself The Red Knight. His banner displayed three lacs d'amour in gold on a field sable. He declared that they were, for the most part, your Grace's subjects, lately come from the wars in Galle. As his pass was good, I saw no reason to keep him.

Ser John snorted, remembering the scene. No one had thought to warn him that a small army was coming his way from the east. He'd been summoned to the gate early in the morning. Dressed in a stained cote of fustian and old hose, he'd tried to face down the cocky young pup in his glorious scarlet and gold, mounted on a war horse the size of a barn. He hadn't enough real soldiers to arrest any of them. The damned boy had *Great*

Noble written all over him, and the Captain of Albinkirk thanked God that the whelp had paid the toll with good grace and had good paper, as any incident between them would have gone badly. For him.

He realised he was looking at the mountains. He tore his eyes away. Again.

He also had a letter from the Abbess at Lissen Carak. She had sent to me last autumn for fifty good men, and I had to refuse her—your Grace knows I am short enough of men as it is. I suppose she has offered her contract to sell-swords in the absence of local men.

I am, as your Grace is aware, almost one hundred men under strength; I have but four proper men-at-arms, and many of my archers are not all they should be. I respectfully request that your Grace either replace me, or provide the necessary funds to increase the garrison to its proper place.

I am your Grace's humblest and most respectful servant,
John Crayford

The Master of the Guild of Furriers had invited him to dinner. Ser John leaned back and decided to call it a day, leaving the letter lying on his desk.

Lissen Carak—The Red Knight

"Sweet Jesu," Michael called from the other side of the wall. It was as high as a man's shoulder, created by generations of peasants hauling stones out of fields. Built against the wall was a two-storey stone house with outbuildings—a rich manor farm. Michael stood in the yard, peering through the house's shattered main door. "Sweet Jesu," the squire said again. "They're all dead, Captain."

His war horse gave the captain the height to see over the wall to where his men were rolling the bodies over, stripping them of valuables as they sought for survivors. Their new employer would not approve, but the captain thought the looting might help her understand what she was choosing to employ. In his experience, it was usually best that the prospective employer understand what he—or she—was buying. From the first.

The captain's squire vaulted over the stone wall that separated the walled garden from the road and took a rag from Toby, the captain's page. Sticky mud, from the endless spring rain, covered his thigh-high buckled boots. He produced a rag from his purse to cover his agitation and began to clean his boots. Michael was fussy and dressed for fashion. His scarlet company surcoat was embroidered with gold stars; the heavy wool worth more than an archer's armour. He was well born and could afford it, so it was his business.

It was the captain's business that the lad's hands were shaking.

"When you feel ready to present yourself," the captain said lightly, but Michael froze at his words, then made himself finish his task with the rag before tossing it back to Toby.

"Apologies, m'lord," he said with a quick glance over his shoulder. "It was something out of the Wild, lord. Stake my soul on it."

"Not much of a stake," the captain said, holding Michael's eye. He winked, as much to amuse the onlookers of his household as to steady his squire, who was pale enough to write on. Then he looked around.

The rain was light—just enough to weigh down the captain's heavy scarlet cloak without soaking it through. Beyond the walled steading stretched fields of dark, newly planted earth, as shining and black in the rain as the captain's horse. The upper fields toward the hills were rich with new greenery and dotted with sheep. Good earth and fertile soil promised rich crops, as far as the eye could see on both sides of the river. This land was tamed, covered in a neat geometric pattern of hedgerows and high stone walls separating tilled plots, or neatly scattered sheep and cattle, with the river to ship them down to the cities in the south. Crops and animals whose riches had paid for the fortress nunnery—Lissen Carak—that capped the high ridge to the south, visible from here as a crenelated line of pale stone. Grey, grey, grey from the sky to the ground. Pale grey, dark grey, black.

Beyond the sheep, to the north, rose the Adnacrags—two hundred leagues of dense mountains that lowered over the fields, their tops lost in the clouds.

The captain laughed at his own thoughts.

The dozen soldiers nearest him looked; every head turned, each wearing matching expressions of fear.

The captain rubbed the pointed beard at his chin, shaking off the water. "Jacques?" he asked his valet.

The older man sat quietly on a war horse. He was better armed than most of the valets; wearing his scarlet surcote with long, hanging sleeves over an Eastern breastplate, and with a fine sword four feet long to the tip. He, too, combed the water out of his pointed beard while he thought.

"M'lord?" he asked.

"How did the Wild make it here?" The captain asked. Even with a gloved hand keeping the water from his eyes, he couldn't *see* the edge of the Wild—there wasn't a stand of trees large enough to hide a deer within a mile. Two miles. Far off to the north, many leagues beyond the rainy horizon and the mountains, was the Wall. Past the Wall was the Wild. True, the Wall was breached in many places and the Wild ran right down into the country. The Adnacrags had never been cleared. But here—

Here, wealth and power held the Wild at bay. *Should have held the Wild at bay.*

"The usual way," Jacques said quietly. "Some fool must have invited them in."

The captain chuckled. "Well," he said, giving his valet a crooked smile, "I don't suppose they'd call us if they didn't have a problem. And we need the work."

"It ripped them apart," Michael said.

He was new to the trade and well-born, but the captain appreciated how quickly he had recovered his poise. At the same time, Michael needed to learn.

"Apart," Michael repeated, licking his lips. His eyes were elsewhere. "It *ate* her. Them."

Mostly recovered, the captain thought to himself. He nodded to his squire and gave his destrier, Grendel, a little rein so he backed a few steps and turned. The big horse could smell blood and something else he didn't like. He didn't like most things, even at the best of times, but this was spooking him and the captain could feel his mount's tension. Given that Grendel wore a chamfron over his face with a spike a foot long, the horse's annoyance could quickly translate into mayhem.

He motioned to Toby, who was now sitting well to the side and away from the isolated steading-house and eating, which is what Toby tended to do whenever left to himself. The captain turned to face his standard bearer and his two marshals where they sat their own fidgeting horses in the rain, waiting for his commands.

"I'll leave Sauce and Bad Tom. They'll stay on their guard until we send them a relief," he said. The discovery of the killings in the steading had interrupted their muddy trek to the fortress.

They'd been riding since the second hour after midnight, after a cold camp and equally cold supper. No one looked happy.

"Go and get me the master of the hunt," he added, turning back to his squire. When he was answered only with silence, he looked around. "Michael?" he asked quietly.

"M'lord?" The young man was looking at the door to the steading. It was oak, bound in iron, and it had been broken in two places, the iron hinges inside the door had bent where they'd been forced off their pins. Trios of parallel grooves had ripped along the grain of the wood—in one spot, the talons had ripped through a decorative iron whorl, a clean cut.

"Do you need a minute, lad?" the captain asked. Jacques had seen to his own mount and was now standing at Grendel's big head, eyeing the spike warily.

"No—no, m'lord." His squire was still stunned, staring at the door and what lay beyond it.

"Then don't stand on ceremony, I beg." The captain dismounted, thinking that he had used the term lad quite naturally. Despite the fact that he and Michael were less than five years apart.

"M'lord?" Michael asked, unclear what he'd just been told to do.

"Move your arse, boy. Get me the huntsman. Now." The captain handed his horse to the valet. Jacques was not really a valet. He was really thecaptain's man and, as such, he had his own servant—Toby. A recent addition. A scrawny thing with large eyes and quick hands, completely enveloped in his red wool cote, which was many sizes too big.

Toby took the horse and gazed at his captain with hero-worship, a big winter apple forgotten in his hand.

The captain liked a little hero-worship. "He's spooked. Don't give him any free rein or there'll be trouble," the captain said gruffly. He paused. "You might give him your apple core though," he said, and the boy smiled.

The captain went into the steading by the splintered door. Closer up, he could see that the darker brown was not a finish. It was blood.

Behind him, his destrier gave a snort that sounded remarkably like human derision—though whether it was for the page or his master was impossible to tell.

The woman just inside the threshold had been a nun before she was ripped open from neck to cervix. Her long, dark hair, unbound from the confines of her wimple, framed the horror of her missing face. She lay in a broad pool of her own blood that ran down into the gaps between the boards. There were tooth marks on her skull—the skin just forward of one ear had been shredded, as if something had gnawed at her face for some time, flensing it from the bone. One arm had been ripped clear of her body, the skin and muscle neatly eaten away so that only shreds remained, bones and tendons still hanging together...and then it had been replaced by the corpse. The white hand with the silver IHS ring and the cross was untouched.

The captain looked at her for a long time.

Just beyond the red ruin of the nun was a single clear footprint in the blood and ordure, which was already brown and sticky in the moist, cool air. Some of the blood had begun to leech into the pine floor boards, smooth from years of bare feet walking them. The leeched blood blurred the edge of the print, but the outline was clear—it was the size of a war horse's hoof or bigger, with three toes.

The captain heard his huntsman come up and dismount outside. He didn't turn, absorbed in the parallel exercises of withholding the need to vomit and committing the scene to memory. There was a second, smudged print further into the room, where the creature had pivoted its weight to pass under the low arch to the main room beyond. It had dug a furrow in the pine with its talons. And a matching furrow in the base board that ran up into the wattle and plaster. A dew claw.

"Why'd this one die here when the rest died in the garden?" he asked.

Gelfred stepped carefully past the body. Like most gentlemen, he carried a short staff—really just a stick shod in silver, like a mountebank's wand. Or a wizard's. He used it first to point and then to pry something shiny out of the floorboards.

"Very good," said the captain.

"She died for them," Gelfred said. A silver cross set with pearls dangled from his stick. "She tried to stop it. She gave the others time to escape."

"If only it had worked," said the captain. He pointed at the prints.

Gelfred crouched by the nearer print, laid his stick along it, and made a clucking sound with his tongue.

"Well, well," he said. His nonchalance was a little too studied. And his face was pale.

The captain couldn't blame the man. In a brief lifetime replete with dead bodies, the captain had seldom seen one so horrible. Part of his conscious mind wandered off a little, wondering if her femininity, the beauty of her hair, contributed to the utter horror of her destruction. Was it like desecration? A deliberate sacrilege?

And another, harder part of his mind walked a different path. The monster had placed that arm *just so.* The tooth marks that framed the bloody sockets that had been her eyes. He could imagine, far too well.

It had been done to leave terror. It was almost *artistic.*

He tasted salt in his mouth and turned away. "Don't act

tough on my account, Gelfred," he said. He spat on the floor, trying to get rid of the taste before he made a spectacle of himself.

"Never seen worse, and that's a fact," Gelfred said. He took a long, slow breath. "God shouldn't allow this!" he said bitterly.

"Gelfred," the captain said, with a bitter smile. "God doesn't give a fuck."

Their eyes met. Gelfred looked away. "I will know what there is to know," he said, looking grim. He didn't like the captain's blasphemy—his face said as much. Especially not when he was about to work with God's power.

Gelfred touched his stick to the middle of the print, and there was a moment of *change*, as if their eyes had adjusted to a new light source, or stronger sunlight.

"Pater noster qui es in caelus," Gelfred intoned in plainchant.

The captain left him to it.

In the garden, Ser Thomas's squire and half a dozen archers had stripped the bodies of valuables—and collected all the body parts strewn across the enclosure, reassembled as far as possible, and laid them out, wrapped in cloaks. The two men were almost green, and the smell of vomit almost covered the smell of blood and ordure. A third archer was wiping his hands on a linen shirt.

Ser Thomas—Bad Tom to every man in the company—was six foot six inches of dark hair, heavy brow and bad attitude. He had a temper and was always the wrong man to cross. He was watching his men attentively, an amulet out and in his hand. He turned at the rattle of the captain's hardened steel sabatons on the stone path and gave him a sketchy salute. "Reckon the young 'uns earned their pay today, Captain."

Since they weren't paid unless they had a contract, it wasn't saying much.

The captain merely grunted. There were six corpses in the garden.

Bad Tom raised an eyebrow and passed something to him.

The captain looked at it, and pursed his lips. Tucked the chain into the purse at his waist, and slapped Bad Tom on his paulder-clad shoulder. "Stay here and stay awake," he said. "You can have Sauce and Gelding, too."

Bad Tom shrugged. He licked his lips. "Me an' Sauce don't always see eye to eye."

The captain smiled inwardly to see this giant of a man—feared throughout the company—admit that he and a woman didn't "see eye to eye."

She came over the wall to join them.

Sauce had won her name as a whore, giving too much lip to customers. She was tall, and in the rain her red hair was toned to dark brown. Freckles gave her an innocence that was a lie. She had made herself a name. That said all that needed to be said.

"Tom fucked it up already?" she asked.

Tom glared.

The captain took a breath. "Play nicely, children. I need my best on guard here, frosty and awake."

"It won't come back," she said.

The captain shook his head. "Stay awake anyway. Just for me."

Bad Tom smiled and blew a kiss at Sauce. "Just for *you*," he said.

Her hand went to her riding sword and with a flick it was in her hand.

The captain cleared his throat.

"He treats me like a whore. I *am not.*" She held the sword steady at his face, and Bad Tom didn't move.

"Say you are sorry, Tom." The captain sounded as if it was all a jest.

"Didn't say one bad thing. Not one! Just a tease!" Tom said. Spittle flew from his lips.

"You meant to cause harm. She took it as harm. You know the rules, Tom." The captain's voice had changed, now. He spoke so softly that Tom had to lean forward to hear him.

"Sorry," Tom muttered like a schoolboy. "Bitch."

Sauce smiled. The tip of her riding sword pressed into the man's thick forehead just over an eye.

"Fuck you!" Tom growled.

The captain leaned forward. "Neither one of you wants this. It's clear you are both *posturing*. Climb down or take the consequences. Tom, Sauce wants to be treated as your peer. Sauce, Tom is top beast and you put his back up at every opportunity. If you want to be part of this company then you have to accept your place in it."

He raised his gloved hand. "On the count of three, you will both back away, Sauce will sheathe her weapon, Tom will bow to her and apologise, and Sauce will return his apology. Or you can both collect your kit, walk away and kill each other. But not as my people. Understand? Three. Two. One."

Sauce stepped back, saluted with her blade and sheathed it. Without looking or fumbling.

Tom let a moment go by. Pure insolence. But then something happened in his face, and he bowed—a good bow, so that his right knee touched the mud. "Humbly crave your pardon," he said in a loud, clear voice.

Sauce smiled. It wasn't a pretty smile, but it did transform her face, despite the missing teeth in the middle. "And I yours, ser knight," she replied. "I regret my... attitude."

She obviously shocked Tom. In the big man's world of

dominance and submission, she was beyond him. The captain could read him like a book. And he thought *Sauce deserves something for that. She's a good man.*

Gelfred appeared at his elbow. Had probably been waiting for the drama to end.

The captain felt the wrongness of it before he saw what his huntsman carried. Like a housewife returning from pilgrimage and smelling something dead under her floor—it was like that, only stronger and wronger.

"I rolled her over. This was in her back," Gelfred said. He had the thing wrapped in his rosary.

The captain swallowed bile, again. *I love this job,* he reminded himself.

To the eye, it looked like a stick—two fingers thick at the butt, sharpened to a needlepoint now clotted with blood and dark. Thorns sprouted from the whole haft, but it was fletched. An arrow. Or rather, an obscene parody of an arrow, whittled from...

"Witch Bane," Gelfred said.

The captain made himself take it without flinching. There were some secrets he would pay the price to preserve. He flashed on the last Witch-Bane arrow he'd seen—and pushed past it.

He held it a moment. "So?" he said, with epic unconcern.

"She was shot in the back—with the Witch Bane—while she was alive." Gelfred's eyes narrowed. "And then the monster ripped her face off."

The captain nodded and handed his huntsman the shaft. The moment it left his hand he felt lighter, and the places where the thorns had pricked his chamois gloves felt like rashes of poison ivy on his thumb and fingers—if poison ivy caused an itchy numbness, a leaden pollution.

"Interesting," the captain said.

Sauce was watching him.

Damn women and their superior powers of observation, he thought.

Her smile forced him to smile in return. The squires and valets in the garden began to breathe again and the captain was sure they'd stay awake, now. Given that there was a murderer on the loose who had monster-allies in the Wild.

He got back to his horse. Jehannes, his marshal, came up on his bridle hand side and cleared his throat. "That woman's trouble," he said.

"Tom's trouble too," the captain replied.

"No other company would have had her." Jehannes spat.

The captain looked at his marshal. "Now Jehannes," he said. "Be serious. Who would have Tom? He's killed more of his own comrades than Judas Iscariot."

Jehannes looked away. "I don't trust her," he said.

The captain nodded. "I know. Let's get moving." He considered vaulting into the saddle and decided that he was too tired and the show would be wasted on Jehannes, anyway. "You dislike her because she's a woman," he said, and put his left foot into the stirrup.

Grendel was tall enough that he had to bend his left knee as far as the articulation in his leg harness would allow. The horse snorted again. Toby held onto the reins.

He leaped up, his right leg powering him into the saddle, pushing his six feet of height and fifty pounds of mail and plate. Got his knee over the high ridge of the war-saddle and was in his seat.

"Yes," Jehannes said, and backed his horse into his place in the column.

The captain saw Michael watching Jehannes go. The younger man turned and raised an eyebrow at the captain.

"Something to say, young Michael?" the captain asked.

"What was the stick? M'lord?" Michael was different from the rest—well born. Almost an apprentice, instead of a hireling. As the captain's squire, he had special privileges. He could ask questions, and all the rest of the company would sit very still and listen to the answer.

The captain looked at him for a moment. Considering. He shrugged—no mean feat in plate armour.

"Witch Bane," he said. "A Witch-Bane *arrow.* The nun had *power.*" He made a face. "Until someone shot the Witch Bane into her back."

"A nun?" Michael asked. "A nun who could work *power*?" He paused. "Who shot her? By Jesu, m'lord, you mean the Wild has *allies*?"

"All in a day's work, lad. It's all in a day's work." His visual memory, too well trained, ran through the items like the rooms in his memory palace—the splintered door, the faceless corpse, the arm, the Witch-Bane arrow. He examined the path from the garden door to the front door.

"Wait on me," he said.

He walked Grendel around the farmyard, following the stone wall to the garden. He stood in his stirrups to peer over the wall, and aligned the open garden door with the splintered front door. He looked over his shoulder several times.

"Wilful!" he called.

His archer appeared. "What now?" he muttered.

The captain pointed at the two doors. "How far away could you stand and still put an arrow into someone at the *front* door."

"What, shooting through the house?" asked Wilful Murder.

The captain nodded.

Wilful shook his head. "Not that far," he admitted. "Any loft at all and the shaft strikes the door jamb." He caught a louse on his collar and killed it between his nails. His eyes met the captain's. "He'd have to be close."

The captain nodded. "Gelfred?" he called.

The huntsman was outside the front door, casting with his wand over a large reptilian print in the road. "M'lord?"

"See if you and Wilful can find any tracks out the back. Wilful will show you where a bowman might have stood."

"It's always fucking me—get Long Paw to do it," Wilful muttered.

The captain's mild glance rested for a moment on his archer and the man cringed.

The captain turned his horse and sighed. "Catch us up as soon as you have the tracks," he said. He waved at Jehannes. "Let's go to the fortress and meet the lady Abbess." He touched his spurs ever so lightly to Grendel's sides, and the stallion snorted and deigned to move forward into the rain.

The rest of the ride along the banks of the Cohocton was uneventful, and the company halted by the fortified bridge overshadowed by the rock-girt ridge and the grey walls of the fortress convent atop it, high above them. Linen tents rose like dirty white flowers from the muddy field, and the officer's pavilions came off the wagons. Teams of archers dug cook pits and latrines, and valets and the many camp followers—craftsmen and sutlers, runaway serfs, prostitutes, servants, and free men and women desperate to gain a place—assembled the heavy wooden hoardings that served the camp as temporary walls and towers. The drovers, an essential part of any company, filled the gaps with the heavy wagons. Horse lines were staked out. Guards were set.

The Abbess's door ward had pointedly refused to allow the mercenaries through her gate. The mercenaries had expected nothing else, and even now hardened professionals were gauging the height of the walls and the likelihood of climbing them. Two veteran archers—Kanny, the barracks room lawyer of the company, and Scrant, who never stopped eating—stood by the camp's newly-constructed wooden gate and speculated on the likelihood of getting some in the nun's dormitory.

It made the captain smile as he rode by, collecting their salutes, on the steep gravel road that led up the ridge from the fortified town at the base, up along the switchbacks and finally up through the fortress gate-house into the courtyard beyond. Behind him, his banner bearer, marshals and six of his best lances dismounted to a quiet command and stood by their horses. His squire held his high-crested bassinet, and his valet bore his sword of war. It was an impressive show and it made good advertising—ideal, as he could see heads at every window and door that opened into the courtyard.

A tall nun in a slate-grey habit—the captain suppressed his reflexive flash on the corpse in the doorway of the steading—reached to take the reins of his horse. A second nun beckoned with her hand. Neither spoke.

The captain was pleased to see Michael dismount elegantly despite the rain, and take Grendel's head, without physically pushing the nun out of the way.

He smiled at the nuns and followed them across the courtyard towards the most ornate door, heavy with scroll-worked iron hinges and elaborate wooden panels. To the north, a dormitory building rose beyond a trio of low sheds that probably served as workshops—smithy, dye house and carding house, or so his nose told him. To the south stood a chapel—far too fragile and beautiful for this martial setting—and next to it, by cosmic irony, a long, low, slate-roofed stable.

Between the chapel's carved oak doors stood a man. He had a

black habit with a silk rope around the waist, was tall and thin to the point of caricature, and his hands were covered in old scars.

The captain didn't like his eyes, which were blue and flat. The man was nervous, and wouldn't meet his eye—and he was clearly angry.

Flicking his eyes away from the priest, the captain reviewed the riches of the abbey with the eye of a money-lender sizing up a potential client. The abbey's income was shown in the cobbled courtyard, the neat flint and granite of the stables with a decorative stripe of glazed brick, the copper on the roof and the lead gutters gushing water into a cistern. The courtyard was thirty paces across—as big as that of any castle he'd lived in as a boy. The walls rose sheer—the outer curtain at his back, the central monastery before him, with towers at each corner, all wet stone and wet lead, rain slicked cobbles; the priest's faded black cassock, and the nun's undyed surcoat.

All shades of grey, he thought to himself, and smiled as he climbed the steps to the massive monastery door, which was opened by another silent nun. She led him down the hall—a great hall lit by stained glass windows high in the walls. The Abbess was enthroned like a queen in a great chair on a dais at the north end of the hall, in a gown whose grey had just enough colour to appear a pale, pale lavender in the multi-faceted light. She had the look of a woman who had once been very beautiful indeed—even in middle age her beauty was right there, resting in more than her face. Her wimple and the high collar of her gown revealed little enough of her. But her bearing was more than noble, or haughty. Her bearing was commanding, confident in a way that only the great of the land were confident. The captain noted that her nuns obeyed her with an eagerness born of either fear or the pleasure of service.

The captain wondered which it was.

"You took long enough to reach us," she said, by way of greeting. Then she snapped her fingers and beckoned at a pair of servants to bring a tray. "We are servants of God here—don't you think you might have managed to strip your armour before you came to my hall?" the Abbess asked. She glanced around, caught a novice's eye, raised an eyebrow. "Fetch the captain a stool," she said. "Not a covered one. A solid one."

"I wear armour every day," the captain said. "It comes with my profession." The great hall was as big as the courtyard outside, with high windows of stained glass set near the roof, and massive wooden beams so old that age and soot had turned them black. The walls were whitewashed over fine plaster, and held niches containing images of saints and two rich books—clearly on display to overawe visitors. Their voices echoed in the room, which was colder than the wet courtyard outside. There was no fire in the central hearth.

The Abbess's people brought her wine, and she sipped it as they placed a small table at the captain's elbow. He was three feet beneath her. "Perhaps your armour is unnecessary in a nunnery?" she asked.

He raised an eyebrow. "I see a fortress," he said. "It happens that there are nuns in it."

She nodded. "If I chose to order you taken by my men, would your armour save you?" she asked.

The novice who brought his stool was pretty and she was careful of him, moving with the deliberation of a swordsman or a dancer. He turned his head to catch her eye and felt the tug of her power, saw that she was not merely pretty. She set the heavy stool down against the back of his knees. Quite deliberately, the captain touched her arm gently and caused her to turn to him. He turned to face her, putting his back to the Abbess.

"Thank you," he said, looking her in the eye with a calculated smile. She was tall and young and graceful, with wide-set almond-shaped eyes and a long nose. Not pretty; she was arresting.

She blushed. The flush travelled like fire down her neck and into her heavy wool gown.

He turned back to the Abbess, his goal accomplished. Wondering why the Abbess had placed such a desirable novice within his reach, unless she meant to. "If I chose to storm your abbey, would your piety save you?" he asked.

She blazed with anger. "How dare you turn your back on me?" she asked. "And leave the room, Amicia. The captain has bitten you with his eyes."

He was smiling. He thought her anger feigned.

She met his eyes and narrowed her own—and then folded her hands together, almost as if she intended to pray.

"Honestly, Captain, I have prayed and prayed over what to do here. Bringing you to fight the Wild is like buying a wolf to shepherd sheep." She looked him in the eye. "I know what you are," she said.

"Do you really?" he asked. "All the better, lady Abbess. Shall we to business, then? Now the pleasantries are done?"

"But what shall I call you?" she asked. "You are a well-born man, for all your snide airs. My chamberlain—"

"Didn't have a nice name for me, did he, my lady Abbess?" He nodded. "You may call me Captain. It is all the name I need." He nodded graciously. "I do not like the name your chamberlain used. Bourc. I call myself the Red Knight."

"Many men are called bourc," she said. "To be born out of wedlock is—"

"To be cursed by God before you are born. Eh, lady Abbess?" He tried to stop the anger that rose on his cheeks like a blush. "So very fair. So *just*."

She scowled at him for a moment, annoyed with him the way older people are often annoyed with the young, when the young posture too much.

He understood her in a glance.

"Too dark? Should I add a touch of heroism?" he asked with a certain air.

She eyed him. "If you wrap yourself in darkness," she said, "you risk merely appearing dull. But you have the wit to know it. There's hope for you, boy, if you know that. Now to business. I'm not rich—"

"I have never met anyone who would admit being rich," he agreed. "Or to getting enough sleep."

"More wine for the captain," snapped the Abbess to the sister who had guarded the door. "But I can pay you. We are afflicted by something from the Wild. It has destroyed two of my farms this year, and one last year. At first—at first, we all hoped that they were isolated incidents." She met his eye squarely. "It is not possible to believe that any more."

"Three farms this year," said the captain. He fished in his purse, hesitated over the chain with the leaf amulet, then fetched forth a cross inlaid with pearls instead.

"Oh, by the wounds of Christ!" swore the Abbess. "Oh, Blessed Virgin protect and cherish her. Sister Hawisia! Is she—"

"She is dead," the captain said. "And six more corpses in the garden. Your good sister died trying to protect them."

"Her faith was very strong," the Abbess said. She was dry eyed, but her voice trembled. "You needn't mock her."

The captain frowned. "I never mock courage, lady Abbess. To face such a thing without weapons—"

"Her faith was a weapon against evil, Captain." The Abbess leaned forward.

"Strong enough to stop a creature from the Wild? No, it was not," said the captain quietly. "I won't comment on evil."

The Abbess stood sharply. "You are some sort of atheist, are you, Captain?"

The captain frowned again. "There is nothing productive for us in theological debate, my lady Abbess. Your lands have attracted a malignant entity—an enemy of Man. They seldom hunt alone, especially not this far from the Wild. You wish me to rid you of them. I can. And I will. In exchange, you will pay me. That is all that matters between us."

The Abbess sat again, her movements violent, angry. The captain sensed that she was off balance—that the death of the nun had struck her personally. She was, after all, the commander of a company of nuns.

"I am not convinced that engaging you is the right decision," she said.

The captain nodded. "It may not be, lady Abbess. But you sent for me, and I am here." Without intending to, he had lowered his voice, and spoke softly.

"Is that a threat?" she asked.

Instead of answering, the captain reached into his purse again and withdrew the broken chain holding a small leaf made of green enamel on bronze.

The Abbess recoiled as if from a snake.

"My men found this," he said.

The Abbess turned her head away.

"You have a traitor," he said. And rose. "Sister Hawisia had an arrow in her back. While she faced something terrible, something very, very terrible." He nodded. "I will go to walk the walls. You need time to think if you want us. Or not."

"You will poison us," she said. "You and your kind do not bring peace."

He nodded. "We bring you no peace, but a company of swords, my lady." He grinned at his own misquote of scripture. "We don't make the violence. We merely deal with it as it comes to us."

"The devil can quote scripture," she said.

"No doubt he had his hand in writing it," the captain shot back.

She bit back a counter—he watched her face change as she decided not to rise to his provocation. And he felt a vague twinge of remorse for goading her, an ache like the pain in his wrist from making too many practice cuts the day before. And, like the pain in his wrist, he was unaccustomed to remorse.

"I could say it is a little late to think of peace now." He sneered briefly and then put his sneer away. "My men are here, and they haven't had a good meal or a paid job in some weeks. I offer this, not as a threat, but as a useful piece of data as you reason through the puzzle. I also think that the creature you have to deal with is far worse than you have imagined. In fact, I'll go so far as to say it's far worse than I had imagined. It is big, powerful, and angry, and very intelligent. And more likely two than one."

She winced.

"Allow me a few minutes to think," she said.

He nodded, bowed, set his riding sword at his waist, and walked back into the courtyard.

His men stood like statues, their scarlet surcoats livid against their grey surroundings. The horses fretted—but only a little—and the men less.

"Be easy," he said.

They all took breath together. Stretched arms tired from bearing armour, or hips bruised from mail and cuirass.

Michael was the boldest. "Are we in?" he asked.

The captain didn't meet his eye because he'd noticed an open window across the courtyard, and seen the face framed in it. "Not yet, my honey. We are not in yet." He blew a kiss at the window.

The face vanished.

Ser Milus, his primus pilus and standard bearer, grunted. "Bad for business," he said. And then, as an afterthought, "m'lord."

The captain flicked him a glance and looked back to the dormitory windows.

"There's more virgins watching us right now," Michael opined, "Then have parted their legs for me in all my life."

Jehannes, the senior marshal, nodded seriously. "Does that mean one, young Michael? Or two?"

Guillaume Longsword, the junior marshal, barked his odd laugh, like the seals of the northern bays. "The second one said she was a virgin," he mock-whined. "At least, that's what she told me!"

Coming through the visor of his helmet, his voice took on an ethereal quality that hung in the air for a moment. Men do not look on horror and forget it. They merely put it away. Memories of the steading were still too close to the surface, and the junior marshal's voice had summoned them, somehow.

No one laughed. Or rather, most of them laughed, and all of it was forced.

The captain shrugged. "I have chosen to give our prospective employer some time to consider her situation," he said.

Milus barked a laugh. "Stewing in her juice to raise the price, is that it?" he asked. He nodded at the door of the chapel. "Yon has no liking for us."

The priest continued to stand in his doorway.

"Think he's a dimwit? Or is he the pimp?" Ser Milus asked. And stared at the priest. "Be my guest, cully. Stare all ye like."

The soldiers chuckled, and the priest went into the chapel.

Michael flinched at the cruelty in the standard bearer's tone, then stepped forward. "What is your will, m'lord?"

"Oh," the captain said, "I'm off hunting." He stepped away quickly, with a wry smile, walked a few steps toward the smithy, concentrated... and vanished.

Michael looked confused. "Where is he?" he asked.

Milus shrugged, shifting the weight of his hauberk. "How does he do that?" he asked Jehannes.

Twenty paces away, the captain walked into the dormitory wing as if it was his right to do so. Michael leaned as if to call out but Jehannes put his gauntleted hand over Michael's mouth.

"There goes our contract," Hugo said. His dark eyes crossed with the standard bearer's, and he shrugged, despite the weight of the maille on his shoulders. "I told you he was too young."

Jehannes eased his hand off the squire's face. "He has his little ways, the Bourc." He gave the other men a minute shake of his head. "Let him be. If he lands us this contract—"

Hugo snorted, and looked up at the window.

The captain reached into the palace in his head.

A vaulted room, twelve sided, with high, arched, stained glass windows, each one bearing a different image set at even intervals between columns of aged marble that supported a groined roof. Under each window was a sign of the zodiac, painted in brilliant blue on gold leaf, and then a band of beaten bronze as wide as a man's arm, and finally, at eye level, a series of niches between the columns, each holding a statue; eleven statues of white marble, and one iron-bound door under the sign of Ares.

In the exact centre of the room stood a twelfth statue—Prudentia, his childhood tutor. Despite her solid white marble skin, she smiled warmly as he approached her.

"Clementia, Pisces, Eustachios," he said in the palace of his memory, and his tutor's veined white hands moved to point at one sign and then another.

And the room moved.

The windows rotated silently above the signs of the zodiac, and the statues below the band of bronze rotated in the opposite direction until his three chosen signs were aligned opposite to the iron-bound door. And he smiled at Prudentia, walked across the tiles of the twelve-sided room and unlatched the door.

He opened it on a verdant garden of rich summer green—the dream memory of the perfect summer day. It was not always thus, on the far side of the door. A rich breeze blew in. It was not always this strong, his green power, and he deflected some with the power of his will, batting it into a ball and shoving it like a handful of summer leaves into a hempen bag he imagined into being and hung from Prudentia's outstretched arm. Against a rainy day. The insistent green breeze stirred through his hair and then reached the aligned signs on the opposite wall and—

He moved away from the horses without urgency, secure in the knowledge that Michael would be distracted as he moved—and so would the watcher in the window.

The captain's favourite phantasms depended on misdirection more than aethereal force. He preferred to add to their efficacy with physical efficiency—he walked quietly, and didn't allow his cloak to flap.

At the door to the dormitory he reached into his memory palace and

leaned into the vaulted room. "Same again, Pru," he said.

Again the sigils moved as the marble statue pointed to the signs, already aligned above the door. He opened it again, allowed the green breeze to power his working, and let the door close.

He walked into the dormitory building. There were a dozen nuns, all big, capable women, sitting in the good light of the clerestory windows, and most of them were sewing.

He walked past them without a swirl of his scarlet cloak, his whole will focused on his belief that *his presence there was perfectly normal* and started up the stairs. No heads turned, but one older nun stopped peering at her embroidery and glanced at the stairwell, raised an eyebrow, and then went back to her work. He heard a murmur from behind him.

Not entirely fooled then, he thought. *Who are these women?*

His sabatons made too much noise and he had to walk carefully, because power—at least, the sort of power he liked to wield—was of limited use. The stairs wound their way up and up, turning as tightly as they would in any other fortress, to foul his sword arm if he was an attacker.

Which I am, of a sort, he thought. The gallery was immediately above the hall. Even on a day this grey, it was full of light. Three grey-clad novices leaned on the casemates of the windows, watching the men in the yard. Giggling.

At the edge of his power, he was surprised to find traces of *their* power.

He stepped into the gallery, and his sabaton made a distinct metallic scratch against the wooden floor—a clarion sound in a world of barefoot women. He didn't try to strain credulity by *willing* himself to seem normal, here.

The three heads snapped around. Two of the girls turned

and ran. The third novice hesitated for a fatal moment—looking. Wondering.

He had her hand. "Amicia?" he said into her eyes, and then put his mouth over hers. Put an armoured leg inside her thighs and trapped her—turned her over his thigh as easily as throwing a child in a wrestling match, and she was in his arms. He rested his back plate against the ledge of the cloister and held her. Gently. Firmly.

She wriggled, catching her falling sleeve against the flange that protected his elbow. But her eyes were locked on his—and huge. She opened her lips. More there than simple fear or refusal. He licked her teeth. Ran a finger under her chin.

Her mouth opened under his—delicious.

He kissed her, or perhaps she kissed him. It was not brief. She relaxed into him—itself a pleasing warmth, even through the hardened steel of his arm harness and breastplate.

Kisses end.

"Don't take the vows," he said. "You do not belong here." He meant to sound teasing, but even in his own head his voice dripped with unintended mockery.

He stood straight and set her on the ground, to show that he was no rapist. She blushed red from her chin to her forehead, again. Even the backs of her hands were red. She cast her eyes down, and then shifted her weight—he watched such things. She leaned forward—

And slammed a hand into his right ear. Taking him completely by surprise. He reeled, his back hit the wall with a metallic *thud*, and he caught himself—

—and turned to chase her down.

But she wasn't running. She stood her ground. "How dare you judge me?" she said.

He rubbed his ear. "You mistake me," he said. "I meant no hard judgment. You wanted to be kissed. It is in your eyes."

As a line, it had certainly worked before. In this case, he felt it to be true. Despite the sharp pain in his ear.

She pursed her lips—full, very lovely lips. "We are all of us sinners, messire. I struggle with my body every day. That gives you no right to it."

There was a secret smile to the corner of her mouth—really, no smile at all, but something—

She turned and walked away down the gallery, leaving him alone.

He descended the stairs, rubbing his ear, wondering how much of the exchange had been witnessed by his men. Reputations can take months to build and be lost in a few heartbeats and his was too new to weather a loss of respect. But he calculated that the grey sky and the angle of the gallery windows should have protected him.

"That was quick," said Michael, admiringly, as he emerged. The captain was careful not to do anything as gross as tuck his braes into his hose. Because, had he taken her right there against the cloister wall, he would still have re-dressed meticulously before emerging.

Why didn't I? He asked himself. *She was willing enough.*

She liked me.

She hit me very hard.

He smiled at Michael. "It took as long as it took," he said. As he spoke, the heavy iron-bound door opened and a mature nun beckoned to the captain.

"The devil himself watches over you," Hugo muttered.

The captain shook his head. "The devil doesn't give a fuck, either," he said, and went to deal with the Abbess.

He knew as soon he crossed the threshold that she'd elected to take them on. If she'd decided *not* to take them on, she wouldn't have seen him again. Murder in the courtyard might have been closer to the mark.

Except that all the soldiers she had couldn't kill the eight of them in the courtyard. And she knew it. If she had eight good men, she'd never have sent for him to begin with.

It was like Euclidean geometry. And the captain could never understand why other people couldn't see all the angles.

He rubbed at the stinging in his ear, bowed deeply to the Abbess, and mustered up a smile.

She nodded. "I have to take you as you are," she said. "So I will use a long spoon. Tell me your rates?"

He nodded. "May I sit?" he asked. When she extended a reasonably gracious hand, he picked up the horn wine cup that had obviously been placed for him. "I drink to your eyes, ma belle."

She held his gaze with her own and smiled. "Flatterer."

"Yes," he said, taking a sip of wine and continuing to meet her stare over the rim like a proper courtier. "Yes, but no."

"My beauty is long gone, with the years," she said.

"Your body remembers your beauty so well that I can still see it," he said.

She nodded. "That was a beautiful compliment," she admitted. Then she laughed. "Who boxed your ear?" she asked.

He stiffened. "It is an old—"

"Nonsense! I educate children. I know a boxed ear when I see one." She narrowed her eyes. "A nun."

"I do not kiss and tell," he said.

"You are not as bad as you would have me believe, messire," she replied.

They gazed at each other for a few breaths.

"Sixteen double leopards a month for every lance. I have

thirty-one lances today—you may muster them and count them yourself. Each lance consists of at least a knight, his squire, and a valet; usually a pair of archers. All mounted, all with horses to feed. Double pay for my corporals. Forty pounds a month for my officers—there are three—and a hundred pounds for me. Each month." He smiled lazily. "My men are very well disciplined. And worth every farthing."

"And if you kill my monster tonight?" she asked.

"Then you have a bargain, lady Abbess—only one month's pay." He sipped his wine.

"How do you tally these months?" she asked.

"Ah! There's none sharper than you, even in the streets of Harndon, lady. Full months by the lunar calendar." He smiled. "So the next one starts in just two weeks. The Merry month of May."

"Jesu, Lord of the Heavens and Saviour of Man. You are not cheap." She shook her head.

"My people are very, very good at this. We have worked on the Continent for many years, and now we are back in Alba. Where you need us. You needed us a year ago. I may be a hard man, lady, but let us agree that no more Sister Hawisias need die? Yes?" He leaned forward to seal the deal, the wine cup between his hands, and suddenly the weight of his armour made him tired and his back hurt.

"I'm sure Satan is charming if you get to know him," she said quietly. "And I'm sure that if you aren't paid, your interest in the Sister Hawisia's of this world will vanish like snow in strong sunshine." She gave him a thin-lipped smile. "Unless you can kiss them—and even then, I doubt you stay with them long. Or they with you."

He frowned.

"For every steading damaged by your men, I will deduct the price of a lance," she said. "For every man of mine injured in a brawl, for every woman who complains to me of your men, the price of a corporal. If a single one of my sisters is injured—or violated—by your Satan's spawn, even so much as a lewd hand laid to her or an unseemly comment made, I will deduct *your* fee. Do you agree? Since," she said with icy contempt, "Your men are so well disciplined?"

She really does like me, he thought. *Despite all.* He was more used to people who disliked him. And he wondered if she would give him Amicia. She'd certainly put the beautiful novice where he could see her. How calculating was the old witch? She seemed the type who would try to lure him with more than coin—but he'd already pricked her with his comment about Sister Hawisia.

"What's the traitor worth?" he asked.

She shook her head. "I do not believe in your traitor," she said, pointing on the enamel leaf on a wooden platter by her side. "You carry this foul thing with you to trick fools. And I am not a fool."

He shrugged. "My lady, you are allowing your dislike for my kind to cloud your judgment. Consider: what could make me to lie to you about such a thing? How many people should have been at that steading?" he asked.

She met his eye—she had no trouble with that, which pleased him. "There should have been seven confreres to work the fields," she allowed.

"We found your good sister and six other corpses," the captain countered. "It is all straightforward enough, lady Abbess." He sipped more wine. "One is missing when none could have escaped. None." He paused. "Some of your sheep have grown teeth. And no longer wish to be part of your flock." He had a sudden thought. "What was Sister Hawisia doing there? She was a nun of the convent, not a labourer?"

She took a sharp breath. "Very well. If you can prove there is a traitor—or traitors—there will be reward. You must trust that I will be fair."

"Then you must understand: my men will behave badly—it is months since they were paid, and longer since they've been anywhere they might spend what they don't have. The writ of my discipline does not run to stopping tavern brawls or lewd remarks." He tried to look serious, though his heart was all but singing with the joy of work and gold to pay the company. "You must trust that I will do my best to keep them to order."

"Perhaps you'll have to lead by example?" she said. "Or get the task done quickly and move on to greener pastures?" she asked sweetly. "I understand the whores are quite comely south of the river. In the Albin."

He thought of the value of this contract—she hadn't quibbled at his inflated prices.

"I'll decide which seems more attractive when I've seen the colour of your money," he said.

"Money?" she asked.

"Payment due a month in advance, lady Abbess. We *never* fight for free."

Lorica—A Golden Bear

The bear was huge. All of the people in the market said so.

The bear sat in its chains, legs fully extended like an exhausted dancer, head down. It had leg manacles, one on each leg, and the chains had been wrought cunningly so that the manacles were connected by running links that limited the beast's movement.

Both of its hind paws were matted with blood—the manacles were also lined in small spikes.

"See the bear! See the bear!"

The bear keeper was a big man, fat as a lord, with legs like tree trunks and arms like hams. His two boys were small and fast and looked as if they might have a second profession in crime.

"A golden bear of the Wild! Today only!" he bellowed, and his boys roamed through the market, shouting "Come and see the bear! The golden bear!"

The market was full, as market can only be at the first breath of spring when every farmer and petty-merchant has been cooped up in a croft or a town house all winter. Every goodwife had new-made baskets to sell. Careful farmers had sound winter apples and carefully hoarded grain on offer. There were new linens—shirts and caps. A knife grinder did a brisk trade, and a dozen other tradesmen and women shouted their wares—fresh oysters from the coast, lambs for sale, tanned leather.

There were close on five hundred people in the market, and more coming in every hour.

A taproom boy from the inn rolled two small casks up, one at a time, placed a pair of boards across them and started serving cider and ale. He set up under the old oak that marked the centre of the market field, a stone's throw from the bear master.

Men began to drink.

A wagoner brought his little daughter to see the bear. It was female, with two cubs. They were beautiful, with their gold-tipped blond fur, but their mother smelled of rot and dung. Her eyes were wild, and when his daughter touched one of the cubs the fearsome thing opened its jaws, and his daughter started at the wicked profusion of teeth. The growing crowd froze and then people shrank back.

The bear raised a paw, stretching the chains—

She stood her ground. "Poor bear!" she said to her father.

The bear's paw was well short of touching the girl. And the pain of moving against the spiked manacles overcame the bear's anger. It fell back on all fours, and then sat again, looking almost human in its despair.

"Shh!" he said. "Hush, child. It's a creature of the Wild. A servant of the enemy." Truth to tell, his voice lacked conviction.

"The cubs are wonderful." The daughter got down on her haunches.

They had ropes on them, but no more.

A priest—a very worldly priest in expensive blue wool, wearing a magnificent and heavy dagger—leaned down. He put his fist before one of the cubs' muzzles and the little bear bit him. He didn't snatch his hand back. He turned to the girl. "The Wild is often beautiful, daughter. But that beauty is Satan's snare for the unwary. Look at him. Look at him!"

The little cub was straining at his rope to bite the priest again. As he rose smoothly to his feet and kicked the cub, he turned to the bear master.

"It is very like heresy, keeping a creature of the Wild for money," he said.

"For which I have a licence from the Bishop of Lorica!" sputtered the bear master.

"The bishop of Lorica would sell a licence to Satan to keep a brothel," said the priest with a hand on the dagger in his belt.

The wagoner took hold of his daughter but she wriggled free. "Pater, the bear is in pain," she said.

"Yes," he said. He was a thoughtful man. But his eyes were on the priest.

And the priest's eyes were on him.

"Is it right for us to hurt any creature?" his daughter asked. "Didn't God make the Wild, just as he made us?"

The priest smiled and it was as terrible as the bear's teeth. "Your daughter has some very interesting notions," he said. "I wonder where she gets them?"

"I don't want any trouble," the wagoner said. "She's just a child."

The priest stepped closer, but just then the bear master, eager to get a show, began to shout. He had quite a crowd—at least a hundred people, and there were more wandering up every minute. There were half a dozen of the earl's soldiers as well, their jupons open in the early heat, flirting with the farmers' daughters. They pushed in eagerly, hoping to see blood.

The wagoner pulled his daughter back, and let the soldiers pass between him and the priest.

The bear master kicked the bear and pulled on the chain. One of his boys began to play a quick, staccato tune on a tin whistle.

The crowd began to chant, "Dance! Dance! Dance, bear, dance!"

The bear just sat. When the bear master's tugging on the chains caused her pain, she raised her head and roared her defiance.

The crowd shuffled back, muttering in disappointment, except for the priest.

One of the soldiers shook his head. "This is crap," he said. "Let's put some dogs on it."

The idea was instantly popular with his mates, but not at all with the bear master. "That's my bear," he insisted.

"Let me see your pass for the fair," said the sergeant. "Give it here."

The man looked at the ground, silenced, for all his size. "Which I ain't got one."

"Then I can take your bear, mate. I can take your bear and your boys." The sergeant smiled. "I ain't a cruel man," he said, his tone indicating that this statement was untrue. "We'll put some dogs on your bear, fair as fair. You'll collect the silver. We'll have some betting."

"This is a gold bear," said the bear master. He was going pale under his red, wine-fed nose. "A gold bear!"

"You mean you spent some silver on putting a bit of gilt on her fur," said another soldier. "Pretty for the crowd."

The bear master shrugged. "Bring your dogs," he said.

It turned out that many of the men in the crowd had dogs they fancied against a bear.

The wagoner slipped back another step, but the priest grabbed his arm. "You stay right here," he said. "And your little witch of a daughter."

The man's grip was like steel, and the light in his eyes was fanatical. The wagoner allowed himself, reluctantly, to be pulled back into the circle around the bear.

Dogs were being brought. There were mastiffs—great dogs the size of small ponies—and big hounds, and some mongrels that had replaced size with sheer ferocity. Some of the dogs sat quietly while others growled relentlessly at the bear.

The bear raised its head and growled too—once.

All the dogs backed away a step.

Men began to place bets.

The bear master and his boys worked the crowd. If he was hesitant to see his bear in a fight, he wasn't hesitant about accepting the sheer quantity of silver suddenly crossing his palm. Even the smallest farmer would wager on a bear baiting. And when the bear was a creature of the Wild—

Well it was almost a religious duty to bet against it.

The odds against the bear went up and up.

So did the number of dogs, and they were becoming unmanageable as the pack grew. Thirty angry dogs can hate each other as thoroughly as they hate a bear.

The priest stepped out of the ring. "Look at this creature of Evil!" he said. "The very embodiment of the enemy. Look at its fangs and teeth, designed by the Unmaker to kill men. And look at these dogs men have bred—animals reduced to lawful obedience by patient generations of men. No one dog can bring down this monster alone, but does anyone doubt that many of them can? And is this lesson lost on any man here? The bear—look at it—is mighty. But man is more puissant by far."

The bear didn't raise its head.

The priest kicked it.

It stared at the ground.

"It won't even fight!" said one of the guards.

"I want my money back!" shouted a wheelwright.

The priest smiled his terrible smile. He grabbed the rope around one of the little cubs, hauled the creature into the air by the scruff of the neck, and tossed it in among the dogs.

The bear leaped to its feet.

The priest laughed. "Now it will fight," it said.

The bear strained against its manacles as the mastiffs ripped the screaming cub to shreds. It sounded like a human child, terrified and afraid, and then it was gone—savaged and eaten by a dozen mongrels. Eaten alive.

The wagoner had his hands over his daughter's eyes.

The priest whirled on him, eyes afire. "Show her!" he shrieked. "Show her what happens when evil is defeated!" He took a step towards the wagoner—

And the bear moved. She moved faster than a man would have thought possible.

She had his head in one paw and his dagger in the other before his body, pumping blood across the crowd, hit the dirt. Then she whirled—suddenly nothing but teeth and claws—and sank the heavy steel dagger into the ground *through* the links of her chain.

The links popped.

A woman screamed.

She killed as many of them as she could catch, until her claws were glutted with blood, and her limbs ached. They screamed, and hampered each other, and her paws struck them hard like rams in a siege, and every man and woman she touched, she killed.

If she could have she would have killed every human in the world. Her cub was dead. *Her cub was dead.*

She killed and killed, but they ran in all directions.

When she couldn't catch any more, she went back and tore at their corpses—found a few still alive and made sure they died in fear.

Her cub was dead.

She had no time to mourn. Before they could bring their powerful bows and their deadly, steel-clad soldiers, she picked up her remaining cub, ignored the pain and the fatigue and all the fear and panic she felt to be so deep in the tame horror of human lands, and fled. Behind her, in the town, alarm bells rang.

She ran.

Lorica—Ser Mark Wishart

Only one knight came, and his squire. They rode up to the gates at a gallop, summoned from their Commandery, to find the gates closed, the towers manned, and men with crossbows on the walls.

"A creature of the Wild!" shouted the panicked men on the wall before they refused to open the gates for him—even though they'd summoned him. Even though he was the Prior of the Order of Saint Thomas. A paladin, no less.

The knight rode slowly around the town until he came to the market field.

He dismounted. His squire watched the fields as if a horde of boglins might appear at any moment.

The knight opened his visor, and walked slowly across the field. There were a few corpses at the edge, by the dry ditch that marked the legal edge of the field. The bodies lay thicker as he grew closer to the Market Oak. Thicker and thicker. He could hear the flies. Smell the opened bowels, warm in the sun.

It smelled like a battlefield.

He knelt for a moment, and prayed. He was, after all, a priest, as well as a knight. Then he rose slowly and walked back to his squire, spurs catching awkwardly on the clothes of the dead.

"What—what was it?" asked his squire. The boy was green.

"I don't know," said the knight. He took off his helmet and handed it to his squire.

Then he walked back into the field of death.

He made a quick count. Breathed as shallowly as he could.

The dogs were mostly in one place. He drew his sword, four feet of mirror-polished steel, and used it as a pry-bar to roll the corpse of a man with legs like tree trunks and arms like hams off the pile of dogs.

He knelt and took off a gauntlet, and picked up what looked like a scrap of wool.

Let out a breath.

He held out his sword, and called on God for aid, and gathered the divine golden power, and then made a small working.

"Fools," he said aloud.

His working showed him where the priest had died, too. He found the man's head, but left it where it lay. Found his dagger, and placed a *phantasm* on it.

"You arrogant idiot," he said to the head.

He pulled the wagoner's body off the mangled corpse of his daughter. Turned aside and threw up, and then knelt and prayed. And wept.

And finally, stumbled to his feet and walked back to where his squire waited, the worry plain on his face.

"It was a golden bear," he said.

"Good Christ!" said the squire. "Here? Three hundred leagues from the wall?"

"Don't blaspheme, lad. They brought it here captive. They baited it with dogs. It had cubs, and they threw one to the dogs." He shrugged.

His squire crossed himself.

"I need you to ride to Harndon and report to the king," the knight said. "I'll track the bear."

The squire nodded. "I can be in the city by nightfall, my lord."

"I know. Go now. It's one bear, and men brought it here. I'll stem these fools' panic—although I ought to leave them to wallow in it. Tell the king that the Bishop of Jarsay is short a vicar. His headless corpse is over there. Knowing the man, I have to assume this was his fault, and the kindest thing I can say is that he got what he deserved."

His squire paled. "Surely, my lord, now it is you who blaspheme."

Ser Mark spat. He could still taste his own vomit. He took a flask of wine from the leather bag behind his saddle and drank off a third of it.

"How long have you been my squire?" he asked.

The young man smiled. "Two years, my lord."

"How often have we faced the Wild together?" he asked.

The young man raised his eyebrows. "A dozen times."

"How many times has the Wild attacked men out of pure evil?" the knight asked. "If a man prods a hornet's nest with a pitchfork and gets stung, does that make the hornets evil?"

His squire sighed. "It's not what they teach in the schools," he said.

The knight took another pull at his flask of wine. The shaking in his hands was stopping. "It's a mother, and she still has a cub. There's the track. I'll follow her."

"A golden bear?" the squire asked. "Alone?"

"I didn't say I'd fight her in the lists, lad. I'll follow her. You tell the king." The man leaped into his saddle with an acrobatic skill which was one of the many things that made his squire look at him with hero-worship. "I'll send a phantasm to the Commandery if I've time and power. Now go."

"Yes, my lord." The squire turned his horse and was off, straight to a gallop as he'd been taught by the Order.

Ser Mark leaned down from his tall horse and looked at the tracks, and then laid a hand on his war horse's neck. "No need to hurry, Bess," he said.

He followed the track easily. The golden bear had made for the nearest woods, as any creature of the Wild would. He didn't bother to follow the spoor exactly, but merely trotted along, checking the ground from time to time. He was too warm in full harness, but the alarm had caught him in the tiltyard, fully armed.

The wine sang in his veins. He wanted to drain the rest of it.

The dead child—

The scraps of the dead cub—

His own knight—when he was learning his catechism and serving his caravans as a squire—had always said *War kills the innocent first.*

Where the stubble of last year's wheat ran up into a tangle of weeds, he saw the hole the bear had made in the hedge. He pulled up.

He didn't have a lance, and a lance was the best way to face a bear.

He drew his war sword, but he didn't push Bess though the gap in the hedge.

He rode along the lane, entered the field carefully through the gate, and rode back along the hedge at a canter.

Tracks.

But no bear.

He felt a little foolish to have drawn his sword, but he didn't feel any inclination to put it away. The fresh tracks were less than an hour old, and the bear's paw print was the size of a pewter plate from the Commandery's kitchens.

Suddenly, there was crashing in the woods to his left.

He tightened the reins, and turned his horse. She was beautifully trained, pivoting on her front feet to keep her head pointed at the threat.

Then he backed her, step by step.

Crash.

Rustle.

He saw a flash of movement, turned his head and saw a jay leap into the air, flicked his eyes back—

Nothing.

"Blessed Virgin, stand with me," he said aloud. Then he rose an inch in his war saddle and just *touched* his spurs to Bess's sides, and she walked forward.

He turned her head and started to ride around the wood. It couldn't be that big.

Rustle.

Rustle.

Crack.

Crash.

It was *right there.*

He gave the horse more spur, and they accelerated to a canter. The great horse made the earth shake.

Near Lorica—A Golden Bear

She was being hunted. She could smell the horse, hear its shod hooves moving on the spring earth, and she could *feel* its pride and its faith in the killer on its back.

After months of degradation and slavery, torture and humiliation she would happily have turned and fought the steel-clad war man. Glory for her if she defeated him, and a better death than she had imagined in a long time. But her cub mewed at her. The cub—it was all for the cub. She had been captured because they could not run and she would not leave them, and she had endured for them.

She only had one left.

She was the smaller of the two, and the gold of her fur was brighter, and she was on the edge of exhaustion, suffering from dehydration and panic. She had lost the power of speech and could only mew like a dumb animal. Her mother feared she might have lost it for life.

But she had to try. The very blood in her veins cried out that she had to try to save her young.

She picked the cub up in her teeth the way a cat carried a kitten, and ran again, ignoring the pain in her paws.

Lorica—Ser Mark Wishart

The knight cantered around the western edge of the woods and saw the river stretching away in a broad curve. He saw the shambing golden creature in the late sunlight, gleaming like a heraldic beast on a city shield. The bear was running flat out. And so very beautiful, Wild. Feral.

"Oh, Bess," he said. For a moment he considered just letting the bear go.

But that was not what he had vowed.

His charger's ears pricked forward. He raised his sword, Bess rumbled into a gallop and he slammed his visor closed.

Bess was faster than the bear. Not much faster, but the great female was hampered by her cub and he could see that her rear paws were mangled and bloody.

He began to run her down as the ground started to slope down towards the broad river. It was wide here, near the sea, and it smelled of brine at the turn of the tide. He set himself in his saddle and raised his sword—

Suddenly, the bear released her cub to tumble deep into some low bushes, and turned like a great cat pouncing—going from prey to predator in the beat of a human heart.

She rose on her haunches as he struck at her—and she was faster than any creature he'd ever faced. She swung with all her weight in one great claw-raking blow, striking at his horse, even as his blow cut through the meat of her right forepaw and into her chest—cut deep.

Bess was already dead beneath him.

He went backwards over his high crupper, as he'd been taught to. He hit hard, rolled, and came to his feet. He'd lost his sword—and lost sight of the bear. He found the dagger at his waist and drew it even as he whirled. Too slow.

She hit him. The blow caught him in the side, and threw him off his feet, but his breastplate held the blow and the claws didn't rake him. By luck he rolled over his sword, and got to his feet with it in his fist. Something in his right leg was badly injured—maybe broken.

The bear was bleeding.

The cub mewed.

The mother looked at the cub. Looked at him. Then she ran, picked the cub up in her mouth and ran for the river. He watched until she was gone—she jumped into the icy water and swam rapidly away.

He stood with his shoulders slumped, until his breathing began to steady. Then he walked to his dead horse, found his unbroken flask, and drank all the rest of the contents.

He said a prayer for a horse he had loved.

And he waited to be found.

West of Lissen Carak—Thorn

A two hundred leagues north-west, Thorn sat under a great holm-oak that had endured a millennium. The tree rose, both high and round, and its progeny filled the gap between the hills closing down from the north and the ever deeper Cohocton River to the south.

Thorn sat cross-legged on the ground. He no longer resembled the man he had once been; he was almost as tall as a barn, when he stood up to his full height, and his skin, where it showed through layers of moss and leather, seemed to be of smooth grey stone. A staff—the product of a single, straight ash tree riven by lightning in its twentieth year—lay across his lap. His gnarled fingers, as long as the tines of a hay fork, made eldritch sigils of pale green fire as he reached out into the Wild for his coven of spies.

He found the youngest and most aggressive of the Qwethnethogs; the strong people of the deep Wild that men called daemons. *Tunxis.* Young, angry, and easy to manipulate.

He exerted his will, and Tunxis came. He was careful about the manner of his summons; Tunxis had more powerful relatives who would resent Thorn using the younger daemon for his own ends.

Tunxis emerged from the oaks to the east at a run, his long, heavily muscled legs beautiful at the fullness of his stride, his body leaning far forward, balanced by the heavy armoured tail that characterized his kind. His chest looked deceptively human, if an unlikely shade of blue-green, and his arms and shoulders were also very man-like. His face had an angelic beauty—large, deep eyes slanted slightly, open and innocent, with a ridge of bone between them that rose into the elegant helmet crest that differentiated the male and female among them. His beak was polished to a mirror-brightness and inlaid with lapis lazuli and gold to mark his social rank, and he wore a sword that few mere human men could even lift.

He was angry—but Tunxis was at the age when young males are always angry.

"Why do you summon me?" he shrieked.

Thorn nodded. "Because I need you," he answered.

Tunxis clacked his beak in contempt. "Perhaps I do not need you. Or your games."

"It was my games that allowed you to kill the witch." Thorn didn't smile. He had lost the ability to, but he smiled inwardly, because Tunxis was so young.

The beak clacked again. "She was nothing." Clacked again, in deep satisfaction. "*You* wanted her dead. And she was too young. You offered me a banquet and gave me a scrap. A *nothing.*"

Thorn handled his staff. "She is certainly nothing now." His *friend* had asked for the death. Layers of treason. Layers of favours asked, and owed. The Wild. His attention threatened to slip away from the daemon. It had probably been a mistake to let Tunxis kill in the valley.

"My cousin says there are armed men riding in the valley. In *our valley.*" Tunxis slurred the words, as all his people did when moved by great emotion.

Thorn leaned forward, suddenly very interested. "Mogan saw them?" he asked.

"Smelled them. Watched them. Counted their horses." Tunxis moved his eyebrows the way daemons did. It was like a smile, but it caused the beak to close—something like the satisfaction of a good meal.

Thorn had had many years in which to study the daemons. They were his closest allies, his not-trusted lieutenants. "How many?" Thorn asked patiently.

"Many," Tunxis said, already bored. "I will find them and kill them."

"You will *not.*" Thorn leaned forward and slowly, carefully, rose to his feet, his heavy head brushing against the middling branches of the ancient oak. "Where has she found soldiers?" he asked out loud. One of the hazards of living alone in the Wild was that you voiced things aloud. He was growing used to talking to himself aloud. It didn't trouble him as it had at first.

"They came from the east," Tunxis said. "I will hunt them and kill them."

Thorn sighed. "No. You will find them and watch them. You will watch them from afar. We will learn their strengths and weaknesses. Chances are they will pass away south over the bridge, or join the lady as a garrison. It is no concern of ours."

"No concern of *yours,* Turncoat. Our land. Our valley. Our hills. Our fortress. Our power. Because you are weak—" Tunxis's beak made three distinct clacks.

Thorn rolled his hand over, long thin fingers flashing, and the daemon fell flat on the ground as if all his sinews had been cut.

Thorn's voice became the hiss of a serpent.

"I am *weak*? The soldiers are *many*? They came from the *east*? You are a fool and a child, Tunxis. I could rip your soul from your body and eat it, and you couldn't lift a claw to stop me. Even now you cannot move, cannot summon power. You are like a hatchling in the rushing water as the salmon comes to take him. Yes? And you tell me 'many' like a lord throwing crumbs to peasants. Many?" he leaned down over the prone daemon and thrust his heavy staff into the creature's stomach. "*How many exactly, you little fool?*"

"I don't know," Tunxis managed.

"From the east, the south-east? From Harndon and the king? From over the mountains? Do you know?" he hissed.

"No," Tunxis said, cringing.

"Tunxis, I like to be polite. To act like—" He sought for a concept that could link him to the alien intelligence. "To act like we are allies. Who share common goals."

"You treat us like servants! We serve no master!" spat the daemon. "We are not like your *men*, who lie and lie and say these pretty things. We are Qwethnethogs!"

Thorn pushed his staff deeper into the young daemon's gut.

"Sometimes I tire of the Wild and the endless struggle. *I am trying to help you and your people reclaim your valley. Your goal is my goal.* So I am not going to eat you. However tempting that might be just now." He withdrew the staff.

"My cousin says I should never trust you. That whatever body you wear, you are just another man." Tunxis sat up, rolled to his feet with a pure and fluid grace.

"Whatever I am, without me you have no chance against the forces of the Rock. You will *never* reclaim your place."

"Men are weak," Tunxis spat.

"Men have defeated your kind again and again. They burn the woods. They cut the trees. They build farms and bridges and they raise armies and your kind *lose.*" He realised that he was trying to negotiate with a child. "Tunxis," he said, laying hold of the young creature's essence. "Do my bidding. Go, and watch the men, and come back and tell me."

But Tunxis had a power of his own, and Thorn watched much of his compulsion roll off the creature. And when he let go his hold, the daemon turned and sprinted for the trees.

And only then did Thorn recall that he'd summoned the boy for another reason entirely, and that made him feel tired and old. But he exerted himself again, summoning one of the Abnethog this time, that men called wyverns.

The Abnethog were more biddable. Less fractious. Just as aggressive. But lacking a direct ability to manipulate the power, they tended to avoid open conflict with the magi.

Sidhi landed neatly in the clearing in front of the holm oak, although the aerial gymnastics required taxed his skills.

"I come," he said.

Thorn nodded. "I thank you. I need you to look in the lower valley to the east," he said. "There are men there, now. Armed men. Possibly very dangerous."

"What man is dangerous to me?" asked the wyvern. Indeed, Sidhi stood eye to eye with Thorn, and when he unfolded his wings their span was extraordinary. Even Thorn felt a twinge of real fear when the Abnethog were angry.

Thorn nodded. "They have bows. And other weapons that could hurt you badly."

Sidhi made a noise in his throat. "Then why should I do this thing?" he asked.

"I made the eyes of your brood clear when they clouded over in the winter. I gave you the rock-that-warms for your mate's nest." Thorn made a motion intended to convey that he would continue to heal sick wyverns.

Sidhi unfolded his wings. "I was going to hunt," he said. "I am hungry. And being summoned by you is like being called a dog." The wings spread farther and farther. "But it may be that I will choose to hunt to the east, and it may be that I will see your enemies."

"Your enemies as well," Thorn said wearily. *Why are they all so childish?*

The wyvern threw back its head, and screamed, and the wings beat—a moment of chaos, and it was in the air, the trees all around it shedding leaves in the storm of air. A night of hard rain wouldn't have ripped so many leaves from the trees.

And then Thorn reached out with his power—gently, hesitantly, a little like a man rising from bed on a dark night to find his way down unfamiliar stairs. He reached out to the east—farther, and a little farther, until he found what he always found.

Her. The lady on the Rock.

He probed the walls like a man running his tongue over a bad tooth. She was there, enshrined in her power. And with her was something else entirely. He couldn't read it—the fortress carried its own power, its own ancient sigils which worked against him.

He sighed. It was raining. He sat in the rain, and tried to enjoy the rise of spring around him.

Tunxis killed the nun, and now the lady has more soldiers. He had set something in motion, and he wasn't sure why.

And he wondered if he had made a mistake.